DEATH.

It's the one experience everyone will share — except for Jak Hamelton, at least that's what the plaque promised.

Three words whirl Jak to a particular garden paradise where a treacherous interaction between Man, Woman and a snake usher death and evil into the world. When a mysterious benefactor named El offers Jak the opportunity to bring the dead back to life and live forever, it sounds like an impossible dream. But after Jak's grandfather unexpectedly begins aging backwards, it appears the dream just might be reality.

However, the weapon Jak's been given to defeat death and evil doesn't even work yet, and the serpent Beelz isn't willing to give up the Earth without a fight. Besides that, there's the poison...

Is it really true that the dead can live forever? What will it take to restore paradise?

Praise for "Jak & the Scarlet Thread"

"I liked *Jak and the Scarlet Thread* because there is a lot of suspense. I didn't want to stop reading it!"
–Davis G., age 12

"An engaging, imaginative, fast-paced story that both parents and kids will stay up late to see what happens next!"
–Karl Bastian, founder of Kidology.org and author of The Order of the Ancient. www.orderoftheancient.com

"Finally a fantasy book I can feel good about my children reading! ...actually causes the reader, kids included, to consider what it was really like when Bible 'stories' happened and then go on to a deeper understanding of the theological implications. Brilliant."
–Kristin G., mom

"Extremely well written! I can't wait for the sequel."
–Christian E., age 12

"I've read a lot of fantasy books in my life. I love to read. However *Jak and The Scarlet Thread* is by far my favorite book of all. It is full of adventure, fantasy, and a little bit of Christianity. The cool thing about it is if I wasn't a Christian I wouldn't be able to tell if it was a Christian book or not."
–Cully H., age 12

"In a genre filled with vampires, witches, and wizards, Nathan Anderson has written a story that is filled with life. *Jak and the Scarlet Thread* is a nonstop thrill ride and the best part is that it dives into the greatest stories of history. Once you start reading it, you will not want to put it down. Watch out Percy and Harry here comes Jak!"
–Terry Cuthbertson, children's pastor, Spring Creek Assembly, creativekidspastor.com

"I really enjoyed the way this book looked at something so familiar to me at a different angle. This book made me laugh and wish against the inevitable."
–Gabe R., age 15

"Good and evil flame into full color through the tumultuous twists and turns of *Jak and the Scarlet Thread*, a gripping read."
–Ellen E., mom

"*Jak and the Scarlet Thread* is a fantastic book for preteens! The book captures the imagination of young people and I highly recommend it. Nathan has a big heart for God and is a gifted writer & communicator."
–Nick Diliberto - Creator of PreteenMinistry.net, a website that provides creative resources for preteen ministry.

"*Jak and the Scarlet Thread* is a good book for children because of the way it brings evil into the world without being violent or scary."
–Joel G., age 9

"Readers young and old will see the familiar Sunday School stories in a whole new light and no one will be prepared for the deadly twists along the way."
–Brian C. Jacobs, author of The Enigma Squad series.

To the Johnson Family,

Follow the Scarlet Thread!

Nathan J. Anderson

JAK AND THE SCARLET THREAD

Nathan J. Anderson

Interior Illustrations by Caitlyn Klawitter

Published by Big Hungry Planet Productions •   www.bighungryplanet.com

ISBN-10: 1456477110
EAN-13: 9781456477110
Library of Congress Control Number: 2010919196

Cover art by CreateSpace

Interior illustrations by Caitlyn Klawitter

This story was written for my children -
Cole, Chase, Logan and Lauren -
each one a unique gift from God.

And dedicated to my wife and best friend, Julie -
without you none of it would have been possible.

Contents

PART ONE – BEGINNING

Chapter 1   The Final Farewell 3
Chapter 2   The Black Thing Under the Couch 7
Chapter 3   The Man with Four Faces 13
Chapter 4   The Creature under the Tree. 19
Chapter 5   The Ancient Plaque 23
Chapter 6   A Disturbing Second Plaque 35
Chapter 7   The Whispering Gate 43
Chapter 8   Pants 53
Chapter 9   Woman 63
Chapter 10 The Two Trees. 67
Chapter 11 Banished to the Birches. 75
Chapter 12 An Army of Goo 85
Chapter 13 A Gift from El. 87
Chapter 14 The War Begins with Rabbits. 93
Chapter 15 The Amazing Hares 95
Chapter 16 The Amazing Hair 101
Chapter 17 The Dance in the Water 111
Chapter 18 The Patch of Silver Sand 117
Chapter 19 Four Shocks in the Morning 123
Chapter 20 Beautiful Evil. 131
Chapter 21 Dreams Do Come True (but sometimes so do nightmares) 135
Chapter 22 The Black Bulge Begins. 141
Chapter 23 Plunging the Dagger Deeper. 147
Chapter 24 The Sickening Rip. 151
Chapter 25 Jak Finds His Father 159
Chapter 26 Secret Meeting under the Banyan Tree 169
Chapter 27 The Scarlet Thread 179

PART TWO – TWISTING

Chapter 28 Smoke on the Water 187
Chapter 29 A Dead Boy's Clothes 197
Chapter 30 The Quelcher 205
Chapter 31 Eve's Brainstorm 215
Chapter 32 The Thing about Cain 223
Chapter 33 The Man with the Missing Finger 235
Chapter 34 The White Diamond 245
Chapter 35 The Wandering Murderer 251
Chapter 36 A Funeral Kidnapping 253
Chapter 37 Dawning of the Day of Sacrifice 265
Chapter 38 The Stinky Card 271
Chapter 39 Squish and Burgers 283
Chapter 40 A Trio of Helpful Giants 291
Chapter 41 How to Avoid Getting Eaten by a Serpent 299
Chapter 42 The Unhappy Bald Giant 303
Chapter 43 Charms & Candles 311
Chapter 44 A Powerful Cup of Tea 319
Chapter 45 Dust Storm 333

PART THREE – CLEANSING

Chapter 46 The Crazy Boat-Builder 343
Chapter 47 Thread Card #2 Finds its Match...Sort Of 349
Chapter 48 The End of the World 357
Chapter 49 Lamech & Lamech 361
Chapter 50 The Watcher in the Waterfall 369
Chapter 51 The Preacher and the Impromptu Zoo 377
Chapter 52 Plunging through the Waterfall 387
Chapter 53 The Smiling Cocoon and a Half-Eaten Candy Bar 395
Chapter 54 The Golden Sword 399
Chapter 55 River Rider 407

Chapter 56 The Gorilla and the Scarecrow........................411
Chapter 57 A Tinge of Red.................................421
Chapter 58 The Whirlwind and the Warm Fuzzies 427
Chapter 59 Pocket Number Three...........................437
Chapter 60 Paradise and Poison 443
Chapter 61 The People at the Bottom of the Stairs................447

PART ONE
BEGINNING

C H A P T E R   I

The Final Farewell

"Pass me the peppers, Jak." Gramma Josie wiped her fingers on her smiley face apron, smearing a pancake batter mustache across one of the faces.

"But you already put some in," said Jak. He handed her the jar of hot peppers from the windowsill. It was cold from sitting next to the frosted windowpane, but he knew the peppers themselves were the home equivalent of a nuclear bomb and flamethrower wrapped into one convenient container.

"Yes, but these last few pancakes for your grandfather need a touch more." She poured the pepper into the pancake batter and mixed it in.

Every Saturday for as long as Jak could remember, Gramma Josie had always made Swedish pancakes a la Mexico - thin eggy pancakes sweeter than sugar but with a zing that would force your morning brain to stand up and salute. But he never remembered her adding as much heat as she did that morning.

"There!" she said, with a final flick of the whisk. "Do you think that's enough?" She winked and scooped a cup of batter onto the griddle.

Jak's mouth went numb just thinking about eating a super-sauced pancake. "It's more than enough. What are you trying to do, kill him?"

Gramma laughed and scooped out another cup. "No, just the opposite. I started putting a smidgen more in his pancakes a few weeks ago, after he went to see the doctor."

"Did the doctor prescribe hot peppers?"

"No, but this is my own remedy. It'll burn the cholesterol right out of him."

Jak chuckled and shook his head. "You're terrible, Gramma. Don't ever do that to me." He tore a small chunk from one of the safe pancakes and tossed it to Macy. The little black and white dog gobbled it down like she hadn't eaten in a week.

"Keep your cholesterol down," said his grandmother, winking at Jak, "and I won't. Now, go on and call your grandfather in from the snow. It's time to eat." She reached for the spatula to flip the pancakes, but her hand never made it above the counter top. Her other hand flew to her forehead and she tried to speak, but nothing came out except slurred gibberish.

"Gramma?" said Jak, jumping down from the stool. "Are you okay?"

She swayed for a moment without answering, then dropped to the floor, hitting her head so hard that it bounced before settling on the linoleum.

"Gramma!" Jak slipped to the floor next to her, grabbed her arm and gently shook it. "Gramma, can you hear me? Are you okay?" But she didn't answer.

A chill crawled down Jak's back and his stomach started to swirl. *This can't really be happening. She's fine, she has to be fine. She can't die, not now.* But her eyes were still closed and her body was as limp as a wet mop

Jak rushed out the back door in his socks. "Gramps!" he shouted. By now the flakes were falling so thick it was hard to see the shed. He jumped down the steps and landed in a pile of snow that was already up past his ankles. "Gramps!" he yelled as he pounded through the shed door. "Something's wrong with Gramma!" A table saw whined as it ripped through a piece of wood, drowning out his voice. He flipped the light switch off and on and yelled again. "GRAMPS!"

A wiry old man with a wrinkled face framed in white whiskers and hair put one hand to his ear as he shut off the saw. "What?" he yelled as the saw wound down.

"GRAMMA!" Jak pointed back to the house. "Something's wrong!"

4

Gramps turned away from the saw and walked briskly toward Jak, his brows furrowed. "What is it? What happened?"

"I don't know, she just fell over."

Without another word, Gramps plunged into the snow and trudged as quickly as he could with Jak back to the house.

Jak could hardly breathe. He'd had nightmares about moments like these, but this was the first time real life *was* the nightmare.

"Josie?" Gramps called, bursting through the back door. As soon as he saw her lying on the floor, his face went gray. "Josie, no, no, no..." He scooped up the phone, his hand trembling so hard he could hardly dial. Almost immediately, a siren wailed in the distance.

Jak hated sirens; they always meant trouble. He tried to swallow the growing lump in his throat, but it wouldn't go down. The only way to get rid of it was for Gramma to sit up and say, "Time to eat!" But she didn't. His stomach swirling, Jak slumped to the linoleum and lifted her head gently onto his lap.

Gramps knelt next to them and caressed Gramma's face, the twinkle in his eyes replaced by a heavy cloud. "Josie? Can you hear me?"

Gramma's eyes fluttered open. She gave a weak lopsided smile, reached for Gramps's hand and squeezed.

"Good bye, boys," she whispered. Then her eyes closed and her head lolled to the side. She was gone.

CHAPTER 2

The Black Thing Under the Couch

"Frankie?" Jak raked an old magazine away from the corner with one of his crutches. It had been six months since the funeral. The doctor said Gramma had died from a stroke, a tiny little blood clot that got stuck in her head and stole her life. He had worn the blue-striped tie Gramma had given him for Christmas, and endured an hour of songs he didn't know plus some guy in a strange white collar droning on and on while Jak's rear end went numb from the hard wooden bench. Finally it was over and he escaped back to normal life, except nothing was normal anymore. How could life be normal when Gramma Josie was dead?

His mom had gotten him a gerbil to try to take his mind off Gramma — not that a gerbil could replace his grandmother — but it was nice having Frankie around, except for one thing: Frankie was a tiny Houdini. So far, he had escaped from his cage exactly thirteen times, and when Jak had come into the kitchen that morning, Frankie had escaped again. The door leading to the basement was ajar, which meant Frankie more than likely had gone downstairs, so he had followed him.

Jak leaned his crutches against the wall and sat very carefully on the fuzzy orange couch. Scratchy wool stuffing and rusty metal springs exploded from every seam, which, on a normal day, would have made navigating the couch a risky venture, but on a dark day like today, the couch was downright dangerous.

He flicked on the blue flashlight his grandmother had given him last year before he went to camp and began to methodically search the floor for a small patch of brown fur. Frankie had to be around there somewhere.

Suddenly, something small and soft brushed past Jak's foot and disappeared underneath the couch. Jak dropped to the floor and was just about to thrust his hand after Frankie when he remembered what lived under the couch: yellow-eyed snakes with green fangs, and big fat hairy spiders with pointy stingers, both waiting for an unsuspecting head to poke around in the dark.

He peered under the orange monster: just as he expected, a sea of spider webs. The thought of reaching into the sticky mess sent shivers down his spine.

The floorboards of the kitchen creaked above him.

"Tess?" Jak called. "Are you up there? I need some help."

"Um, I'm kind of busy!" she called back.

Jak didn't know what she could possibly be busy with. His cousin was only two years, three months and fourteen days older than he was, but as soon as she turned fifteen, she had become a different person. The last thing he saw her doing was painting her fingernails with disgusting smelling pink nail polish. *Maybe the stench will knock Frankie out. That'll make him easier to catch.*

"Frankie got out again, and I need you to help me. Bring the box."

He kept a long yellow shoebox next to the gerbil cage in the kitchen to help trap Frankie. Sometimes he would run right to it, and then it was easy to scoop him up.

A flurry of paws scurried down the stairs, and Jak turned, smacking his bandaged ankle against the concrete. He grimaced and bit his lip as pain bounced through the bruises. *How long was it going to take for his foot to heal?*

Jak took a deep breath. "Macy, if you come down here, you can't eat him, okay?"

"Why don't you get Macy to help you instead of me?" Tess plunked down the stairs, a sullen look on her face. "After all, she is a hunting dog."

"Yeah, right! The only thing she's ever hunted for is sandwiches in my lunch bag. Where's the box?"

8

"What box?" said Tess, blank-eyed.

Just then Macy stuffed her nose under the couch and growled.

Jak whipped around. "You see him, girl?" He dropped to the ground again, careful to keep his ankle from hitting the floor, and shone the light under the couch.

Through the thick blanket of cobwebs, he could see the faint outline of a ball of fur huddled against the wall. Ignoring the imminent threat of snakes and spiders, Jak stretched his hand as far as he could underneath the couch, but his arm wasn't quite long enough.

Jak jerked his hand back out. Spider webs coated his fingers like a weird sort of sticky glove, but nothing had bit him. Shuddering, he scraped his hand across a dusty couch cushion, peeling off the mess in sticky clumps. He had tempted fate and won, but wasn't about to do it again. He scanned the basement around him, looking for something longer than his arm, when his eyes landed on his crutches.

"Tess, get on your knees on that end of the couch. I'm going to sweep my crutch underneath and force him out this side. Is Gramps upstairs?"

A loud crash on the floor directly overhead answered Jak's question.

"Yeah," said Tess. "He was making pancakes a minute ago, but now I think he's scraping the batter off the floor."

That's another thing that had changed in the past six months. Since his mom worked every Saturday at the hospital, Gramps took over Gramma's tradition of making the traditional Saturday breakfast, Swedish pancakes. He made a different sort of pancake than Gramma had, called them "Swedish Surprise," a fitting name not because they were anything special, but because when you ate them, you were always surprised at how awful they tasted. Most of the time, they were burnt black on one side, raw on the other, and filled with lumpy flour landmines so that when you bit into them, all you could taste was clods of white paste. Judging from the bowl that had just thudded to the floor above their heads, today's Swedish Surprise might feature dirt.

"Gramps!" shouted Jak.

Footsteps moved in the direction of the basement, and the door creaked open.

"Jak? You call for me?"

"Yeah. I've got Frankie cornered under the couch, and I need you to come and help me catch him."

"Alright. Just a minute. Do you want the box, Jak?"

9

"Yes! Bring it down."

Gramps eased down the steps one at a time while Jak waited as patiently as he could.

"Whoa," said Gramps "It's dark down here. What happened to the other light?"

Jak stiffened. "Uh...it broke."

"Broke? How?"

"Yeah...well, it just...uh, it just shattered one day." Jak didn't want to talk about the broken light above the couch and the part he had played in its demise, so he changed the subject as quickly as he could. "Go to the other end of the couch with the box. I'm going to sweep my crutch toward you and force him into the box. Okay?"

"Alright. Just make it quick, 'cause I've got pancakes on the griddle upstairs."

Jak didn't think an extra ten minutes would make any difference in the quality of Gramps's pancakes. He aimed the flashlight back under the couch and inserted his crutch underneath until it hit the wall to the left of the gerbil. Gently, he moved it toward Frankie until it bumped him. The gerbil startled and scampered a few inches; Jak moved it again, and the gerbil scampered a few more inches.

"It's working," Jak whispered.

"What's that burning smell?" asked Tess, wrinkling her nose.

"What smell?" said Gramps.

"Shhh," said Jak. "Don't scare him, or we'll be here all day trying to catch him."

"All day? I don't think so," said Tess. "I..."

"Shhh!" said Jak.

Suddenly, the crutch stopped moving. This was not part of Jak's plan.

He peered under the couch once again and saw a black thing blocking the crutch. Frankie had skirted around it and sat nibbling something on the other side.

Great. Now what? He pushed against the black thing. It didn't move, so he pushed harder. Still nothing.

Frankie began to scamper toward the front of the couch.

"Tess, go to the other side of me and catch him if he comes out."

"I'M NOT TOUCHING THAT RAT!"

Frankie moved again. He was going to get away, Jak just knew it. It was now or never.

He yanked the crutch as hard as he could, and both the black thing and the gerbil slid across the floor like hockey pucks on ice. The black thing thudded into the shoebox while the gerbil completely missed and somersaulted to the side.

"Get him, Gramps!" shouted Jak.

But before Gramps could move, Frankie scooted across the floor and escaped through a gerbil-sized hole under a wall of cabinets.

Jak groaned and slumped to the floor. "We'll never get him out from under there. What was that stupid black thing anyway?"

"I don't know," said Gramps. "It shot into the box too fast for me to tell." He tilted the box upside down, and a thick rectangular object thudded to the ground.

Jak crawled over and lifted it up. It was solid, yet sagged a little in his hands.

He leaned against the couch, careful to avoid the particularly sharp springs that stretched their necks toward his back, and opened the cover.

It was a picture book. Nestled into four fabric pouches sat four pictures, two by two, one pair set above the other. They looked like old baseball cards, except no one wore a uniform, and several of the men were sporting impressive beards.

"What is it?" asked Gramps, settling down next to Jak.

"It's a picture book." Jak shone the flashlight on the pages to get a better look. "Who are these people, Gramps?"

Gramps took his horn-rimmed glasses out of his shirt pocket and peered at the page. He frowned and shook his head. "Not sure."

"Those look more like baseball cards than pictures," said Tess.

"Yeah, but if they're baseball cards, that's the weirdest looking team I've ever seen," said Jak.

He flipped the page and found several more pouches, each filled with a card just like the ones on the previous page.

"Keep going, Jak," said Gramps. "It looks like there are paper pages under all those pictures."

Jak turned a whole section of cards until he opened to a crisp page, completely white except for a name written in blue ink at the top:

Josefina Maria Leon.

Gramma's name sent each of their stomachs tumbling. Gramps leaned back against the couch and bit his lip, staring hard at the wall of cabinets. Tess closed her eyes, and Jak sat frozen.

The smoke alarm in the kitchen began blaring, but Gramps didn't move.

"How did this get under the couch?" Jak whispered.

"Must've fallen off the shelf," said Gramps. "It's been so long since I've seen it that I forgot about it. Gramma got the book when she was a little girl, a gift from her father." The muscles in his jaw moved in and out like the gills of a fish breathing underwater.

Jak pushed Macy's nose out of the way and turned the page. A faded red bookmark sprawled across an elegant drawing of a tree with dark clusters of fruit hanging from the branches. At one time, the colors of the picture must have been vibrant and alive, but age had faded the leaves of the tree until they were almost as dark as the fruit, and only the slightest tinge of green remained. He couldn't tell if it was a crab apple or cherry tree, or maybe it was something else. Below the picture, a sea of words sloshed together, and Jak couldn't figure out why it was so hard to read. Maybe he needed more light.

He adjusted the book, but that didn't help.

Jak frowned. "I can't read it."

"Of course you can't. It's written in Spanish," said Tess.

"Spanish?"

"Yeah," said Tess. "Gramma was born in Spain, remember? Great-grandpa must have given it to her when they moved to Mexico."

The smoke alarm kept blaring, and the smell of smoking pancakes slowly burned its way even down into the stale basement air. Gramps reluctantly got up.

Jak didn't know much Spanish, but he knew enough from his grandmother's kitchen cookbook language lessons to read the first line. *"En el principio..."* But that was as far as he got.

As soon as he began to read, the letters on the page grew fat and fuzzy like a caterpillar, and the room began to swirl. He could see Gramps, Tess, Macy and the book, but they were turning faster and faster, like they were on a merry-go-round.

A pair of feet began tromping down the stairs, accompanied almost instantly by a howling wind. Then the couch spring that had been digging into his back disappeared, and the basement vanished.

CHAPTER 3

The Man with Four Faces

Jak lay flat on his back, his right heel throbbing, surrounded by a swirling mist and a troop of shadowy trees. His eyes darted back and forth from one black trunk to the next, and panic began to rise in his throat. *What happened to the basement? Where am I now? And what's wrong with my foot?*

He rolled to his side and reached for his heel. The Ace bandage that had been wrapped around his sprained ankle had almost ripped away. Now his foot was wet and sticky, and burned like fire. When he pulled his hand away, blood dripped in bright red streams down his fingers. *What was going on?*

Jak used his crutch to push himself up from the ground. But as soon as he moved, a huge black snake reared, hissing through the mist, and snapped at the air above his feet.

He stopped and lay perfectly still, his eyes glued to the creature's head.

The head was as big as a football, with eyes that glowed electric yellow, crooked black lines radiating from the pupil to the lid. Teeth as sharp as shards of glass pushed between the lips of the snake while a reddish drool dripped in strings out the mouth and down the neck. It slowly nosed through the air, flicking a forked black tongue in and out as if it were searching for something.

A cold sweat broke out on Jak's forehead as he realized why his foot hurt so much. The red drool stringing from the snake's teeth wasn't drool at all; it was blood, and it belonged to him. The snake was searching for *him*.

He began to inch backwards. He had to get away; he had to find a place to hide, and fast.

Suddenly, an apple thudded into one of the snake's eyes, and the head recoiled, causing the monster to hiss, blinking and snapping even more furiously at the air.

"Get...get out of here!" a voice shouted as a second apple sailed over Jak and hit the snake square in the face again.

Screeching like a giant fingernail scraping down a blackboard, the snake snapped at the air once more, then dropped to the ground and slithered away through a patchwork of tree trunks.

Jak hadn't realized he had been holding his breath, but as soon as the snake was gone, his lungs gasped for air. His skin was cold, and he began to shake, either from the snake or from his foot, he couldn't tell.

Gramps dumped his remaining arsenal of apples to the ground and knelt next to Jak, shifting his eyes between the boy and the misty path on which the snake had retreated. "You alright?"

A couple of years earlier, Jak would have burst out crying, but he was twelve now, almost thirteen, and crying was no longer an option—especially in front of his grandfather.

"The snake..." said Jak, trying to collect himself. But the questions kept bumping into each other, and he didn't know where to start. "My foot...it really hurts. Where are we? And where did the snake come from?"

Gramps placed a warm hand on Jak's shivering arm and stared into the mist in the direction the snake had fled. He shook his head. "I don't know, but it's gone now. Which foot hurts?" He pulled a pair of horn-rimmed glasses from his shirt pocket and perched them on his nose.

Jak groaned and pointed. "The one I sprained."

Gramps leaned down for a closer look.

From the expression on his grandfather's face, Jak knew his heel must look pretty bad.

"Jak!" Tess hurried toward him. Her hair had fallen across her face, so he couldn't see her expression, but from the tone of her voice, Jak knew she was scared. She didn't get scared very easily, but landing in a place like this was enough to frighten anybody. Macy bounded past her and began licking Jak's face.

"Macy," said Jak, mustering a small smile, "you're here too."

"What happened?" asked Tess, tucking the loose strands of hair behind her ear. "Where are..." Her words melted away as she stood staring at his foot. Then she dropped to her knees and began peeling away the remaining shreds of his bandage. "Jak," she gasped, "your heel! It's all bloody. What did you do?"

As soon as her fingers touched the wound, the pain twisted Jak's stomach inside out. "I...I don't know," he groaned. "One minute we were in the basement, and the next—"

"We have to stop the bleeding," she said, interrupting him and gripping his heel like a vise. "Gramps, I need a strip of cloth."

Gramps fished around in his pocket and came up with a faded blue bandanna that looked as if it belonged in the rag pile. "I only used it once, so it should be okay."

"That'll work," she said. "Rip it into strips."

Gramps silently obeyed, and Tess began wrapping the fabric around Jak's heel. She must have thought it was more important to do the job quickly than gently, for every yank sent another jolt of pain through his leg.

He instinctively jerked his foot away, but Tess wouldn't let go. "Hold still," she snapped, "or I won't be able to wrap it." He gripped the rubber handle of his crutch as hard as he could in an attempt to ignore the pain.

This was not the way Jak had planned on spending his Saturday morning. They were supposed to be in the basement catching Frankie, not stuck in some weird woods with a giant snake. He took a deep breath and tried to focus on the bigger problem. They still had no idea where they were or how they got there.

The mist hung wet and cold on his face, and it was eerily silent around them, as if they had landed in the middle of a graveyard. He shuddered at the thought. They sat in a sparse woods on the edge of a clearing dotted with what appeared to be fruit trees. In the soupy mist, it was hard to tell exactly what kind of trees they were, but the round shadowy shapes nestled amongst the leaves and branches looked like fruit.

A cold wind burrowed into their ears, causing Jak to pull the collar of his T-shirt halfway up his head to protect himself. The wind twirled the mist around a hill in the middle of the clearing. At the top of the hill, an unlikely pair of trees stood like a pair of mismatched socks: one tall and stately, the other short and squatty.

Suddenly a thunderclap cracked directly above them and sent a shiver through the earth. Startled, Tess dropped a strip of bandanna while Jak and Gramps both jumped.

"Must be a storm comin'," said Gramps, eying the sky above them. It looked a sick shade of blue, but there wasn't a cloud in sight. As the thunder rumbled away, a throaty whistle edged into the air above them. Macy whined and began to prance nervously around Jak.

Jak tilted his head up, looking for the source of the sound. Whatever it was, it was too far away to see.

"Do you hear that?" asked Jak, still searching.

"Hear what?" said Gramps, cupping his hand around his ear.

A black speck suddenly appeared high in the sky and dropped straight down like a bomb, growing larger and larger as it approached the ground. In a moment, a collection of spinning black clouds engulfed the taller of the two trees, crackling, popping, and spinning the leaves dizzy. The wind began to twist and howl around them, clutching at their clothes and whipping their hair sideways.

Gramps sprang into action. "C'mon!" he said, just loud enough to be heard over the whine of the wind. "We have to get back!" With Tess still holding Jak's heel in her hand, Gramps grabbed Jak under the arms and began to pull him deeper into the woods.

Jak looked back at the twister to see which way it was moving, but it hadn't moved at all. Instead, the clouds stayed in the same spot, swirling around the tallest tree on the hill.

Strange.

With no warning, a lightning bolt exploded sideways from the tornado and knocked Gramps ten feet back, only to land with a *thump* on his rear end. His eyes went wide with the impact, and he held his hands to his gut like he had been shot.

"Gramps!" screamed Tess, almost dropping Jak's foot.

Jak struggled to stand so he could help his grandfather, but the old man lifted one hand in a wave and started to crawl back toward them.

Jak breathed a sigh of relief. For a moment, he thought he had lost Gramps too.

A silvery whispering on the hill snapped Jak's attention back to the tornado. It sounded like a voice, but he didn't see anyone near the tree. The clouds above grabbed his attention though; there was something strange about the way they stretched and groaned. They almost looked like...faces.

He sat up in shock. "Did you see that?" he asked, pointing to the tree.

Tess was using the extra seconds to tug at a final knot in the last swatch of bandanna. "See what?" she asked without looking up.

He pointed again. "Faces...up there, in the clouds."

She stopped tying and stared at the tree. "I don't see anything."

"There!" Jak pointed to a spot in the tornado that bore a stark resemblance to a lion.

"What is it?" said Gramps, crawling up next to Jak. He was breathing heavily, and sweat ran down his forehead, as if it had taken every ounce of energy to make it back.

"Faces," said Jak. "In the clouds. They're all over. Look, at the top, there's a bull. See the horns?" But as soon as Jak could name them, the faces melted away in the whirl of the clouds.

Gramps squinted into the tree. "I don't see anything, son."

"There's nothing there, Jak," said Tess, shaking her head.

"They were there," Jak insisted. "I saw them."

Tess looked at Gramps, concerned. "I think he's hallucinating. He must be in shock."

"Look!" Jak pointed to the tree again.

The face of a man stretched out of the tornado, and then an entire body stepped out and onto the ground. But the body wasn't human, nor was it animal. Rather, it was both. It stood as tall as a small tree with giant wings protruding from its back, covered in shiny brown and gold feathers that ruffled against the torrent of wind. The legs were thick, ending in split hooves that stamped the ground, and were covered in black hair—not hair like a person's, but more like a cow's. From the waist up, the creature was human: a barrel-chested man with heavily muscled arms, short wild black hair, a strong nose, and black eyes. Tiny bursts of light rippled through the entire body as if he were plugged into an electric outlet. He twirled a bolt of lightning in his right hand so fast that the jags of light almost blurred together as they crackled.

The face turned toward Jak, and their eyes connected for a moment, black on blue. But then the head twisted to the left, way beyond the distance any human head could turn, and kept spinning until it locked into the face of a lion, framed with a golden mane. And then it twisted again and became a bull, complete with curved horns and a black hide that matched the legs. The head twisted a third time, revealing a golden-eyed eagle.

Suddenly, the creature snapped his wrist, and the lightning bolt disappeared with a crack. His wings twitched and folded in, and the bull legs strode toward the four stunned onlookers.

The canine member of the audience started barking and lunged for the four-faced creature.

"Macy! Get back here!" shouted Jak.

But she didn't pay any attention until the head of the lion spun around again and roared so loudly that Jak thought his eardrums would burst. Macy yipped and stumbled over herself as she retreated behind Jak.

The lion-headed creature stopped directly over Jak and peered into his face with two tawny eyes, a low growl escaping from its throat.

Jak's heart almost crawled out of his chest. Either this was an extremely bad dream, or this guy had a great costume. He pinched his arm because now would be a good time to wake up, but the creature didn't disappear. Instead, the human head twisted around again, and the creature bent down until it was so close Jak could smell its breath — hot, sweet breath, like a flower on fire.

"Poison." Its voice was deep and sounded like a river of voices rushing toward him all at once. The man became silent, staring straight at Jak expectantly, as if waiting for him to either say something or faint with fright.

"Poison?" asked Jak slowly. He wanted to turn away, to break the gaze, but he mustered up every bit of courage he had. "Wh-what poison?"

The man-beast frowned, and his eyes narrowed. "I do not have permission to say, but I have orders to fulfill." He stretched out his arm and pressed a gigantic hand against Jak's forehead. "Go back, Jak. Further back." Then he shoved hard .

A black curtain descended over Jak's eyes as his whole body fell backwards.

CHAPTER 4
The Creature under the Tree

Jak opened his eyes into two narrow slits and squinted at the blue paint on his bedroom ceiling. A warm breeze sailed through his window, and he could hear the leaves rustling in the trees.

He breathed a sigh of relief, rolled over, and closed his eyes. It had all been just a dream. There was no snake, no swivel-headed monster-man, and no black book. *Maybe I can fall asleep again and have a better dream.*

He wriggled on his bed, trying to get comfortable, but his covers must have slipped onto the floor because the mattress felt funny.

Suddenly, he felt something soft and hairy crawling across his cheek, and his eyes flew open.

A giant brown spider sat perched next to his nose, waving two front legs at his eyebrows.

"Ugh!" He swatted the spider from his cheek and jerked upright in his bed—except he wasn't in his bed. In fact, he wasn't even in his bedroom. For that matter, he wasn't even in a house, he was outside.

The spider skittered into the grass next to one of his crutches and disappeared. At the same time, Macy jumped up and slobbered her tongue across his cheek. He could hear Gramps murmuring, "Well, I'll be jiggered. Where in tarnation did we go?"

That was a good question. Jak's head spun from side to side in utter confusion. They couldn't be in the back yard because the last time Jak checked, the back yard was still drowning in rain water. This sky didn't have a cloud in sight, and the ground was dry.

Jak pushed himself up on his knees to get a better view.

They were halfway up a hill covered with long grass. It wasn't the dry brown pokey kind that grew in the vacant lot by the grocery store, but rather a soft deep green grass—the kind that invited you to lie down and take a nap. The grass grew thick, dotted here and there with sprays of white daisies and purple violets. At the bottom of the hill, the grass began to thin out and merge with what appeared to be a white sand beach peppered with black rocks. It had to be a beach because beyond it rolled an unending expanse of sparkling blue water with no other shore in sight.

A short distance down the beach, a wide river churned into the sea. Judging from the froth where the black of the river met the blue of the sea, the current was strong.

Up the hill, a line of trees stretched in either direction as far as Jak could see. They weren't pine trees, but the other kind, with normal leaves, like the giant oak in the back yard at home. Beyond the woods, a range of foothills swelled and disappeared into the horizon, looking very much like something out of a painting that someone would hang above a fireplace.

Behind Jak and Gramps, a small grove of cherry trees gathered together like a clutch of hens in a barnyard, each with glossy green leaves and covered in clusters of bright red fruit. Set apart, as if shunned by the others, stood a lone cherry tree. The cherries of this tree were dark red, almost black, and the leaves were dark green.

As far as he could tell, they were alone. Nothing moved except the grass and the flowers, blown by the wind—no birds, no bees, nothing. Jak scanned the ground, looking for more oversized bugs or any other creatures that might be stalking the area. He shuddered at the thought of encountering one of those gigantic black snakes again, but all he saw was the black book. It was sprawled upside down, pages pressed into the grass, with a skinny red satin bookmark flapping in the breeze.

The book. His grandmother's book. Thinking about his grandmother twisted his stomach back into the knots he'd been trying to untie for six months.

The bottom branches of the black cherry tree began to shake and rattle, pulling him back to the present.

Jak tensed and backed away. The tips of the grass touched the lowest branches of the tree, so he couldn't see what was causing the shaking. But if the spiders were as big as his hand, he had to be prepared for anything.

He raised the crutch in the air like a club and waited, but the only thing that came out from the branches was a shriek: "Somebody help me! My hair is stuck!"

Jak put the crutch down at the sound of Tess's voice, but before either he or Gramps could crawl under the tree to assist, one of the branches snapped, and Tess emerged, looking like she had gotten into a fight with an army of sticks and twigs. The gray bark of broken candy-bar-sized cherry branches stood out like barrettes against her dark brown hair.

She fumbled with the snarls, trying to untangle the stems and leaves and talk at the same time. "What happened? Where are we? What did you do?"

Jak's mouth dropped open and he raised his hands, palms upturned as if to plead his innocence. "I didn't do anything. I just read the first few words of Gramma's book. But then the sentence sort of crawled off the page, and I got dizzy, and we were here." That wasn't quite true, because he had actually ended up in the woods with the snake and the four-faced man, but nobody else had mentioned it, so he kept it to himself.

"But where is *here?*" said Tess.

Jak shrugged his shoulders. "I don't know." He stuffed his hands in his pockets and stared toward the ocean, feeling a little guilty and a lot confused. If only he hadn't followed Frankie that morning.

He knew the basement was real, and the cherry grove they were in now was real. But the clearing with the snake? Had that been real too? It had been so realistic that Jak thought twice about whether or not it was just a dream. *But my foot's okay now, right? Except for the sprain. But what did the man mean when he said I have to go back? Back to what?*

CHAPTER 5

The Ancient Plaque

Most of the sticks were out of Tess's hair by now, and she turned her attention to plucking bits of grass from her otherwise clean light blue T-shirt. "So you just read a few words from the book and we got zapped somewhere else?"

Jak nodded. "I know it doesn't make sense, but that's what happened. It's not my fault."

"What was the first line of the book anyway, Jak?" said Gramps, his eyebrows lifted in anticipation.

"DON'T SAY IT!" Tess shouted.

Gramps stared at her in surprise. "Why not?"

"Why not?" She slapped her shorts, and the remaining strands of grass flew toward the ground. "Because five minutes ago we were trying to catch a rat in the basement, and now we're stuck on a hill in the middle of nowhere."

"He's NOT a rat," said Jak.

"I don't care what it is!" shouted Tess in exasperation.

"Settle down, Tess," said Gramps.

Tess crossed her arms and gazed at the ground.

"Now," said Gramps slowly. "Why don't you want Jak to tell me what the book said?"

Tess lowered her voice. "Because we don't know what will happen if he blurts it out again. Maybe we'll get transported somewhere else, somewhere worse—like in the middle of a volcano or stuck in the ocean."

Or back in school, thought Jak. All things considered, being incinerated in a volcano almost sounded better than sitting through another one of Mrs. Whoople's math classes.

"I don't think so," said Gramps. "We've already been transported. Maybe if we read it again, it will take us back home... or maybe it'll help us figure out what to do next."

"Oh, alright," she said, rolling her eyes. "But, Jak, just whisper it in his ear."

Jak looked around for his other crutch but could only see long green grass. "Do you see my other crutch lying around anywhere?" asked Jak.

Both Gramps and Tess shook their heads.

Great. As much as Jak hated the crutches, they did help him get where he needed to go. Sometimes he only used one crutch, but it required hopping with his good foot, and since he wasn't a rabbit, it didn't take long for him to tire out.

"Gramps, will you come over here instead?"

"Certainly," said Gramps.

Jak glanced at Tess. She looked like an unhappy cat who had just been tossed in a barrel of pickle juice and wasn't sure what to expect next. Whatever it was, she seemed certain she wasn't going to like it.

Extra quietly, he whispered the same three words he had read in the book: "*En el principio.*"

"*En el principio?*" said Gramps, except that Gramps didn't whisper. If anything, he spoke louder than usual.

"Gramps!" said Tess.

A guilty expression crossed his face. "Sorry." He hesitated before going on. "Nothing happened anyway. What's '*el principio*' mean?"

"It means 'the beginning,'" said Jak tentatively. He hoped Tess wouldn't blow up while they were talking. Sometimes being with her was like playing with lit firecrackers.

"So '*En el principio*' means?"

"'In the beginning,'" said Jak.

"The beginning of what?" asked Gramps.

The three stood silent.

"Probably the beginning of a really bad day," said Tess glumly, crossing her arms and turning to face the ocean.

"Maybe what's happened is like one of those books where people get sucked into another world through a wormhole in space," said Jak.

"Oh yeah? What happens to those people?" asked Tess.

"In one book I read, a dinosaur tried to eat them, and in another they were marooned on a desert planet for sixty years, and in another—"

Tess shook her head. "You can stop now, Jak. You're not helping."

But Jak had already stopped. He pushed himself to his knees and stared at what he saw behind Tess. The broken branch of the black cherry tree left just enough space to reveal a tarnished plaque screwed into the ancient trunk.

"What are you looking at?" Tess turned and followed his gaze.

"There's something on the tree," said Jak. He dropped his crutch and crawled underneath the branches.

The plaque was black with splotches of green tracing the edges. It looked very old, but the words on the plaque shone with a dull copper light, as if a million hands had rubbed the age away from the letters.

> Follow the scarlet path to find the place
> where the dead live again
> and the living never die.
> If not, the black fruit will send you home.
> But beware. Death follows the eaters.
>
> Bring the book.
> El

Death, death, death, Jack was sick of thinking about death. As he read the plaque, every scary movie he'd ever seen about the undead ran through his mind. Blank-eyed zombies and half-wrapped mummies was how they usually showed up. He definitely did not want to go to a place where the dead come back to life. He shivered. They had to get out of there, and it looked like the black cherries would do the trick.

"What is it?" asked Tess. She pulled the branches back and stuck her head under the tree.

Jak pointed to the metal plate. "It's a plaque, some kind of message."

Gramps tried to bend over to poke his head under the tree as well but only made it halfway. He grimaced and grabbed his chest, sucking air slowly between his teeth. "Read it to me," he said.

Jak took a deep breath and read the plaque out loud. When he got to the end, a new round of sweat greased his palms as he realized what would happen if they went home. "We're stuck," he said, a note of despair in his voice. "If we stay here, zombies will attack us, but if we go home, we'll die!"

"Zombies?" Gramps scratched his beard and squinted at the sky. "I don't think so. Sounds to me like the dead people will come back to normal life—you know, a real flesh-and-blood body like they used to have."

"No death?" asked Jak, suddenly very interested in what Gramps had to say. "People who are dead now will come back to life and nobody will die? Ever?"

Gramps nodded. "That's what it sounds like to me."

Jak felt a twinge of hope and read the plaque again. His grandfather was right; it did sound like a place where death never showed up. If he could find that place then not only would he never die, but maybe Gramma would come back from the dead too! His heart began to beat faster as the thought took root and began to grow. The only thing was, he hadn't seen any path, just the grassy hill above them and the ocean below.

He backed out from underneath the tree, careful not to scratch his face on the black twigs sticking out from the branches or to accidentally sit on his twisted ankle. "But to get there, we have to follow some path," he said, "and we have to take the book."

The book lay next to the black cherry tree, open faced and upside down, the pages smushed into the grass with the red satin bookmark flapping in the wind.

He nudged the spine with his lone crutch.

"DON'T TOUCH THAT THING!" Tess bent over and yanked Jak's crutch away from the book.

"What? What's wrong?" said Jak.

Tess narrowed her eyes and whispered. "It might do something weird again."

Jak jerked the crutch back out of her hand. "You're being a little paranoid, Tess. There must be some reason this El guy wants us to take the book."

Suddenly, Tess stood up as if she had gotten an idea. "Come on."

"Where are you going?" asked Jak.

"Home. Grab a black cherry. I don't know how this works, but the plaque says they'll send us home."

Jak balked. "Yeah, but it also said that if we eat them, we'll die."

"Tess," said Gramps. He stared at her for a moment before continuing. "I know it sounds crazy, but getting plucked out of the basement and ending up here is crazy too. Aren't you even a little bit curious about a place where dead people come back to life?"

"No." Tess flipped her hair back behind her ears. "It's impossible, Gramps. There's no such place. Dead is *dead.*" She hesitated, and her face softened. "I know. I miss Gramma, too, but she's gone, and there is nothing we do can bring her back."

"But what if we could?" said Gramps. "What if we could bring her back?" His bright blue eyes were wide and wild, and, with his gray hair sticking up in the back, he looked every bit like a mad scientist on the brink of a great discovery.

Tess stared back at him and then shook her head. "That's impossible." She fingered one of the black cherries. "I just want to go home."

"But if we go home, we'll die!" said Jak.

"Everybody dies someday," said Tess.

"I know that," Jak replied, "but what if it means we die NOW, as soon as we get home? Maybe the burning pancakes set the house on fire. If we eat the black cherries, we might get home just in time to burn to death in the kitchen."

Tess didn't answer; she only rubbed at another spot on the black cherry. Jak could tell she was wavering.

"And if there really is a place," Jak pondered, "where we won't die and where dead people come back to life, we at least have to try to find it."

"In case you haven't noticed, there is no path." Tess pointed around the grove. "That sign is ancient. If there really was a path, it's long gone by now. I mean, what are we supposed to do? Wander around looking for graveyards with dead people digging themselves out? And have you thought about the fact that we don't even know who this El is? For all we know, he could be looking for his next meal. Maybe every time he gets hungry he zaps somebody here and then lures them into a giant boiling pot of people stew."

"Seems if that's what he wanted, he would have just plunked us straight from the basement into the pot, doesn't it?" said Gramps, cocking one white eyebrow.

The tension hung thick between them, an unspoken tug-o-war with Gramps and Jak on one side and Tess on the other.

"Gramma never would have done something like this," said Tess. "She would have gone straight home. She..."

Jak tuned Tess out, leaving Gramps to deal with her. He watched Macy running from tree to tree, sniffing whatever it is that dogs sniff. Suddenly she stopped, snorted, and began scrabbling at the dirt with her front paws.

While Gramps and Tess continued arguing, Jak stood and hobbled toward the dog. "What is it, Macy?" He bent down and inspected the spot where Macy had scraped the crust away. Underneath lay an earth brown stone, flat on the top and squared off at one edge.

Jak brushed away more dirt, revealing three more square edges. It was a stone brick! He ripped up the grass next to the brick and swept away the dirt, revealing three more stones just like the first. They were pieced together like one of those fancy sidewalks in downtown St. Paul.

Strange, he thought. *A sidewalk in the middle of the hill? Why would anyone put a sidewalk in the middle of a hill?* He stopped in mid-thought. *The path from the plaque! This must be it. But if this is the path, which way does it lead?* It would take a lot of digging to answer that question.

He stretched his fingers wide and placed his palm on the first brick. *Do you really lead to a place without death?* As soon as the question formed in his mind, a gust of salty wind howled up from the ocean and tore across the field, slapping the grass hard to the ground.

Jak dropped low to keep from getting blown over, nervous that he had unwittingly unleashed something new.

The wind began to rip up grass and dirt, spewing green and black chunks across the field like a lawnmower that had drunk too much coffee. In its wake stood a brown brick path, three feet wide and stretching all the way up the hill to the edge of the woods. Then, just as suddenly as it had come, the wind disappeared. All that could be heard now was the crashing of the breakers on the beach below

Jak stuck his head up. His freak-o-meter was bouncing between "wow" and "scary." On one hand, it was exciting to see the wind mow a path through the field, but on the other, it terrified him. He had no idea how it had happened, but there was no denying the fact that a road of brown bricks now led up the hill toward the woods.

"I think we just found the path," he said, his voice trembling.

Tess virtually exploded. "Jak Hamelton, what did you do this time?"

"I didn't do anything!" said Jak, getting to his knees. "Macy found a brick in the dirt. All I did was touch it."

"Stop touching stuff!" Tess glared at him in exasperation.

"But don't you get it?" said Gramps, his eyes dancing like he had just found Christmas. "This is it! It's like the yellow brick road, except instead of leading us to Oz, it'll take us to the place without death."

Tess looked at Gramps, then at the path. "The plaque says it's supposed to be scarlet. There's nothing scarlet about these stones."

Gramps laughed. "After what just happened, how could it NOT be the path?"

Tess twirled her hair between her fingers and gave a deep sigh. "Alright, fine. If this is that important to you, we can follow it, at least for a little while."

"Then we have to take the book," said Jak, pointing behind him.

Tess bit her lip and sighed again. "Alright, but I'm going to be the one who picks it up."

She circled the upside-down book like it was a snapping turtle, then stretched out one foot and flipped it over with her toe. The front cover flopped open to the cloth pages in the beginning, but when Tess stooped to pick it up, her hand flew to her mouth and she gasped.

"What's wrong?" Jak hopped to her side.

"They're gone! The cards are gone," she said, recoiling from the book as if it had a disease.

"What do you mean they're gone?" asked Gramps, fumbling in his shirt pocket for his glasses.

Jak held up the book so Gramps could see. "They're *gone* gone. They're not here."

There was now only one page of cloth, and it held three empty pockets. He turned the page and came to the first paper page, the one with his grandmother's name on it, but this page was different too.

Jak caught his breath.

"What is it?" Gramps slid his glasses onto his nose and read over Jak's shoulder. "Well, I'll be jiggered!"

The page looked the same as before, except now, under *Josefina Maria Leon*, in the same blue ink, was written *Jak Joseph Hamelton.*

Not only that, but the words on the next page had all transformed from Spanish to English.

"I want to go home," said Tess, twirling her hair around her finger twice as fast as she normally did. "This is just too weird." She took a step backwards. "I know the two of you want to stick around and see what happens, but I at least want the option of eating the cherries. I mean, what happens if the book suddenly whisks us somewhere else, somewhere really dangerous? Just because you don't have any reason to go home doesn't mean I don't." She stopped, as if she realized how much her words had stung Gramps. "What I mean is," she continued in a softer tone, "can we at least pick four cherries and put them in our pockets? Then if something bad happens, we can eat them and go home."

"Yeah, go home and die," said Jak, closing the book.

Tess rolled her eyes.

"Alright," said Gramps. "Go ahead and pick the cherries. It won't do any harm to pluck 'em from the tree."

Tess went back to the black cherry tree. The branches were so loaded with fruit that they dipped and bowed to the ground. She chose one cluster near the end of the branch closest to her and plucked it from the tree. The branch twanged back into the air, and several cherries dropped to the ground next to her feet. As soon as they hit the grass, they began spinning, hissing, and spitting, like lit fireworks.

Tess jumped back. The grass where she had been standing wilted and turned brown. Then the whole mess of broiling cherries and grass began to smolder and burn until nothing was left except a charred circle on the ground.

The three of them stood silent and unmoving, staring at the scorched dirt. Tess glanced at the four cherries she held in her hand and then very carefully handed one to Gramps. "Don't drop it," she instructed. She held out the other two to Jak, dangling them by the stem in front of his nose. "You get two, Jak—one for you and one for Macy."

But Jak backed up a half a step and didn't take them. He had seen what had just happened. "I don't want any of them."

"You have to." She thrust the cherries toward him again.

"Why?" he said, burying his hands in his pockets.

"Because Macy listens to you, Jak. If we get in trouble, she has to come quickly, or she might get left behind."

"But I can hardly walk, Tess. How am I going to hold *one* cherry, much less two?"

"Put them in your pocket."

Jak's jaw dropped. "Are you serious? You saw what they just did to the ground. What if they do the same thing in my pants?"

She fixed Jak with her trademark 'I'm-the-grown-up-and-you're-the-little-boy' stare. "Do you want Macy to get trapped here?"

As much as he hated to admit it, Jak knew she was right. Even though Macy was officially Gramps's dog, she listened to him more than anyone. He took the cherries from her hand and put them in his pocket, silently wishing he had worn fireproof underwear. "Where is Macy anyway?" He hadn't seen her since the wind tore up the grass. "Macy!" Jak called, but she didn't appear. So much for Macy listening to him.

He was just about to put two fingers in his mouth to whistle when a bark sounded in the distance, toward the sea. They looked down the hill and saw a black and white speck on the beach barking at the water, or rather at something *in* the water. A black form flew into the air above the waves and crashed back down.

"Hey, look!" Jak pointed to the sea. "A dolphin!"

Suddenly, the air above the sea erupted into a column of green and silver flames twenty feet long. The black body shot out of the water toward the beach. It unfolded four legs and landed on the sand in a full gallop, its mouth agape, heading straight toward Macy.

Without even thinking, Jak took a step forward to run down the hill. He had to get down to the beach. Whatever that animal was, it was going to eat Macy.

But as soon as his right foot touched the ground, he crumpled, pain ricocheting through his sprained ankle.

"Jak," said Gramps, taking a step toward him.

Jak ignored the pain and struggled to get up so he could see what was going on. "I'm fine. What's happening to Macy?"

Gramps peered down the hill. "Macy's running up the hill. She's in the grass now. She's got a good head start. The creature's still on the beach. I think she'll be okay."

"What is that thing?" asked Tess, squinting toward the beach.

"I don't know," said Gramps. "Some kind of water dog, maybe."

"Water dog?" said Jak, standing upright once again, his chest pounding. He shook his head. "I don't think so. More like a shark with legs."

"But the flame," said Tess. "That silver flame! Where did it come from?"

By now Jak had regained his footing and could see down the hill. He could barely see the top of Macy's white ears bounding through the grass. Gramps was right in saying she had a good head start; however, her short legs were no match for the creature's long stride, and the gap was closing quickly.

In any other situation, this would have been funny, because one of Macy's favorite past times was chasing rabbits. Any chance she got, she shot out the door for hours at a time, frightening every long-eared rodent she could find. But now she was the rabbit, and she was running for her life. Macy's bark changed from the normal defiant challenge to a frightened yelp.

Jak shuddered and wished he could run down to help her, but Macy was on her own, and Jak didn't think she was going to make it. The creature was too fast, gaining too quickly. Whenever he watched nature shows, this was the point where he always turned off the TV. He hated the pounce and hated the kill even more. Once the TV was off, he could pretend it never happened, but this was different.

Macy was just a few feet in front of the creature now, and he knew there was no way she could get away. The black body flung itself into the air, massive paws poised to pull her down. At that moment, a scream pierced the air.

The creature whipped its head around and looked up the hill straight at Jak. That's when Jak realized *he* was the one who had screamed. Macy shot to the left, and the creature landed hard on its side, then bounced up and changed course, this time heading straight up the hill toward the grove. It bellowed, as if angry over the lost prey, but now charging toward another. Suddenly an orange burst of flame shot out in front of the animal, just like a dragon in a movie.

A dragon? A dragon!

"The fire! It's coming from that animal. C'mon!" said Jak, hopping as fast as he could with one crutch. "We have to get back, behind the trees."

The grove wasn't the best fortress against a creature who could breathe fire, but it was all they had, and it was better than being out in the open. They crouched in the grass and peeked out between the branches of the largest cherry tree they could find.

The creature careened to a halt beside the black cherry tree. It pawed at the ground and shook its head, sending a sputter of sparks toward the cherries.

"It's definitely not a dog," whispered Tess.

Jak hesitated, a little nervous to say what he really thought it was, but he mustered his courage and said quietly, "I think it's a dragon."

"A dragon?" said Gramps, both eyebrows arching up.

"It can't be a dragon," said Tess. "It doesn't look anything like a dragon. Besides, dragons aren't real." But she stopped short as the creature snorted a purple flame.

"Go and tell *him* that," said Jak, cocking his head toward the dragon.

Up close, the creature's head resembled that of a small horse. A long pink tongue hung out and lapped at the air like a dog, as if it was drinking in smells. The animal put its head back and wailed a forlorn cry that sounded something like a cross between a wolf's howl and a lion's roar.

"He must not be able to see very well, the way he keeps tossing his head back and forth," said Jak. "I've seen Macy do that when she's lost the scent of a rabbit."

"I don't like being sniffed out." Tess shivered. "Makes me think he wants to eat us."

Gramps tapped Jak on the shoulder and pointed to the field on the other side of the grove.

The flowers moved as if a light breeze had blown over them. But through the long grass, Jak could make out the form of a cat creeping toward them— not a nice little house cat, but a mean-looking golden wildcat, as big as a coffee table. And he looked hungry.

Jak's shoulders slumped. They were stuck between being barbecued or torn to shreds.

CHAPTER 6

A Disturbing Second Plaque

Jak touched Tess's arm and pointed behind them. As soon as she saw the cat, Tess's face turned stark white. She dug the black cherry out of her pocket and hissed, "Eat it."

Jak shook his head and pointed again, this time down the hill toward Macy.

Tess shook her head and mouthed the words, *"I'm sorry. . .we have to go."*

But before they could do anything, the cat leapt into the air, landing silently on padded paws just two feet away from their hiding place.

Jak was wrong. The creature wasn't as big as a coffee table; it was as big as the orange couch in Gramps's basement. They slunk even further into the grass, not that it made any difference. A pair of bright yellow eyes eyed them up and down, accompanied by a quiet growl.

It was going to be death by cat.

But instead of taking a swipe at them, it made another tremendous leap straight over the cherry tree and landed on top of the dragon, dropping it to the ground with a snort and a thud.

Even though Jak had been terrified just a minute earlier of being scorched to death by the dragon, he didn't want to watch the beast get torn apart by the cat. But he couldn't take his eyes away.

The cat opened his mouth wide near the dragon's neck, and Jak cringed, waiting for the teeth to rip open the dragon, but it never happened. Instead, a red tongue darted out of its mouth and licked the dragon's muzzle, then the big cat rolled over and started purring.

Jak stared on in disbelief, dumbfounded.

In turn, the dragon licked the cat's face with his own tongue, poked his head back into the grove, and continued flitting his tongue under the branches of the tree next to their hiding place.

Tess tapped Jak and Gramps on their shoulders. When she had both of their attention, she pointed to the black cherry in her hand and then pointed to her mouth.

Jak shook his head. There was no way he was going to leave Macy behind. Besides, after what he'd just witnessed, he was certain neither the dragon nor the wildcat wanted to hurt them, but he knew he would have a hard time convincing Tess of that without proof, so he did the only thing he could do. He stooped under the branches of the tree and hopped into the field, in full view of both animals.

The dragon snorted a green flame and trotted straight toward Jak. His hinged jaw was open at a wide angle, revealing an army of teeth behind his wagging pink tongue. He stopped right in front of Jak and flopped onto his haunches like a giant dog. Then he brought his snout so close that Jak could feel the hot breath stinging his cheek. With no warning, the tongue shot out of the creature's mouth and swiped directly across Jak's face, almost knocking him over. Then the creature rubbed his head against Jak's shoulder, and a rumble shook its body.

Jak laughed and ran his hand through the creature's mane. "See?" he called through the branches. "He wants to be friends."

Gramps stooped under the branches and into the field, but Tess remained hidden.

"What about the cat?" she asked, poking her head out from between the branches.

The golden cat growled quietly and lifted his head to look at Jak, but instead of pouncing, it only licked its paw for a moment and then laid back down in the sun as if bored with the whole situation and needed a nap.

"He's going to sleep," said Jak. "You can come on out."

Tess crept out from behind the tree, watching the dragon like a hawk with every step she took. "Are you sure that thing is not going to eat us?"

"Tess, look at his teeth," Gramps said. "They're flat like cow's teeth, not sharp like..." He glanced over to the cat before finishing his sentence, hushing his voice a little "...like a tiger's. This animal was made for grazing, not hunting." But at that moment, the wild cat yawned, revealing a mouthful of teeth that looked a lot like the fire breather's.

Strange, thought Jak before turning his attention back to the dragon. "He's like a big dog, Tess, Come on, feel his head."

She wasn't convinced and stayed by the tree, but the dragon wasn't about to be ignored, and in one quick motion, he bounded to her side and licked her from chin to ear, drenching her with as much affection as saliva. Tess started to scream, but she stopped as it became obvious the only thing the dragon wanted to do was drag his tongue across her face. She gave a slight smile and patted the animal lightly on the head. "Okay. You win."

Up close, the creature looked like some odd mix between a Great Dane, a horse, and a giraffe. His head was like that of a small horse: boxy on one end and tapering down to the snout. It was attached to his body by a long neck, like a mini-giraffe, so his eyes were a full head above Gramps's. He had long lips, short, sleek black hair, and cow brown eyes crowned with a white diamond perched in the middle of his forehead.

A short black mane sprouted on the top of his head and wound its way down the creature's back like a cape, ending just before a long tail with the same black fur. His body was the same size as a Great Dane's, solid, yet lithe, rippling with muscle. His legs were lanky and long, like a horse's legs, but instead of hooves, he had extra-long dog feet.

A rainbow of scales covered the bottom of the creature's neck, flanks, and legs. They were dark and iridescent, the same as the wings on the green beetles that showed up on Gramps's porch every spring. Jak expected the scales to be hard and rough, but instead they were smooth and supple to the touch, like a leather couch.

But the most amazing aspect of the animal had to be the fire. With almost every breath, sparks flew from the creature's mouth. When he snorted (which he seemed to do often, making Jak wonder if he had some kind of cold), flames the same variety of colors as his scales blew out his nose.

"This is the craziest animal I've ever seen," Gramps said.

"Yeah. He's like a dragon," said Jak, "except he doesn't look or feel like a dragon." Jak ran his hands down the creature's mane. "He's soft and warm." The fire breather's tongue washed his cheek again, and Jak couldn't help but laugh. "And friendly."

The creature's muzzle nuzzled the pocket with the black cherries in it, and Jak pulled one out and held it aloft. "Are you hungry?"

Tess pulled his hand back. "Don't give him that one! You might need it." She plucked a cherry from the branch above her head. "Give him this one instead."

Jak looked at Tess, slightly annoyed, and then dangled the freshly picked cherry in front of the fire breather's nose. His lips curled back and pulled the fruit into its mouth, crunching the flesh, pit, and stem at the same time. When he nuzzled Jak again, Jak picked another red treat and fed it to the beast.

"I wonder why he doesn't pick cherries himself," said Tess. "He's certainly tall enough."

"Maybe he just wants me to feed him," Jak said, picking another cherry. "I think he likes me."

"Don't get too attached, Jak," Gramps said. "He's a wild animal, and I'm sure he'll probably be on his way in a few minutes. He's probably just curious and hasn't seen anything like us before."

Jak stroked the fire breather's skin, watching the iridescent scales change colors as the flanks moved in and out with the animal's breath. "I think I'll call him Scorch."

Gramps laughed. "Yep. The best way to keep from getting attached to an animal is to name him."

A bark sounded in the distance. Macy stood on the stone pathway, half-way up the hill, staring at the woods at the top of the hill, her tail pointed straight up in the air.

Jak had seen that stance a thousand times before. She smelled something, and it would only be a matter of seconds before she followed her nose and rocketed up the path. Jak whistled, but she ignored him.

"We have to get up there, or she's going to run."

But it was too late. Macy charged up the hill and disappeared into the darkness of the woods.

"C'mon," said Jak. He hated to leave the fire breather, but he knew if they didn't get Macy right away, she might get lost or, even worse, run into an animal that really *did* want to eat her. He grabbed his crutch and began to hobble up the path.

"Jak!" Tess called after him. "It'll take you a month to get up there limping like that."

He swiveled on his good foot and peered at Tess in frustration. "Well, what am I supposed to do then? It's not like you or Gramps can give me a piggy-back ride."

Just then, the fire breather came alongside Jak and lay down next to him. He craned his head back and gently bit Jak's sleeve, pulling him toward his broad back.

"What is he doing?" asked Tess.

"I...I don't know," said Jak.

"I think he wants to give you a ride," said Gramps.

The suggestion surprised Jak. He had always wanted to ride a horse, but his mom was allergic to hay, so they avoided stables at all costs. This wasn't a horse, but the thought of riding the fire breather sounded just as much fun... as long as he didn't get burned.

He swung his bad leg around the fire breather's back, and the creature gently lifted itself off the ground. Jak grinned. *This is way better than riding a horse.*

The cape of fur on Scorch's back was still damp from the ocean, but it made for a comfortable seat nonetheless, and was certainly better than walking — especially with just one crutch. It was also long enough that Jak was able to hang onto it like reins.

"I'll take your crutch, Jak," said Gramps. "It'll make a good walking stick. That just leaves the book."

"We're taking it with us?" asked Tess, sounding surprised and not too pleased about it.

"Of course," said Jak. "We already talked about this. That's what that El guy said on the plaque, didn't he? We have to take the book with us."

Tess crossed her arms in a huff. "I'm okay with taking this path for a little while, but I'm not carrying that book."

"Then I'll carry it," said Jak.

"How?"

Jak thought for a moment. He couldn't let go of Scorch's fur, or he would fall off his back. If only he had brought his school backpack, then it would be easy. "Um, I'll stuff it in my shirt."

"Your shirt?"

"Yeah." He made sure his shirt was tucked into his jeans and held out his hand for the book.

"Okay, but only on one condition," said Tess sternly, raising an eyebrow.

"And that is?"

"You have to promise not to open the book. I don't want to all of a sudden get zapped to the North Pole or the middle of the ocean somewhere. Promise?"

Jak was itching to read more, but if this was the only way Tess would compromise, he didn't have a choice. "Fine. I promise."

"Cross your heart and hope to die?" She made an X on her chest with one finger.

Jak didn't hope to die, but that was part of the promising ritual, so he had to do it. "Hope to die." Jak crossed his chest too.

He took the book and stuffed it down his shirt until it sat snugly next to the waistband of his pants. It was a little uncomfortable, but at least it would be safe.

Another bark echoed in the woods, followed by a yip.

Tess eyed the cherries hanging above her. "I wish I had a bag. I'd pack up some of these cherries. Who knows what we'll find to eat later on. We might starve to death."

"Here...take my jacket," said Gramps. He unzipped his yellow windbreaker and handed it to Tess.

She laid the thin jacket on the ground and piled bunches of cherries on top. Then she folded it up and tied a big knot with the sleeves and tail of the coat. "Alright," she said, hefting the makeshift lunch box. "I'm ready. Let's go."

Now that they were all packed up, the only problem was that Jak wasn't sure how to get Scorch to go. He tried rocking back and forth, but that didn't work. He even tried the age-old "Giddyap," but the dragon creature just looked at him like he was talking nonsense.

"Maybe you should kick him," said Gramps.

"Are you crazy?" said Jak. "I'm on his back. Where do you think I'd end up if I kicked him?"

"That's how cowboys do it."

"Well, horses can't breathe fire." It was bad enough having a messed-up ankle. Jak had no desire to add third-degree burns. "Do you think there's an ON button somewhere?"

"Did you try telling him what to do?" said Gramps.

"He's an animal," said Tess. "He doesn't understand English."

"Maybe not, but he sure knew I needed a ride." Jak didn't know what else to try, so he grabbed tight onto Scorch's mane and said, "Scorch, find Macy."

Immediately, Scorch surged up the path, his head sweeping back and forth, tongue lapping the air the same way it had when he was looking for them behind the cherry trees. Gramps and Tess could hardly keep up.

At the edge of the field, where the path plunged into the woods, another plaque, as old and green as the first, sat plastered on a tall red rock. Jak could barely read the words as Scorch zoomed past, but as soon as he read them, alarm bells began ringing in his head.

C H A P T E R   7

The Whispering Gate

He sat up straight. *Did that plaque say what I think it said?* The first plaque had promised that the path led to the place where dead people come back to life, the place where the living never die, but this new plaque said:

Following will cost your life.

That doesn't make any sense, thought Jak. *How can we be dead and alive at the same time?*

Scorch swept deeper into the woods, fifty feet ahead of Gramps and Tess. Almost right away, the sun disappeared, lost in the deep green foliage high above their heads, and the path changed from brown bricks to dirt. Jak expected it to be cold and spooky, but it was quite the contrary. The shadows felt like a warm blanket in a safe corner of a house where you could curl up and take a nap.

But as calm as the place seemed, Jak was anything but relaxed. The message from the second plaque rolled around his stomach.

43

"Jak!" called Tess. She sounded like she was at least a mile away.

Jak pulled back on Scorch's mane, and the beast reluctantly slowed to a walk. Gramps and Tess finally caught up and panted to a stop behind them.

"Slow that thing down, would ya, Jak?" Gramps wheezed. He bent over and put his hands on his knees. "Or else you're gonna give me another heart attack."

But Jak hardly heard him. "Did you see that plaque?"

"What plaque?" asked Tess, looking around.

"On that big red rock!" Jak pointed back to the entrance to the woods.

Tess shook her head and shrugged.

"I didn't see a thing," said Gramps. "I was too busy just trying to breathe."

"It said 'Following will cost your life.' I don't get it. The first plaque said this path is supposed to keep us from dying, not make us die."

"I told you so!" said Tess. "We should just eat the black cherries and go home."

Macy's howl echoed through the woods, causing Scorch to stamp his feet and strain forward.

Jak looked down the path, but he couldn't see the dog anywhere, no matter how much he squinted and strained his eyes. He was torn. It seemed that no matter what he chose, eating the black cherries or following the path, he would end up dead. He turned back to Tess. "If you want to go, Tess, you can go, but I'm not leaving until I find Macy."

"I didn't say I'm leaving." Tess looked at the ground and tucked a stray strand of hair behind her ear. "All I said was that it makes more sense to go home."

Gramps straightened, still trying to catch his breath. "Home? We just started, for Pete's sake. Let's keep going."

"But...," said Jak, nervously twisting on Scorch's back and pointing towards the field again, "what about the second plaque? We're going to get killed trying to get to the place where nobody dies!"

Gramps shook his head. "Didn't say you'll die."

"Yes, it did," said Jak, nodding his head.

"No...it said it will cost your life."

Jak looked at Gramps with a confused expression on his face. "Isn't that the same as dying?"

"Could be." Gramps cocked one bushy eyebrow. "But not necessarily."

Jak scratched his head. "But that doesn't make any—"

Macy howled again, and Scorch leapt forward before Jak could say "sense."

He yanked on Scorch's mane. "Slow down, boy. Gramps and Tess can't go as fast as we can."

Scorch slowed to a brisk walk, slow enough for Gramps and Tess to keep up but fast enough to push them along.

Jak kept a sharp eye out for the black snake. He was still pretty certain that the four-faced man and the snake had just been a dream, but it didn't hurt to keep his eyes open. He patted Scorch on the neck, hoping that if the snake did show up, the fire breather would blast him to smithereens.

Gradually the salty smell of the sea was completely replaced by the piney fragrance of the wooden giants. Jak kept a sharp eye on the trees, but nothing attacked them from the woods; they didn't even see any other animals. The higher up into the hills they went, the more he began to recognize elm and oak trees and purple and white sprays of familiar woodland flowers, but there was also something very different about the place.

"This isn't like home at all," said Jak.

By this time, Scorch had let Gramps and Tess catch up, and they walked together.

"Really, Sherlock?" said Tess, smirking. "You just noticed that?"

He shot Tess a look. "I mean there's something different about the air and the light. They're more..." Jak couldn't think of the right word.

"They're more *alive*," said Gramps in between breaths. "More invigorating."

"How can light be *more* alive?" asked Tess. "It's not even alive in the first place."

"I don't know. It just is," said Jak.

Gramps wiped the sweat from his forehead with his bandanna. "How 'bout if we take a short break? I haven't walked this far since I got lost in the parking lot at the mall." He stopped, stretched his arms, and twisted from side to side, then tried unsuccessfully to touch his toes. "I feel a lot better than I did this morning, but I could go for a rest."

Jak needed a break too. Although he was grateful for the ride, sitting that long without moving his legs meant that fluid pooled in his sprained ankle, and it was throbbing. Plus, Jak's pants were wet with seawater and sweat. Unsurprisingly, Scorch's body was hot. A rainbow of sparks flew from his mouth every few feet.

Apparently, Scorch needed a break as well because he lay down on the ground. But as soon as Jak dismounted, Scorch shot up and galloped off into the woods.

"Hey! Where're you going?" Jak called after him, but Scorch was lost in the trees.

"You might be walking the rest of the way," said Gramps, lying down on the ground and closing his eyes.

"I hope not." Jak took the book out from his shirt and laid it on the ground. It felt a little damp from the sweat, but other than that, it was okay. He then slowly unwrapped the Ace bandage from around his ankle. As the pressure released, a cool breeze bathed the hot skin, sending goose bumps up his leg.

The ankle hadn't changed much since yesterday. It was still swollen to twice its normal size and still black, blue, and yellowish green. He tried to flex his foot, but a jolt of pain shot through his ankle. *Not yet.* The doctor said it was a severe sprain that might need surgery to heal properly. He wished for the thousandth time they had played kickball instead of hide-and-seek. Then he never would've fallen in the river.

Tess handed him a red cherry. "Want one?" she said, her mouth full. "They're really good."

"Yeah, sure." He sank his teeth into the flesh of the fruit, and a flood of the cherriest flavor he had ever tasted washed through his mouth. At the same time, he felt a layer of tiredness melt away.

A bark muffled through the woods, but Jak couldn't tell if Macy was in trouble or still just chasing a phantom rabbit. Either way, she was still ahead of them, and they had to keep going.

"Gramps, you ready?" asked Jak, poking him in the stomach with his left foot. There wasn't as much padding as there used to be. Gramps had lost about fifteen pounds since Gramma died.

"Hmm?" Gramps mouth twitched as he raised his head off the ground and peered at Jak through half-closed eyes.

"Time to go." He wrapped the bandage around his ankle again and stood.

Gramps sat up and rubbed the muscles in his feet, careful to avoid a corn at the base of his right big toe. "Wish I'd worn my sneakers instead of these dadburned slippers."

"Yeah," said Tess, "and I wish I'd grabbed a stack of pancakes."

Jak grabbed his crutch from where it lay next to Gramps. "I think I'm going to need my crutch. Scorch didn't come back." He wasn't looking forward to hobbling along with one crutch, but that was the only way he could make the journey.

Gramps stood and rubbed his eyes. "Wonder how those pancakes are doing at home all by themselves."

"Probably the same as always," said Jak.

"What does that mean?"

"Lumpy and burnt to perfection."

Gramps raised an eyebrow. "Are you saying you don't like my pancakes?"

"No." Jak smiled. "Just that I'm always surprised the fire truck doesn't show up every time you make them."

"Well, if it did show up, the firemen would jump out with plates and forks in their hands, ready for a feast. Matter of fact, I bet they'd ask me to come and cook at their next pancake breakfast."

"You mean so they could practice putting out fires?"

"Shhh," said Tess. "What's that noise?"

"Where?" whispered Jak.

"There's something in the woods."

Jak held his crutch like a club again, remembering the message from the second plaque. He wasn't going to lose his life, at least, not if he could help it.

They listened hard but heard nothing.

Suddenly, a dark form darted out of the woods, straight toward Jak, bowling him to the ground.

It all happened so fast that Jak dropped the crutch and instinctively spread his hands out to keep from hitting the ground hard, but he was happy. "Scorch, you came back!" He was dripping with water, pink tongue waving like a flag in the air. The fire breather nuzzled Jak with his head and knelt.

"The river that flows into the sea must be down there somewhere," said Gramps.

Jak put his hand out and touched Scorch's back. It was soaking wet. Riding him would be like sitting on top of a sponge, but he would rather have a wet rear end than to have to hobble through the woods.

The dirt path continued up the ridge, where the trees began to thin in an unnatural way. Instead of growing randomly, there seemed to be a sort of pattern, trees growing in lines and squares. And it wasn't only the trees. The shrubs and the flowers both began to appear in clumps, hedges, and trellises. It was obvious someone loved the place very much and spent a great deal of time tending the plants.

At the top of the hill, they stopped. No one said anything, and all they could do was stare.

Below them lay a valley, lush and green. It was filled with fruit groves and flowers scattered in a wild, yet captivating pattern throughout the garden, as if an eccentric gardener had thrown seeds everywhere in a crazy plan that actually worked. Another ridge, higher than the one they were on, towered to the left, except that instead of a gentle slope edging into the garden, it was a sheer cliff. A river as wide as the Mississippi thundered over the edge. Halfway up the cliff, part of the river hit another section of rock and flowed toward the sea, but the rest crashed into the valley. A cloud of mist swirled above the treetops.

"Wow," said Tess, entranced. "I wish I had a camera."

Gramps nodded and whispered, "It's beautiful."

"Who do you think planted this?" said Tess. "It just kind of showed up out of nowhere."

"Maybe it was that El guy," offered Jak.

A bark echoed through the valley.

In the awe of seeing such a beautiful garden, Jak had almost forgotten about Macy. But seeing the vastness of the valley reminded him that if he didn't find her soon, he might never find her.

"Is Macy down there, Scorch?"

Scorch's tongue still wagged back and forth the same way it had since they left the cherries. A blue flame erupted from his nose, and he stretched a paw forward on the path.

Jak took that as a 'yes.' Unless Scorch was leading them on a wild goose chase, he assumed they must still be headed in the right direction.

"Let's go," he said.

Scorch struck out, jogging lightly over the path as they zigzagged down the hill. But as they zagged around a clump of birch trees, the path stopped, blocked by a tall arched gate. There was no fence attached to the gate. It was just a frame and a closed door, either inviting them to walk through and continue down the hill or warning them to stay away, Jak wasn't sure which. He tried to slow Scorch down to think for a moment, but the fire breather kept going until they reached the gate. As soon as they arrived, Scorch stopped abruptly and knelt down to the ground.

Jak assumed this meant he was supposed to get off, so he did.

"DON'T TOUCH IT, JAK!" shouted Tess, her hands cupped in a megaphone as she ran down the hill after him.

Jak looked back and flung his arms out in both directions to show that his hands weren't going anywhere. "I didn't," he insisted. "I'm just looking."

She trotted up next to him, her cheeks flushed pink from running. "Yeah, well, every time you touch something, weird things happen."

Gramps puffed in and bent over, his hands on his knees. "It's almost as hard going down the hill as it was going up." He eyed the gate. "What is this thing anyway?"

"I'm not sure," said Jak. "Looks like some sort of gate."

The posts on either side of the door were as fat as dictionaries and stretched straight up in the air until they reached the top of Gramps's head. Then they angled in, reaching for each other until they touched and formed a peak on the top, about ten feet from the ground. A giant door, two feet wider than the path, hung on weathered brass hinges, solid and shut. A matching brass door knocker rested in the middle of the door. The entire gate, except for the brass, was painted royal blue. It seemed very new, yet very old at the same time.

Jak peered around the gate, but there was nothing there except trees, grass, and flowers. The path was gone, just like that.

A ripple of excitement flooded over him as he realized what that meant. *The path ends here, so this must be the entrance to the land without death.* He wondered if it could really be that easy. So far, it hadn't cost him anything except a hike through the hills.

Etched into the wood of the gate were black swirls, whorls, lines, and letters that looked like a mixed-up alphabet soup from every language of the world. Every square inch was covered with different patterns.

"Look at this," said Jak, pointing to the frame.

"What is it?" said Gramps, pulling his glasses out of his pocket.

"Pictures, letters, everywhere, carved into the wood."

"What do they say?" Gramps put his glasses on and peered at the carvings.

"I don't know. I can't read them."

Jak touched one of the carvings on the door. It glowed a faint red, and a quiet voice whispered something in the air.

He snatched his finger from the wood and looked around but saw no one. Jak knew Tess didn't want him to touch the gate, but he had to find out. After glancing behind him to make sure Tess wasn't looking, he touched another carving. It, too, glowed, and a deeper voice whispered this time.

Tess stepped back abruptly from the door, her eyes wide. "What was that?"

"I think it's coming from the carvings," whispered Jak.

"Here's one I can read," said Gramps, pointing to a spot near his head.

Jak stood on the tiptoes of his left foot and scrutinized the letters, with no luck. It was just a jumble of letters with some weird symbols he didn't recognize. "You can read that gibberish?" asked Jak in disbelief. "It looks like some kind of hieroglyphics to me."

"Yah sure, you betcha. It's Swedish," said Gramps, with a hint a pride in his voice. He pointed to the letters and sounded them out. "*I begynnelsen...*"

His fingers were only a hair's breadth away from the inscription. Jak gently bumped Gramps's elbow so his fingers touched the wood. Immediately, the words glowed red, and a man's voice flowed out of the gate, echoing the words Gramps had just spoken.

"Whoa!" Gramps's eyebrows shot up in amazement.

"What was that?" asked Tess, inspecting Gramps's post now.

Gramps's eyes narrowed, and he glanced at Jak

Jak knew his grandfather was well aware of what Jak had done. Jak gulped and looked away, pretending to inspect another carving on the gate.

"If you touch the inscriptions, they glow and talk to you," said Gramps. "Right, Jak?"

"Yeah," said Jak, his face flushing a light shade of red. "That's pretty cool, Gramps. What did that guy say? I couldn't understand a word he said."

"He said, 'In the beginning.'"

"In the beginning?" said Jak, turning around in surprise. He hadn't anticipated that. "That's what the book said."

"I bet that's what every single one of these inscriptions says," said Gramps, running his hands lightly over the wood. A sprinkling of whispers followed his finger.

Jak wondered what was so important about 'the beginning.' *The beginning of what?*

Tess stood off to the side, apparently reluctant to touch the talking gate.

"C'mon, Tess. You touch one," said Jak. "It's not going to bite you. It's just wood." To make his point, Jak stretched out the fingers on both hands and touched as many letters and pictures as he could at the same time. Red light flickered, and a chorus of voices spoke, but instead of fading away, they grew louder and began to repeat themselves.

He pulled his hands away, but the voices continued to swell.

This wasn't supposed to be happening. As soon as his fingers left the wood, the voices were supposed to stop.

It was as if the gate had come to life. More carvings pulsed with light, followed by more voices, chanting the phrase over and over again in a thousand different languages. Then the door creaked and began to swing inward.

They scrambled back, readying themselves for whatever might come through it, but nothing did. As soon as the door hung wide open, the voices and light faded away. Beyond it lay a white gravel pathway leading down the hill into the valley.

"Hmph," said Gramps, stepping closer to the door. "That path wasn't there before."

Jak peered around the gate once again, expecting to see the white path meandering down the hill, but the hill looked the same as before—just grass, flowers, and trees. He peeked through the doorway again, and the white gravel reappeared. "And you can't see it when you look past the gate either. Only if you look through the doorway."

Adrenaline flowed through him. *This must really be it! This is the path to the place without death! Soon, I'll get to see Gramma again. Would she look the same as she did that last day in the kitchen? Or would she be young like the pictures of her wedding day?*

Several yips, howls, and roars filled the air from the valley, and Scorch's head snapped up. A low growl rumbled from his throat, and he looked at Jak.

Maybe it wasn't the place with no death. One of those yips was Macy, but the rest were definitely not.

"I have to go. Meet me at the bottom." He jumped on Scorch's back and wrapped his fingers in the long black mane. "Go. Find Macy."

Scorch took off through the doorway and down the white path faster than he had gone all day, faster than Jak had ever gone without riding in a car. The trees zoomed past as they wound down the hill and emptied into a field of orange tulips next to the river.

An enormous stone bridge spanned the flowing water. Scorch flew across it and picked up the path on the other side.

The growls and chirps were louder now. A chorus of barks and whistles careened through the air—a dogfight for sure, or worse. Jak's stomach twisted into a knot as he imagined Macy, torn to shreds, her life dripping into the ground.

The path burst out of the trees into a clearing, and when Jak saw what was there, he immediately scrunched down and yanked as hard as he could on Scorch's mane.

"Stop, stop!" he whispered frantically.

The fire breather faltered as if he was not sure what to do, but he had slowed down enough for Jak, who slid to the ground and hopped back to the safety of the trees.

The entire clearing was covered with animals, and not just the petting zoo types like goats and sheep and chickens, but a wild animal zoo, with lions and tigers and bears, except all the animals roamed free. There were no fences and no glass. And in the middle of the animals stood a man, completely naked.

CHAPTER 8

Pants

Jak hoped the man hadn't seen him. Maybe this was El, and Jak had blundered into his bedroom as he was getting ready to step in the shower, although he doubted there was a shower in the clearing. He hated to think what would happen if El found out Jak had just seen him naked, but it wasn't his fault the guy didn't have any clothes on. *Didn't his mother ever tell him not to run around outside in his birthday suit?*

He heard a familiar bark and glanced back toward the clearing. He had to get Macy out of there before something pounced on her and gobbled her up. And then the three of them had to get out of the clearing before El saw them. *Maybe we should just eat the black cherries and go home.*

Holding his hand up like a shield so he wouldn't see the man again, he scanned the menagerie, looking for a black and white ball of fur amidst the sea of colors that brayed, growled, bleated, and howled in the clearing.

A lion sprawled not far from where Jak hid, finishing up a meal of something white. Jak caught his breath. *Macy?*

The lion's long red tongue slurped up the white fur trapped in its paws, but the white fur shot up and butted the beast square in the nose.

Jak breathed a sigh of relief. It wasn't Macy; it was a lamb, and it was alive, at least for the moment. He had seen house cats play with mice before eating them, but he had never envisioned a lion would do the same thing with its prey.

The lion responded to the butting lamb with another lick, which sent the little animal tumbling, but the lion stuck out a paw and caught the lamb before it rolled away. The lamb sprang out of the lion's paw and butted it again, this time in the side. In response, the lion growled, but it didn't sound like an angry or hungry growl—more like a laughing growl.

Jak kept waiting for the lion to stop playing and begin lunch, but it never happened. Instead, the lamb plopped down next to the lion, snuggled into the mane, and lay his head down like it was time for a nap.

That's weird. The lion must be old or toothless... or saving the lamb for a snack.

Still using his hand as a shield, Jak roved his eyes back toward the middle of the clearing, continuing to search for Macy. Zebras, giraffes, crocodiles, camels, monkeys, cows, squirrels, and plenty of other spots and stripes Jak didn't recognize populated the clearing. He couldn't believe the number of animals that roamed free without any snapping or chewing going on.

When he finally spotted Macy, he groaned. She sat smack dab in the middle of the clearing, enjoying a good head scratch from none other than the naked El. *How am I going to get her now?*

Without any warning and obviously unable to contain himself any longer, Scorch shot into the clearing, braying his own special mixture of howl and growl. Jak's fingers were intertwined in Scorch's mane, so the fire breather's sudden movement dragged Jak into the clearing as well, and a subtle entrance it was not. Every head turned, including El's.

Jak braced himself, ready for anger and embarrassment to come flying his way. He unwound his fingers from Scorch's mane and stood to face the man. He looked about the same age as some of the college guys who used to coach his baseball team back in Minneapolis, with a dark brown fringe of a beard covering his face. His eyes matched the green hue of Scorch's scales, and his skin matched the brown of the chocolate stain on Jak's shirt, but he didn't seem angry. If anything, he was curious.

El stepped toward Jak and reached out one hand, fingering Jak's T-shirt, as if he was trying to figure out what it was.

"This...skin? This is your skin?" The words dripped out of his mouth like the first trickles from a dry spigot.

Jak shook his head, still unsure of what the man would do. "No. That's my shirt."

"Shirt?" El's eyebrows scrunched. There didn't seem to be a place for the word "shirt" in his brain, but then a great smile cracked his face, and two rows of perfect white teeth laughed at Jak.

"Ah, shirt, I know. Shirt. It's like skin, but not skin." His fingers fell away from Jak's shirt and moved to tussle Scorch's mane. "I see you have discovered another leviathan."

"Leviathan? Is that his name?" said Jak.

"Yes. Do you like it?"

Jak nodded.

"I gave them the honor of a name when the great light hung lower in the sky." El pointed to the sun which now hung directly overhead.

Another iridescent form darted from the trees and nuzzled Scorch. It looked exactly like Scorch, except the mane was red instead of black.

"Ah, here is the other—a perfect match for the one that came with you. They all have matches, you know. Every single one."

It was true. There were two of everything in the clearing.

"Except for me." He frowned and sighed, looking off into the distance. "I do not have a match. You are the first creature such as myself I have found, but I do not think you are my match either." After an awkward silence, El turned once again toward Jak. "But now it is time to give you a name." He grabbed Jak's jaw with both hands and pulled his face up to look directly into his eyes. "You shall be called—" But before he could finish his sentence, footsteps crashed down the white path.

"Hey! You get your grubby hands off of him!" Tess barged into the clearing with Gramps huffing a ways behind her. Macy trotted over to greet her, but she didn't stop charging toward Jak and El.

Jak held his hands palms up toward Tess. "It's okay! He's not hurting me."

"What's he doing then?" Tess demanded.

El inspected the girl and then threw his head and chest back. "I am naming him."

By this time, Jak could tell Tess had finally realized that the man was naked. Her face turned red. She stepped behind Gramps and looked toward the ground, muttering a quick "Oh."

"I have it!" El announced. He put both hands on Jak's shoulders and looked him square in the eyes. "You shall be called Boy. Yes, Boy it is. I like it." He nodded his head up and down, as if congratulating himself on such a fine name.

"Uh, sir?" Jak pulled away from the man's grasp. "I already have a name."

"You do?" El's mouth hung open, shocked that something would have a name that he had not given. "Who named you?"

"My mother." Jak hadn't thought about his mother since leaving the cherry grove near the beach. She would be home from work in a few hours. He wished there were some way he could send her a message to let her know he was okay.

"Mother?" said the man. "El has not yet brought me Mother. What is Mother?"

Jak's mind jarred back to the conversation. "You mean you're not El?" he sputtered.

"Me?" The man put his hand on his chest and smiled like the idea of him being El was the funniest thing he had ever heard. "El? Of course not!" He laughed. "I am only the ruler and the namer. El pulled me from the dirt, just as he pulled all creatures from the dirt. But he gave me the job of ruling over the creatures and giving them honor and meaning with a name. And if your name is not to be Boy, what is it?"

"Well, I am *a* boy, but my name is Jak. What's your name?"

The man stuck his chest out again. "My name is Man."

"Man?" said Jak. That didn't make any sense. "That is what you ARE, but what is your name?"

"The name given to me by El himself is Man," insisted the man. "I like it. Do you not like it?"

Jak could tell this conversation was going nowhere, so he nodded his head, "I like it. It's nice."

"Good. Now, for the other two, do they have names as well, or shall I name them?"

Gramps stepped forward and stuck out his hand. "I already have a name — Clarence Thompson. It's nice to meet you."

Man looked at Gramps's extended hand and knit his brows together for a moment before imitating him and extending his own.

56

Gramps grabbed it and pumped it up and down vigorously. "Clarence, Clarence Thompson."

Man nodded his head. "That's a nice name. Did you get it from Mother?"

"Yes I did."

"Mother does a nice job of naming. Clarence and Jak."

Tess still hid behind Gramps, so Man craned his neck around Gramps's shoulder. "And you? Do you have a name?"

Tess kept her eyes pasted to the ground. Her ears were as red as the fruit on the tree behind Man. "Yes," she said, sounding as if she wished she could crawl into a hole in the ground. "My name is Tess."

"Tess, Tess, Tess. Clarence and Jak." Man rolled the words around on his tongue like he was tasting every letter. "Very nice. I assume Mother named you as well?"

"Yeah, but my mother is different from Jak's mother."

"And my mother," said Gramps, "is a different woman from both Tess and Jak's mothers."

"Woman?" Man's eyebrows arched. "I have not met Woman yet. Is Woman furry like dog or smooth like leviathan?"

"Neither," said Jak. "Well, maybe both." This was hard to explain, so he pointed at Tess.

"Tess, she's a woman." Jak had never called Tess a woman before and squirmed at what he had just said, so he hedged. "She's not really a woman. She's a girl."

"I am too a woman!" Tess looked up for the first time and wrestled Jak with her eyes.

"Alright, whatever." It wasn't worth arguing about at the moment, so he let it drop.

"Girl!" Man said. "That's the name I was going to give you. I like it. Do you like it?"

Jak nodded, but Tess went back to her staring contest with the grass.

"Good," Man said, nodding. And then he continued, almost talking to himself, "Three more creatures, but no match." Suddenly he clapped his hands together, and his eyes focused once again on them. "It is time for eating. Come." He spun on his heels and strode to the tree laden with red fruit about the size of grapefruit. "This I have named pomegranate. The sweetness runs wild in your mouth." He plucked four good-sized pomegranates and tossed one to each of them. "Eat! It is good. El has called it good...and it is!"

Jak had heard of pomegranate, but he had never actually tasted one before. He bit into the flesh and tore off a chunk. Immediately his face contorted, and he spat it out on the ground. It wasn't sweet at all; it tasted more like a rotten lemon.

Man laughed. "Not like that. Like this." He turned his pomegranate over in his hands, testing with his fingers for a soft spot, then dug his thumbs in and tore off the flesh. "You ate the outside. Not even the pigs will eat that. But look inside." He scooped a handful of little red balls from inside the fruit and poured them into his mouth. His eyes closed, and he sighed.

Jak looked at his remaining pomegranate. Sure enough, inside the rind sat a small army of red corn-kernel-sized balls holding onto a fibrous white membrane. He put his fingers in and swirled around until he could pour some out into his palm, and then he poured the palmful into his mouth.

A river of sweet redness spurt into the back of his teeth. "Mmmmm." He had never tasted anything so good before, except for the cherries they'd devoured at lunchtime. Quickly, he broke apart the rest of the pomegranate and emptied it of the kernels. Gramps and Tess did the same.

"You like?" asked Man, laughing. "See? I told you it was good."

Jak nodded his head and tried to say "Yes," but it came out as "Yesh." A trickle of red juice ran down his chin. He swiped it away with his hand and onto his jeans, leaving a bright red stain that looked like blood.

"Ah, good," said Man, wiping his mouth with a leaf from the tree when he had finished. "Next, we explore."

"Explore?" said Jak. "Where are we going?" If Man had suggested exploring before eating the pomegranates, Jak would have said he needed to rest, but for some reason, he was bursting with energy and ready to go exploring.

"I don't know," said Man. "I came up from the dirt only this morning, so no matter where I go, I am exploring."

Came up from the dirt? What was Man talking about? "What do you mean?"

"I mean the garden is new, the creatures are new, the sky is new, the great light is new. It's all new to me—fresh. The grass has never been crumpled, and the air has never been breathed, and I intend to crumple and breathe all over this garden. Come, let's go. There's a lot of air just waiting for us. I can smell it."

Man bounded across the clearing and down another white path that appeared to lead toward the waterfall. Jak and the others followed at a much slower pace. By this time, Jak had realized that the white gravel paths weren't gravel at all; they were crushed sea shells. Different hues of blues and greens kept sparkling like tiny gems as they walked.

"Are you coming?" Man hollered back through the trees.

"We'll be there in a minute," Jak hollered back.

"What's a minute?" Man hollered in return.

"Never mind," hollered Jak once more. "We're coming,"

As soon as he had left, Tess almost exploded. "This guy is crazy...and he's naked! Doesn't he have any clothes?"

"I don't think he knows he's naked," said Jak.

"And if he does know," said Gramps, "I don't think he cares."

"Well, I care," said Tess. She strode to a giant tree with roots clinging to the ground like a wooden spider and plucked a handful of leaves, each as large as her head.

"What are you doing?" said Jak.

"I'm making some pants for him." She inspected the leaves.

Gramps chuckled. "Are you going to call them Leave-i's?

"Very funny, Gramps." She jabbed her pointer finger through the top of each leaf several times, making a neat row of holes across the fattest part of the leaf. Then she looked up and started searching the branches of the trees.

"Now all I need is a vine."

"Can you look for one on the way?" asked Jak. He was afraid they would lose Man if they waited much longer. "He wants us to follow him."

"I suppose."

Macy and Scorch and the red leviathan zigzagged back and forth across the trail as Jak hobbled, and Gramps and Tess walked after Man. A web of vines were slung through the thick foliage above their heads like a mass of tangled telephone wire. Tess grabbed one about the thickness of a pencil, and tried to snap it in half, but it was so strong that all she could do was bend it in half.

"Do you want some help?" offered Gramps.

"It's too tough. I don't think you could get it either," said Tess, letting go of the vine.

"Tools, my dear," he said. "Even monkeys use them." He dug his red Swiss Army knife out of his pocket and handed it to Jak.

"Me?" said Jak. He took it hesitantly. It had been a while since he'd used a knife. He stared for a moment at the big knife, but then looked at the scar on his thumb and passed over it in favor of the little knife on the other side.

Someday he'd pull out the big knife again, just not today. He cut two clean slices in the vine and handed a piece the length of a belt to Tess.

"Thanks, monkey boy." She threaded the belt through the holes on the leaves, tied the two vine ends together, and held up her creation

"There. Definitely better than running around naked."

Gramps nodded his head. "Not bad, Tess. Think you could make me a pair?"

"Eww!" Tess made a face. "I think you'd better stick with the pants you have."

"Hey!"

All three of them jumped at the sound of Man's voice. It floated down toward them from the treetops. They scoured the branches but saw nothing through the dense green. The leaves right above Tess rustled, and Man's head appeared, along with two upside-down chimpanzee faces. "What're you doing?"

"We're following you," Jak said.

Man did a back flip down from the branches and landed solidly on both feet. Scorch slid to a stop next to him and licked his hand.

"No you're not." Man shook his head and pursed his lips. "You're standing here talking about something called 'pants.'" He leaned in and narrowed his eyes like he was going to inquire about a great secret. "What are pants?"

Tess held up the leafy creation. "These are pants—well, more like shorts—but I made them for you to wear."

"For me?" Man's eyes sparkled. "Thank you! I have never had pants."

"I know," said Tess matter-of-factly.

Man took them from her hand and pulled the leafy skirt down over his head and laid it around his neck like a necklace. "I like pants. Come! The waterfall is not far. I can smell it."

"But..." said Tess, but it was too late. Man had already started sprinting down the path ahead of them. Tess let loose a giant sigh. "Gramps, you have to tell him how to wear pants."

"Alright, I'll try," said Gramps, rubbing his beard, "but like I said, I don't think he cares if he runs around naked or not."

Man was right. The smell of waterfall grew stronger with every step. The path emptied out into another clearing, except this one lay at the edge of the river and was covered with little yellow flowers and fat green grass growing as high as Jak's calf. But Man was nowhere to be seen.

Suddenly, Macy took off through the grass, as if she followed an invisible trail. Then her tail pointed straight in the air and she began barking. The two leviathans trotted up beside her, snuffled something on the ground, and then threw their heads back and joined her with twin smoky brays.

"What'd you find, guys?" asked Jak. He limp-jogged with one crutch through the grass until he stood next to them. "You'll never believe this!" he called back to Tess and Gramps. "It's Man, and he's asleep!"

CHAPTER 9

Woman

"Asleep?" said Tess. "But he just ran down the path two minutes ago. How could he be asleep?"

"I don't know, but he's out cold."

Man's chest moved in and out as if he'd been lying there for hours, unhurried and unaware he was being watched.

"I thought he wanted to get to the waterfall," said Jak, "but I guess he was tired."

"How could he fall asleep so fast?" said Tess.

"I don't know," said Jak. He wondered if Tess was going to ask him and Gramps to slip the pants down from Man's neck to his waist while he slept. He nudged Man's shoulder with his toe. "Man, are you really asleep?"

A snore erupted from Man's throat and answered Jak's question.

"So what do we do now?" said Tess.

"Well," said Gramps, "we came this far, so we might as well go smell the waterfall. It sure looked beautiful from the top of the hill."

The roar was much louder now. The falls had to be around the bend in the river.

As soon as they started heading upstream, Scorch and his mate dove head-first into the rushing blue. Once their heads submerged, Jak couldn't tell where the leviathans had gone. Both sets of iridescent scales matched the dance of the underwater hues, and it didn't help that they could hold their breath for what seemed an eternity.

A fountain of matching blue flames shot into the air further upstream and then disappeared around the bend. Macy took off barking and disappeared around the bend as well.

Jak couldn't stop thinking about what Man had said about El pulling him up from the dirt. It didn't make any sense. "Gramps," said Jak, almost shouting because of the tremendous tumult of falling water, "what do you think Man meant when he said El pulled him from the dirt? Was he trapped under it? Like stuck in a hole or something?"

"That's a good question, Jak. You should ask him."

Jak was hoping for more than that from his grandfather, but it didn't appear he had anything more to say, which was just as well because the storm of the waterfall ahead drowned out everything except its own voice.

He had seen plenty of waterfalls in his life, but this waterfall beat them all. The cliff towered above them like a drowning skyscraper. Part of the water that slid over the edge landed on a ledge halfway up and flowed toward the sea, making it a split falls. The rest crash landed in a frothy pool at the bottom.

Jak liked that name – Split Falls; maybe Man would let him name it.

But it wasn't the height or the sound that was different. It was something about the water itself. It was cleaner, or brighter, or something he couldn't quite decide—more like a rush of bubbling diamonds jumping off the cliff.

Scorch and the red leviathan clambered out of the pond and shook the water from their manes.

Jak felt a finger tap him on the shoulder and turned to see Tess holding what looked like a raspberry, except that it was the same size as a golf ball. She pointed to a bramble crawling along the ground and halfway up the base of the cliff, covered with a thousand berries just like it. When he pulled it apart, it fell into juicy red orbs. He popped one in his mouth and bit down. The skin burst apart, and a fountain of juice exploded in his mouth for the third time that day. Once again, it felt like liquid energy squirting straight from the berry to his body.

"Gramps!" Jak shouted. "You've gotta try this!" But Gramps had his mouth full, and telltale bright red juice already stained his beard.

None of them noticed the sun ambling across the sky. They were more concerned with trying the varieties of fruits and berries hanging from the trees and vines around the cliff. By the time they wandered far enough away from the waterfall to talk, the sun had already started to touch the tallest trees on the ridge.

"Let's go back and see if Man's awake," said Jak. He was full and ready to go back to the clearing.

Gramps patted his stomach and burped. "Sounds good to me."

They retraced their steps and arrived back at the grassy bank near the trail as the sun turned orange. Man no longer lay in the grass but sat upright, leaning on one arm, talking and laughing to himself. The pants still hung around his neck.

Jak smiled. Even though Man was strange, he liked him. Who else would sit in the grass laughing at his own jokes? But then he froze in his tracks and felt the blood rush to the tips of his earlobes.

Man was not talking to himself, nor was he talking to an animal. He was talking to a woman—a very beautiful, very *naked* woman.

CHAPTER 10

The Two Trees

Jak's pulse quickened, and he turned his head toward Man, but he didn't really want to look at him either because he was naked too.

"Jak, Clarence, Tess...you're back!" Man was a quick study when it came to social graces; he stood and pumped Gramps's hand just as Gramps had pumped his earlier. "I never made it to smell the waterfall. I found something else to name, and once I named her, I couldn't leave her. She is so..." Man glanced back at the woman and sighed deeply. "...so beautiful. She makes my skin tingle. A perfect match."

The woman stood up from the grass, took Man's hand in hers, and bowed her head slightly to Jak. "Hello. It is nice to meet you." Her voice was warm and gentle, like a soft shower. Her skin matched the milky candy-bar brown of Man's, and her eyes shared the same stoplight green, only with flecks of hazel and blue.

"It...it's nice to meet you too," Jak stammered. He could tell Gramps and Tess were also having a difficult time finding a safe place to rest their eyes. He finally settled on looking Man straight in the face.

"I have named her Woman," Man said, "and she is much better than any of the animals I named earlier today. Is she like Mother?" Man asked.

"Yes," said Jak, "she is like my mother. They are both women."

"Women...women are good," Man said, nodding his head up and down. "El has said so, and I agree."

"El? He was here?" asked Jak in surprise.

"Yes. He left not long ago. I remember waiting for you to come out of the woods, and the next thing I knew, El was patting my side with his fingers, and I woke up from a deep sleep. Woman was lying next to me, and I didn't know what she was, but El asked if I liked my new companion. 'I made her just for you,' he said, 'to help you.' He said I am going to need lots of help. And then he was gone, and it was just Woman and me." He kissed her on the cheek. "I like her very much. We were just talking about pants." He fingered the leafy pair of shorts hanging around his neck. "Tess, would you make pants for Woman too?"

"Uh, sure," Tess said. "I can get some more leaves on the way back."

"Good. I want to take Woman back anyway, to give her a pomegranate."

Scorch pranced up to Man and nuzzled his head into Man's side. Man ran his hand down Scorch's back, and the animal responded with a purr that sounded something like the deep clicking of a socket wrench.

Man laughed, "...and to show her the creatures I named this morning. This is Leviathan."

Now it was the woman's turn to run her hand down Scorch's back. "She is smooth and soft, very beautiful," she said.

In his head, Jak did a double-take over what Woman had just said. *She? Scorch isn't a she. He's a he!* "The black leviathan is a male, not a female," he said.

Woman shook her head, sending her long, straight, black hair bouncing in all directions. "No, she is a she."

Man nodded his head in agreement, "Yes, she is a she."

"What?" said Jak, astonished. "You mean to tell me Scorch is really a girl?"

"No." Man laughed. "Not a girl. Tess is a girl. This leviathan is a female. Is that not good?"

"Good" or "bad" weren't exactly the words swirling in Jak's head. It was more of a jolt than anything. He needed a minute to mentally go back and rewrite the day, scratching out the parts that joined "he" and "Scorch" and replacing them with "she" and "Scorch."

"No...I mean, yes, it is good. I just thought she was a male," said Jak.

Man ran his hand over the red leviathan's head. "This is a male, but this..." Man ran his hand over Scorch's back again. "...is a female." He looked back at Woman and took her hand. "A beautiful female."

"All the animals are beautiful, each in his or her own way," Man said, "and they are ours to care for. That's what El told me. Come on! I want to show you the tree." He beckoned toward the garden and started to lead her down the seashell path.

"We'll catch up," said Tess. She made motions to Jak and Gramps to stay behind with her. As soon as Man and Woman were out of earshot, she burst. "What is going on here? Why is everybody around here naked?"

"I'm not naked," said Gramps.

"I didn't mean you. I meant them!" Tess jerked her thumb in the direction of the path. "It's like they don't even care."

"Maybe they don't know," Jak said.

"How could you not know you're naked?"

Jak shrugged his shoulders. "Maybe walking around with no clothes on for them is the same as walking around with clothes on for us."

"Why don't you ask them?" suggested Gramps.

"That'd be weird," said Tess. "What would I say? 'Excuse me, but did you notice that you're naked?'"

"Sounds about right," said Gramps.

"At least they want another pair of pants for the woman," said Jak.

"But she's going to wear it around her neck just like he is," said Tess.

"At least it will cover her top."

"You're right about it being a bit awkward though, Tess," said Gramps.

"It's like they're two little kids," said Jak.

"Well, not quite," said Gramps. "It's more like two people who haven't lived much life."

"But they're adults, Gramps!" said Tess. "It's not like they were born yesterday."

Gramps bit at his whiskers and raised his eyebrows. "All I'm saying is that the best way to get an answer is to ask a question." He bowed his head and waved his hand majestically toward the seashell path. "After you."

Tess rolled her eyes again and crossed her arms as she stomped down the path.

As they walked, Jak searched the canopy of leaves above them for just the right vine for the pants Tess was going to make for Woman, but his mind was really churning over three questions: *Is this the place with no death? How is following the path going to cost me my life? What did Man mean when he said El pulled him from the dirt?* And now a fourth question joined the three: *Do Man and Woman know they are naked?* He hoped he would get some answers before more questions popped up, or he was sure to start losing track.

By the time they broke into the clearing, Tess had finished the pants, and Man and Woman had already slurped their way through half a pomegranate.

"Ah, you made it!" said Man, tossing the rind in a pile next to the tree.

"Yes, and with a fresh pair of pants." Tess held up the pants to her waist and smiled. She had a plan. If it went well, she would skip asking them the naked question, but if it didn't... "See? You put them on like this." She had decided the best way to get Woman to wear the pants correctly was to model them for her. Tess bent over and stepped both feet through the vine-waistband and then pulled the pants over her shorts up to her waist. "Just like that." Then she pulled them back off and held them out.

Woman's eyes danced as she took the pants from Tess. "Thank you, Tess." She stepped into the pants just like Tess had and pulled them up to her waist. She smiled as she looked down to her hips, now covered in leaves.

Tess let out the breath she had been holding and she relaxed. It was a small victory, but a victory nonetheless. She thought she would have a go at a leaf shirt that afternoon. Before she could give that much thought, though, Woman grabbed the pants and yanked them up over her chest until the waistband rested around her neck, just like Man's pants. She twirled in a circle. "Do you like it?"

Tess sagged a little but nodded her head. "Yeah. It looks great."

"Good!" said Man and clapped his hands together. "Come! I want to show you the tree."

"But isn't this the tree right here?" asked Jak, pointing to the pomegranate tree.

"Yes, very good, Jak. That IS a tree. You learn quickly. But there are many more trees in the garden. The one I want to show you is this way." Man spun on his heels and bounced down the hill, grabbing Woman's hand and sending the pants around both of their necks bouncing along with them.

"Wait!" Tess called after them, but it was too late. Her naked question would have to wait.

This time, Man led them beyond the pomegranate tree into the woods. The trees in this section towered above any of the fruit trees, brushing the sky and swaying in the wind, just like the giant pines had down by the sea, except that these had fat, green, deciduous leaves shaped like distorted gingerbread men instead of pine needles. Laughter drifted back from Man and Woman as they darted through the giants.

"He's hard to keep up with, isn't he?" Gramps wiped his brow with a well-worn bandanna. "Yes," said Jak. He hopped along with one crutch as fast as he could. Every time the top of the crutch dug into his armpit, he wished Man would slow down.

"It's like trying to follow a couple of ADHD monkeys," said Tess.

Scorch and Macy ran ahead of them on the seashell path, sniffing and snorting, a rainbow of sparks blowing out of Scorch's nostrils

"ARE YOU COMING??" Man's voice filtered back through the forest.

"Sounds like he's already a mile ahead of us." Jak cupped his hands around his mouth and yelled as loud as he could, "YES, WE'RE COM—"

But before he could get the sentence all the way off his tongue, a dark red form bowled Jak over, sending him face down in the dirt. He spat the dirt out of his mouth, pushed himself up, and was greeted by a long red tongue. The male leviathan licked his cheek and then turned on his tail and sped off to join Scorch and Macy.

"Why do they do that?" asked Jak, brushing himself off.

"Do what?" said Gramps.

"Keep knocking me down. First Scorch jumped me back in the woods at lunch, and now he jumped me." Jak was still trying to get used to the idea that the red leviathan was a "he" not a "she."

"I guess they like you," said Gramps, shrugging his shoulders.

They followed Man's and Woman's laughter down the path through the giant trees. Macy often circled back to bark at Jak to hurry up. It was a lot easier to hurry up whenever he came across a vine hanging down over the path, because then he could swing like Tarzan as far as the vine would take him. When he was on a vine, it didn't matter if his ankle was sprained or not. He felt free until he hit the ground again.

Soon the ground tilted upward, forcing them to climb a gentle slope. The big trees thinned out, replaced by clumps of magnificent pink flowers and yellow birches. At the top of the slope, a blast of sunshine marked the exit. Jak blinked his eyes against the light as he pushed himself into the open glade. He could see Macy, Scorch, and the male leviathan playing tag and could just make out Man and Woman peering up at something. As his eyes adjusted, he got a funny feeling in his stomach. There was something remarkably familiar about this spot. And then it dawned on him. "We're back at the clearing!" he said, wondering what had gone wrong..

"What do you mean, back at the clearing?" asked Tess, blinking back the sunlight. "We just walked through the woods. How could we be back at the clearing?"

"We must have gone in a circle." He pointed with his crutch. "Look! There's the pomegranate tree, and over there are the two seashell paths."

"Wasn't that fun?" called Man. He and woman strolled over to the trio. He had a big smile on his face. "I love going through the woods to get to the tree!"

"Why didn't we just walk through the clearing?" asked Tess, making no effort to hide her frustration. "It would have been a lot faster."

"Faster, yes, but the view is much better through the woods."

Jak rubbed his right arm and shoulder. He could have done without the scenic route. His armpit was sore from the crutch, and his ankle was beginning to throb again. He shifted the book in his shirt. *I should have given the book to Gramps to carry for a while. That would have made the trek a little easier, but it's too late now. This tree had better be worth it.*

"So where's this tree you wanted to show us?" asked Jak.

Man pointed to the top of a hillock near the end of the path.

Two trees stood quietly together, set apart from the other trees in the garden, but as different from each other as milk and oil.

One tree stood erect and straight, like a sentry guarding a treasure. Golden veins flowed around the burnt brown bark like a network of veins running through a person's arm. They ran straight up the trunk and extended into each branch, exploding in clusters of spiny emerald-green leaves that looked something like twin starfish. But unlike most of the other smaller trees in the garden, no fruit hung from its branches.

The other tree hunched short and squat, with gnarled, knotty roots spreading like an old woman's hand into the ground, a firm and ancient grip on the dirt. The leaves were dark green, almost black with a heavy luster. They were the same size and shape as an egg, but with serrated edges.

Jak recognized the squatty tree straightaway. "Hey! This is the same as that black cherry tree." He dug the two cherries from his pocket. They were slightly bruised and a bit squashed, but they were still whole. He held them out to the fruit dangling from the branches, and it was a perfect match.

"Cherry? Hmm. I like that name," said Man. "El gave this tree a different name, but we could also call it cherry."

"What did El call it?" asked Woman, curiously eying the tree.

"He called it The Tree of Knowing Good and Evil."

"Cherry is a lot easier to say than that," said Jak.

"And that other name doesn't make any sense," said Tess. "The Tree of Knowing Good and Evil? What does *that* mean?"

"I don't know," said Man, "but I do know that El said we may not eat the fruit of this tree. He warned us that we may look and touch, but not taste or eat."

"Why?" asked Jak. "Is it poisonous?"

"I am not sure what that means, poisonous," said Man, crinkling his brow in confusion.

"It means that if you eat it you will die," said Jak.

"Then yes," said Man. "It is poisonous. El said if we eat it, we will die."

Jak's thoughts raced back to the first plaque. "That's the same thing the plaque said. When we got here this morning, a tree just like this one had a sign on it that said if we ate the black cherries, death would follow us."

"So you, too, have been warned of death," said Man. "Do you know what death is?"

Jak, Gramps, and Tess stood silent for a moment until Gramps answered, "Yes." His voice trembled. "Death is a thief. One moment a person is with you, living and breathing and laughing, and the next, she's gone. All that's left is a cold, lifeless body. "

Woman shuddered and drew close to Man. "That sounds awful."

Gramps nodded his head. "It is, but it happens to everyone. Sooner or later, everyone dies."

"Why does everyone die?" said Woman.

Gramps shrugged his shoulders again. "Maybe somebody ate the fruit of this here tree."

"We will stay away," pronounced Man sternly. He turned his attention to the other tree. "Now *this* tree is different." He stroked its trunk in the same affectionate manner he had stroked Leviathan's mane. "This tree is full of life."

"What's so special about it?" said Jak.

"This tree GIVES life. When you eat the fruit of this tree, it fills you with... with... well, try it for yourself, and you will see."

"But it doesn't have any fruit," said Jak, staring up at the branches.

"No fruit? Of course it has fruit!" Man stepped up to the branches and plucked one of the smaller leaves from the middle of a cluster of the starfish-shaped ones. It hadn't yet reached maturity. Instead of emerald green, it was purple, with short little nubs where the starfish arms would be someday. "See?'

"But that's just a leaf," said Jak.

Man smiled and snapped the leaf in half. Pink juice ran down his fingers as he pulled the leaf apart. It was as thick as a pancake and full of pink pulp. "Then when you eat the leaf of this tree it fills you like no other fruit in the garden." He plucked four more purple leaves, handed one to each of them and then held his up in the air, like a toast at a wedding. "To life without death!" He took a big bite and motioned for the others to do the same.

Jak had never eaten a leaf before unless you count lettuce and spinach or the one time some older kids in his neighborhood forced him to eat an oak leaf, which actually tasted better than the spinach. But none of them fit into the category of "tasty" or hardly even "edible," so he couldn't imagine eating a leaf on purpose, and he certainly couldn't imagine one filling him up.

However, this leaf smelled strangely good, kind of like the strawberry wafers he always begged for at the grocery store. He nibbled on one edge. *Not bad.* He crunched off a section. *Not bad at all.* He took a large bite and almost immediately felt an electric shock zinging down his spine.

CHAPTER 11

Banished to the Birches

The zing caught him by surprise. The colors of the garden swam and mushed into a puddle. He reached out to steady himself, but his hand found only air. He felt himself tipping over.

Two hands caught him and steadied him on his feet. At the same moment, the puddle of colors cleared into deeper greens, browns and blues, as if he had discovered a whole new spectrum of colors. The zing shot through his entire body, washing him with a wave of energy that rippled through his arms, feet, and head, leaving him tingly all over. "Whoa!" he said, blinking hard. "What just happened?"

Man smiled. "It was the your first bite from the tree. You will get used to it by the second bite."

Jak had goosebumps all over his body, making the hair on his arms and legs stand straight up.

"I feel tingly all over."

"Me too," said Tess, a slight smile on her face. It was the first time she had truly smiled all day.

"Amazing!" said Gramps.

"Isn't it?" asked Man. "I told El the same thing when He gave me a leaf this morning." Bubbling with excitement, he turned to Woman. "Woman, do you like it?"

Still chewing, Woman had her eyes closed and a contented expression on her face. "It is...thrilling."

Yes, "thrilling" was just the right word. It was almost like a drug, and Jak wondered if the leaves would be legal back in Grantsburg.

"El calls it The Tree of Life," said Man, "and he said we may eat as much as we please, although a few bites fills me so full of tingle that I cannot eat any more."

Gramps finished chewing his second bite and smiled contentedly. "I sure wish I had a tree like this in my back yard instead of that wormy crab apple tree." He took another bite and closed his eyes.

Jak looked at the leaf again and realized that what he had mistaken for a young leaf was actually the fruit. On one end of the purple fruit, an oval about the size of a quarter lay embedded under the skin. He bit the pink flesh away until he exposed a flat wrinkled brown seed. "I guess it isn't a leaf," said Jak, more to himself than to anyone else. He felt a little foolish, but nobody seemed to care that he had made a fuss about eating a leaf that wasn't a leaf.

"Come," said Man. "El will be here soon."

Jak lifted the seed out and put it in his pocket to have a closer look later on.

"El?" asked Tess. "He's coming here?"

"Yes," said Man. "He told me he would be back when the big light has almost gone from the heavens." He pointed to the ridge where the sun had almost sunk beneath the trees. With the fading sunlight, the sky had changed from bright blue to a brilliant sunset in the west.

"Look! The heavens are pink and red and orange!" said Woman. "It's beautiful."

Jak and Tess exchanged a glance. The woman acted as if she had never seen a sunset before, yet she had to be at least twenty years old. *Had she spent her life under the dirt, like Man? Maybe they lived in underground caves until today. But wait... that can't be right unless they lived in different caves, because Man never met Woman until this afternoon. What is going on here?* Jak was glad El was finally coming. He had so many questions, and he knew El was the only one who could answer them.

"He said he would meet us by the pomegranate tree," said Man.

"Do we have to go back through the woods, or can we just walk across the clearing?" asked Jak, hoping for the latter. His right armpit were still stinging from the trip through the woods, and he was hoping to stay right where he was.

"We can walk across the clearing," said Man. "Besides, I think the light has faded from the woods."

Indeed, the woods had been enveloped in darkness. A mist had risen, coating the leaves and grass with a sprinkling of moisture. Gramps, Man, and Woman walked ahead, talking about the many fruit trees in the garden. Tess lagged behind with Jak and the animals. Scorch put her neck beneath Jak's arm and acted as a living crutch, a welcome relief from the uncomfortable wooden one. He transferred the old crutch to his left hand and used it as a walking stick.

"What do you think this El looks like?" asked Tess.

"Oh, I don't know." Jak shrugged his shoulders. "Probably old and bald with a long white beard, like a wizard or something. What do you think?" Their feet collected water as they slowly trod through the grass, soaking through their tennis shoes and socks until their toes felt squishy.

Tess pursed her lips. "Well, if he's a good man, then he'll be wearing a long white robe, and have flowing white hair and a trim beard. He'll be tall and good looking, and he'll carry a staff of some kind."

"Yeah, and what movie is that from exactly, Tess?"

She ignored Jak and kept talking. "But if he's bad, he'll be wearing a long black robe and have a pointy black goatee with greasy black hair and dandruff."

Jak stopped and peered into the shadows. He thought he had seen something flash in the woods. "Did you see a light over there?"

Tess stopped and stared in the same direction. "Yeah! Over there!" She pointed toward a faint glow in the eastern portion of the garden, near the entrance to the scenic route they had taken through woods. They peered through bushes as best as they could, but they couldn't get a clear view of what was causing the light.

"It's him!" called Man, pointing in the same direction. "It is El."

Jak began to walk faster. El was there! The one who had put the plaque on the tree and the plaque on the red rock by the woods, the one who had brought them there in the first place. *Maybe now it will all make sense.*

Suddenly, a sound like rushing water filled the garden. As it washed across Jak and Tess, exhilaration and fear gripped them.

A confused expression came across Man's face. He looked like he was about to say something, but nothing came out of his mouth. After a moment, he finally managed to get out the words, "He says you must leave the clearing. You must go back to the bridge and wait."

"Wait?" Jak hobbled forward, leaning on his crutch. He had been wanting to talk with El all day, and if he didn't get to ask him his questions, he thought his head would blow up. "Wait for what?"

"Wait for him to leave."

"But we want to talk with him!"

The sound of rushing water filled the garden again, and an uncomfortable dread began gnawing at Jak's gut.

"He says you will talk with him," said Man, "but not now, not like this. He says that as you follow the path, you will begin to understand."

"We already followed the path," said Jak, "and it led us here."

"I can't believe this," said Tess, giving a sigh of disgust and pushing her hair behind her ears. "He rips us away from home, plops us on a hill in the middle of nowhere, and now he won't even talk to us?"

"Yeah, and how come you can understand him and we can't?" asked Jak, "All I hear is a river."

"I don't know," said Man, shaking his head.

The light had not moved and had not changed in intensity. It remained hidden in the trunks and leaves of the eastern woods.

"Man, ask him why he brought us here," demanded Jak.

The silvery water sound began again even before Jak had finished speaking.

"He says he has no more to say on this matter," said Man. "Follow the path, and soon you will talk with him."

"But why can't we see him right now?" asked Jak. His ears had turned pink, and he pulled at his shirt collar, suddenly hotter than he had been all day.

"Jak," Gramps murmured, "I think we'd better back up now and head back to the bridge."

"But—" protested Jak.

Gramps clamped one hand over Jak's mouth, and with the other, he grabbed Jak's shoulder and gently steered him in the direction of the seashell path leading to the bridge. Scorch hesitated, looking between the light on one side of the clearing and the woods on the other. Then she trotted under Jak's right arm again to support him, followed by her mate.

As soon as they walked around the bend in the path, the darkness above the clearing was swallowed up by a dome of warm white light, and the sound of rushing water flooded the garden.

"This is dumb," said Jak as they reached the other side of the bridge. A small copse of birch trees formed a ring to the left of the seashell path, like a makeshift campsite. Someone had placed three piles of dried grass in three different sections of the campsite, and each pile had a dark blue blanket folded neatly on top. Jak threw his crutch at a patch of red flowers, then took the book out from underneath his shirt and plopped both himself and the book on top of one of the beds, frowning ferociously.

"This is more than dumb," said Tess, plopping down next to him. "Dandruff and greasy black hair would have been better than a big light bulb who tells us to go away."

Gramps sat down on the other side of Jak. "Don't be too hard on him, Tess. We don't know why he did what he did."

"Doesn't matter," said Jak, "It's obvious he doesn't really want us here."

"That's not what he said," said Gramps. "He said if we follow the path, then we'll be able to talk to him."

"What path?" Jak shot back. "The only other paths we've seen are the one to Split Falls and the wild-goose-chase scenic route Man took us on to get to the Two Trees. There aren't any other paths."

"I don't have an answer for you, Jak," Gramps replied.

"I'm hungry," said Tess. She lay down on one of the beds next to where Macy, Scorch, and the male leviathan had curled up together. "All we've had to eat all day is fruit, and I'm sick of it. I want some real food—some barbecued chicken or a burger."

Suddenly, Macy shot up and stared across the bridge with a low growl vibrating from her throat.

The leaves above them rustled, and a pair of black monkeys with white mustaches almost as big as their faces dropped to the ground. At the same time, a red baboon with light brown fur radiating out from each cheek and almost as large as Jak, traipsed across the bridge. All three were chattering in monkey gibberish, and each held a round, flat piece of wood, like a platter, of sorts; the baboon held two since its hands were bigger. On the topside of each piece of wood sat a pile of food, with steam rising in small spirals.

The primates monkey-walked to the three humans. Once they reached Jak, Tess, and Gramps, they let out an odd series of grunts, their eyes imploring the humans to accept their gift.

Jak couldn't help but smile.

"Looks like this place comes with room service," said Gramps, accepting a plate from one of the mustached monkeys.

Tess groaned. "No meat though."

The little monkeys, having delivered their loads, shimmied up the birches, swung to the top of a giant oak, and leapt across the river.

The aroma made Jak's mouth erupt with saliva. His ankle was throbbing, and he was still angry, but he was also hungry. The baboon handed him a plate and put the second plate on the ground for Macy, then immediately scrambled back over the river, his bright red rear end bobbing up and down like a moving stoplight across the bridge.

Macy barked and dug into the brown and green pile of moist kibbles that crowned her plate. At the same time, Scorch and her mate dove into the river, apparently to find a meal of their own.

"Hey," said Jak, "there's a note on my plate."

"Mine too," said Tess. A piece of green paper with black edging folded into a triangular tent stood next to a mound of puffy orange stuff that looked like sweet potatoes. It read "Enjoy."

"The monkeys here must be pretty smart," said Gramps. "I don't know any monkeys back home who can serve dinner and write notes."

"C'mon, Gramps," said Jak, not sure if his grandfather was being serious or not. "You don't really think the note is from the monkeys, do you?"

"Who else would it be from?" said Gramps.

Jak didn't think Man and Woman would have sent anything except maybe a basket of fruit, which, in this garden, wouldn't be anything special because fruit trees were all over the place. He couldn't figure out who would have known to send food, so he pushed it to the back of his mind and began inspecting his plate.

In addition to the sweet potato, there was corn on the cob dripping with butter, a brown and white fruity bread laced with dark brown caramel-looking sauce, and a pile of black beans.

Beans? How are we supposed to enjoy beans? Jak wondered. He shuddered at the thought. He also noticed there were no eating utensils. "How are we supposed to eat this stuff with no silverware?"

"Here." Gramps handed him a thick leaf that would serve quite nicely as a spoon. "Dip in and enjoy, just like the sign says."

Everything except the beans, Jak thought. Jak scooped up some orange stuff and chewed. His taste buds were immediately happy. The flavor was better than any other sweet potato he had ever eaten in his life; it was like a zesty soup compared to thin gruel. He tried the corn, and the result was the same.

"Try the beans," said Gramps, wiping a kernel of corn off his mustache.

"Are you kidding?" said Tess. "I can't stand beans."

"It's different than fruit. Isn't that what you wanted?"

"I said *meat*. I would hardly consider beans as an acceptable alternative to grilled chicken," she grumbled, pushing them even further away from everything else on her plate.

"You'll like these," said Gramps.

"No, I won't."

Gramps shrugged his shoulders. "Suit yourself," he said, shoveling in a leafful.

"Why would we like beans if we never liked them before?" asked Jak.

"Oh, I just think you will."

Jak's curiosity was piqued. He picked up a bean and nibbled just a bit between his teeth, expecting a bitter burnt black beany buffet, but he got something much different. He popped the bean into his mouth and chewed slowly.

"Did you eat one?" Tess asked, surprised.

Jak raised his eyebrows and nodded. "Chicken! Tess, it tastes just like chicken!"

"What?" said Tess. "You're joking!"

From the look on her face, Jak could tell she was trying to decide if he was telling the truth or just pulling her leg. He scooped up some more with the makeshift spoon and poured them in his mouth.

"That's why I thought you might like them, Tess," said Gramps. "They taste exactly like grilled chicken."

Tess picked up a bean and tentatively placed it on her tongue.

"You have to chew it," said Gramps. "It's not a vitamin. I promise you'll like it."

She closed her eyes, scrunched her nose, and bit down on the legume. Her eyes immediately flew open. "You're right! It's good, just like teriyaki chicken!"

Gramps smiled and nodded. "Yep. Thought you'd like it."

Jak had no idea what the white fruity bread with the sauce was, but it was the best dessert he had ever had. It was sooo good! If he hadn't been so angry with El, he would have laughed because that's what Man had said all day, "Good, El said it was good." He began to think maybe everything here was good except for El himself.

He looked at the book lying next to him on his pile of grass. El was the one who told them to bring it, so maybe they were *supposed* to read it. Maybe it held the clues to why they were there and what they were supposed to do.

While Tess was focusing on her teriyaki chicken-beans, he flipped the book open to the page with the tree on it. There he read the words that had started it all: "In the beginning..." This time, he kept reading, the whole time keeping one eye on Tess and one eye on the page.

"In the beginning, El made the heavens and the earth..."

He made it all the way through the first chapter, a story about El and how he had made everything from the sun and stars down to the bugs and birds. But that was as far as Jak could go because the page wouldn't turn to the second chapter, as if it was glued shut.

Scorch and the red leviathan returned, dripping, but looking quite satisfied. They lay down next to him and began licking their faces clean and combing each other's fur.

Jak sighed, closed the book, and put his plate on the ground next to him. He didn't know what to think of El.

"Full?" asked Gramps.

"Yep. Boy, that was good." He stretched and leaned back with Scorch lying behind him. Her stomach was soft and warm, the perfect pillow. Jak propped his sprained ankle up on a rock. It had been a long, exhausting day. Just a mere sixteen hours earlier, he had been in his own bed, but now he wasn't even certain he was on the same planet. His mom would be home by now too. Her twelve-hour shifts at the hospital always turned into fifteen-hour shifts, so he was sure she would have gone straight to bed and hadn't even noticed he was gone yet. On weekends like that, when she had to work so much, Jak became somewhat invisible. For all he knew, she wouldn't even notice him missing till Monday. It was a lot better now that they lived with

Gramps. Not as many bills to pay, mom said, but the weekends were long. Someday maybe things would change, maybe even his mom and dad would get back together.

He gazed at the stars; they looked different than the stars at home. They still sparkled blue and red and yellow, but he didn't see any familiar constellations. He began to mentally draw lines between the stars, creating his own.

Suddenly, a bright white light, ten times more brilliant than any of the others, flashed in the sky and flung itself toward the western horizon.

Jak sat up. "Gramps, look!" he shouted, pointing at the sky.

Gramps craned his neck and peered up. "Well, I'll be jiggered!"

Jak expected it to burn out quickly, like a normal falling star, but it didn't. It stayed the same intense white until it disappeared among the treetops. "I've never seen one stay so bright so long," said Jak. "Do you think it was a comet?"

"No, I don't think so," said Gramps, stroking his beard. "I didn't see a tail. Must've been a meteor."

"It looked like it fell into the sea."

"I doubt that, Jak," said Gramps. "Meteors normally burn out before hitting Earth."

"Yeah, but that one was so bright," said Jak

"There's another one!" said Tess, pointing up.

Another falling star, not quite as bright as the first, appeared in the same spot and shot off in the same direction. Then there was another and another, until a blizzard of shooting stars filled the sky, all flying in the same direction as the first until they vanished from sight into the trees.

Gramps stood looking at the sky, his mouth wide open. He had spent the past ten years watching the nighttime sky as an active member of the Grantsburg Astronomical Society, GAS for short. Jak had always derived much pleasure from asking Gramps, "Do you have GAS tonight?" but the reality was that Gramps only had GAS once a month. A meteor shower like this one would have sparked great interest for the members of GAS.

"What were they, Gramps?" asked Tess.

"I...I don't know," said Gramps, scratching his head. "Must've been a group of meteors, but I've never seen anything like it."

They continued watching the sky, but no more meteors sparked through the sky.

Jak yawned and his mind wandered back to that last day in the kitchen with his grandmother. Whenever he thought of that morning, a mixture of pleasure and guilt filled him. He loved remembering her, but he always searched for something he could have done differently, something that could have saved her. *Maybe if I'd caught her before she hit her head...or maybe if I called 911 right away...maybe, maybe, maybe...* But no matter what scenario he played out in his head, the result was the same: his grandmother was dead and gone, and there was nothing he could do about it. But, according to El, maybe now he could.

Jak rubbed his eyes and yawned again. It was late. He laid his head back down on Scorch's warm, soft belly. Her head looped around and rested on his lap. He had discovered earlier in the day that she liked it when he scratched the white spot on her forehead, so he scratched the spot now, and a deep rumble erupted from her stomach. The purring and rhythmic breathing worked like a gentle lullaby, gradually blending in with the throb of his ankle and the rush of the river, sending him off to sleep.

CHAPTER 12

An Army of Goo

The meteors didn't burn up before hitting the Earth. Instead, each one fell hissing into the ocean beyond the cherry grove and dissolved with a sizzle into puddles of luminescent jellyfish goo that slowly followed the waves toward the beach. The first meteor that coursed through the sky was also the first to reach the land and ooze its way onto the sand. A pile of light lurched upward and formed a man-sized tower of flickering yellow light. It grew stronger and more robust, a mesmerizing cascade of brilliant light, crackling like a live electric wire in a rainstorm.

The cascade focused its brilliance on a spot at the top of the tower, and a lopsided blob bulged up and burst out of the neck into the shape of a rotten pumpkin. It spun the rotten pumpkin-shaped blob, and three orbs spit out on strings, like three balls attached by three rubber bands to the same paddle. The orbs were immediately sucked back into the grotesque head and became two large, hollow eyes and a stubby, flat nose. At the same time, a hole widened in the middle of the head, leaving a gaping jack-o-lantern grin. A pair of rubbery arms and legs wriggled out of the chest and trunk and planted the body in the sand.

By this time, the second and third piles of goo had crawled onto the beach and begun their own lurch upward.

The rotten pumpkin head twisted around and observed an entire flotilla of goo washing into the beach. "Good," it rasped. "We are all here."

One by one, each of the jellyfish goo creatures took their stand on the beach until an army of giant glow-stick ghosts, none as majestic as the first, hovered over the sand, flickering and angry.

The pumpkin-headed creature flowed among them like a sergeant, inspecting the ranks as they piled up, gurgling and blubbering until the beach was littered with conversation. Apparently satisfied, the creature stopped the inspection and flowed back to its original position on the beach. When it got there, it rose into the air, flapping its rubber arms. "Look at me!" it cackled. "I am the foremost creation of the enemy, his pride and joy."

The lights on the beach pulsed in a jeer that swept up and down the beach.

Suddenly, the creature inflated like a balloon, rose to twice its height, and exploded, spewing its own head, arms, and legs to the ground where they flopped like a pile of dying fish. The now-deformed body transformed itself back into the brilliant cascade of light and poured over the twitching appendages, grinding them into the dirt. "And so we will do to them," the voice roared. "The enemy will fail, but we will succeed. The enemy will fall, but we will rise. We have escaped the clutches of the tyrant, and now the tyrant will be cast down! And it begins here. We will grind the adoration of his creatures back into the dirt from which they were drawn! They will be our slaves, and Earth will be ours. The enemy will lose all that is dear to him, and we shall reign forever!"

The crowd roared its approval, and a deafening chant began, "Lu-ci-fer! Lu-ci-fer!"

The brilliant light pulsed, and the crowd shushed.

"Move out," he growled. "Spread among the enemy's creation and destroy whatever breathes, except for the humans. We will squeeze Yahweh's handiwork until the blood flows down his face."

The crowd erupted into hoots and hollers once again, and the Lights began to flood over the grass and up the hill.

CHAPTER 13

A Gift from El

❦

"I'm going to call him Red," announced Jak.

It was a beautiful day. The air was warm yet crisp and the sun was peeking through the leaves as they gently waved in the breeze. The plates from last night's dinner had disappeared, which meant that either the monkeys had returned or something else had visited them during the night. Gramps's blanket sat folded again on top of his pile of grass, but he was nowhere to be seen.

"Uhn," Tess groaned, putting one hand up to block a ray of sunshine that had just blasted her in the eyes. She groggily sat up, looked around, and then sighed with disappointment. "Are we still here? I was hoping maybe it was all a dream and I'd wake up back in math class." She rubbed her eyes and yawned. "Who'd have thought I'd ever miss math class? But it sure beats this place." She glanced at Jak. "Who're you going to call Red?"

"Scorch's mate, the red leviathan," Jak said as he sat next to the three animals. He had his hand on Red's long neck and was gently scratching the iridescent scarlet scales.

Red heaved a contented sigh.

"Did you stay up all night thinking of that name?" said Tess. She made no attempt to hide the sarcasm in her voice.

"Good morning!" came a shout. Man and Woman ambled across the bridge holding hands, followed by Gramps, whose eyes were glued to the ground.

Jak couldn't help but smile, both amused and embarrassed, when he saw them. Except for the pants still hanging around their necks, Man and Woman were still completely naked. He felt the blood rushing to his face again and turned to look at something else. "Good morning," he said.

"Yes, it is a good morning. El said so, and he is right." Man grinned like he had a secret. "I have two things for you," he announced. "One is a gift from Woman and me for all of you, and the other is a gift from El for Jak."

"A gift?" said Jak.

"No." Man shook his head. "*Two* gifts."

Jak loved gifts just like anybody else, but after being pushed away by El the night before, the last thing he expected was a gift from El, unless it was something awful like a chunk of coal or a dead rat. Thinking of a dead rat made him wonder what Frankie was up to at the moment. There would be plenty of food from the box of oatmeal that had spilled behind the downstairs pantry, so at least the little fur ball wouldn't starve to death.

"Open your mouth and close your eyes," said Man.

"What is it?" asked Jak, skeptical.

"Just do it." Jak opened his mouth but only closed his eyes halfway. He never trusted anybody who was going to put something in his mouth. He shot a glance at Tess; she stood with her arms folded across her chest, her eyes wide open.

"Girl, aren't you going to close your eyes?" asked Man.

Jak almost burst out laughing. He knew Tess would hate being called a girl, but that's what she was, and there was nothing she could do about it except grow up.

"I'll let Jak go first," she said with an edge of ice in her voice.

"I don't think this is going to work," said Gramps.

"But it is wonderful! He will like it!"

"Yes, but you can't stuff the whole thing in his mouth unless you break it apart first."

Man thought for a moment. "Yes, you are right."

Jak couldn't see much, but he heard something being smashed in half with what he guessed was Man's hand.

"Now," said Man, "close your mouth and open your eyes."

A giggle bubbled from Woman. "He means to open your mouth and close your eyes."

"They are," said Jak. He caught a glimpse of something red and dripping before shutting his eyes all the way and hoped it was watermelon.

Man dropped the red dripping thing into his mouth.

It *was* watermelon—really good watermelon, juicy and sweet and better than any watermelon he had eaten before. His dad used to say that watermelon has more water in it than water does. Once, when Jak was about six years old, he had tried to collect all the juice from a watermelon his dad brought home from a roadside stand to see if his dad was right, but he had gotten distracted by the seeds his dad kept spitting at him and never did figure it out. It had been a long time since he and his father had eaten watermelon together. It was a long trip from Seattle just to share a watermelon.

"Good, yes?" asked Man.

Jak opened his eyes and nodded his head.

Man nodded his head along with him and said, "Yes, it is good. Would you like some, Tess?"

"Sure," she said, but before Man could help her, she scooped some out of the rind and fed herself.

Man looked at her quizzically for a moment, as if trying to figure her out, but then he turned and waved his arm graciously toward Woman. "And now, gift number two—a gift for Jak from El."

Woman's hands were behind her, hiding whatever it was. She brought her arms out front and held out two of the twin starfish leaves from the Tree of Life. He knew it wasn't the fruit from the Tree of Life; the fruit was purplish and smaller. These were definitely leaves.

"Is this dessert?" he said.

"I don't think so," said Man. "What is dessert?"

"I mean, am I supposed to eat them?"

"No, no!" Man shook his head quickly and made a face like he had just eaten a live slug. "These are not for eating, although I suppose you could try, but they don't look very good for eating to me. El said to wrap them around your ankle, the one that you hang in the air and never put on the ground."

"Wrap them around his ankle? Why would he do that?" asked Tess.

"I don't know," said Man, "but that is what El said. I brought a small vine for tying."

Jak sat down and unwrapped his ankle. It always felt better in the morning because he had elevated it all night to allow the swelling to go down. But around lunchtime, he could count on it throbbing and aching and looking like a puffy bruised softball. Normally he would lie down and put his leg up for a while, but yesterday had been so busy that he wasn't able to elevate it till he went to sleep. His ankle didn't look any better this morning. The skin was still swollen and hot, filled with dark purple and green fluid, and tender to the touch.

Macy, Scorch, and Red crowded around, a medical team of long slurping tongues.

"Oooh, Jak," said Woman. She looked at her own ankle and pressed the skin and then reached out and gently touched Jak's. "That does not look good. What happened? Did El make you like this?"

Jak's stomach clenched as he thought about the day he had twisted his ankle. He didn't like talking about it very much.

"No," he said slowly. "It was an accident." He swallowed, tempted to leave the explanation at that. It would be a lot easier, but it wouldn't be completely honest. "A bunch of us were down at the park by the river playing hide and seek, a game where one person has to find everyone else who has hidden. There's this willow tree that stretches sideways across the river, and it has a great hiding spot on this one branch with lots of leaves to hide in. I've always been the only one who can get out there since everybody else is too big, so that's where I hid. But there's this little second grader who is always following me around. He saw where I was hiding and climbed up after me. I told him to get down, but he wouldn't listen." Now Jak was coming to the part he didn't like to talk about. *It was an accident,* he told himself. He took a deep breath and continued. "So I started shaking the branch a little, just enough to scare him back down." He stopped speaking again, dreading the next part of the story.

"And..." said Man, prodding Jak on.

"I wasn't trying to do it, even though some of the other kids said I was, but I wasn't, honest."

"Do what?" asked Man.

"The branch sort of started shaking more than I expected, and the boy... well...he fell into the river. I didn't mean to do it, honest! I tried to catch him, but he was too far away, and then I lost my balance and I fell out of the tree too. The water was dark and fast and I couldn't find him. The current was pulling me under and then my foot got stuck in some rocks and I couldn't get out and I couldn't breathe."

Man was staring intently at him. "How did you get out?"

"A fisherman saw me and got me unstuck. "

"What happened to the boy?" asked Woman.

"Some kids on the shore threw him a rope. He was crying, but okay."

"And your ankle?"

"It got super twisted up in the rocks. The doctor said I might not ever be able to walk normally again." He almost felt like he deserved the sprained ankle for what he had done.

Woman furrowed her eyebrows together. "Maybe this will help." She bent down and carefully wrapped one of the twin starfish leaves around the top of his ankle and the other around the bottom.

Man circled the vine around both leaves and tied them together until the leaves stayed snug against his leg. "There," said Man, standing up straight again. "Now we will see what El will do."

CHAPTER 14
The War Begins with Rabbits

Lucifer led the Lights slurping along the dirt pathway in the dark through the forest and hills, scouring every branch and leaf, hungry for blood and flickering with anticipation. But every time they attacked a creature, it ended up being just a pine cone or a clump of grass bending in the breeze.

He had a vague idea of what the humans looked like, but he wasn't sure what other breathing creatures Yahweh had made. It didn't matter though. He would kill them one by one until all that were left were the humans. And these he would wrap with chains and bolt to his throne for mere entertainment. He was certain a whip would make them dance. He chuckled dryly to himself at the thought. *The enemy is such a fool.*

The sky gradually grew brighter until another light crested over the horizon and filled the valley with a warm yellow glow.

Lucifer gazed at the newcomer with hatred; it rivaled his own brightness. He sulked as the light rose higher in the sky, the desire to kill rising with it, yet it seemed to only be another of Yahweh's breathless creations. There had to be something that breathed here somewhere, he could sense it.

He billowed over the edge of the ridge where the trees had begun to thin out. Across the valley, a waterfall crashed over a cliff into a pool at the bottom. Down the hill, a large blue gate stood in the middle of the field, with an open door swinging back and forth in the wind. Suddenly, he felt something move behind him.

Lucifer snapped around and zeroed in on a pair of creatures hopping through the grass. He shot out two gooey tentacles, snatched them by their ears, and held them aloft, exhilarated at the find.

The animals twitched their whiskers and finished munching the grass in between their teeth.

He brought them close and inspected the oddities. They were small, soft, and warm, with two short legs in front and two strong long legs in the back. Grayish-brown fur covered their bodies, and they each had a poufy white tail, soft black eyes, and long ears. Neither seemed afraid; they appeared perfectly content to hang by their ears. He would change that.

He squeezed them tight in his tentacles, dripping small droplets of sticky tar-like light onto the ground, and raised himself twenty feet into the air. "I have found the first!" he bellowed, inflating his presence fatter and taller until he was a mound of pulsing yellow light.

The other Lights flocked to the ridge, pushing each other out of the way so they could be near enough to witness the first killings of Yahweh's creation.

The two creatures snuggled together in the mesh of his tentacles, as if they had found a fantastic place to take a nap. Lucifer sneered at them. *Stupid creatures couldn't even tell they were breathing their last breaths.* A shiver of excitement rippled through him as he pictured the first bloodshed in this new world; Yahweh would be furious, and that made him very, very happy.

A spidery Light raised one skinny leg and shouted. "What're you waitin' for? Kill 'em!"

"Yes, spill the blood!" shouted a fat purple blob. "Spill the blood!"

The crowd picked up the chant. "Spill the blood! Spill the blood!"

Lucifer raised his prize high and screamed into the night, "It begins now!" He wrapped his tentacles tight around the creature's heads until only their long ears poked out. Then he squeezed tight and mashed his hands together until he was certain their skulls had cracked and nothing remained except an oatmeal of flesh and bone.

The creatures were dead, and the war had begun!

CHAPTER 15

The Amazing Hares

Jak and the others headed to the pool at the bottom of Split Falls for the day. The air was warm, making it a perfect day for swimming, so that's exactly what they did. They swung on the vines that hung from the cliff, splashed in the water, ate fat raspberries, and lay in the sun telling Man and Woman their story.

Jak didn't think the two really got much of what they were talking about, as they were from a different world, but they understood enough to know that the book was important and that Jak and the others couldn't go back home yet without dying.

As nice as it was to swim in the pool, it was also a bit awkward. For one thing, the wild animals were not wild. Just like Macy, Scorch, and Red, they wanted to be near the humans. At any given moment, an elephant might squirt a trunk of water in their face or a badger would try to curl up in their laps. Jak, Tess, and Gramps could not get used to the fact that just because an animal growled at you it didn't mean it wanted to eat you. It might mean, "Throw me a banana," or "You're sitting on my raspberry," or "Would you please scratch my back?" That was a lot different from back home where a growling animal meant danger. Tess almost hurt herself trying to escape up an apple tree when a woodchuck sidled next to her and surprised her by rubbing her arm with his whiskers.

The second reason it had been a little awkward had to do with clothing—or rather, lack thereof. Man and Woman obviously didn't feel the need for swimming suits; although they did remove their pants from around their necks and lay them carefully on the bank. "We don't want to ruin them," Woman explained.

Jak, Tess, and Gramps, however, kept their pants on. Jak untucked his shirt, carefully pulled out the book, and laid it at the base of a river birch. Then he and Gramps tossed their shirts on the bank of the river.

"Why don't you take the rest of your clothes off?" asked Man, squirting water in the eyes of a hippo that was nudging him for a nose rub. "I think it would be much nicer for you."

"And much easier," said Woman.

"Thanks for the invitation," said Gramps, "but we'll leave them on."

This was the moment Tess had been waiting for. The question burned on her tongue and she could hold it back no longer. She swam up next to Woman, who was gently stroking the back of a frog sunning itself on a lily pad.

"Woman?" she said timidly.

Woman turned toward her, drops of water trickling down her long black hair and smiled. "Yes, Tess?"

Tess took a deep breath and plunged in. "Do you... I mean... uh, doesn't it bother you to be naked all the time?"

"Naked?" asked Man, swimming up next to Woman. Man sank into the water so just his eyes and the top of his head poked out, imitating the crocodile floating next to him.

Tess sagged a bit. She had been hoping to have a private conversation with Woman, but there was nothing she could do about it now. "Yes, naked. You don't have any clothes on." There, she had said it, and for the first time she could look Man in the eyes. "If I walked around with no clothes on, I'd be... well, everybody I know would be embarrassed."

"Embarrassed?" said Woman, crinkling her forehead.

"Yeah, you know." But by the blank stares they each gave her, she realized they didn't know, so she explained. "Embarrassed means you feel ashamed, like you want to hide under a rock, or want to run away because you don't have any clothes on."

Woman gave a quick frown. "Why would we be embarrassed? What is there to be embarrassed about?"

"Yes," said Man, wiping the water from his mouth with the back of his hand and nodding his agreement with Woman. "El made us just the way we are. There is nothing to hide, nothing to be ashamed of." He dipped back down and shot another mouthful of water, this time at the crocodile. The croc dove under the surface.

"But..." said Tess, feeling like she was losing ground. "There are certain things, certain parts of our bodies, that we need to hide from almost everyone. That's why we wear clothes."

"But hiding is not a good thing," said Woman, shaking her head. "Look what happened to Jak and his ankle when he tried to hide."

Man disappeared under the water in a flurry of bubbles.

A moment later, Woman started laughing and then toppled over and disappeared too.

Tess looked at Gramps and Jak and threw up her hands in despair, "What are we going to do about those two?"

Gramps and Jak just grinned and shrugged.

❧

Lucifer released his tentacles and dropped the mangled mess on the ground. But instead of a mangled mess falling from his tentacles, the two creatures hopped happily back into the grass and began munching again.

Lucifer and the other Lights stared dumbfounded at the two munchers.

"What?!" Lucifer bellowed. He was certain he had thoroughly killed them. He scooped them up again and wrapped his tentacles around their necks. *This time,* he thought, *I will pop their little heads off!*

He squeezed so hard that their heads should have flipped backwards and tumbled into the grass, but they didn't. The creatures only twitched their noses and stared at him with placid brown eyes.

He whipped his tentacles around and smashed them to the ground as hard as he could, but they dropped to the grass as if he had gently put them down.

Lucifer bellowed in rage. The two orbs where his eyes should have been bulged, and he blasted the long-eared creatures with white hot radiance, but not a patch of fur or blade of grass suffered from the blast—not even the lightest singe. Instead, the two hopped under a hedge of yellow-flowered bushes and disappeared.

He whipped around, fuming, and shot into the sky, inflating himself into a swirling bright yellow cloud as large as a house. Wriggling white tentacles burst out of the cloud and pointed down the hill, past the blue gate.

"This world is ours for the taking!" he screamed. "Nothing will stop us! Go!" He pointed down the hill again. "Do not come back until every inch has been splattered with the blood of his creation! The first killer will receive a special position in the new kingdom."

Lucifer's words worked like an electric shock. Fat blobby Lights zoomed down the hill, running over the smaller Lights in the attempt to get down the hill before the others, causing a cascade of whining as the stragglers slid down after the others.

Lucifer descended back to the ground and compressed himself into a solid tower of gleaming yellow. He waved a tentacle slowly through the air. He sensed something. He paused for a moment to listen. Something was down there in the valley, something somehow connected to him. The something or some*one* smelled of blood and evil, and it drew him like a fly to a pile of manure. He glided down the hill and past the blue gate.

I will find it, he declared, *and I will kill it.*

But by the time he had reached the bottom of the hill, some of the Lights were already returning. As soon as they saw him, they veered off the path, blubbering and going as dim as they could, trying to hide behind fat-trunked trees or wide patches of hedges and shrubs. One lopsided black Light about the same size and shape of a lamppost must not have been looking where it was gliding because it zoomed straight into Lucifer, entangling its long, stubby arm in one of Lucifer's tentacles.

"Imbecile!" Lucifer spat. "I gave the order to attack the valley. What are you doing back here already? Cowards!"

"Uhhh..." The black Light shifted uncomfortably and then stammered in a thin, weedy voice, "Um, we found more creatures, we did, in the clearing. Yes, we found them, but... but we can't—"

"Out with it!" shouted Lucifer. "You can't *what?*"

"We can't kill anything," it complained. "Nothing will die. A fat creature with a horn on its nose sat on me when I tried to strangle it, and a long-necked creature kicked the Light next to me and sent it straight into a tree. And then I tried a smaller creature with a bushy tail and long teeth, but it bit me."

Lights of all shapes and colors, taking advantage of the black Light's unfortunate collision with Lucifer, wound quietly and quickly back up the hill.

Lucifer's attention shifted as he realized what was going on. He was about to turn and blast a few more Lights, but before he could do anything, a troop of the biggest, most influential Lights in Lucifer's army sidled up next to him.

"Lucius," purred a fat, blotchy purple tower that resembled a humongous rotten grape. "It cannot be done."

"Stul," Lucifer said, "of all my officers, I expected more from you."

"It cannot be done," Stul insisted. "We have no influence over these creatures. It does not matter if they are creations who breathe or creations who don't. We have no power here, Lucius."

"Certainly there must be another way, Lucifer," said a tall thick black tower who looked very much like an oversized gravestone.

"Do you have something in mind, Reaf?" snapped Lucifer.

"Nooo," Reaf admitted, flitting back and forth. "Not yet, but we just got here. Certainly we will think of something in time, once we know more about the creations."

Lucifer reluctantly allowed himself to be convinced. His defeat with the pathetic little long-eared creatures still pricked at his overblown ego. Not even he had been able to spill blood in Yahweh's creation, so he couldn't really expect his legions to be any more successful.

"What would you have us do, sir?" Stul asked, interrupting his thoughts.

"Get back to the beach and take the rest of these slackers with you." Lucifer paused, looking toward the valley. Whatever it was that beckoned him forward would have to wait.

CHAPTER 16

The Amazing Hair

By the time the sun kissed the tops of the trees, Jak and the others were exhausted and headed back to the clearing. That's when Jak noticed that the ache wasn't there. True, he had lounged around in the sun for part of the day, but his ankle always throbbed by day's end, and this time, he felt nothing.

The leaves were still wrapped tight around his foot. The vines had held, even in the water. He gently pressed the area that had been swollen that morning, but it didn't hurt. Jak put his foot on the ground and slowly put his weight on it until his heel stood flat on the grass, then lifted the crutch into the air. He was standing on his own two legs, without the help of that annoying crutch! *But how?* he wondered. *The doctors told me it would take months. How did it heal so fast?*

He took a tiny step forward, and there was no pain.

Jak smiled and took a bigger step, but this time he was rewarded with a dull ache that raced through his ankle. He leaned back on his crutch. . He still didn't have all of his strength, but it was better than it had been. He hobbled to catch up with the others, but decided to wait and tell them later about his progress. Secretly, he hoped maybe it would even be stronger by the time the day was done. That would be more impressive.

Man led them straight to the Tree of Life. Even though the Tree of Knowing Good and Evil stood right next to the Tree of Life, the five of them gathered as far as possible away from it, as if even being near the tree might allow a sliver of death to slide into them.

The purple fruit was obvious now that Jak knew where to look. The tree was covered with hundreds of them, nestled among the twin starfish leaf clusters.

Jak looked at the leaves more closely than he had the day before, wondering if he should pick some more. *But they were a gift from El, so the tree must belong to him. But he also told Man to eat the fruit from the tree, so why not take the leaves? Besides, he would never even know.*

"It is time for the zing," said Man. He plucked five pieces of the fruit, gave one to each of them, then held his fruit up and said, "To life without death."

They bit into the fruit, and, once again, the delicious sensation prickled through Jak's back up into his head and down his spine. "That's what you should call this fruit," said Jak, "zingers."

"Zingers?" said Man. "I like it! You are good at naming things—Split Falls, cherries, and now zingers. I had not thought of naming the fruit of this tree, but zingers it is."

They stood quietly, each savoring the moment. A mist began to sprout from the air. Where it came from exactly was hard to tell, as it just kind of appeared like a natural sprinkler system.

"The air has begun to cool. El will be coming soon," Woman said softly, braiding the ends of her hair. "I do not understand why you could not be with us last night. It was wonderful, being with El."

There was an awkward silence.

"What is he like?" asked Jak. "Is he old and bald?"

"No," said Woman, shaking her head and smiling. "El is nothing like that at all."

"How about a black goatee and greasy hair?" asked Tess.

"No, nothing like that either. He is more like..." Woman stared into the sky, trying to think of just the right word. "He is like light. El's hair and face and body are made out of light."

"Is he mean?" asked Jak, taking one last bite of zinger.

"Oh no! El is very kind. We talked about Man and me meeting each other by the river, about meeting you, about taking care of the animals and the garden. He said he will have something special for us tonight."

Jak didn't want to ask the question because he was afraid of the answer, but he asked it anyway. "Did he say anything about us staying? About us seeing him tonight?"

Woman shook her head.

Jak sighed. He would just have to wait. The group began to drift away toward the pomegranate tree to wait for El, leaving Jak by himself. If he was going to take a leaf, now was the time. He turned around to make sure no one was looking, then reached for a twin cluster, but as soon as his fingers touched the stems, he changed his mind. *Maybe El won't know, but maybe he will.* Jak didn't need to give him any more reasons to send them back to the bridge.

But the same thing happened that night. El insisted that only Man and Woman stay in the clearing, and sent Jak and the others away. This time they brought with them big poofy pods they had discovered that morning on the way to the river. The pods were like giant milk weed pods that grew on plants as tall as corn, but instead of corn cobs, the pods flopped from the sides, each filled with soft white fibers, perfect for sleeping on.

The same mustached monkeys and the red baboon came with food, an assortment of papaya and pomegranate and red beans that tasted like chicken enchiladas. Another sign that read "Enjoy" (this time it was red) stood on each of their plates.

Even though the red bean enchiladas were wonderful, Jak fumed as he shoveled in the last of the beans. He was so angry he didn't even want to tell Tess and Gramps about how well his ankle was doing.

"Do you think he doesn't like us?" he asked. "We've been here—wherever here is—for two days, and the guy won't even talk to us. Why did he bring us here if he doesn't want to see us? It doesn't make any sense."

"It doesn't make any sense to *you*," said Gramps. He yawned and settled back on the bed. "I've been around long enough to know that just because I don't understand something doesn't mean it's bad." He yawned again, leaned his head back on his pod-pillow and closed his eyes. "It could mean—" He stopped talking and, a moment later, broke into a gentle snore without finishing his sentence.

"It could mean El is wacko," said Jak, finishing the sentence for him, though he knew that probably wasn't what Gramps was going to say.

A gentle whoosh came across the bridge, and the warm glow of the light that came with El—or maybe the light that actually *was* El—danced above the clearing. The sound of the rushing river flowed next to them, but it was not actually the river at all. It was the voice of El, flowing through the trees and dancing along with the glow.

Jak stared at the light. It wasn't fair that they had to stay here while Man and Woman got to stay in the clearing. Jak glanced at Gramps and then at Tess. "Let's go," he whispered, fed up with the whole ordeal.

"Go where?"

"To the clearing."

Tess looked at him, her eyes narrowed. "We just came from the clearing. We're not supposed to be there right now."

"I know, but it can't hurt to take one look at El, can it?" said Jak. "They won't even know we're there. We'll just go to the last bend in the path and have a peek around the corner."

Tess thought for a second. "Okay, I'm game, but what about your foot?"

His foot wasn't much better than it had been at zinger time. "Scorch will help me if I get too tired, right, Scorch?"

At the sound of her name, the leviathan raised her head and pranced up. Red and Macy got up at the same time, and the five of them set off down the path toward the clearing.

The darkness made it a lot harder to walk in the seashells than Jak expected. The shadows made the path seem solid in places where it was shifty and shifty in places it was solid. He had to root around with his crutch to make sure it was firmly planted in the seashells before he placed his weight on it.

Crunch, swing forward, probe... crunch, swing forward, probe. *At this rate, the sun will be up before we even get to the bend in the path,* Jak thought.

It had been comfortably cool at the bridge, but the closer they drew to the clearing, the hotter it got. Sweat began to bead up on Jak's forehead. "I'm hot," he complained, wiping his face with his shirt.

"Me too," said Tess, "and I'm having a hard time catching my breath. I feel like I just ran a lap around the track at school."

Jak took a deep breath and let it out. "I need a break."

They sat on the seashells and rested, silent, both wondering if this was such a good idea.

Jak looked down the path toward the bend. "Tess," he whispered hoarsely. "What?"

He pointed to where the white of the path disappeared into the black of the woods. Small tendrils of light crawled around the corner and evaporated into wisps that blew away in the wind.

"What is it?" she asked, a touch of fear in her voice.

"I don't know."

One of the tendrils reached further than the rest, coming all the way to Jak's arm, a beautiful golden yellow and orange-, the same hues as the sunset, moving together like swirls of smoke. A sudden burst of breeze batted the tendril, and it melted away.

"Let's go find out," said Jak. They still had a ways to go before they reached the clearing, and if this was any indication of what El was like, it was going to be amazing.

The closer they got to the corner, the brighter and fatter the tendrils became. By the time they rounded the bend, a brilliant cloud engulfed them. The light whirled around them, bathing their bodies, caressing their skin like liquid sunshine.

Tess reached out her fingers and tried to touch it. "It's beautiful."

Jak was mesmerized, and a feeling came over him like he never wanted to leave that place, he wanted to stay and bask in the light forever. It felt like home and apple pie with ice cream and...

Suddenly Jak clutched his throat. He couldn't breathe! It wasn't the same feeling you get from running fast and hard, but more like he was drowning. He tried to cough but couldn't get any air into his lungs. He dropped his crutch and fell backwards onto the shells.

More bursts of light exploded toward them until the trees blazed white and the temperature soared like a giant oven door had just been thrown open.

Jak shut his eyes and scrabbled backwards, aware of nothing except the blinding white and his burning lungs and skin. He had to get back around the corner, away from this strangling, burning light.

The next thing Jak knew, he and Tess were lying flat on their backs in the same spot where they had stopped to rest, gasping for air. The light was gone, but the tendrils still made their way around the corner and wisped down the trail.

The animals seemed fine. Red sprawled on the ground next to them scratching one ear while Macy and Scorch busied themselves with trying to lick air into Tess and Jak.

Jak's mouth felt dry and grainy, and a layer of ash that tasted like burnt socks coated his tongue. He coughed and spat the ash on the ground.

"Wh-what happened?" asked Tess, stupefied. "I...I couldn't breathe. I couldn't see anything except that... that light! I couldn't tell where I was or what I was doing." She spat on the ground too. "I don't think El liked it that we tried to sneak into the garden."

"But how could he have known?" said Jak. "He didn't see us. There's no way he could have found out." He stopped and sucked in another lungful of air. "What I can't figure out, though, is how Man and Woman can stand to be with him. They made it sound like it's wonderful, but that was just... just awful."

"Let's go back to the bridge," said Tess. "I'm exhausted."

Jak's ankle throbbed again, and he realized he must have stepped down on it in his frantic attempt to escape the light. It was going to be another night of trying to get to sleep with a lullaby of ache. He picked up his crutch and turned around. It was strange really. An hour earlier, the only thing Jak wanted was to meet with El and ask him a thousand questions, but now meeting El was the last thing he wanted to do.

The next morning, Man and Woman arrived at the bridge at the same time Jak was checking the leaf bandage around his ankle. In the night, the leaves had withered and curled, taking on a brownish hue instead of the lively green. He wasn't sure if it was because the light clouds from the night before had burned them to death or because they had wilted on their own. He unlaced the vines and peeled the dry leaves away from his skin. In spite of stepping on his foot the night before, the swelling had definitely gone down. The green and purple bruises had faded to yellow and brown, and he could finally wiggle his ankle.

Man was so excited he could hardly stand still. Neither he nor Woman had any burn marks on their skin, and their breathing seemed just fine, so apparently their meeting with El had been a success.

"Gifts! More gifts!" he said, holding something aloft in his clenched fist.

Woman had her hands behind her back. Her hazel-green eyes sparkled, and she gave a tremendous smile.

"Gifts for who?" said Jak.

"You mean for *whom*," said Tess, obviously enjoying the opportunity to correct him.

Jak gave her an exasperated look. Ever since she had won that spelling bee in the sixth grade, she acted like she was some kind of prize-winning English teacher, always going around correcting everyone.

Man kept talking. "He gave a gift to Woman and me and another gift for you, Jak."

After what had happened the night before, Jak wasn't sure why he'd be getting a gift from El. All he could think was that El must not have noticed their intrusion. He hoped it was more leaves because then his ankle might be totally better by that night or the next day.

Man held out his hand. Cupped in the palm sat a pile of objects, yellow, black, brown, and green, some pointy, and some blunt. They looked like seeds, but Jak didn't know why Man would get so excited about that. Certainly he must have seen seeds before.

"They are called seeds." Man took his time saying the word "seeds," squeezing every ounce from each letter. "Here's what you do. You dig a little hole in the ground." Man bent over and, with his fingers, dug into the dirt on the bank of the river. "And then you drop a seed into the hole." Man dramatically plucked a seed from his palm and inserted it into the hole. "And then you cover the seed up with the dirt." He pulled the pile of dirt over the hole and patted it down. "And then you wait." He stood and smiled. "El said that soon the seeds will grow. They'll come up out of the dirt, but they will be different, something called plants—not a tree like these in the woods and not like the fruit trees, but plants that grow new kinds of food. But first we must prepare a place for putting the seeds so they have room to grow. El calls it *work*, and that is what we get to do today."

Gramps, Tess, and Jak stole glances at each other while Man was explaining about his seeds, but said nothing about the fact that they already knew all about seeds.

"Sounds great," said Gramps. But by the way he said it, Jak wasn't sure if his grandfather was telling the truth or not. After all, gardening had never been his forte. As a matter of fact, Gramps was a well-known plant murderer.

Once Gramma had planted sweet corn in between the garage and the shed, a place that was easy to water and got plenty of sun. The shoots came up nice and green, and by July, the corn was up to her knees, just like it was supposed to be. Gramps had promised to help her weed because Gramma's hip was bad and she had a hard time bending over. He did a decent job, too, until the day Gramma and her friends went to Minneapolis to go shopping.

He was a little behind in weeding, which meant the weeds were extra tough, so he decided that instead of pulling the weeds by hand, he would use a hoe. After all, farmers had been getting rid of weeds with hoes for thousands of years. But when Gramps used a hoe, it was more like a logger cutting down a tree with an ax than a farmer teasing a weed from the soil. When Gramma came home, she discovered the weeds were gone from the garden, but so was the corn. It might be better if Gramps wasn't a part of this garden.

"And here is the second gift, the one from El to you, Jak," said Man. He motioned for Woman to step forward. When she brought her arms in front of her, she did not have two leaves in her hands. In fact, she didn't even have one leaf. She held a bag, woven from bands of red and blue threads with a wide shoulder strap and a flap with a wooden button.

"It is for the book," she said with a touch of reverence. "El said you will soon need this."

Jak's face fell when he realized there were no leaves. In that moment, he also remembered that he had forgotten to put the book back in his shirt yesterday when they finished swimming. *El must have seen it and thinks I'm irresponsible, leaving the book out in the open like that.* Irritated, he took the bag and slung it around his shoulders. "Thanks," he said, but the tone of his voice didn't sound very grateful.

"Aren't you going to open it?" asked Man.

"No." He paused, then added sheepishly, "I don't have the book here. I forgot it under a tree by Split Falls." He feared it was soaking wet and ruined from the mist, but he was afraid to say so.

A smile cracked Man's face again. "Oh, but I think you should open it now."

Jak didn't think it was worth arguing about, so he turned the wooden clasp and lifted the flap.

Inside the bag was the book, safe and dry, along with two more leaves.

Jak smiled and slid the bag from his shoulder, plopped down, and lifted the leaves carefully to his ankle. Maybe El didn't hate him after all. "It feels so much better today," he said. "I don't understand it, but the leaves did something. Last night I could almost walk on it again."

"You could?" asked Tess, surprised. "Why didn't you say something?"

Jak shrugged. "I don't know." But he did know. The truth was that he had been angry with El.

"And it looks much better too," said Woman. "The leaves have drawn out some of the twisting." She crouched next to him and helped him tie the vines around the fresh leaves.

When they had finished wrapping his ankle, Man, unable to contain himself, set out toward the clearing. "Come on, let's go plant these seeds."

They spent the morning clearing a patch of dirt between the pomegranate tree and the entrance to the path leading to the sea.

Jak leaned the new book bag with the book and the two black cherries inside it against the pomegranate (He had transferred the cherries the night before, thinking it much safer that they travel in the bag instead of his pocket) and then removed his shoe from his left foot. He was sick of wearing it and didn't think he really needed it anyway, especially in the dirt. Gramps decided to go barefoot as well, but Tess kept her tennis shoes on.

Planting was hard work but good work, and it was much easier than Jak remembered from helping Gramma dig her garden. Digging was especially easy for Macy, Scorch, and Red. Their tongues and tails wagged happily as they dug, yipping and braying, through the dirt. Whenever Macy dug holes in the yard at home, Jak or Gramps yelled at her, so it felt strange to be encouraging her to dig holes here.

The diggers' claws made holes fast, but the holes tended to be big enough to bury large rocks and needed to be filled in most of the way before they were the right depth to bury the seeds. Eventually, they worked out a system. Jak led Macy, Red, and Scorch in ripping out the grass and digging. Man and Gramps followed, filling in the holes until they were the right depth, and Woman and Tess dropped seeds in the holes and then led a pair of elephants in filling the dirt in over them. Several times throughout the morning, Red and Scorch galloped away toward the river, only to return a few minutes later, shaking a shower of water from their manes over everyone in the field.

It was while digging that Jak noticed that the leviathans' paws were different from Macy's. He had assumed they were the same as dog paws, with claws extending from in between the pads, but they weren't. Their claws were attached to long toes that extended from their feet, with a thick webbing of flesh attached to each toe, like duck feet, except that they could close their toes together. *No wonder their feet make such great shovels,* he thought.

"Hey," said Jak, when the fourth clod of dirt in a row hit him in the face. "Watch where you're throwing that. You're hitting me in the head!" He couldn't help but wonder if the three animals were playing a game of "Hit Jak with the Dirt" because almost every single toss of earth peppered his head or his chest.

Every time he got hit, it reminded him what Man had told him when they met two days earlier about coming up from the dirt. He still didn't have a clue what he meant. The only thing he could think of was that Man had been trapped in an underground cavern and El pulled him out.

By noon, they had cleared and planted a section as big as a school classroom. They took a lunch break underneath the shade of the pomegranate tree. Man had snatched Jak's shoe and run down the path leading to the river. He returned with the shoe sloshing full of water so they could wash the dirt from their hands. They now sat munching on the juicy pomegranate kernels and resting. Woman sat cross-legged with Red's head on her thigh, running her fingers through the silky red mane as she ate. Macy and Scorch lay on either side of Jak, chewing on a couple of fruit rinds the leviathans had brought back from one of their excursions to the river.

Jak was just getting ready to ask Man about coming up from the dirt when Man spoke,

"What is evil?" He sat with his eyes transfixed, staring across the clearing at the Tree of Knowing Good and Evil. "I do not understand. El has said everything is good."

"I have wondered the same thing," said Woman, pouring another handful of pomegranate kernels. "All that is around us is good—the trees, the fruit, the water. There is nothing here that El has called evil, yet if we eat of that tree, we will know good *and* evil. How can we know evil if everything is good?"

Gramps put down the pomegranate he was working on. "Be glad you don't know evil," he said, still chewing. "If evil were here, you would know because it would suck the life out of you. Believe me, you wouldn't like it."

Suddenly, Tess sat straight up with a shocked expression on her face. "Gramps," she said, pointing to his head, "since when do you have brown hair?"

CHAPTER 17

The Dance in the Water

"Brown hair? He reached up and pulled his hair down as far as he could, but it was too short for him to see it.

Tess marched over to Gramps. "You've had gray hair forever, but now, look." She pulled up a shock of pepper-brown hair mixed in with the salty gray. "Some of your hair is brown now."

"Same thing with his beard," said Jak, amazed. This was impossible!

Gramps stuck his lip out as far as he could to look at his mustache. "How much brown is there?" he said.

"Enough that I could see it in the shade from the other side of the tree," said Tess.

"You mean Clarence used to have different color hair?" asked Man, looking at him curiously.

"Sure did," said Gramps. "I used to have hair darker than Jak's."

"What happened to it?"

"I got old. My hair got old, my eyes got old, and my heart got old. Everything's falling apart, I guess, although I do feel pretty good today - the arthritis in my hands isn't acting up a bit. Maybe it's all the pomegranate. I read once that pomegranates are good for arthritis."

"Pomegranates...," repeated Jak to himself. His mind was spinning a million miles an hour. "Gramps, it was the zingers!" He dug the book out of the red and blue bag he had received that morning and turned to the page with the picture of the Tree of Knowing Good and Evil. Tess looked a bit apprehensive with the book open but didn't say anything. "Here... read this."

Gramps put on his glasses and peered at the page. "Hmph! I just got these glasses a month ago, but I can't read a thing on that page." He sighed. "I guess I'm getting old faster than I used to."

"Now," said Jak, "take your glasses *off* and try to read."

Gramps looked at Jak as if he had just asked him to eat a tarantula. "You know I can't read without my glasses."

"I know, but just try it, okay?"

So Gramps put his glasses in his pocket and tried again. "Well, I'll be jiggered! Look at that! I can read every word on that page!"

"The problem," said Jak, excitement lacing his voice, "isn't that you're getting older, Gramps. You're getting *younger*. Your hair is turning from gray to brown, just like it used to be, and you can't feel the arthritis because the arthritis isn't there."

"So," said Tess, "you're saying that Gramps is getting younger because he's been eating the zingers?"

"Think about it, Tess. How could my ankle get better just by wrapping leaves around it? But it is. I bet I'm going to be able to run on it tomorrow. It's got to be the Tree of Life."

Gramps gave a low whistle. "Well, I'll be jiggered," he said again, rubbing his whiskers as if he was trying to feel the brown in it.

The five of them stared at the two trees on the hill: one that gave life, and the other that brought death.

They finished lunch and got back to work, each looking forward to eating zingers in the evening. Gramps kept rubbing his beard and touching his head so much that his hair was turning brown as much from dirt as it was from the zingers. By late afternoon, they had finished planting another classroom-sized section of what Tess thought were corn and pea seeds.

Jak felt like they could probably plant at least a few seeds in his ears because of all the dirt Scorch, Red, and Macy had thrown at his head. With all the uncertainty of the past two days, it felt good to do something useful and productive, but he still wanted to know when El was going to tell them why they were there. "Did El say anything about tonight?" he asked Woman as they gathered by the Tree of Life when the planting was done. Man had retrieved another shoeful of water, and they were taking turns rinsing dirt off their hands before they ate.

"Yes and no," said Woman. "He said he would be coming a little later to gaze with us at the bright lights in the night sky, but. . ." She shook her head. "But he said nothing about you staying." She bit her lip. "But perhaps he will let you stay tonight."

Jak sighed, realizing he would just have to wait—again.

Eating the zingers had a new meaning that night. After the discovery of Gramps's brown hair and disappearing arthritis, it was no longer just a nice treat at the end of the day. The two nights previous, Gramps had not eaten much. "The effect is so powerful that I can only do a few bites," he had said, "I'm afraid I'm going to have another heart attack." But tonight was different.

As soon as Man finished lifting the zinger and saying, "To life without death," Gramps dug into the zinger and ate the whole thing. He said he was even considering swallowing the seed, but he didn't.

After they had eaten the zingers, they stood for a while watching a pair of peacocks as the sun began to touch the trees at the top of the ridge near Split Falls. The male spread his feathers in a tremendous blue and green sideways fan and turned in circles in the direction of the female. He voiced a loud vibration, trying to get the female's attention.

"He's doing the mating dance," Gramps whispered to Tess and Jak.

"Doesn't look like the female's very interested," said Tess.

"Females never look very interested," said Gramps. "That's why the males have to keep on trying. Eventually he'll win her over."

The peacocks moved to the edge of the clearing and then out of sight.

"Let's go down to the quiet spot on the river at the edge of the pool," said Man. "We can wash ourselves while we wait."

The temperature had not dropped much yet, so it felt good to jump into the cool water and wash the dirt of the day away. When they had finished, they lay on the bank and let the warm breeze and the last rays of sunshine dry them while they watched the horizon turn orange and pink.

Red and Scorch continued swimming, but they kept quieter than usual. Normally they splashed and dove and jumped. It was obvious they were made for the water, but they were doing something different now. Scorch did not move around the pool, but stayed in the middle, rotating like a statue on a lazy Susan, her eyes fixed on Red.

Red swam in a slow clockwise circle, swimming around Scorch several times, getting closer with every revolution. His mane was erect, sticking into the air like a giant Mohawk. Short blue flames licked out of his mouth. When their noses were just about to touch, Scorch darted back and began swimming away. For a moment, it appeared that Red was going to let her go, but he threw his head back and brayed, then shot off after her.

It was not a haphazard race. Scorch swam around the edge of the pool in ever-shrinking circles, followed exactly by Red, both swimming so fast that it was hard for the audience on the bank to follow the leviathans' bodies with their eyes. 'Round and 'round they went, churning the water into a whirlpool. Every so often, Red's head surfaced and blasted a red or blue or green flame into the air above him.

When the circle could shrink no more, they abruptly flipped their bodies upright in the water and faced each other, locked in a gaze, swimming a slow circle dance in the middle of the pond until they were close enough to touch each other's noses. Their long necks straddled side by side, and suddenly they flipped their heads back, lighting the evening sky with twin columns of fire, one blue and the other green. No roar or growl escaped their mouths, just the sound of breath being forced from their throats and the crackle of the flames. Then they sank beneath the surface and could be seen no more.

"Wow! What was that?" said Jak.

"I bet it was the same thing we just saw with the peacocks," said Gramps.

"A mating dance?"

"Yep."

"How do you know that?"

"Oh, you can tell from the look in a man's eyes. It's the same look Red had in his."

The sky was dark now, and a myriad of stars shone in the sky above them. Jak wondered if there would be a meteor shower like the night before.

"Look at all the lights," said Woman. "So many colors! Aren't they beautiful?"

They were so intent on watching the heavens that they never noticed the two leviathans slip out of the pool and streak down the path toward the sea.

It had been a long day, and Jak's mouth was spending more time open than closed because of a continual series of yawns. El still had not arrived, but Gramps, Jak, and Tess decided to return to the birch copse by the bridge. "We'd probably get sent there anyway," said Jak.

Man and Woman stayed where they were by the pool, holding hands and drawing imaginary lines between the stars while they waited.

Red and Scorch galloped down the trail, nipping at each other's tails and nuzzling on the run. A powerful force ran through their blood and drew them toward the salty water. Their animal brains didn't know why, but the beach next to the ocean was the place where the eggs had to be laid, the place where they would hatch, the place where they would teach the infant leviathans to swim and jump through the waves. The ocean beckoned, so to the ocean they ran in a full-tilt gallop toward the future.

CHAPTER 18

The Patch of Silver Sand

The army of defeated Lights gathered on the beach. They hovered over the white sand in groups, muttering about the sharp hooves and horns and teeth of the various creatures they had tried to attack in the garden.

Lucifer flowed back and forth at the place where the sand met the grass, trying to think of a way around this most unfortunate circumstance. There had to be a way to destroy El's creation, and he was going to find it.

"But what can we do?" purred Stul. He floated like a lazy purple rock next to Lucifer, picking at the blotches that covered him until they popped and blew purple goo onto the grass. "It is clear that the creatures are heavily guarded by the enemy's servants. I can feel his power laced through the very fiber of this place."

"I know that," snapped Lucifer. His temper was short. "I knew that the moment we entered this world. Do you think I am stupid, Stul?" Lucifer's light glowed in bright bursts of yellow and white, and Stul backed away.

"Lucius," Stul cooed. "I am merely pointing out our disadvantage."

"I have no disadvantages," said Lucifer, spouting a slurry of glowing spittle into the air.

"Then what are we to do?" said Reaf, irritated and pacing back and forth opposite Lucifer, "We cannot just sit here on the beach forever. The enemy has repulsed us, and we have been cast out of our home in the first world. You know as well as I do that we cannot overcome Yahweh."

At the sound of the name, a hiss erupted from Lucifer, and he blazed white hot. "Silence!" he thundered.

Reaf dared not flinch.

"Do not speak the name again. The coward is afraid of my power and my presence. He does not deserve his position and has bullied me out of what should be *mine*." Light dripped from his lips and steamed into the sand.

The entire beach had gone silent, and everyone was staring at Lucifer.

A tall, thin red Light shuffled forward, prostrated itself low before Lucifer, and spoke in an even-keeled, thin voice, "Master, our friend Reaf does bring up a good point though. How shall we enslave the new creatures and gain dominion? Share your wisdom with us."

"Yes, what will we do?" A murmur spread through the glowing towers, echoing the same question.

The murmur broke open a window in Lucifer's mind, and he remembered something El had said before the war had begun. *Why have I not thought of this before? The fool has created the exact tool we need to pierce a hole in the enemy's protection and bring death to this place!* All he had to do was find a way to use it to his advantage. He quickly inflated to twice his height. "There is a way!" he announced.

The Lights went silent.

"From what I gleaned while still in the court of the enemy, there is a certain tree..." Suddenly, Lucifer stopped speaking, snapped around and focused his attention up the hill toward the woods.

The leviathans galloped out of the trees at the same moment that a million bubbles of light popped and faded from the beach. The scent of the sea wafted strongly on their tongues, and together they waded down the hill through the grass. A new scent also ran in the breeze, something they had never smelled before—or rather, never *felt* before. It was wild and strong...

and dangerous. They emptied onto the beach and licked the air with their tongues – something was not right.

☙❧

Lucifer watched the red creature step carefully onto the sand, one foot at a time, testing every step as if it expected the ground to suddenly cave in under its weight. It then dropped to its haunches and crawled slowly forward, wagging a long pink tongue back and forth, straight toward the spot where Lucifer now lay disguised as a patch of silver sand.

The creature stopped at the patch and licked the ground, as if it was trying to figure out exactly what the strange spot was. As soon as the tongue touched him, Lucifer was flooded with memories from the animal, memories of what he knew must be the man and the woman, two more who resembled the man, and another who resembled the woman. It was the first clear glimpse he had of the rulers of creation, the chosen resting place for the heart of the enemy—the humans. A wave of revulsion and hatred swept through him, and he had a hard time restraining himself from rising up and storming back into the valley to kill them, but he knew that would not accomplish his goal, nor would it even be possible... yet.

He streamed up the tongue of the red creature into its head and slowly approached its mind. He did not want to scare the creature, so he washed a warm glow around the animal's mind and waited until it became aware of his presence.

The red creature was a stupid animal. It had no ability to form thoughts, so his communication was limited to channeling feelings through head nuzzles and tongue licks, both of which Lucifer could clearly see it spent freely on its mate and the humans, especially the woman. Still, it could recognize speech and, though limited by the smallness of its mind, it had some understanding, an understanding that could perhaps be twisted.

Suddenly, the seed of a plan sprouted in Lucifer's thoughts, and he shivered with delight. This creature, this stupid creature would give Lucifer exactly what he wanted. All it needed was a little push. He probed forward, further into the creature's mind. *"Peace,"* he whispered, long and slow. *"I mean you no harm."*

The creature pulled back and almost retreated completely, but it didn't. Its mind stayed, crouched in a position similar to the creature's body, waiting.

"I come with a gift." Lucifer's voice remained soft and soothing. *"A gift you will enjoy more than anything El has given you."*

The animal remained crouched and unmoving. Lucifer continued, reassuringly. *"Speech, my friend, the ability to talk and reason, like the woman and the other humans do. Yahweh has made you a stupid creature. It was not fair, I know, but he did it anyway."*

The creature did not know what "stupid" meant, but it did not matter because it recognized the words "speech" and "Yahweh." Lucifer could sense that a warning was sounding in the animal's instinct, an alarm to pull back, to run away, but the creature stayed.

Lucifer laughed to himself, realizing the first noose had drawn tight. *"And it wasn't fair that Yahweh put Man over you, was it? After all, you are able to think on your own. You do not need a ruler over you, do you?"*

A swirl of feelings moved in the leviathan's gut, desire mixed with confusion. Again, the warning sounded in his instinct. This time, the red creature pulled his tongue up out of the sand. Lucifer immediately lost the connection and found himself back in the sand, watching while the animal paced in a circle as if it were thinking, trying to decide.

Anger flared in Lucifer, but he restrained himself from reverting to a pillar of light and attempting to blast the creature. If he was going to win this world and dominion over everything in it, he knew he would have to be patient.

The red creature trotted back to the silver patch of sand and stuck his tongue into it once more.

Lucifer immediately flowed back into the animals' mind and continued his persuasive purr. *"I can give you wisdom, I can give you speech, and I can give you power. Let me go with you and teach you what Yahweh has kept from you."*

One last time, a warning buzzed in the animal's brain, but this time, the animal did not resist; the offer was too tempting. Lucifer could feel the animal's intense desire for speech churning inside.

Suddenly, the creature lay down in the sand, and the wall that denied Lucifer entrance beyond the animal's mind came tumbling down.

Lucifer rushed through the entire body, bursting through its eyes in a short-lived twin explosion of light. He had gained entrance.

The red creature rose to his feet and trotted away, but not toward the surf. Instead, he backtracked through the grass and up the hill toward the woods. His mate took two steps toward the ocean, then two steps back toward the grass, then looked back and forth a few times before reluctantly giving up on the ocean and trotting after her mate.

The patch of silver sand was gone.

CHAPTER 19

Four Shocks in the Morning

The first thing Jak noticed when he woke up the next morning was his ankle. He was in the middle of a dream about chasing the ice cream truck with Tess through Grantsburg. As they ran, a humongous icicle fell from the sky and pinned his pant leg to the ground. Tess kept running, darting around other giant icicles spiked into the ground, but Jak was stuck. He ripped at his pant leg until it tore apart and then took off after Tess and the truck, pant leg flapping in the wind, dodging the towers of ice.

That's when he woke up and realized he really *was* running, except instead of dodging icicles, he was dodging trees. In a panic, he dropped to the ground, fully expecting a river of pain to rush through his ankle, but it didn't. In fact, it felt normal, almost good, like stretching a muscle that had been cramped in one position too long. He lifted his foot in the air and twisted it around in a circle.

The swollen yellow and brown bruises were gone, replaced by normal healthy pink skin. The leaf wrap hung limp to the ground, brown and withered. Either most of the vine rope had fallen off in the night, or he had ripped it apart in his dream.

Jak jumped up, tested his ankle with a few practice jumps, and then ran back to the campsite as fast as his legs would carry him.

The sun was just beginning to heat up the droplets of dew on the grass, sending steamy swirls snaking their way through the leaves.

"Hey!" he shouted, taking a sharp right turn in the seashell path and veering into the birch copse. "Wake up, you guys! Check it out! I can run again, and my ankle is all better."

That's when Jak got the second shock of the morning.

The pile of dirt in which Man had planted the seeds was no longer just a pile of dirt. Two plants stood six inches tall, vibrant, green, and leafy. He fingered the leaves in surprise. *Nothing grows that fast—at least nothing back home.*

And that's when Jak got the third shock of the morning.

Down the hill trotted Red and Scorch. Jak expected to see beads of water running down their sides from their normal early morning dip in the river, but they were dry. Scorch's tongue lolled out of her mouth, and she panted.

He had never seen her pant before, as she always cooled off in the river before she got too hot.

"Good morning, Scorch. Morning, Red."

Red ignored him as if Jak wasn't there and trotted straight ahead across the bridge.

Odd. Normally it was a race to see if Scorch or Red would be the first to lick his hand.

Scorch lowered her head after Red disappeared across the river and rubbed against Jak's side in a way she never had before. It was a mournful rub, as if she was sad about something.

He reached down and scratched the white diamond on her forehead in the place where the mane thinned out. That always kick-started the purring motorcycle in her belly, but no rumble came. She pulled away, glancing back once or twice as she followed Red over the bridge.

Something was wrong. The butterflies started flitting in his stomach, and that's when he got the final and biggest shock of the morning.

Tess rolled over and cracked her eyes open. Her hair was splayed in a thousand directions, as if she had stuck her hand in an electric outlet during the night. Though this may have shocked someone else, Jak had seen her like that plenty of times. The shock came when a strange man climbed out of Gramps's bed.

He looked to be in his early forties, with rumpled walnut-brown hair and a trim figure, including a noticeable bulge in his biceps. His shoulders were as square as his face, made more distinct by the full brown beard that followed the contour of his chin.

When Tess saw the man, she gasped and scrambled to where Jak stood. "Who are you?" she demanded.

Macy propped her head up from one of the pods by Jak's bed and growled.

"Who am I? What kind of question is that?" asked the man in surprise. "Most people begin the day by saying, 'good morning' or 'how did you sleep?', not by demanding to know who you are." He plucked a large dry leaf that looked like a dead Tree of Life leaf from the front of his shirt and dropped it on the bed. "I'm hungry. Come on, let's get some breakfast."

"No way! Not until you tell us who you are," said Tess, her eyes wide and wary.

"What's wrong with you, Tess? Are you dreaming?" The man took a step closer, and Tess backed away. "Pinch her, Jak," said the man. "Make sure she's awake."

The voice sounded like Gramps's, except the rasp that always sat at the edge of Gramps's words wasn't there. The face had the same square jaw and twinkling blue eyes, but the rest of him looked different. For a moment, Jak thought he looked kind of like a younger version of Gramps, but he knew that wasn't possible. *Or is it?* he thought, glancing down at his healed ankle.

Jak cocked his head. "Are you Clarence Thompson?"

"Am I Clarence Thompson? Well, I used to be, but from the way you're looking at me, I'd guess you wouldn't believe me no matter what I said." The man dug in the back pocket of his pants and pulled out Gramps's wallet. "Here's my driver's license with my picture on it."

Jak looked at the license. It was Gramps alright, but the gray and withered Gramps he remembered, not this man standing before them. "Okay, if you're really Gramps," said Jak, trying to figure out a way to prove who this man was, "tell me what we were trying to catch before we got blasted to this place?"

"We were trying to catch your gerbil, Frankie," said the man.

"And whose name is written in the book?"

"Your grandmother's, Josefina Maria Leon. And as soon as we got here, your name, and—"

But that was all Jak and Tess needed. They rushed over to the new improved Gramps and began poking his muscles to see if they were real.

"Gramps, you look so different," said Tess, "You're young! You look like my dad."

Gramps touched his face. "I do?"

"Yeah. Remember how much of the zinger you ate last night?" said Jak. "Wow, you really got zinged. How come you had a Tree of Life leaf on your shirt?"

"Well, I saw how much better your ankle was getting from those leaves, and..." Gramps stopped and stared at Jak. "Where's your crutch, Jak?"

Jak smiled. "I don't need it anymore." He lifted his bare foot up so Gramps and Tess could see. "It's all healed. That's what I was yelling about this morning when I woke you up."

"You're serious?" asked Tess. "You can walk?"

Jak took several steps forward and then began jumping up and down to show them. "Yep."

"Well, I'll be jiggered," said Gramps, scratching his new head of hair. "I kept the leaves you threw away. I figured maybe something was left inside them that could help my heart, been laying them on my chest every night. I even put one on the corn on my foot. From the combination of the zingers and the leaves, I'd say they've done a pretty good job. Your grandmother would be mighty surprised to see me now!"

Gramma.

Jak couldn't help but wonder what would have happened if Gramma had been able to eat a plateful of zingers and lay the leaves on her head. He also couldn't help but wonder what would happen if they dug up the grave and squeezed zinger juice through her lips. *It is the Tree of Life, right?*

Before he knew it, the words escaped his lips. "Do you think Gramma—"

"No," Tess interrupted, as if she could read his thoughts. "She's dead, Jak. Nothing can bring her back. That's just the way it is, and it's best we don't even think about it."

"But it's the Tree of Life," he argued. "You don't know what could happen."

"You can't bring somebody back from the dead!" said Tess, her eyes flashing. "Maybe if we had found the zingers and the leaves before she died, but now it's too late."

Through Red's eyes, Lucifer saw the boy on the other side of the bridge, and so spurred Red quickly past him without stopping for so much as a morning lick of his hand. Speed was of the utmost importance if his plan was going to work. He knew it would only be a matter of time before one of the humans discovered the differences in Red. Even if Lucifer pulled completely back, the changes in Red's behavior could not be hidden. He could feel the juices of resentment toward El and the man growing in the animal.

Lucifer understood the rules. As the rulers of Earth, Man and Woman determined the fate of all those on the planet. If they discovered the hitchhiker within Red, Lucifer would be forced to leave, and he and his horde would be banned from ever returning to this world. If that happened, his chance to conquer would be lost, perhaps forever.

Red broke into a gallop, and it wasn't long before the clearing came into view.

It was perfect. Woman was alone, reaching up into the branches of a tree, sorting between the large red fruits that hung there, but Man was nowhere to be seen.

Lucifer directed Red straight to Woman and approached her in the same way he had seen Red approach her in the memories, licking her hand.

"Good morning, Red," said Woman, mussing his mane. "Where did you and Scorch go last night? We looked, but we couldn't find you." She began to peel a pomegranate.

It was now or never. Lucifer lifted Red's head as high as it would go and looked Woman straight in the eyes. "We went to the sea," he said. His voice was low and melodic, like the waves of the sea itself.

Woman's eyes went wide, and her mouth dropped. "You…you can talk?"

Lucifer smiled as best he could, forcing the muscles in his face to rise unnaturally upward in imitation of the humans. "Yes. El met us at the sea last night and gave me the gift of speech."

A look of comprehension came into Woman's eyes, and she nodded her head slowly. "So that's why El came late. Can you and Scorch both talk?"

"No." Lucifer bowed his head slightly, just enough to feign humility. "Only me for now."

"Where is Scorch?" Woman looked past Red to the trail behind him.

"She is not far behind. We crossed the bridge this morning, and I have so many questions. Since you and Man are so wise, perhaps you can answer some of them for me."

She nodded her head, obviously flattered, which was exactly what Lucifer wanted. "Of course."

"Is Man here?" asked Lucifer, glancing around the clearing.

"He went to the waterfall to gather some of the berries that grow next to the pool."

Good, he will be gone for a while, Lucifer thought. Everything was playing into his hand. At this point it was hard to differentiate between the feelings swirling through Red and those swirling through Lucifer. In fact, the agitation and excitement flowing through both of them seemed to act as a glue, binding them together as one creature.

"The first question is about the fruit," said Lucifer, with a feigned innocence that suggested he was a schoolboy asking a question of his favorite teacher. "Did El really say you cannot eat fruit from any of the trees?"

Woman looked at him with a funny expression. "No, of course not! He gave us the fruit as our food."

"Oh, that makes more sense," said Lucifer. "I thought El was being overly strict about not eating *any* fruit, especially since it all looks so tasty. But I admired you and Man for making your own decisions."

"It's only the fruit from *that* tree that we cannot eat." She pointed to the Tree of Knowing Good and Evil. "El said we cannot even touch it or we will die."

"Really? That is what he said?" Lucifer stopped for a moment and shook his head slightly from side to side. "I do not know if I should tell you this or not, but last night, when El gave me speech, he told me about that tree." He turned his head from side to side to make sure no creature stood near them, then moved closer to Woman and lowered his voice. "He said it was a secret, but I think you deserve the truth. Come with me."

Red began padding across the clearing toward the hill where the two trees stood, with Woman in tow, still speaking almost in a whisper. "The truth is that you will not die if you eat the fruit from the Tree of the Knowledge of Good and Evil. El said the only reason he does not want you to eat from the tree is because the fruit will open your eyes to see what you cannot see right now. You know how the fruit from that other tree fills you full of life?"

Woman nodded, hanging on his every word.

"The fruit from this tree will fill you full of wisdom so you will be just like El. Then you will understand both good *and* evil."

Woman's eyes lit up. "We talked about evil yesterday. Man and I do not understand what it is, but we want to know. Clarence said we will not like evil, that it is not good."

Lucifer shook Red's head again, making a mental note that Clarence must be one of the other humans he saw in the memories. "That is what El told him to say because El does not want you to be like him. There is no such thing as death, Woman. Don't you see? If you become like El, then he will no longer be able to control you. You will be as wise as he is." He plucked a black cherry from the Tree of Knowing Good and Evil with his teeth. It swung between his lips for a second like an ominous black pendulum. Then he tipped his head back and it dropped into his mouth. He closed his eyes and chewed slowly. "Mmmmm. It is so good and sweet, even better than the zingers. But I understand if you are afraid to eat it."

"No," said Woman. She put down the pomegranate. "I am not afraid. It is only that I haven't even thought about eating it." She fingered a bunch of the cherries, caressing them as if she were tasting them with her fingers. Then she grasped one of the cherries and pulled. A wonderful aroma filled the air as it broke away from the branch, sweet and succulent.

"Even the smell begins to fill one with knowledge," said Lucifer, forcing a deranged smile once again.

Woman brought the cherry close to her nose. She stuck out her tongue far enough to touch the dark red skin and gave a tiny lick. Her cheeks flushed pink and her eyes reflected a very short struggle in her soul. "To the knowledge of good and evil," she whispered. Woman opened her mouth and bit down on the juicy fruit. Immediately, goosebumps prickled up her skin and a contented smile crossed her face.

A shiver swept through Red's body as Lucifer laughed to himself. His plan had worked; he had done all he could do. The final step of handing the scepter of creation over to him was up to Woman.

CHAPTER 20
Beautiful Evil

"Woman! Where are you?" called Man. He stood in the dirt of the garden, surrounded by rows of plants six inches tall, holding a large leaf filled with berries. As soon as he saw her and Red by the Tree of Knowing Good and Evil, he waved.

"What are you doing over there?" he shouted. Woman had never gone to the Two Trees by herself, especially not the Tree of Knowing Good and Evil.

"Man!" called Woman, waving him over. "Come here! I have to show you something."

Man put his trophy of berries on the ground and ran to the hill. "What is it? Did Red bring you something from the woods?"

Keeping her hands behind her back, she shook her head. "No, but I have discovered something wonderful about The Tree of Knowing Good and Evil. It will help us. It will make us wise, as wise as El. I tasted it just now, and it is true." Triumphantly she held out the black cherry she had just bitten

Man's face clouded over as he looked at the cherry, and he went pale. "But El told us not to eat from this tree. He said we'll die if we do. Don't you remember?"

"I know, but Red told me why." She placed a hand on Man's arm. "El does not want us to be like him. He knows all about evil, and we know nothing. He's keeping it to himself so we're stuck depending on him. There's no such thing as death!"

"What?" said Man, shocked. "How do you know this?"

"Red told me."

"Red? But Red is a beast...he cannot speak."

"That's why El wasn't here till late last night. He met Red and Scorch at the endless water Jak told us about and gave Red the gift of speech." Her eyes lit up as if she had just shared the greatest news in the world.

Man turned and inspected Red. "You have speech?"

Lucifer closed Red's eyes and bowed his head. "It is true."

"What did you and El speak of?"

Lucifer faked a troubled expression in his eyes. "I am sorry to say it, but he told me about this tree and about you and Woman." He glanced furtively around the clearing again and then added quietly, "But I don't think I should say anything more about it."

"No! You have the gift of speech, do not go silent now. What else did he say?" demanded Man.

Lucifer hesitated. "He said that if you eat the fruit from the Knowing Good and Evil tree, your eyes will be opened, and you will become just like he is. Then you will see what you cannot see right now." He sighed and turned his face askance. "I am afraid my tongue has said more than it should."

"No," said Man, "You have said just enough."

Woman reached up, plucked another black cherry from the tree, and extended her hand to Man. "It is delicious—even better than the zingers. And when you eat it, then finally we will know the beauty and wisdom of evil, just like El."

Lucifer licked his muzzle and stared hungrily as Man took the fruit and turned it in his hands.

Man squeezed the skin while a storm battled in his gut. El had said "No," but Woman wanted him to eat it very much. And he *did* want to know about evil. He didn't think Red was correct in saying there is no such thing as death.

After all, Clarence had talked about death. But perhaps it wasn't as bad as Clarence made it out to be.

Woman caressed his arm and smiled in the way that melted Man to his core. "What are you waiting for?" she said.

Man smiled back. He could not resist her. "To the knowledge of good and evil," he said, and raised the fruit to his mouth.

CHAPTER 21

Dreams Do Come True
(but sometimes so do nightmares)

Jak, Macy, Tess, and the much younger Gramps were halfway down the trail toward the clearing when a gentle breath of warm wind burst in their faces, as if the world had just exhaled. It was immediately followed by a cold, brisk breeze that sailed through the trees and bit into their skin. It caught them by surprise since this was the first time the weather had been anything but warm and sunny. They had gotten used to the consistent steamy warmth of the garden, but this felt more like a chilly October morning in Minnesota. Even the trees, which were normally full of the clamor of birds and bugs, stood silent, as if someone had pressed nature's mute button.

Macy whined while Jak licked his lips. The air tasted pasty and old. He squinted through the treetops at what was supposed to be blue sky, but it wasn't the same blue. It looked sick and pallid, as if at any moment it might dry up and blow away. "Something is wrong," he said. "Look at the sky."

"It's the sun," said Tess. "It's like somebody drained all the color out of it." She folded her arms around herself and shivered. "I'm freezing! I wish I'd brought your windbreaker."

"Something strange is going on," said Jak. He pulled the book bag closer to his chest to keep as much warmth as he could trapped by his body. "Just before you woke up, Scorch and Red came down the path from the sea and by our sleeping spot. Scorch looked exhausted. I've never seen her like that before. Her tongue was hanging out, and she was panting. And Red trotted right on by without even stopping to lick my hand. Either he didn't see me or he just plain ignored me."

"Did Scorch stop?" said Tess.

"Just for a second. She rubbed her head against my side like she was sad and then followed Red toward the clearing."

"Maybe Man can tell us what's happening," said Gramps.

But when they got to the clearing, Man and Woman were nowhere to be found, and neither were any of the animals. The place was completely deserted.

"Wow," said Jak, looking at the plants that sprouted the night before. "Lots of plants, but no Man."

"Maybe they went down to the falls," said Tess.

"It looks like they just came back from the falls," said Gramps, pointing to the leaf full of berries from Split Falls that Macy was sniffing.

"Maybe they went back to get more," said Jak. "There's not enough in the leaf for all five of us, six if you include Macy."

"Fair enough," said Gramps. "Let's head to the falls."

But when they got to Split Falls, Man and Woman were not there.

"We could spend all day trying to find them," said Tess. "There're lots of places we haven't explored yet. I say we go back to the clearing and find a warm spot to wait for them to come back."

"I think we should keep looking," said Jak. He couldn't help thinking about Red and Scorch. If something strange was going on, Man and Woman might need help. "How about combing the woods from here back to the clearing? If we find them, great, but if not, we end up back at the clearing anyway." Jak's suggestion would have been near to impossible for Gramps's heart or Jak's foot the day before, but things were different now. He flexed his right foot and smiled. Today was a new day, and he was ready to go.

It wasn't hard to comb through the woods, especially since it was more like a garden than an unkempt forest with dead branches blocking their way. However, the woods tilted sideways, and it seemed to take a lot longer to get back to the clearing that way. By the time the sun was high in the sky, they still had not made it back. Obviously, they had made a wrong turn somewhere.

A small river bubbled past, so they stopped for a lunch of apples and blueberries before they turned around and climbed back up the hill. It was a long, tedious climb, and by the time they made it back to the clearing, the sun had almost touched the trees on the western ridge.

Tess heaved herself on the ground and lay flat on her back, her arms extended to the side like she was flying. She groaned. "I'm exhausted."

"Me too," said Jak.

"Me three," said Gramps.

They lay there quietly, soaking in the last warm rays of afternoon sun.

"Well, we made it to the clearing at least," said Jak.

"Yeah, six hours later," said Tess. She closed her eyes and sighed.

"At least we know Man and Woman aren't on that side of the garden," said Jak. "What about the trail Man took us down the first day he showed us the Two Trees?"

"Can't we wait for a while? I'm tired," said Tess.

"Well, you go ahead and rest, but I'm going to poke my head in the trees."

With Macy at his heels, Jak headed toward the entrance to the trail on the other side of the Two Trees.

It looked darker than Jak remembered. Instead of a warm and friendly arch of branches inviting him into the woods, it looked more like a wide-open mouth, ready to gobble him up as soon as he got close enough.

Macy barked, and Jak stopped. Her nose was stuck to the ground by the base of the hill.

"No, Macy. It's not time for the zingers," said Jak. "We'll eat some tonight, when Man and Woman come back." But Macy did not move.

"C'mon, girl," said Jak.

Still, she did not move.

"What's up, Macy?" Jak walked back to the hill and bent down to see what Macy was sniffing. What he saw filled him with dread.

At the base of the hill, two black cherries had rolled to a stop in the grass. Each bore a different set of teeth marks laying the flesh bare all the way down to the pit.

Jak shot up. "They ate it! Man and Woman ate the black cherries!"

"What?" said Gramps in disbelief, scrambling to his feet faster than he ever would have been able to before.

"The cherries!" said Jak. "They're here on the ground, half-eaten and still wet."

A combination of fear and anger roiled in his gut. *Why would they do that? The rule was no eating from the Tree of Knowing Good and Evil or they would die!* Jak ran to the top of the hill and looked down the other side, anticipating two bodies dead on the ground, but instead of two human bodies, he saw a different body wrapped up in a furry black ball.

"Scorch! What are you doing here?"

The leviathan pulled her head up from where it had been curled around her body and looked at Jak with sad eyes.

"Come here, Scorch. What's wrong?" Jak held out his hand.

She continued looking at him as if trying to decide to stay where she was or get up and amble over to Jak. She must have decided it was worth the risk because she stood up and tentatively stepped toward him, her head hung low.

Macy barked again. She had moved from the cherries at the bottom of the hill to the path near the entrance of the woods, and now she stood barking into the shadows. By this time, Tess and Gramps had arrived at the base of hill.

"I hear someone crying in the woods," said Tess. "It sounds like Woman."

Scorch crested the hill and nuzzled Jak's hand but then pulled away again.

"Jak," Tess continued, "if what El said is true, they might be dying right now."

"I know," he said, "but what can we do? If El is in there, we can't help them." Jak remembered the brilliant cloud in the woods that had almost strangled them the night they tried to sneak into the clearing. He didn't want to go anywhere near that light ever again, but if Man and Woman were dying, they had to at least try to help them. Jak took one last look at Scorch. "I'll be right back. Don't go anywhere." He ran down the hill and, together with Tess and Gramps, plunged into the woods, but they didn't run very far, because to go any further would have been an intrusion.

A faint glow glimmered in the rising mist a short distance ahead of them. Jak was pretty sure it was El. He looked different from what Jak expected. The first time they had seen him, they hadn't really seen him at all, only the brilliant light on his way to the clearing to meet with Man and Woman. And the second time they hadn't really seen him either, only the strangling cloud on the path. But this wasn't a brilliant light. This light was more like a human star wrapped up in a burlap sack . Streaks of light burst from pinholes in the burlap and burned holes in the grass or trees or whatever they touched.

Man and Woman had pulled the pants Tess had made for them over their hips, just like they were supposed to be worn, and Woman had woven a crude shirt for herself from leaves as well. They stood apart from each other, separated by a pile of sheepskin. Jak couldn't hear what they were saying, but Woman continued to sob, and Man clenched and unclenched his hands again and again.

Red slunk on the opposite side of El, dark lightning flashing in his eyes and his lips curled as if the very presence of El repulsed him.

Then the burlap sack light pulsed once and disappeared, and El was gone.

Suddenly a twin howl shook the garden and Red's body dropped hard to the ground. Jak heard a thud behind him as well and whirled to find Scorch writhing on the ground.

Her legs spasmed and sucked into her body until just the feet remained, if they could even be called feet; they were nothing more than four twitching flippers. The black mane lay in clumps across the ground, scraped clean away as she thrashed through the seashells. The tip of her tongue flickered through an arsenal of sharp yellow teeth and began to split like the skin of a sausage bursting over a flame. Each flicker scraped a chunk of bloody pink skin away until all that was left was a forked black tongue.

"Scorch!" Jak ran to her side and reached out his hand to try and calm her down, but as soon as his fingers touched her head, she lunged at him and snapped.

Jak yanked his arm back in time to keep all five fingers, but the sudden jerk threw him off balance and sent him tumbling backwards.

Before he could move, Scorch writhed toward him and lunged again. This time, she caught Jak's right heel in her mouth, crunched into the bone, and began shaking her head violently back and forth.

His mind raced back to the dream. It was real, and it was happening right now.

139

C H A P T E R   2 2

The Black Bulge Begins

Lucifer could not get away. The presence of El drew him in like a magnet, and no matter how hard he pulled, he could not escape this meeting. But this time, he had won. Both of the humans had eaten the black fruit, and in doing so, Man had transferred the authority of Earth to his grasp.

The sweetest part was that, even though Lucifer was now the ruler, the creation still belonged to El. Lucifer could spend countless days twisting and destroying the very things El loved most, especially the humans. If only he could get away from El, he could enjoy this glorious moment.

Yet, there was also a certain satisfaction from being with El. He looked sick and worn out, a remnant of his former self and no longer the glorious flaming power he used to be. He had been reduced to a sack-wrapped glow in the shadows of the trees. Certainly this was because of the revolution and because of the current victory in the much-celebrated garden over the much-loved human. If Lucifer had been in a different place with different company, he would have laughed long and loud. The Almighty Yahweh had been beaten.

El spoke to him and the humans, but he did not listen. He did not care what El had to say. When this meeting was over, he would leave the body of the red beast and stream back to the beach to gather his army and begin the perversion of creation.

They would begin with the helpless creatures like lambs, rabbits, small cats, and hummingbirds, and then make their way to the larger creatures like mastodons and giraffes. They would pluck them apart, limb from limb, as easily as pulling a stem from an apple. Whatever would produce the most pain and agony, the most screaming, the most wailing, that is what they would do. The blood would flow, and the gift of life would flit away.

The sobs of the woman broke Lucifer out of his daydream and, with no warning, he suddenly dropped to the ground hard. A jolt like lightning pierced his legs, leaving him feeling like they were burning away from his body. He looked down and saw that his legs had dissolved into four convulsing flippers, scrabbling at the dirt.

His whole body convulsed with pain shooting into every fiber. The lightning raced up and invaded his belly and chest and seemed to explode out his back.

Red howled in agony, rolled over, and scraped across the ground, leaving his red mane in scattered patches. The lightning flowed into his mouth and pounded at his teeth and tongue, stretching and shaping like the mallet of a sculptor, driving him crazy with pain.

Then the lightning left, and it was over.

Lucifer lay still on the ground, his sides heaving and his head pounding. He tried to stand, but he could not, so he craned his neck around to snap at El, but El was gone, as were Man and Woman.

Lucifer had not had the chance to leave the leviathan's body before the lightning had come, but now that El was gone, he began to do so, disconnecting himself piece by piece from the mind of the beast. The creature had been a willing and effective tool. It would almost be a pity to destroy him along with the other leviathan.

But as much as Lucifer struggled to pull his consciousness from the body, it would not budge. Lucifer could not disconnect from the animal's body. The best he could manage was a burst of light from the creature's mouth that settled in a solid column on the ground. From that vantage point, he looked at what had become of Red. It was a pitiful sight. The creature was no longer beautiful and elegant; he was now ugly, deformed and mindless. His fur was completely gone, revealing broken scales spread in bloody patches across his body.

Even Lucifer was shocked at the transformation. Reefs of long, pointed teeth extended up from the bottom jaw and down from the top. Red's snout was smashed inward like someone had struck him with a sledgehammer. The eyes weren't much better. The lids were gone, revealing two pale, yellow orbs spasming in their sockets. The light sucked back into Red's body, and Lucifer lay there trembling with fury.

What had El done to him?

He roared and lashed out his tail, snapping a sapling in half. His legs were now useless stumps, forcing Red to twist his body back and forth, churning up piles of dirt and sod as he slid down the hill.

⊗⊗

Excruciating pain bolted up Jak's leg, but he could not pull it away. It was trapped firmly in the vise-grips of Scorch's teeth.

"Scorch, stop!"

But she continued whipping her head back and forth, as if she was in a trance and couldn't break out of it. Gramps scooped up Jak's book bag and threw it at her, hitting her square in the face. There was a dull *thud* as it connected with her head, but it was enough. Scorch opened her mouth and snapped her thick head in the direction of the bag.

Jak knew he had half-second before she turned her attention back to him, but he was in shock. *Why is she attacking me? I'm her friend! I would never hurt her.*

"Jak!" Tess screamed, "Get up!"

But he could not move. The beast rammed her nose into the bag and sent it flying through the air and then opened her mouth and split Jak's ears with a shriek he had only heard once before, in his dream. It was the same raw shriek, the sound of an animal ready to make its first kill.

The sound worked on Jak like a key in a rusty lock, sending a shiver sweeping through his body and releasing the pent-up energy in every muscle he had. This was it, and he knew he had to move or die trying.

He grabbed the trunk of a sapling behind him and pulled with his arms while pushing with his good leg. Jak shut his eyes for a moment and winced.

Every nerve in his right foot screamed as he dragged his body across the ground, but he had to keep going.

The leviathan ducked her head back down and began scraping along the ground toward Jak, the forked black tongue flickering in and out, lapping up the trail of blood Jak left behind on his retreat.

For the first time, Jak saw her for what she had become. The beautiful long-legged leviathan had transformed into an ugly, rough-skinned killing machine slinking through the dirt.

An apple sailed through the air above Jak's head.

"Git! Get out of here," Gramps shouted. He had a shirtful and was throwing them at Scorch. It wasn't the most effective weapon in the world, but his aim was true. The apples continued to pelt her in the face until she finally backed off and slithered away across the clearing. Gramps ran after her, shouting and continuing to throw apples, making sure she would not return.

"Jak!" shouted Tess, running toward him. "Are you okay?" Her eyes widened in shock as she saw the damage Scorch had done. "Oh, Jak! Your foot."

Jak lifted his foot just enough to see the raw flesh, dripping with blood.

Tess dropped to her knees and immediately squeezed his heel like a vise.

"Ouch!" Jak yelled. It felt like a knife had stabbed him in the foot all over again.

"Sorry," said Tess, "but I have to stop the blood." She glanced around. "We need to find something to wrap your foot."

But there wasn't anything. The only things near them were seashells, sticks, and leaves, and none of them would do for a bandage.

Tess looked at her own foot for a moment, then kicked off the shoe, slid the sock off her foot, and began tying it tightly around Jak's heel. "You need it more than I do."

Jak gritted his teeth and leaned back on his elbows, his mind a whirl of pain and confusion. *What had happened to Scorch? And what else in my dream is going to come true?*

The evening mist continued to roll up from the ground, circling silently around them, blurring the flowers and trees into black shadows, just like in the dream.

Gramps ran back, breathless. "She's gone. Is he okay?" He peered at Jak's leg and gave a low whistle.

Tess glanced up with a worried expression in her eyes. "No. I think the bone is crushed in his heel, and the rest...well, you can see for yourself."

Tears threatened to roll down Jak's cheeks, prompted by the pain, but mostly from the sense of betrayal. "Why did she do it?" he said, taking deep breaths to keep the tears away. His head swam, and he bit his lip. "I was trying to help her."

A low throaty hum began to fill the air, and Jak glanced at the sky. According to the dream, the tornado should show up at any second.

"We need more cloth to wrap his foot," said Tess. Gramps fished around in his pocket and, as Jak expected, came up with his faded blue bandanna.

"I only used it once, so it should be okay," said Gramps.

Tess held the handkerchief like it was a dead mouse for a second and then began ripping it into strips and wrapping it around Jak's leg.

Jak gritted his teeth again, and his attention split between the agony and the dream.

But then a third thing entered his mind, something different. There was something happening in his heel. A cold prickling spread through his veins, like an evil spider had crawled into his leg and was clawing its way toward his heart. This was new; there weren't any spiders in his blood in the dream.

Suddenly, a veil began to close in his mind, and his eyes rolled back in his head.

"Jak!" Tess slapped him across the face, fear running across her face. "Do not faint on me. Do you understand?"

His eyes snapped into focus, and he blinked several times. "Yeah, I'm okay," he mumbled. But the clawing had not gone away. He lay on his back, trying not to twitch as Tess worked on his leg, but he was confused about what the spidery thing was.

A black speck appeared high in the sky, pulling Jak's attention away from his leg. The humming was growing louder by the second.

"Tess, I'm going to the Tree of Life," said Gramps, getting to his feet. "He needs a zinger or a leaf or both." He turned and began running for the tree, but before he even got to the base of the hill, the hum turned into a roar, and the tornado swept down from the sky, engulfing the Tree of Life. The black clouds crackled and popped, spinning the leaves dizzy and spitting out sharp blades of electricity into the air. The wind began to howl around them, clutching at their clothes as if they were stuck in a giant vacuum cleaner.

A lightning bolt shot out sideways from the cloud and knocked Gramps ten feet behind them. He doubled over, clutching his hands to his stomach.

"Gramps!" shouted Tess. She leaned up on her knees, almost dropping Jak's foot in the process.

Jak sat up. According to the dream, Gramps was going to be fine, but he had to be sure.

Gramps held up one hand to indicate he was okay, then started crawling back to them, his clothes and hair ruffling in the torrent of wind.

Jak breathed a sigh of relief but abruptly turned and glued his eyes to the twister, watching nervously for the four-faced man.

"I'm sorry, Jak. I can't make it!" shouted Gramps above the din of the tornado. He sat down next to him, panting, with beads of sweat running down his face. "We've gotta get away from this wind." He slid his arms under Jak and began to lift him.

"No, wait!" shouted Jak. He struggled out of Gramps's hands, staring at the tornado. As if on cue, the clouds on the top pinched together, forming a beak and a bird's head. "Look!" He pointed to the tree. "An eagle!"

Tess and Gramps leaned into the wind and peered at the tornado.

"Eagle? There's nothing there," shouted Tess.

The eagle had faded away, but at the same time, a pair of horns and the snout of a bull formed at the bottom of the cloud.

"There!" Jak pointed to the bottom. "Another one!"

"Where?" said Gramps, squinting his eyes and frantically searching the cloud.

"In the clouds. Don't you see the faces? There was an eagle, and now a bull." But then the bull melted away.

Tess looked at Gramps. "He's in shock. He's hallucinating."

"No," Jak insisted. "They were there! I saw them." A black bulge began to form in the middle. *This is it. He's coming.* Jak stabbed the air with his finger. "Look!"

CHAPTER 23
Plunging the Dagger Deeper

Thrashing through the woods proved to be an arduous chore. Red's body had been accustomed to bounding around trees and over bushes, but now he was forced to crush them or try and go around them.

Lucifer cursed the woods and cursed El for trapping him in the flesh and blood of the leviathan. Luckily, he was headed downhill.

At the bottom of the hill, a fast-flowing stream jagged its way through the rocks. As soon as his body hit the water, it instinctively knew what to do. The stream was about ten feet wide and just deep enough that his flippers had room to move. When Lucifer flexed them and thrust back, he found that they easily propelled him upstream. That's where he would find the waterfall and then the river leading to the sea.

The cool water felt good on his aching back and face. The scales were raw and covered in blood where the fur had been scraped away. To make matters worse, his mouth was sore, not only from the rapid growth of his teeth, but also from accidentally piercing his lips from the daggers that now erupted from his face.

As he swam, the images from Red's memory kept coming back to him. There was something peculiar about the other three humans, particularly the smallest one with the brown hair and the limp. He had passed this human on the way back from the sea.

Lucifer reached further in the memories and could suddenly smell the little man. He stopped swimming for a second, shocked. It was the same scent he had detected when they first attacked the garden, the scent of blood mixed with evil. This human could have been captured as a slave even then. He cursed and spat a black flame. It was too late now. But there was something about this creature that gnawed at Lucifer. His instinct compelled him to capture the little man as soon as possible. But later. It would have to be later.

He churned the water once again with his flippers. Before long, he came to a rough wooden bridge spanning the stream. It hung low over the water—too low for him to swim under—so he clambered up the embankment and thrashed across a black gravel path leading to the east. Suddenly, in the middle of the path, he stopped and jerked his head in all directions, his forked tongue darting in and out, tasting the air.

The almost exact same scent as the little man, blood mixed with evil, rose strong on his tongue. He looked to the ground and there, dug into the gravel, were two pair of footprints, set wide apart as if the ones who owned the feet had been running. Lucifer's eyes glowed. The prints were fresh, and belonged to Man and Woman.

He stared down the path as far as he could, straining to see the two fleeing figures, trying to bring the world into focus, but it remained a blurry mess. He cursed Red's weak eyes and opened the leviathan's mouth wide, shooting out a burst of brilliant yellow light twenty feet down the path. Lucifer hung there, suspended like a glowing tower, dripping bright globs onto the black path, but he was tethered to the leviathan and could go no further.

The leviathan's body sucked the light back into its mouth with a loud smack and continued scrabbling across the path. *I will deal with the humans later,* he thought. For now, he had more pressing matters to attend to.

He thrashed his way upstream to the river at the top of the cliff, tumbled over Split Falls, and entered the river leading to the sea. The current ran fast, and it wasn't long before it spit him into the ocean.

Lucifer quickly swam to the beach, where clumps of Lights glowed like giant piles of multicolored seagull droppings. He churned his way through the sand to the first clump he found.

"Get up," he growled. "Assssssemble the army. It isss time for war!"

Something was wrong. Lucifer shook Red's head violently, trying to knock the extra S out of his mouth. The teeth were so large that they got in the way of his tongue as he spoke.

A diarrhea-brown Light eyed him over and cackled. "Right away, yer stinkin' majesty." He spewed a series of disgusting brown colors as he and the other Lights laughed at the leviathan. "Yer nothin' but a stinkin' red-bellied mud crawler!"

At this, Lucifer roared, opened the leviathan's mouth wide, and blasted the brown Light with a burst of blue flame. The Light disintegrated into a pile of brown mush that looked like the bottom of a coffee pot that had boiled too long. Lucifer streamed from Red's mouth and flashed with all his brilliance into a gleaming yellow tower, hovering over the brown stain on the beach.

"Fool!" he howled. "Does not even recognize the voice of his master."

The other Lights immediately dropped prostrate to the ground, bowing and trembling, each hoping it would not be the next to taste the wrath of the angry blue flame.

The leviathan's body loped up the beach toward the grass line. Red's mouth was still open wide, dripping great droplets of yellowish saliva through its teeth and onto the sand.

Lights flocked toward the beaming light of Lucifer, bowing, murmuring, and wondering what had happened.

"Lucius!" purred Stul, oozing to a halt next to Lucifer. "What is this?" he said, pointing a gloopy stump toward Red's body.

Lucifer snorted. "Yahweh gave me a coronation gift."

The purple blob blinked lavender for a moment. "A coronation gift? You mean to say you have done it?"

Pride washed through Lucifer, and he swelled as large as he could, which amounted to a large lump about the size of a dumpster. He raised one oozing tentacle into the air like a fist and bellowed, "THE ENEMY IS DEFEAT-ED! THE EARTH IS OURS!!"

The beach erupted with cheers and whistles that lasted for a full five minutes before the tentacle cut them off like a conductor silencing an orchestra.

"I now rule this world, and no one—NO ONE—can take it away from me." Lucifer's voice echoed down the beach. "Evil has been released, and I will use it just as I will use you, to wreak havoc on the humans and all the enemy has made."

There was one matter of great importance though. He wanted the Tree. Not the Tree of Knowledge of Good and Evil, for it had already played its part. The tree he wanted was the Tree of Life. Now that the humans had released death into the world, he also wanted the power to extend life if he so chose. It could be a powerful tool in manipulating or torturing the humans, and he was certain if he did not act fast, the enemy would try to keep that power for himself. "But first," Lucifer continued, "there is a certain tree in the garden that I must have."

Something rustled in the grass behind Red, interrupting Lucifer's speech. The dark form of the female leviathan tumbled out onto the sandy beach and thrashed through the sand. She was just as deformed as Red was. Hard ridges ran down her back where the black mane had once stood proud, and her iridescent scales had grown cloudy and grayish green. She snapped at the air and blew a pitiful plume of blue fire his direction.

Good, thought Lucifer. *She is seething with anger. She will be useful.*

"Can we start with this beast here, sir?" said a stubby orange Light. "I'm itching to rip a tail off."

"No," growled Lucifer. "The creature is off limits for now."

Scorch dragged herself through the soft sand and began digging a hole with her rear feet. Lucifer glowed bright yellow in pleasure. Soon, he would have a small army of leviathans which he could use to harass the humans as well. He broke into a dark laugh. "And now," he said, "it is time to plunge the dagger deeper into the heart of El."

Each Light leaned forward with anticipation, awaiting their instructions and eager to take part.

"CAPTURE THE TREE OF LIFE AND DESTROY THE REST OF THE GARDEN!" Red sucked in the light of Lucifer and let loose a blast of orange flame that stretched all the way to the cherry grove, setting it on fire.

One of the Lights formed a hole in its top and sucked air through itself, sounding a horn deep and long. Immediately, the beach was drowned in spurts and hisses as the Lights soared into the air, forming a grotesque rainbow headed toward the garden.

CHAPTER 24

The Sickening Rip

The bulge stretched into the face of a man, a cloudy black mask at first, followed quickly by his entire body. It was the same man as the one in Jak's dream — same flecks of light rippling through his body, the same wild black hair and beard, the same bull legs and eagle wings, and the same lightning bolt sword whipping around like a fan blade on fire.

A look of pure terror swept across Tess's face. She pulled back behind Gramps and covered her mouth with one hand, gasping. "What is it?" she said.

The face of the man turned toward Jak, and their eyes locked for a moment, but then the head twisted to the left until it morphed into the lion's head and mane. Then it spun to the bull, and when it twisted a third time, it revealed the eagle. Suddenly, the man snapped his wrist with a crack, and the lightning sword disappeared. The golden wings twitched, folded in, and the creature strode toward them, spinning its head back to the face of the man.

Jak tensed. He reached out to grab Macy before she went after the man, but it was too late. She growled and shot from behind him, snapping at the creature as it approached.

"Macy! Get back here!" Jak shouted. But she stubbornly kept barking until the head of the lion spun around and roared, sending her yipping in retreat.

The lion-headed creature stopped directly over Jak. The human head flipped around again and he bent down until it was so close that Jak could smell his flower-on-fire breath. *This was the point in the dream where the man said something about..*

"Poison." The man's voice flowed like a chorus of rivers. He stared unblinking into Jak's eyes.

Jak flinched, partly from the agony of his foot, but mostly because of the man's gaze. Even though Jak had lived through all this before in a dream (if it really had been a dream), his mouth went dry, and he could hardly breathe.

"P...poison?" Jak finally stammered. He blinked but did not turn away, not sure what would happen next. If it continued like the dream, he would be sent back to the cherry grove by the sea, and it would start all over again. But if not, he had no idea what would happen, and he wasn't sure he wanted to find out.

The roar of the spinning clouds suddenly settled into a whistle of shifting wind, and the man's voice transformed into one singular voice, deep and gruff in an earthy sort of way, like the way a tree might talk in Ireland. "There is not much time." He knelt next to Jak, except he no longer had the legs and feet of a bull, nor the wings of the eagle. They had disappeared and left in their place a thick human form. He was still a giant of a man, but smaller, and dressed in black breeches and a grizzled navy-blue tunic cinched together with a wide black leather belt. He moved one hand gently down Jak's mangled leg. His other hand held a fistful of spiny leaves that looked exactly like the leaves from the Tree of Life. "The last gift of the tree. Help me, girl," he said to Tess.

She hesitated a moment, staring at the man as if she was evaluating whether he was a friend or enemy.

Jak couldn't blame her, for he would've done the same thing.

After a second, she must have decided he was a friend, because she knelt next to the man and asked, "What do you need me to do?"

The man placed one hand under Jak's knee and with the other grabbed the end of Jak's foot near his toes and raised the leg off the ground. "Hold his leg like this."

Jak winced at his touch. Tess put her hand next to the man's hand and held on.

The man began draping the leaves over and around Jak's leg and heel, tying them tight with a length of thin green vine.

As soon as the leaves touched his skin, the pain slacked off to a bearable ache, and the strange crawling in his blood seemed to creep a little more slowly. "It must be tight, or the leaves will not even have a chance to draw the venom out."

"Venom?" said Jak, suddenly feeling even more nervous than he had been. "Is Scorch poisonous?"

"Scorch?" the man asked, arching an eyebrow.

"The leviathan," explained Gramps.

The man's eyes grew even darker. "There is venom in his lips."

"She's a girl," said Jak.

The man glanced up. "Male or female, it makes no difference. The leviathan and its mate are one. They now carry the same poison and the same curse."

"But she didn't do anything," said Tess.

"She has been twisted, as has her mate and all of creation." The man tied the last knot in the vine and ran his hands over the bandage to make sure it was tight. Then he closed his eyes and muttered a few words Jak could not hear. "That's enough, girl. Our work is done."

Tess let go and moved back to where Gramps stood while the man lowered Jak's leg to the ground. It now sported a deep green leafy cast, similar to the first one he and Woman had put together, and the pain had reduced to a light throb.

The man looked intently at Jak. "El gave me a message for you."

Jak's stomach dropped, certain he was in for an "I told you to stay away from me" speech accompanied by some sort of outlandish punishment for trying to sneak into the clearing.

"He makes a gift of these words: 'Yahweh is my protection and my strength.'"

"Yahweh?" said Jak. "Who is Yahweh?"

A look of surprise crossed the man's eyes. "That is his name."

"Whose name?"

"El's. El is a title proclaiming who he is, but Yahweh is his name. Remember his words. You will need them." He stood and beckoned to Jak with one hand. "Stand."

"I…I don't think I can."

A rumble came from the black clouds.

The man glanced at the clouds and back again. "You do not have a choice." He lifted Jak up as if he was a piece of straw and set him on his left foot. "You must go. Now."

"Go where?" asked Jak. He had no idea what the man was talking about.

In two giant steps, the man retrieved the book bag from where it had been tossed in the grass and handed it to Jak. "Do not lose this, boy. You will need it as well."

A thunderclap sounded from the tornado around the tree, and another form stretched out from the cloud coalescing into a lion's face, and a silvery flowed down. "Brother, the darkness is coming," said the voice. "Send them now and return to us or it will be too late."

"Who's coming?" asked Tess, standing up. "What are they going to do?"

"The door has been ripped away, and the carnage of creation begins here in the garden. Soon they will search for you as well. He has seen you and will not stop until he has found you."

"*Who?*" insisted Tess. "Who is coming?"

But in spite of her demand, the man did not answer her. "Follow the path past the lip of the waterfall." The man pointed to Split Falls. "Go as far as you can toward the hills. I will find you and tell you El's plan."

A volley of lightning spat from the cloud, and a voice descended once again. "Brother."

Without even saying goodbye, the man pivoted and began sprinting toward the tree. The lightning sword erupted from his hand while a pair of giant wings sprouted from his back, propelling him forward until he was once again united with the swirling black cloud. A rumble shook the ground as he left.

"Come on! Let's go," said Gramps, grabbing Jak's arm.

"Go where?" asked Tess. "There's no path up Split Falls. It's just a cliff filled with vines, and Jak can hardly walk."

"I know, but I also know we've just seen Scorch turn into a monster and a four-faced man step out of a tornado. I'm inclined to think he knows what he's talking about, so let's go." He paused and looked her straight in the eyes. "Do you have a better idea, young lady?"

"Yes." Her face had turned to steel. "Let's eat the black cherries and go home!"

"But the man said he'll meet up with us and tell us the plan!" said Jak.

"What plan?" exclaimed Tess. "We've been here plenty long enough already. Let's go home!"

Jak knew arguing with her wasn't going to work, so he tried a different tactic. "I've been walking with one good leg for the past couple of weeks," said Jak. "I think I can manage." He didn't have his crutch with him, so he'd have to try to limp on his bandaged foot.

But the moment his bad foot touched the ground, it felt like a lightning bolt seared up his leg. He pulled his injured foot up, feeling sick to his stomach, and stood for a second, gaining his bearings before venturing forward once again. This time he hopped with a one-legged jump, trying as best as he could to keep his injured leg still, but it was impossible. He might as well have been trying to balance an egg on his head. But he didn't have a choice. He had to get going, pain or no pain.

"Tess," said Gramps, "get on the other side. We'll have to help him."

Tess sighed in frustration and draped one arm around Jak from the right while Gramps did the same from the left, forming a pair of human crutches.

Jak was thankful to have them. It wasn't a perfect situation, but at least his body didn't hit the ground so hard now when he jumped. He began to breathe a little more easily. They made their way across the clearing and onto the seashell path toward the falls. The moist air from the river felt good in his lungs. But not for long.

A cold blast shot down from above, and the temperature dropped even further than it already had. A horn sounded in the distance toward the sea, and another rumble shook the garden, stronger than the first, followed by a sharp splintering of rock. Behind them, a crack split the earth and slowly widened like a giant mouth, swallowing whatever stood in its way.

"Go, go, go!" shouted Gramps.

"We need to eat the cherries!" Tess shouted back. Gramps shook his head as they pulled Jak along the path even faster. The pomegranate tree disappeared into the hole, along with an orange tree and a mango tree. The crack kept growing, moving swiftly toward the white seashell path on one side and the hill of the Two Trees on the other until it reached the beginning of the path. Huge chunks of grass and dirt laced with the shells disappeared into the ever-widening gorge.

Suddenly, a chorus of eerie high-pitched laughter ripped through the sky and bounced off the cliff walls. A volley of bright orange fireballs swooped down and hurled themselves into the trees on either side of the path, setting them on fire. The earth shook, and the crack lurched another ten feet toward them, swallowing an entire section of seashell. The edge was now less than a car's length away, nibbling at the path piece by piece.

Dread washed through Jak as he realized they weren't going to make it.

Just then, a sharp bark snapped Jak's head the other direction. Macy darted to a tree on the other side of the path, then shot out the other side with the end of a vine trailing behind her.

"Not now, Macy! Get up the path and..." Jak trailed off. This was exactly what he needed! He grabbed the vine and swung fifteen feet down the path. "Good girl, Macy. Now find me another one!"

Macy darted into the woods and emerged holding a new vine. Jak snatched it from her mouth and sprung through the air while Gramps and Tess ran alongside him.

"Tess," said Gramps, "go to the falls and see if you can figure out what the man meant about a path up the cliff."

For once, Tess did exactly as she was told without any objections and sprinted ahead.

Another crack split the air, and the ground where they had just been standing dropped out of sight. By the time Jak landed, Macy had another vine in her mouth, and he pushed off into the air once again. He and Gramps were at least two vines ahead of the gorge, as long as it didn't speed up or suddenly take a huge section of ground all at once.

When they reached the pool, Jak's leg was throbbing, and the leaf cast was tinged with red. He desperately wanted to stop and let the pounding settle down, but he couldn't; he had to keep going.

Ahead of him, Tess perched like a monkey on the face of the cliff. She was holding a gnarled vine in one hand and pointing to the bottom of the cliff with the other.

"There's a path!" she shouted over the crash of the waterfall. "Behind the vines are some steps carved into the rock."

Gramps swept back a veil of thick green vines and revealed a shallow white staircase, the same color as the seashell path, carved into the rock that angled up toward the lip of the cliff.

Jak stared at the steps. If he had been a mountain goat, perhaps the staircase would have been big enough, but this was impossible. "Seriously?" he said. "We're going up that? I don't even think Macy could make it up that." But the little dog ran ahead of them and disappeared up the steps.

"We don't have a choice," said Gramps. "I'll help you." He wrapped one hand around a vine, his other hand around Jak's arm, and began pulling him up the steep incline.

The steps zigzagged up the cliff, mossy and slick with the mist of the falls. With only one good leg, Jak had to hop up each step, and he slipped almost every time. Whenever he put his hand out to steady himself against the cliff wall, his hand slid down the slippery moss. In addition to that, water dribbled down his face, and he had to wipe his eyes every few seconds. "Gramps, this isn't working," he shouted. "I'm going to try doing it a different way."

Gramps nodded his approval, and Jak turned around and began scooting up the cliff on his rear end. Gramps held the scruff of his collar in one hand while Jak pushed with his good leg and pulled himself up with a vine at the same time. It was slow progress, but they kept at it, step by slippery step until they were halfway up. Through the curtain of vines, Jak caught a good view of the pool. The gorge had hit the edge of the water by now, the same spot where they had lain counting the stars the night before, and the pool was draining violently into the hole in the earth.

Suddenly, Gramps's foot slipped, hit Jak in the back, and shoved him off the steps. The collar of his shirt jerked and gave a sickening rip as Jak shot over the edge.

CHAPTER 25

Jak Finds His Father

Jak clung desperately to the vine in his hands, but he swung, twirling, straight toward Split Falls. The vine jerked and gave way, dropping him straight down until the vine caught again. He swung sideways into another curtain of vines hanging next to the tons of water spilling over the edge of the cliff.

He gasped, feeling like he had just been punched in the stomach. Slamming into a pile of vines hurt more than he thought it would.

"Jak," shouted Gramps, holding onto two vines and struggling to keep his balance on the steps. "You okay?"

Jak could hardly hear him, but he nodded his head with a weak smile and shouted back. "Yeah, I think so."

The same slick green moss that grew on the steps grew here as well, and he could barely get his foot to stay in one of the few crevices the cliff offered him. He had to find some good footholds because it was the only way he could shift some of his weight off his arms and onto his good leg.

It was now so cold that the spray of the falls began to ice over in Jak's hair. Fifty feet below him, the end of the vine twirled in the grass at the edge of the rapidly draining pool. Fifty feet above him, Tess's head poked out over the cliff. She was yelling something, but the falls were so loud that he could only guess what she was saying.

He wanted to tell her that he was okay, but he was stuck. There was no way he could swing back to the stairs, and there was no way he could get to the top. If he were able to use both legs and if his hands weren't so cold, then he might be able to climb the remaining fifty feet, but he had never been able to climb with just his arms, much less when they were frozen, wet, and tired. But what choice did he have? He either had to try it, or give up and hang there on the cliff till he got so tired he fell to his doom. The message the four-faced man had given him from El flashed through his mind. *Yahweh is my protection and my strength.* If there was ever a time he needed strength, it was now.

In his mind, he flipped a coin. If it was heads, he would climb, and if it was tails, he would stay. The quarter flipped up and around in his imagination and landed heads up.

He took a deep breath, gripped the slick vine as tightly as he could, and pulled with all his strength. His body lifted from its perch and moved up the cliff a foot. He grabbed another toe hold and did it again.

As he climbed, the book bag began to dig into his left shoulder, and he wished he had given it to Tess back in the clearing. He considered wriggling it free and letting it fall to the path below but decided against it in the off chance that El showed up to help him. He wouldn't be very happy if Jak had tossed the book into the waterfall. Besides, it was Gramma's book, and he didn't want anything to happen to it.

Suddenly the water at the base of the falls gurgled like a giant drain had been unplugged and the steady roar of the falls changed to a gloppy *glurg glurg glurg.*

Jak locked his foot into a crevice in the rock and looked down.

There was nothing left. Instead of dangling in the grass, the end of the vine he was climbing now swirled in a churning whirlpool of mud.

His fingers suddenly went numb, and the creepy-crawly thing in his blood reared its head again. It was almost as if it was whispering to him, *"You'll never make it, Jak! You might as well quit, Jak! Just give up, Jak!"*

He blinked and shook his head, trying to regain his focus. One slip and he'd be taking a permanent mud bath.

A faint voice filtered down from the rim of the falls. "Hang on, Jak!"

Jak looked up and saw Gramps's face peeking down over the edge of the cliff right next to Tess's and Macy's. *If only Gramps were a superhero, then he could fly down and get me. Or better yet, if only I were a superhero, then I could fly up on my own.*

Thirty more feet. He could do it...he *had* to do it. He reached up, but before he could get a firm grip, his foot slipped on the moss, and he plunged straight down. His hands scrabbled at the vine, but his fingers were so cramped and cold that they were more like two wooden blocks. Instinctively, he swung his right arm in a quick circle, scooping the vine up and around, forming a loop around his hand. His body jerked to a stop, and he dangled like a yo-yo. With the sudden lurch, the book bag slid off his left shoulder.

Jak grabbed at the strap but missed, and it raked down his arm. His fingers caught the bottom of the bag, tipping it upside down. The book shifted and began tumbling through the fabric. The two black cherries dropped out like two miniature bombs, headed for the mud pit. The book would be the next to go, and then Jak himself if he wasn't careful.

Jak bent his left leg and pressed the flap shut. He felt a solid thud as the book stopped short of falling out. Very carefully, he inched his left hand down, grabbed the top of the bag, and pulled it into his arms. *Whew.*

"Jak!" shrieked Tess. Her voice was faint.

He slung the strap over his shoulder again and waved with his left hand. He was as okay as he could be. How much ground had he lost? Ten feet. Jak sucked the mist through his teeth and forced the fingers on his left hand to once more reach up and grab, reach and grab, reach and grab. His biceps burned as if someone was pressing a blow torch into them, but he had to keep going.

"A few more feet, Jak!" Tess shouted.

Suddenly he heard a series of loud snaps above him, and the vine began to slide in spastic jerks down the side of the cliff. He flailed at a small tree embedded in the rock, but the roots ripped out, spraying dirt in his eyes. The vine totally gave way, and for a split second, he was weightless.

But in that moment Gramps might as well have put on a spandex suit and cape, because Jak felt a strong hand clamp onto his shoulder and haul him over the lip of the cliff. SuperGramps carried him back from the river to a safe spot under a balding river birch.

Jak lay down on a pile of dry leaves. His arms were shaking, his hands were raw, and he felt like he was going to throw up. Tess and Macy crouched together with Gramps and Jak under the tree. All four were cold, wet, and miserable—but at least they were alive.

"Jak," said Tess. Her eyes were red, and there were streaks down her cheeks like she'd been crying. "Don't ever do that again."

Jak opened his mouth and was just about to say it wasn't his fault, but then he realized that Tess *had* been crying. She was scared, and for once, she had let it show. "I won't," he said instead.

She grabbed his hand for a moment and then let it go, rubbing her nose and looking away.

The tree was far enough back from the edge of the cliff that Jak didn't have a clear view of the valley and the garden. He had to know what was going on. "Gramps, will you help me up?"

"Where are you going?" asked Gramps.

"I have to see what happened," said Jak, struggling to his feet.

Gramps hesitated as if unsure whether or not this was a good idea, but then wrapped one arm around Jak "Alright," he said, and together they approached the cliff.

Jak took one look and hardly recognized what he saw. "It's gone! Half the garden is gone!" Beyond the Tree of Life and the Tree of Knowing Good and Evil, the garden still glowed green, although a much paler green than the day before, but in the other direction it was as if someone had dumped a giant bucket of brown over everything.

The river was gone, the forest was gone, and the seashell paths were gone. In fact, the entire western edge of the garden had been replaced by a sea of mud for as far as Jak could see. Coarse, ugly spires of rock jutted up through the mud like upside-down sugar cones, and yellowish foam slapped angrily against what used to be a shore. Now it was really just a ragged mishmash of torn sod and exposed roots at the base of the hill that still housed the Two Trees.

Jak hardly had time to wrap his mind around the giant mud pit before a flash of light shot into the sky from the west and exploded into the Tree of Life. Short lightning bolts whirled from the spinning clouds around the tree and spit the ball of fire into the mud. But as soon as the first flame had been doused, a howling whine like a troop of fighter jets filled the air, and three more flashes of light ripped into the tree from opposite sides, only to be deflected by the lightning into the mud.

Another howl, and four more shot in, followed by an entire volley from all directions, impossible to count, screaming and attacking the tornado. It was almost as if the fireballs were alive, from the way they darted in and out and kept pounding at the cloud. The cloud had transformed as well; it was now a mass of spinning lightning bolts that sent the fireballs careening one by one into the muddy sea.

When the last ball of fire hissed into the water, the horn bellowed again, and the valley became eerily quiet. The only sound was the crashing of the waterfall into what used to be the pond.

"What's happening, Gramps?" said Tess, coming up behind them. Tears streamed down her face as she twisted her hair around one finger. "The fireballs and the mud and Scorch and that, that giant man thing, and Man and Woman...what's happening?"

He wrapped his arms around her and rocked her back and forth like he had when she was a little girl.

"Something must've gone wrong, Tess—terribly wrong—between El and Man and Woman." He released her and led them back to the river birch.

"Yeah," said Jak, sitting down and making sure to keep his bad foot up. "Did you notice how strange Man and Woman were acting? I mean, besides the fact that they were actually wearing pants the right way, something was definitely wrong. Woman was crying, and Man seemed mad. And there was obviously something wrong with Red, too, slinking around the way he was."

"But all they did was eat the black cherries," said Tess. "What's so bad about that?"

"I don't know," said Gramps, shaking his head, "but it made a huge difference, that's for sure."

She dug her hand in the pocket of her shorts and pulled out her black cherry. Unbelievably, it still gleamed glossy purplish black, with not a bruise or a blemish.

"What are you doing?" said Gramps, watching her very carefully.

Tess sniffled. "I don't think we have much of a choice. It's terrible being here – Jak almost died! We need to go home."

"Tess," Gramps said, suddenly sitting up straight, "the black cherries are the whole problem in the first place. Don't you see? If Man and Woman had left them well enough alone, like El told them to, none of this would have happened. The answer can't be for us to eat the black cherries too. Remember the plaque back on the hill? It said, 'Death follows the eaters.' I've seen more death in my seventy years than I care to remember—some from war, some from accidents, and some from disease and old age—but it never matters how it happens, the result is the same. The dead are gone...forever."

Gramps cheeks went pale as he spoke. "Your grandmother's ancestors crossed the sea to the New World hundreds of years ago looking for the fabled Fountain of Youth, the same kind of thing the plaque talked about. I think we've found it, except it's not a fountain. It's a tree—that tree down there." He pointed over the cliff. "We can't get to that one anymore, but the plaque said to follow the path to the place where the dead come back to life. I'm guessing that path leads to another Tree of Life, maybe an entire grove of them."

He dug the black cherry out his pocket. In spite of living in the pocket for the past three days, it was still shiny and perfect, just like Tess's. "Here's what I think we should do with the black cherries." Gramps reared his hand back and threw the cherry into the middle of the river.

The water around it boiled and hissed as the cherry spun itself in quick circles and then disappeared, spit by the river over the edge of the cliff.

"Gramps!" said Tess.

"I'm not going back, Tess," he interrupted. "These past six months have been the loneliest days of my life, and if there's a chance—just a chance—to get Josie back, I've got to stay."

Tess turned to Jak with a pleading expression in her eyes. "Jak, you still have two cherries. You could give Gramps one, and you and Macy could split the other."

Jak hedged, thinking it probably wasn't the best time to tell her that his cherries had escaped kamikaze style into the mud pit. "Um, well..." He bit his lip and looked toward the ground. "I *did* have two cherries."

"You *did?*" Her eyes grew wider. "What does that mean?"

Jak couldn't hide it anymore, so he just blurted it out. "I lost them. They dropped out of the bag when I was climbing up the cliff."

Tess slumped and sighed, running her hand across her face. "Great! That's just great. Now what do we do?"

"Well," said Gramps, "the man said El has a plan. Maybe we should hear him out."

Jak was torn. On one hand, he couldn't deny that the Tree of Life had miraculously aged Gramps backwards and healed his foot, but on the other hand, El hadn't exactly been friendly, at least, not by Jak's standards.

He pulled the seed from the first zinger he had eaten out of his pocket and turned it in his fingers, inspecting the wrinkles and creases pitted throughout each side. *Maybe there is another tree.* He remembered the seeds Man had planted by the river and how fast they had grown. *Or maybe I can grow another Tree of Life right here!* Making sure Tess and Gramps weren't watching, he dug a hole as deep as his finger, pushed the seed in, and piled the dirt back on top. Now he just had to wait.

"The man said we were supposed to travel as far as we could into the hills," said Gramps, shading his eyes against the weak yellow sun and peering into the distance. "How's your foot, Jak?"

"It hurts, and I think it's bleeding again." Besides, he didn't want to go yet. He had to see if the tree would grow. Jak's stomach growled, and he scanned the land around them looking for fruit, but there was none to be found. All the trees looked faded and lifeless. "Do you guys see any food around?" said Jak. "I'm starving."

"Just a bunch of spoiled oranges," said Tess, pointing behind them to a naked orange tree. The ground underneath its branches was littered with rotten-looking, squishy fruit.

"That's weird," said Jak, his stomach growling again. "I haven't seen any rotten fruit since we got here. And the other side of the river looks like the vacant lot next to the grocery store with all the burn weed. I haven't seen any burn weed since we got here either."

A sudden waft of warm air made Jak look up in time to see a giant pair of wings blotting out the sun. An eagle the size of a truck circled and landed right next to Jak. As soon as it was on the ground, the wings folded into his back, and the golden-eyed head twisted to the side. Close-cropped wild black hair and piercing black eyes rolled into place, and the thick form of the man stepped forward once again. He was dressed in the same blue tunic and black breeches, but this time he also had a brown knapsack looped around one shoulder.

He took one look at Jak's little mound of dirt and shook his head. "It won't work, boy. What you have on your leg now is the last gift of the tree in this age."

"What do you mean it won't work?" Jak demanded. "The seeds Man planted by the river grew overnight."

"Yes, but I promise you that day is gone." He dug his thumb and one finger into the mound and extracted the seed. Then he dropped it into Jak's palm. "Take it as a remembrance of the way the garden was. The leaves will grow again and heal again, to be sure, but not for a long time. Give me your foot." The man knelt next to Jak and began to unwind the vine that held the leaf cast together.

"I think it's still bleeding," said Jak. "It feels kinda mushy."

"Does it hurt?"

"It did, especially when I was hopping, but now it's not so bad."

The leaves fell away and a warm liquid dripped from his leg onto the ground, but it wasn't blood. It was water. The skin was raw and red, with deep scarred tooth tracks etched in his toes up past his ankle. But at least the bleeding had stopped.

Jak twisted his foot in circle. It snapped and popped like a bowl of rice cereal, but it didn't hurt as much as Jak thought it would. He tested it on the ground with part of his weight. A sprinkle of pain bounced back and forth, but it was not so bad that he couldn't limp. He hobbled to Gramps, then turned around and hobbled back to the man. "That's all I can do. I can limp."

"Good," said the man. "That is what I was hoping for."

"What does it mean?" said Gramps.

"It means the boy will live." The man hesitated and stood up. "For now."

A chill ran down Jak's spine. *For now?* "Is it gone? The poison, I mean?" said Jak.

The man shook his head as he threw the leaves in the river. They twirled slowly in the current and then disappeared over the edge. "The poison still runs in your blood. The leaves have drawn a portion out, which is why you are not dead yet."

"But can't you get the rest of it out?" asked Tess. "Isn't there something you can do? What about the fruit from the Tree of Life?"

"Did you not hear me?" said the man, cocking his left eyebrow. "I said the leaves were the last gift of the tree. The tree is now off limits. Besides, it would not help." He shook his head.

"What do you mean, the tree is off limits?" asked Jak. It made no sense to him. "We were able to eat the fruit before, so why not now?"

"Yes, that was before, but this is now," said the man. "That is why my brothers and I are here – to guard the fruit of the tree."

"From what?" said Jak.

"Not from what, but from whom. We guard against Man and Woman and their offspring." He paused. "And others," he added so softly Jak could hardly hear him.

"Man and Woman?" said Tess. "But why?"

"Why?" His eyes flashed. "That is my question as well. All this..." He swung his arm toward the valley and his face grew dark. "If we'd had our way, we'd have stormed into the garden and ripped the fruit out of the man's hand, but El wouldn't allow it. 'The choice belongs to Man,' he said. And that...," the huge man pointed once again to the valley, "...that is what Man chose." He breathed heavily, glaring at them for a few moments before lowering his arm and sighing. "I do not know how this poison will affect Jak. Perhaps it will be no different from the poison that now runs in all human veins."

"Wait," said Tess. Her face twisted into a something-isn't-right-here expression. "The poison in Jak is no different from the poison that runs in all human veins? What does that mean? Scorch didn't bite me, and I'm human."

"She did not need to." The man stood straight once again. "The moment Man bit the fruit, poison twisted his heart and filled the very fluid of his life. Rebellion is in your blood, and death is your destiny."

"My blood?" said Tess. "What does Man eating the fruit have to do with me?"

The man furrowed his brow. "You do not know?"

Tess and Jak exchanged glances.

"Know what?" asked Jak with a touch of hesitation.

"Man is your father."

CHAPTER 26

Secret Meeting under the Banyan Tree

Jak was glad he hadn't been standing up because he probably would have fallen over in shock. And from the way Tess reacted, she probably would have fallen over, too.

"What are you talking about?" said Tess. "My father's name is Victor Thompson, and he lives in Grantsburg, Wisconsin."

"And who is his father?" asked the man.

"That would be me," said Gramps, raising his hand.

"And who is your father?"

"Hezekiah Thompson."

"And his father's father's father?"

"Well," said Gramps, stroking his thick brown beard, "Now you're getting back there a ways."

"Yes," said the man, "and if you keep digging backwards, you will come to—"

Jak could see where the man was headed, and his mind struggled to make sense of it, but it still didn't make *any* sense. "Man?" said Jak.

The man nodded his head. "Correct."

Jak's mind felt like it had just been squeezed through a cheese grater. It was all too impossible to believe.

"So...you're saying we went back in time?" said Jak, incredulous.

"Yes," the man said nonchalantly, as if it was nothing more significant than a conversation about how good raspberries tasted.

"How far back?"

The man raised one bushy black eyebrow. "To the beginning."

Suddenly it all came rushing together: the book, the gate, and the freshness of the garden. The thought rocketed through Jak's head, spinning his mind upside down and inside out. That explained quite a bit. For example, why Man didn't mind running around in his birthday suit. He'd never had clothes and never needed them because there wasn't anyone else around.

"But how could that be?" asked Tess. "I mean, we're here and he's here all at the same time, but technically we haven't even been born yet."

"I don't know," said the man. "It just is. El has arranged it so."

"How old is Man?" asked Jak.

"Three days."

"Three days old?" said Tess. "He's got to be older than that! He's full-grown, and he looks at least twenty."

"Three days, and only three days."

"But that means he was born the same day we got here," said Jak. "How could he grow up in three—" One of his many questions slipped into his mind like a key and unlocked a mental door that slowly swung open. "Man wasn't born at all," said Jak.

"Not as you know it," said the man.

"He was pulled up from the dirt," said Jak. "El made him out of a pile of dirt, like a snowman, except he's a dirt man."

"Yes."

A very strange picture was being painted in Jak's head: round balls of black dirt being heaped on top of each other and then suddenly coming alive as Man. The whole thing was almost too bizarre to comprehend.

"But I don't understand," said Tess. "The garden—"

Suddenly, the man held up his hand to stop her, scanned the sky, and tilted his head to the side as if he had heard something beyond the reach of the humans' ears. "Too many evil eyes are marching through the air," he whispered. "Come with me, under the banyan tree."

A banyan tree had wrapped itself around an oak fifty yards upstream and now spread twenty feet in either direction. It was an odd thing, more of a super thick vine than a tree, strangling the host and spreading roots to the ground like pillars to create its own support. But in doing so, it also created a vast leaf-covered roof big enough to hide several elephants.

The man ducked underneath and settled cross-legged on the grass next to the fat trunk of the oak. The trunk cut out some of the wind, but a portion still sneaked around and bit into their skin. The golden wings erupted once more from the man's back, and he covered them like a giant tent.

The effect was immediate. The cold bite of the wind disappeared, and their shivering lessened. The man broke open a knapsack and lifted out a round speckled loaf of bread and a curled white flask that looked like it had been made out of a ram's horn.

Food! Jak's stomach growled again, and his mouth spouted a river of saliva.

The man dug deeper into his tunic and pulled out a package. He began to unwrap it. "And this," he said, talking to Macy, "is for you." He pulled out a meat-laden bone and tossed it to the dog.

She barked and pounced on the bone.

He then cut three steaming slabs of bread and covered them with butter, thick slices of white cheese, and red berry jam. "We have little time. You're going to need all your strength, so eat up.

They needed no prompting; they were starving. It was nothing like eating the zingers or even the giant raspberries at the bottom of Split Falls. There was no zing and no sudden burst of energy, but it felt good to finally put something in their stomachs. The bread was hearty, almost like eating meat, with a slight oat-like crunch, and the horn was filled with a hot, sweet broth, like a combination of hot chocolate and chicken noodle soup, except it tasted good.

"What are we going to need all our strength for?" asked Jak, wiping jam from his chin. His fingers tingled as the warmth began to edge back into his hands.

"Yes, what's going on?" said Tess. "Who's destroying the garden? Where are Man and Woman?"

"And who are you?" said Jak. He was tired of thinking of the man as the weird four-faced creature.

The man nodded his head with each question as he handed the flask to Gramps. "My name is Guardian, and I am a servant of El." He bowed his head slightly. "The long and short of it is that Man and Woman were made to rule creation, and it was good. The only thing they were forbidden to do was eat from the Tree of Knowing Good and Evil — that's it. They were warned that if they ate from the Tree, death would follow. It was not a difficult rule; it did not require strength or courage, only obedience, and they would've been safe. You found the black cherries in the clearing?"

They nodded their heads, their mouths full and chewing.

"They chose not to heed the warning, thought knowing the difference between good and evil was just what they needed to become as wise as Yahweh." He snorted. "But there is no such thing as wisdom apart from Yahweh. One taste of the fruit, and they got exactly what they asked for. Now they know evil very intimately, for it has invaded every corner of their hearts, killed their spirits, and will soon enough kill their bodies." He pointed over the cliff. "And you can see in the valley the price they are paying."

"Are you saying El wrecked the garden just because they didn't do what he said?" said Tess.

"Who said anything about El wrecking the garden?" Fire flashed through Guardian's eyes. "El warned them what would happen if they ate the fruit. You yourselves told them about death. Eating the black cherries was the same as issuing an invitation for death to stomp into the universe. That means Man is no longer king of this creation and El himself has been shut out from his own creation. If he were to come here now in all his glory, Earth would writhe in his presence. It could not endure his beauty nor his brilliance. But you know this already, Jak and Tess." He gave them a stern half-smile, and one eyebrow cocked up.

"What do you mean?" said Jak innocently, but knowing all too well that Guardian was referring to the night they had gone back to the clearing. His cheeks flushed hot, and he had to confess. "Y-yes," Jak stammered. "We know."

"You do?" said Gramps, surprised.

Jak didn't want to admit to his grandfather what they had done, but it didn't feel like he had much choice. "Tess and I sneaked to the clearing one night after you fell asleep."

"You did what?" Gramps almost spit his sandwich out.

"But we never made it," Jak added quickly. "The light choked us, and we had to turn back."

"That is why El could not allow you to be with him in the garden," said Guardian. "You already carried the poison in your blood. Thousands of generations of humans have passed it along to you. That which is tainted cannot stand in his presence, which is why he will not visit his creation in his full glory again... until the time is right." His eyes narrowed. "A new power now rules, and it is he who has destroyed the garden. He will continue to pervert El's creation as long as he is allowed."

"A new power?" asked Jak. The image of Red ignoring him that morning and then slinking in the woods near Man and Woman popped into his mind. "Who is he?"

Guardian paused for a moment, clenching his jaws ferociously before speaking. "A rogue servant named Lucifer. He rebelled against Yahweh in the other realm and attempted to overthrow the Mighty One. He was defeated and cast out but led his army here. However, Lucifer had no power here because Man and Woman ruled, and the creation was good. Therefore, evil could not dig its claws into the Earth. But when Man and Woman rebelled against Yahweh and sought out the knowledge of evil, it sank into their hearts and poisoned their blood... poisoned your blood." He stopped, took a deep breath, and shook his head. "That is why the Tree of Life is off limits to the human race. If you ate its fruit, it would give your bodies unbounded strength, and you would live forever."

"What's wrong with that?" said Gramps, running his fingers through his newly sprouted head of hair.

Guardian cocked his head and locked eyes with Gramps. "A living body with a dead spirit is as good as a well-dressed corpse."

Gramma Josie flashed into Jak's mind—not the smiling Gramma Josie, but the cold, waxy one in the casket. She had her best dress on, the dark blue one with the white lace, but it didn't make any difference. She was still pale and plastic, nothing at all like the green pepper-and-onion-loving fajita queen he had known. A shiver washed down his spine, and that familiar pit dug into his stomach.

"So there's no hope of finding another tree that will keep us from dying and no hope of Gramma coming back to life?" asked Jak. "Then what's the point? We've been dragged back to the beginning of time, my foot's messed up more than ever, plus this poison is crawling around in my blood ready to kill me, and we can't go home because we'll die there too. This is a stupid waste of time!"

Guardian folded his arms across his chest and stood perfectly still, his black eyes piercing into Jak. "What did the plaque say, Jak?"

Jak sighed. "The plaque talked about life that never ends and dead people coming back to life."

"Precisely, and so shall it be, but for the time being, humans are stuck. There's nothing you can do about death and the evil that pounds in your veins. There is nothing you can do about Lucifer and his horde." The giant leaned in close and whispered, "But El has a plan."

Guardian beckoned with his finger for the three to come close. "Listen to me now," he continued to whisper, "there are many books similar to the one you have in your bag, Jak. Many people have traveled to the garden from all over the world and witnessed the rise and fall of Man just as you have. Some have eaten the black fruit and have gone home, but those who stayed traveled on the same path upon which you are about to embark." He raised his head up above the safety of his wings like a periscope and spun it in all directions before bringing his head back down into the huddle. "But this is the first time that El has decreed that it is time to finish working out the plan. That is why you are here." He tapped Jak on the chest several times with a thick forefinger.

"Me?" said Jak in shock.

"Yes, you."

"But what can I do? I'm just a kid."

"The dream you had when you first came here was no dream, boy. It was real."

At the mention of a dream, Tess perked up, obviously curious and a bit perturbed that Jak hadn't mentioned it before. "What dream?" she demanded.

"Tell you later," said Jak.

Guardian shifted his gaze back to Jak and continued, "El tested your mettle, and you tested well. You have been brought here for a reason." He bent in so close that Jak could smell the fire on his breath as he whispered. "To carry the book."

Goosebumps erupted on Jak's skin. He liked the feeling of having passed a test, especially one he didn't even know he was taking, but he wondered what the big deal was about carrying the book and why El would choose him to do it. He could hardly get *himself* anywhere with a bum foot. He pressed against the rectangular outline of the book through the cloth of the book bag still slung around his shoulder. "Carry the book where?" he asked.

Another explosion rocked the valley, and Guardian's wings shuddered against the blast.

"I don't have time to explain, and even if I did, I could only tell you a bit of the story because that's all I know. You must take it to the plains of Megiddo, to the place Yahweh shows you."

"But I don't know where it is. I've never even heard of Magoo...what'd you call it?"

"Megiddo," said Guardian. "Take this." He reached into a pocket hidden in the folds of his cloak and handed Jak a small bag that looked like a miniature gunny sack, woven in the same blue and red pattern as the book bag.

Jak lifted the flap and pulled out a familiar-looking deck of cards.

"Hey! These are the cards we first saw in the book back in Gramps's basement. What are they?"

Guardian spun his head completely around again, checking for unwelcome ears, before leaning in and whispering, "This book will have the power to break Lucifer's grip and send death and evil to their graves."

"Why didn't you tell us that before?" said Jak, starting to stand up. "Let's do it."

But Guardian shook his head and pushed him back down. "No! It does not yet have the strength to do so. First it must be completed."

"You mean I have to write in it?"

"No. It has to do with the people on some of the cards. I am told their words give the book power. You must follow the path to find the people, capture their words, and then place the cards in the pockets of the book. When it is completed, it will have the power to rid the Earth of the three. Then you are to bring it to Megiddo."

"And where is that?" asked Jak.

Guardian stared at him in silence for a moment. Then he looked to the ground, took a deep breath and let it out. "I do not know."

"You don't know?" Tess exploded. "Then how are we supposed to get there?"

"I am sorry, but I can only answer some of your questions. There are many parts of this story I do not know. But this is the part I do know, so I have shared it with you."

Jak didn't know what to think. His mind was overwhelmed with all that had happened. Gramps was young again, his foot was healed and then chewed up by an animal that used to be his friend, they had met a lion/bull/eagle man, not to mention a three-day-old full-grown naked man made of dirt, and to top it off, the garden had been destroyed by fireballs. He was scared, and his leg hurt, and he wished a little that the cherries hadn't fallen out of the book bag. There was no way he could limp to Magoodo, not to mention the fact that nobody even knew where Magoodo was.

The whine of an approaching squadron began again, and the western horizon filled with a thousand glowing fireballs headed toward the garden.

Guardian retracted his wings, and the cold wind bit once more into their skin. "I must go now, and so must you. You still have an advantage in that Lucifer does not yet know where you are and knows nothing of your journey. At some point, he will figure it out, for he is cunning, and when he finds you, beware. Whatever you do, do not give him the book."

Great, thought Jak. *In addition to a bum leg and an impossible journey, now there's some deranged enemy ready to pounce on me.* "But what if I don't want to carry the book to Magoodo?" said Jak.

"It's Megiddo," said Guardian, correcting him like Tess would as he stood to his feet. "You always have a choice. You may eat the last black cherry and go home and die." He stopped speaking and stared at Jak for a moment. "But I tell you again, you are the one El has chosen. He does not choose on a whim."

"But why can't you carry it?"

The giant pressed his lips together and shook his head slightly. "I am not human. Man invited the poison in, so a man must take it out as well."

The storm around the Tree of Life rumbled and belched a black cloud into the air.

Guardian spun his head around, revealing the eagle and bull faces as he did so. "I must go. My brothers need me." Suddenly, Guardian's legs swelled until they were thick and covered with charcoal-black hair. His feet split into hooves, and his whole body inflated until he once again towered his original size.

"But I can't do this!" Jak pleaded. "I can hardly walk!"

The giant knelt until he was at eye level with Jak, then took his massive hand and pulled Jak's chin until they were looking directly at each other. "This is not a game, Jak. If you do not do this, the living are doomed to die, and the dead will stay dead forever. Remember, Yahweh is your protection and your strength. Now, follow the path." With that, Guardian launched himself into the air.

Jak panicked. He still had no idea what path they were supposed to follow. The white seashell paths had been destroyed, and there was nothing at the top of the cliff either. "But there is no path!" he shouted.

Guardian's head spun around as he winged through the air. "The Thread, Jak! Follow the Scarlet Thread!" And then he disappeared into the mist of Split Falls as quickly and mysteriously as he had come.

CHAPTER 27

The Scarlet Thread

Jak stood at the edge of the banyan tree, staring into the mist where Guardian had disappeared. His head was swimming. El had chosen him to take the book to Magoodo or Migidoo or whatever it was, but he could hardly walk, and he had no idea how to get there. He was supposed to be following some scarlet thread, but he had no idea where to find that either. He didn't have a hole in his pocket that needed mending or a loose button to fasten to his pants. He needed a path. What good was a thread going to do?

An explosion sounded in the distance, and a bright light flashed in the valley. The second attack had begun, and he knew they didn't have much time.

"What did he say about a thread?" said Gramps.

"I don't know." Jak shrugged his shoulders.

"He said to follow the Scarlet Thread," said Tess. "So where is it?"

"I don't know that either," said Jak. "Where am I supposed to find a scarlet thread? What color is scarlet anyway? Green?"

"No, it's red—deep red, like blood," said Tess.

Jak knew the color of blood well enough since it was spattered all over his pants, but he hardly thought the threads in his pants were what Guardian had in mind. He was completely confused and growing increasingly frustrated by the minute.

"How 'bout this?" asked Gramps. He held up the book bag. The pattern in the bag alternated blue and red, a deep red, like blood.

"Yeah, that could be it," said Jak. "Maybe there's something inside." He dumped the bag upside down and laid the book on the grass, a little more reverently than before. After all, this was the book that was supposed to save the world.

There was nothing in the bag besides the back side of the design—no notes, no mysterious drawings, nothing. He picked the book up again and was about to put it back in the bag when he noticed something flopping out of the pages. It was the bookmark—a *scarlet* bookmark!

He flipped the book open to the spot where the bookmark was. It was the first paper page, the one with the picture of the Tree of Knowing Good and Evil. He realized that the ink of the picture hadn't faded at all. That's exactly what the tree looked like, dark and foreboding. He picked up the bookmark.

"If that's the Scarlet Thread," said Tess, "we're not going to get very far. It's only six inches long."

"I know," said Jak, "but I don't know what else to look for. Are we supposed to find a thread that points us in the direction we're supposed to go, or is it like following a string through the woods?"

This was obviously going nowhere, so he threw the bookmark down toward the book on the ground, but it never made it. Instead, it stopped directly above the book, hovering in the air and turning in a slow circle. "Whoa!" said Jak.

"What is it?" asked Gramps.

"The bookmark," he whispered, pointing to where the bookmark floated.

As it turned, it quivered and grew longer and wider until it was the same size as a baseball bat. Then it twirled into the leaves above their heads and whizzed through the branches of the banyan tree, humming and whirring and wrapping itself into a living red spaghetti noodle knot. Then it shot out of the tree, hummed up the river and around the bend until they could no longer see the end.

Macy whined and hid behind Jak.

"Well, I'll be!" stammered Gramps.

"That was weird," said Tess.

"*That's* the Scarlet Thread," said Jak. "This has to be the path Guardian was talking about."

"The one that will cost your life if you follow it?" asked Tess.

A series of explosions lit the sky above the valley once again.

"I don't think it'll be much more dangerous than sticking around here," said Gramps. "We better get moving. I don't want to meet this Lucifer fellow."

Neither did Jak. He threw the deck of cards in the bag along with the book while Tess gathered the flask, still half-full of broth, and the remains of the bread, cheese, and jam. They left the cover of the banyan tree and began making their way along the bank, following the Thread.

It was slow going, especially for Jak, who could only limp. It wasn't so much the pain that slowed him down, although there was plenty of that. It was the fact that he wasn't physically able to go any faster. His right ankle didn't obey the way it once had. It wouldn't swing forward the way it was supposed to, and his foot wouldn't bend the way it was supposed to. And there was the constant sense of that alien spider kind of thing lurking in his foot, pushing toward his heart. Maybe it was death. He didn't know. He just knew it was there, waiting to take him over.

He shuffled through the grass as fast he could, but still Tess and Gramps had to wait for him. Macy carried the bone in her mouth and trotted along behind. He hoped she didn't find any rabbits on the way because they couldn't stop to track her down.

Light pulsed through the Thread as they followed, like a marker tracking their progress and encouraging him to keep going. When they finally made it to the bend in the river, Jak expected to see the Thread stretching off into the distance, but it didn't. Instead, it stopped almost immediately at a weeping willow suspended over the water. Memories of the willow in the park and the boy falling into the river flooded through him along with guilt for what he had done. He took a deep breath and kept walking. He had to keep going.

"This is it?" said Tess. "This is as far as we go?"

"No," said Gramps, "I don't think so. Over there, under the branches." He pointed to the tree's long wispy branches that brushed the top of a boat, moored to the trunk of the tree. "I think we found ourselves a ride."

❧

A bright yellow flame erupted from Red's mouth, singeing the bottom branches of an oak tree that loomed like a skyscraper over the banks of the mud pond. This was not the way it was supposed to work. Creation was rightfully under his rule, and he should be able to do as he liked. They had succeeded in blasting half of the garden into a mud hole, but they still could not kill the creatures, and they could not capture the Tree of Life. The black tornado was an impenetrable wall.

He ran his tongue through his crooked teeth, slobbering yellow slime onto the ground where it congealed with the dirt and formed a steaming slobber pie.

"Ssstul, Reaf, Ssslie, Egar!" Lucifer roared through Red's mouth, spraying spittle everywhere, "Get over here, NOW!"

A parade of four putrid Lights oozed their way, muttering and cursing, to a rock about a stone's throw away from the hill of the Two Trees.

Lucifer lay coiled in a heap on the rock, soaking in the rays of the sun and boiling in his own anger. "We have been cheated!" he growled. "*I* am now the ruler. It isss *I* who deccceeived Woman and ussshered death into the world, therefore *I* ssshould be able to control it." The flippers that used to be his front legs twitched as he spoke.

The group of Lights sputtered in front of him.

"We've tried everything, Lucifer," said Slie in a fat, milky voice, his black light blinking slowly on and off, "but the creatures won't die. The trees and the grass, yes, but the creatures continue to live. We've squeezed and pushed and burned, but it's no use. It's just like the way it was before death came."

"Ssshut up, Sslie," spat Lucifer. "I know that. I need ideass, not usseless prattle of what hasss failed."

No one said anything for a moment until Stul slid forward. "Lucius, what was it that the enemy told the humans in the beginning?"

Lucifer's eyes stared without blinking, like giant yellow bowls of Jell-O. "He told them they were the rulerss." A spark flew from his nose, landed on Stul's face and slowly burned its way through the purple goo.

"But there was something else," said Stul, flicking it away. "You overheard more while we were still in the court of the enemy, but I cannot remember what it was."

Lucifer thought back to the gatherings of the council in Yahweh's court. The creatures would be Yahweh's highest creation, loved more than anything else, and they were... *to fill the Earth*. He snorted, blasting a hole in Egar's belly. Egar flashed a deeper shade of red and grunted, quickly oozing the hole shut. "They were to multiply!" shouted Lucifer. He licked his lips, sending another glob of yellow slobber to the ground. "The number of foolss will grow. We will bide our time until the humanss sspawn, and then convinccce them to *dessstroy each other*."

A memory flickered in Red's brain of the little man in the garden. "But there are three other humans. There is another man, woman, and a little man. Sssend a troop of Lightss to find them, esssspecially the little one. He belongsss to *me*."

The boat was a fat canoe, sleek at the front and back, yet wide in the middle. It rested on top of the water, bobbing like a cork. Three paddles lay in the boat, an open invitation for them to get in.

Jak was grateful for the chance to sit. The top of his body was fine, and he didn't mind paddling. In fact, he enjoyed it. Gramps sat in the steering seat in the back, Tess took the front, and Jak and Macy sat together in the middle. As soon as they pushed out into the river, the Thread zoomed off once again upstream.

Jak looked over his shoulder at Split Falls one last time and was startled when a pair of bright Lights hovered slowly up through the mist, twisting this way and that, as if they were looking for something.

"Go, go, go," said Jak quietly, dipping his paddle deep into the dark water. "We've got company, and I don't think they're friendly."

"What is it?" said Tess, turning her head to look. As soon as she saw the Lights, she started paddling so fast she almost dropped her paddle in the water.

"Shh," said Gramps. He had taken a look backwards as well and now pushed hard against the water, yet hardly making a splash.

Beads of sweat sprouted on Jak's forehead. The Lights were twenty feet in the air, spinning around like tops. Suddenly they stopped twirling and began zooming up the river, straight toward the canoe, screaming an alarm that sounded like a cat had just been sat on by a sumo wrestler.

"Faster!" shouted Jak. "They see us!"

The water erupted as three paddles churned the boat around the bend.

Jak craned his head around one more time, expecting to see the Lights buzz around the corner, but nothing came. He held his breath and counted to ten, but still the sky was empty. They stopped paddling and listened, but the wild screaming was gone, and the only thing they could hear was the waves slapping against the side of the boat.

PART TWO
TWISTING

CHAPTER 28

Smoke on the Water

Jak twisted around and tried to force his vision to go around the bend in the river. Surely the Lights had seen them, but they were nowhere to be found. "Where'd they go?" he said.

"I don't know," said Gramps, frowning. "They should've shown up by now, unless..." He scratched his beard as if he was pulling ideas through his whiskers.

"Unless what?" asked Tess.

"Unless they went to get reinforcements."

Gramps, Tess, and Jak immediately sank their paddles back into the water and began paddling furiously. The last thing they needed was for Lucifer's entire army to find them.

They paddled hard into the night, occasionally stopping to listen for cat-like screeching, but they didn't hear it again. When all the stars had come out, they finally stopped, exhausted, along the bank of the river to rest for the night.

Jak found three wool blankets stuffed in the prow of the canoe, so they laid them out on the grass and tried to sleep, but no one slept very well.

As soon as light cracked the horizon, they packed up and got back on the river, cold and miserable. The leftover bread, cheese, and broth for breakfast cheered them a little, and by mid-morning, the sun had finally warmed them up enough that the shivering melted away. The only excitement they had was when another pair of meteors darted through the sky. The canoe was near the bank, so they hid under a sumac bush until the fireballs disappeared over the horizon.

It was obvious now: Lucifer was hunting for them.

The river stayed as wide as a four-lane highway, and the Thread continued to lead them upstream until a large finger of water forked away to the right and gushed downstream to the east. At this point, the Thread took an abrupt turn to the east as well, so Gramps dug his paddle on the left side of the boat and guided them into the new river. It was a lot easier going downstream than upstream, so Jak and Tess took a break from paddling while Gramps steered.

Jak rubbed his arms and hands. They were tired, and an uncomfortable prickle permeated his whole body, like an itch he couldn't scratch. It felt good to rest, to just sit and watch the bank flow by the boat. It didn't seem as cold on this river; the further downstream they went, the warmer it became. The flowers and trees had lost their vibrant color, and there were just as many weeds as flowers. Things were definitely changing.

Jak closed his eyes and soaked in the sunshine, but he couldn't get his mind off the mysterious prickle that nagged him.

"So, Jak," said Tess, craning her neck around, "Guardian said something about finding the people on the cards he gave you. That's a lot of people."

"The way I understood it," said Gramps, guiding them around a large rock in the middle of the water, "is that he talked about finding *some* of the people on the cards, not necessarily everybody."

"How do you know who you're supposed to find?" said Tess.

"I don't know," said Jak. He took the deck of cards out of the book bag, and he and Tess spread them on the floor of the canoe. Each card had a picture of a person, a blue line winding around the card edge, and an empty black box on the bottom. "I guess we're supposed to follow the Thread and find them on the way," said Jak, looking at the faces on the cards.

"But the cards don't even have names written on them," said Tess. "What are you going to do, wander around holding the card up to people's faces and saying, 'Excuse me. Is this you?'"

"There has to be some way of knowing who to talk to," said Jak. "Ouch!" he cried, slapping at his neck. Something had bit him. When he looked at his palm, he found a bloody mosquito the size of a quarter smeared over his hand.

"It's a mosquito," he said, scratching his neck. "A big one. That's the first mosquito I've seen since we've gotten here." He washed his hands in the river and wiped them as dry as he could on his pants. While he was waiting for them to dry completely, he bent over and inspected a card with a picture of an older man. The man on the card looked like he had spent most of his life outdoors. He had a dark face, hazel eyes, black hair, and a trim beard. His head and chin were both streaked with gray.

"Agh!" Tess slapped her arm and wiped her hand on the canoe. "Yuk. Another mosquito."

Jak picked up the card to get a closer look. As soon as he touched it, the card began to squirm and wiggle in his hand like he was holding a frog.

He gasped and grabbed the card with both hands to keep it from falling into the river. A red line began to race around the edges of the card, following the blue line, sometimes intersecting, sometimes sliding alongside, until it completely surrounded the card. Then, just like that, the card stopped wriggling.

Tess stared at the card with her mouth agape. "What was that about?"

"I don't know." Jak shrugged. "A red line traced around the edges. See?" He held the card up. "Maybe this is one of the guys we need to find. None of the other cards have a red line on them, do they?"

"No, not yet. Here..try this one." She handed him a card with a black-haired man carrying a drum and some sort of harp. When the card stayed still, she gave him another. This one had a picture of a man with short brown hair and a scraggly brown beard. He held a lamb in his arms and was smiling, but his card didn't do anything either. The fourth card featured a sour-looking man with a scar on his cheek; Jak was glad that card sat silent when he touched it.

They made their way through the pile, Jak holding each card to see what would happen, but nothing did—until the very last card. The man on the last card looked about fifty years old, with dark brown hair and beard, and crow's feet wrinkles on his temples angling back from a pair of bright brown eyes. He held a wooden mallet in his hand and had a big smile pasted across his face as if he had just told a good joke. As soon as Jak picked the card up, it jumped and wiggled, and then, just like with the first card, a red line snaked around the edge.

"Two cards. That must mean you're supposed to look for two people," said Tess. She sighed. "I guess that's not so bad."

The boat slid into a section of the river shaded by huge trees that draped themselves over the water.

Suddenly, at the same time, both Gramps and Tess slapped at mosquitoes.

"I think we've got trouble," said Gramps.

A swarm of mosquitoes hovered in the shade over the river like vultures. They flew straight toward the canoe and began stinging their necks and ears and hands, any exposed flesh they could find to feast on.

"Aagh!" said Jak, hitting himself in the cheek and ankle at the same time. "I can't get them away from me!" As soon as he swatted one away from his arm, another one stung him in the forehead, and when he slapped that one, another one buzzed into his ear.

Macy whined and crawled under the seat, protecting herself by curling into a tight ball.

"Paddle!" said Gramps. "We have to get out of the shade before they eat us alive!"

They dug their paddles into the river, racing for the sunny spot at the end of the trees and trying to ignore the bloodsuckers that buzzed around their ears.

The Thread hurried ahead of them. As soon as it burst into the sunshine, it took a sharp right and zoomed up the bank of the river.

"We're almost there!" said Jak. "And the Thread just headed onto the shore!"

They churned like madmen until the canoe burst out of the shadow. A strong smell of smoke wafted over the river, forcing the cloud of mosquitoes to quickly thin out. From over the hill, several white plumes billowed into the sky.

As soon as Jak saw the smoke, panic began to rise in his throat, and the mysterious prickle grew stronger, to the point where it was even painful.

Gramps steered them toward the shore

"The fireballs!" said Jak. "They must have landed on the other side of the hill. We can't go ashore here."

"But that's where the Thread went," said Gramps.

"I know," said Jak. "But I don't want to go anywhere near those fireballs. Remember what Guardian said about Lucifer hunting us down?"

"Yes, but what else did he say?" asked Gramps. "What are the words El gave to you?"

Jak scratched at a mosquito bite on his arm. "He said, 'Yahweh is your protection and your strength.' But what good are words going to do against fire? We need some firepower of our own—a tank or machine gun or something like that."

"Well, before we start building a tank, let's see what's on the other side of that hill," said Gramps.

The canoe slid softly into the grass at the edge of the bank, and Macy immediately jumped out and began her traditional frantic tour of smells. Jak was grateful to leave the mosquitoes behind but reluctant to follow the Thread over the hill. As soon as his foot touched the ground it began hurting him to walk—not just his bad leg, but his whole body, like the spidery thing in his ankle had turned into boiling oil coursing through his blood. This was more than mere apprehension. "I don't feel so good," he said. His eyes closed, and he began to sway.

Gramps came alongside him and gripped his elbow. "We've just gotta make it over this hill, son."

They followed the Thread up the grassy slope and the pain subsided, replaced by a dull ache in his bones. As they approached, music drifted faintly through the trees, accompanied by the smell of food. At the crest of the hill, they could see a village, decorated with shocks of corn and green flags that fluttered in the breeze.

The Thread floated down into the valley and settled over the village. A field lay in between the hill and the village. A grid of fires blazed in one section of the field, each with a tripod erected above it and a flat grate hanging over the flames. Tables laden with food surrounded the fires, and people were cutting and sorting and peeling, apparently preparing for a feast. In the middle of the field, a tremendous pile of grass and sticks was stacked in the sun. A group of laughing children, surrounded by a small zoo of animals, played a ballgame of some kind on the side of the field nearest the hill.

Jak breathed a sigh of relief. *So it isn't the fireballs after all.*

Crack!

A ball the size of a large grapefruit rolled in front of Macy, and she jerked back, but when the ball did not move, she began nosing it.

A boy who looked a little older than Tess ran to pick it up, but stopped short when he saw them. He looked like an athlete; his shoulders were broadening into manhood, and he sported curly brown hair, tan skin, and bright green eyes. He looked at them quizzically for a moment, and then spoke. "Hullo. Are you comin' to the feast?" He pointed down the hill at the fires. "We've got corn roastin', and it's just about time to eat."

Tess stood dumbstruck, staring at the boy.

Gramps narrowed his eyes and inspected the boy for a moment before nodding his head. "Sure, that sounds good."

"Alright then. Follow me." He stooped to pick up the ball and then started down the hill shouting, "Hey, Mum! We've got guests!"

A stout woman at the edge of the village looked up from a kettle she was stirring. She smiled and called out, "Bring 'em o'er here, Nal."

Nal led them to the large table next to the kettle and they sat down. The woman stirring the kettle wore a dark green robe with animals of various colors embroidered on the hems. Her hair was long and dark, and hung behind her shoulders in a white plait. A large man with jet-black whiskers and lively green eyes sat at the table next to a smaller man with a braided brown beard, both with drinks in their hands. The large man eyed them over with the same intensity Gramps had inspected the boy. "Where 'er ya from?"

"Oh, that's got to wait, Jared," said the woman, shaking her head. "For goodness sake, they've just sat down."

"No, it can't wait," said the man. He stood, grabbed Gramps's wrist, flipped it around, and examined it. "Humph." He sat down again, apparently satisfied with what he saw, and took a swig from his cup.

"Excuse his manners," said the woman, blushing as she placed a mug in front of each of them. "He's a bit too careful." She shot the man a disapproving look, then settled herself in a chair across from them.

Jak lifted his mug. Steam wisped from the top along with the delicious smell of apple cider. "Now then," she said, pushing a few stray strands of hair back behind her ears, "my name is Beertael, but you can call me Beerta. You've met my Nal, and this is my husband Jared." She put her hand on the arm of the man with the jet-black whiskers. "Welcome to East Eden. What're yer names and what village are you from?" She looked at them expectantly, taking a careful sip from her mug.

192

"I'm Clarence Thompson," said Gramps, "and this is my grandson Jak and granddaughter Tess. We are from Grantsburg, Wisconsin, in the United States of America."

Tess tried to smile, but she had just taken a swig from her mug, and her entire face had puckered up like a grape in the sun. She was obviously drinking something different than apple cider.

"Grantsburg, you say? I haven't heard of that one," said Beerta, daintily wiping her mouth with a dried leaf napkin. "Have you, Jared?"

He shook his head. "No, but new ones're popping up almost every day. I was expectin' you to say somethin' like that though."

"Why is that?" asked Gramps.

"Because of the way you're dressed. It doesn't take a scholar to figure out you aren't from 'round 'ere. What er you doin' so far away from home?"

Jak glanced at Gramps, not sure how much they should say about what they were doing. These people seemed nice enough, but there was always the chance they could be on Lucifer's side. Before he had a chance to decide what to say, Beerta interrupted his thoughts.

"You wouldn't happen to be followin' the Thread, would you?" asked Beerta.

Shocked, Jak went red in the face and stammered, "Um, uh...yeah." He bit his lip, hoping he hadn't just blown their cover. *How had she known?*

Jared gave a low whistle. "Thread followers, eh? Haven't seen many of them lately."

"Has been a while, hasn't it?" Beerta agreed. " I thought I saw a sparkle in the air when you came over the hill. Where's the Thread now?"

Bewildered, Jak pointed straight up. "It's right above us."

"Oh." Beerta glanced up and tilted her head in several directions until she finally stopped with her right ear almost touching her shoulder. "Yes! There it is."

"You mean you can't see it?" said Jak. "It's right above us. You can't miss it."

"No," said Jared. "YOU can't miss it, but we can. It's nothin' more than a mist to us."

"Sometimes we can see it fine," said Nal, who was squinting up at the sky with his head cocked to the left, "but most often it's like a sheet of water in the air."

"So we're the only ones who can see it right now?" said Tess.

"Yes, dear, more than likely," said Beerta. She straightened her robe around her. "I s'pose you've come from Eden, then?"

"I'm not sure," said Gramps, "but we've come from the west."

"Yep, that'd be Eden. I noticed you limpin' yer way down the hill," said Beerta to Jak. "Are you 'urt?"

Once again, Jak did not know how much to say. "Yeah, something happened this morning."

"Not going to get much better if you keep walkin' on it like that," said Beerta, "Let me have a look."

Jak didn't have anything to hide about his foot, so he plunked it up on the bench. It was then that he noticed the bleeding, only it wasn't just his injured foot that bled. Patches of dried blood criss-crossed both feet.

"You can't be trompin' through the brush barefoot," said Jared, "unless you'd like prickers and thorns lodgin' in yer 'eel."

Jak had left his shoe in the garden after Man had used it to ferry water from the pool. He hadn't needed it there, but evidently here he did.

"But that isn't the only thing. Look at this 'eel," said Beerta. She traced her finger through the tooth tracks in Jak's skin. A mountain range of angry red scars ran from the ball of his foot up to his calf.

"That's why the boy's limpin'." Beerta looked at Jak with motherly concern. " If you don't mind me askin', what 'appened?"

Jak hesitated, but they seemed trustworthy, so he decided to chance it. "Well, we went back to the clearing in the garden, and I found Scorch. She's a leviathan, and—"

"Leviathan, you say?" said Jared with surprise.

"Yes," said Jak, nodding his head. "Something was wrong with her. And then we heard Woman crying in the woods, so we went in to help them because we thought they were dying, but they weren't." Once Jak started telling the story, he found he could not stop.

"El and Man and Woman were in the woods, and Man and Woman were upset. Then, all of a sudden, Scorch fell down. She was in awful pain, writhing on the ground, so I went to help her, but she...well, she turned on me, snapped at my hand, and I fell, and then she grabbed my heel in her teeth and thrashed it back and forth." Jak stopped. He didn't like thinking about it again.

"And yer still alive?" said Beerta.

"Of course he's alive, or he wouldn't be talkin' to us right now," said Jared.

"Yes, of course," she said, flustered and slightly embarrassed. "What I meant is that nothin' is wrong with the boy, he's 'ere talkin' to us just fine."

"He's got a limp, Mum," said Nal, pointing to Jak's right foot.

"I know that," said Beerta, "but the poison... I would think the poison would be especially strong in him, you know, because of the bite."

Jak nodded his head. "It is—or at least that's what Guardian said."

"Ah," said Jared, fingering his beard and nodding his head. "So you've met the servant then."

Jak nodded his head again. "Yes. He wrapped some leaves from the Tree of Life around my ankle, and they drew some of the poison out."

"He gave you some leaves from the tree?" asked Jared, his eyes opening wide. "He 'ardly even lets us look at it."

"He said this was the last gift the tree was going to give."

"So it really does work!" said Beerta. She sighed. "I wish we could get a few of those leaves 'ere. All that weedin' sets my back to achin'."

"What color is this Scorch you're talkin' about?" said Jared.

"She's black, for the most part," said Tess. Her face was finally back to normal now, and she could talk without puckering. "At least she was before her mane came off."

"Her mane?" said Nal.

"Yes. She used to have a beautiful black mane that went from her head to her tail, but it got scraped away when she changed. She's ugly now—just four flippers instead of legs, a smashed-in face, and teeth like knives," said Tess.

Beerta and Jared exchanged glances, and Nal looked down at the table.

"She's the one then," said Beerta.

C H A P T E R   2 9

A Dead Boy's Clothes

"She's the one what?" asked Tess.

Jared leaned forward and put his elbows on the table. "'ave you seen this black leviathan since the garden?"

Jak shook his head. "No."

"We 'ave." He paused. "More than we would 'ave liked."

Beerta had grown strangely quiet.

"Nal 'ad a twin brother," Jared continued.

"I '*ave* a twin brother, Father," said Nal.

Jared sighed. "Alright then. Nal 'as a twin named Enoch. Five years ago, they was out playin' by the river...all the younguns were there...when the black beast slithered out of the water and tried to snatch 'em, but they all got away and ran home 'cept our Enoch...he disappeared." Jared stared straight at Jak. "Never found his body, not even a bone."

Nal leaned forward. "That's 'cause 'e's not dead, Father."

"The black one's a child stealer," said Jared forcefully. "Been doin' it for almost four hundred years."

"Four hundred years?" said Tess. "But we just left the garden yesterday morning."

"Maybe so, but it's been four hundred years of stolen children and five years of sorrow for us."

The numbers flashed in Jak's head; 400 years had passed since they had left the top of Split Falls—400 years in a day. "Are you sure this is the same leviathan?" said Jak. "Tess is right. We just left the garden yesterday, so how could four hundred years have gone by?"

The man with the braided beard wiped his whiskers with the back of his hand. "Did you say you're followin' the Thread? That Thread does funny things with time, or so I've heard. It might be that you left Eden yesterday mornin', but for us, it's been over four hundred years."

"Yeah, but wouldn't Scorch be dead by now? Four hundred years is a long time."

"We're not sure the beast *can* die," said Jared. "We've tried to kill 'em before but can't find a soft spot in their scales. Our spears bounce off without doin' nothin' at all."

"But there must be some way to get rid of her," said Tess.

Jared raised an eyebrow. "Then the next time the black one shows her ugly head 'round here, *you* go and try to ram a spear up her nose."

"Maybe that's why the only thing wrong with you is the limp. Because for you, it just happened yesterday mornin'," said Nal. "Whenever someone gets bit by the beast and lives to tell about it, they're fine for a day or two, but then they turn dark and moody. Their skin turns yellow, their eyes become bloodshot and sink into their heads, and then they get mean."

"Nal, that's enough," said Beerta. "The poor boy's been through enough without your stories."

"But it's true, Mum. I've seen it. Remember Tam? And Soath? And—"

"Hush now! Not another word!"

"The poison of the beast is more than we can bear," said Jared. "The other one is no better. He doesn't steal children, but he sets entire villages on fire with his mouth, and none his tongue has tasted have survived. You can always tell when he and his men have been afoot, because you'll find a corpse in the wood with the legs and arms torn off, nothing left but a pile of flies and maggots to honor the dead.

"What other one are you talking about?" said Tess.

"The other leviathan—not the black one, but the other. We call him Beelzebub, the Lord of the Flies."

"Is he....red?" asked Jak.

"Yep, from snout to tail. Have you seen 'im then?"

Jak slumped in his chair. That explained it then. He had seen Red hit the ground just before Scorch did, but by the time he turned around to check on him, Red had disappeared. He had hoped maybe it was just Scorch that had been changed during the rebellion, but now he knew better. "The last time I saw him he was with Man, Woman and El in the woods."

"And it isn't just him either," said Jared.

"You mean there are more leviathans?" said Tess.

"Yes, some little 'uns, but I don't mean them. There are other creatures, filled to the gills with evil. Sometimes you see them darting through the air, like a fire in the sky."

"We've seen them before," said Jak. "We saw them when we were in the garden. They first came two nights ago, but we thought they were meteors. And we saw some more this afternoon."

Jared shook his head. "That can't mean anythin' good. The fathers say these fiery creatures are Beelzebub's servants and do whatever he tells 'em to do."

"But Red can't talk," said Jak.

"That I don't know," said Jared, "but whether he can talk or not makes no difference. Either way, the evil ones still come with those scum Beelzin'" Jared spat on the ground. "Whenever they get the chance, they destroy or steal whatever lies in their path, whether it be man or beast, home or field."

"That's enough dreariness for now," Beerta broke in. "Let's talk about somethin' a little more cheery. After all, this is a celebration. Jak, what do yer parents think about yer comin' here?"

"I don't know," Jak answered slowly. "My mom's gone a lot working, and my dad... well, Dad isn't around much either."

Beerta blushed. "Oh, I'm sorry to hear that. That must make you and yer sister sad."

"I'm not his sister," said Tess. "I'm his cousin."

"Oh." Beerta blushed again. "I'm sorry. I mean, not sorry you're his cousin, I'm sorry that—"

"That's alright," Gramps reassured her. "You look like you are getting ready for a party."

Beerta smiled gratefully. "It's a double celebration, Remembrance Day and a birthday party."

At that moment, a commotion began on the other end of the field where the ballgame was going on. The children had stopped playing and now whooped and jumped up and down around a large cart pulled by two black horses. A small caravan of men and woman pulled up behind the cart, all of them either riding donkeys or walking.

"He's back!" Nal jumped out of his seat and ran toward the wagon.

"Nal, don't forget our guests!" But Nal either didn't hear his mother, or chose to ignore her because he kept going.

"They've just returned from the annual pilgrimage to Eden. Every year before Remembrance Day, the eldest father goes to Eden to visit the Tree of Life. He is not allowed to touch it, but—"

"Can't touch it?" roared Jared angrily. "Can't hardly get close enough to see it with that blasted Guardian swingin' that lightnin' sword every which way."

"But even just seein' the servant is enough for him, I think," said Beerta. She picked up a towel and began wiping the table where Nal had spilled his drink.

"I s'pose," said Jared. "He never complains about it."

A man and woman stepped down out of the cart, and everyone burst into applause and whistles. They disappeared into the crowd, which now began moving en masse toward the roasting grounds.

Beerta turned her attention back to her guests. "Did you see them, the man and woman who got out of the cart?"

"Yes," said Jak, Tess, and Gramps together.

"It's his birthday. Well, actually his birthday was a few days ago, but since it is so close to Remembrance Day and since it's such a special birthday, we are celebrating them together this year." She put the towel back on the table. "Come now. We must get you cleaned up. You can't attend the celebration with blood on yer clothes! Just wouldn't be proper."

Beerta led them away from the grounds into the village. The houses stood close to one another, and were made out of some sort of stone or mud, whitewashed so that the entire village looked like a collection of square bones.

Some had two stories, but most were just a single floor. She was considerate enough to walk slowly so Jak could keep up, occasionally looking back, but not saying anything more about his limp.

"Four hundred years," said Jak, sweat breaking out over his face as he walked. "I can't believe it. Wasn't it just yesterday that we woke up next to the bridge in the garden?"

"Yep," said Gramps. He grabbed Jak's right arm to help him make the trek down the road. "But apparently we've made quite a journey in less than two days."

"I want to talk with the guy who's having a birthday," said Jak.

"How come?" said Tess.

"Because Beerta said he's the oldest guy around. Maybe he knew Man or Woman, or maybe he knew someone who did."

Suddenly, a burst of pain flashed through Jak's entire body, and his knees buckled, sending him stumbling toward the ground. Gramps caught him and laid him in the shadow of one of the bone houses. Jak's breath came short and shallow, and the faces of Gramps, Tess, and Beerta grew blurry.

It felt like the same twisting pain he had when he sprained his ankle, except it vibrated through his whole body. He couldn't move and could hardly think. Someone far away was calling his name...

"Jak!" A hand slapped across his face, and the blurred faces became clear once again.

Jak inhaled quickly and coughed.

"Jak, are you okay?" said Tess, her forehead creased with worry.

He sat up on one elbow, rubbed his eyes and gave a slight groan. "Yeah...I think so." The pain had slipped away again, but it had been less than an hour since the previous episode when they got out of the canoe. *It's getting worse,* Jak thought.

"It's the poison. Must be the poison," said Beerta, wringing her hands.

"Is there a doctor in the village?" said Gramps.

"There are some healers, yes, but there is no cure for the poison. Whenever someone gets bitten, the only thing we can do is celebrate his life while he is still alive and then wait for...well, you know." She glanced at Gramps with a troubled expression on her face, and then looked away.

"I'm okay now," said Jak. His head hurt and his stomach felt queasy, but besides that and the insistent ache in his heel, the rest of him felt alright. He shuddered as he sat in the dirt. Nal had said that everyone who was bitten by Scorch went mad and died. For the first time, he considered the possibility that this was happening to him. The words Guardian had given him came to mind. *Yahweh is my protection and my strength.* He hadn't even made it through one day on the journey and it already looked like he was going to keel over. *Does El even care what is happening to me? If he did he would send Guardian with a zinger or even just a few more leaves.* But Jak doubted that would happen. El wouldn't even talk to him, so why would he send Guardian with a zinger? He rubbed his eyes again and sat all the way up. "Let's keep going."

Gramps helped Jak up, and they followed Beerta to a one-story house. They pushed aside a striped brown and green cloth curtain and entered a well-lit room. The walls only reached as high as Gramps's head; above the walls was an open space, with four posts supporting a roof, making it look like they were in a pavilion. A pile of rolled-up fleece blankets lay on a reed mat in the corner next to a large wooden basket, and a brown blanket hung from ceiling to floor in the other corner. In the middle of the room was a stack of thin wood slats and a half-finished basket.

"Excuse the mess," said Beerta, blushing once again. "I'm in the middle of makin' a new harvest basket for the winter fruit." She picked up a brown woven cloth from a small basket on a shelf made out of rocks near the door and handed it to Tess. "For your face and hands, dear. You can go first," She pointed to a wooden bowl by the brown blanket. "Wring it out outside when you are finished and give it to Jak. You two make sure to get behind yer ears. Nal always forgets his ears." She poured water into a basin, and Tess began to wash.

Beerta made Jak sit on a stool while she gently washed the blood and dirt from both of his feet with a second bowl of water. Then she had him stand on a mat. She put her hands on her hips. "You're a bit smaller than Nal, but let's see if I can't find you somethin' clean to wear. Hmmmm," she said, tapping her finger against her chin.

"A bit smaller than Nal" was a nice way to say Jak was small for his age. He kept hoping that maybe when he turned thirteen, he'd finally hit a growth spurt—if he even made it to thirteen.

Beerta thought for a second and then walked over and lifted the lid from the basket in the corner. She slowly pulled out a dark blue tunic and black pants and smelled them.

"These belonged to Enoch," she said. "They've been sitting in that basket for five years now, just collectin' dust and waitin' for him to come and put it on, but he doesn't come." She wiped her eyes with the back of her hand. "You're not much bigger than he was. Try them on." She pointed to the room beyond the brown blanket hanging from the ceiling.

"But I can't," said Jak. "They're special."

"Which is exactly why you should wear them tonight — it's a special occasion. Please." Her eyes pleaded with him.

Jak looked at Gramps; he didn't know what to do. When Gramps nodded in approval, Jak took the tunic and pants from Beerta and went behind the cloth. It was strange to think about wearing a dead boy's clothes, not to mention the fact that the only clothes Jak wore that were this loose-fitting were pajamas. The pants were a little bit short, but other than that, they both fit perfectly.

When he walked out from behind the curtain, Beerta's hands flew to her mouth.

"They're beautiful," she said, wiping tears from her eyes. "You look so handsome."

Jak's ears burned red with embarrassment.

A horn blast like a trumpet sounded in the village.

"It's time," said Beerta, handing him a pair of sandals. "Come."

CHAPTER 30

The Quelcher

Beerta swept past them, and they followed her back the way they had come. The sun had settled in the west, and a handful of orange and pink fingers still held the sky, but the brightest stars had already peeked into the darkening eastern horizon.

The sounds and smells of the roasting grounds reached them before they arrived, a constant buzz of conversation and laughter washed in a buttery corn-on-the-cob aroma wafting through the breeze. A warm glow danced in the darkness and when they got there, Jak could see the reason why. Large torches blazed atop wooden stakes that had been driven in the ground, clearly showing that the crowd had swelled considerably; some sat on mats or blankets on the ground, some sat at tables, and some stood near the fires.

Beerta led them to a mat nearest the huge stack of brush. Nal and Jared were already sitting down, although Nal looked like he could hardly keep his rear end on the mat.

"I'm sorry, Mum. I just had to go and say hello." But when he saw Jak, his expression suddenly went icy. "Why is he wearing Enoch's clothes?"

"Because he needed some and because they fit and because I wanted him to wear them."

"But they're Enoch's!"

"Naloch," growled Jared. "Leave it be. The ceremony's about to begin."

The horn sounded again, this time two long blasts, and the crowd fell silent. A portly man in a dark brown robe and black sash hoisted himself atop a table near the grid of fires.

"Today is the Day of Remembrance!" he shouted.

"Remember the day!" the crowd shouted back.

"In the beginning, El created all and said it was good," said the man.

"And it was good!" echoed the crowd.

"But we craved the knowledge of evil, so we ate the fruit and knew evil."

A chorus of drums boomed ominously.

"The evil now crawls in our blood, and we are doomed to die."

Great, thought Jak. *This is some celebration. Why is it that everywhere I go, people insist on talking about death?*

"Share now the names of those who have gone before us." The speaker spread his arms wide in an invitation to the crowd.

A man on their right stood. "Kittim," he said.

Then a woman on the other side of the crowd rose and said, "Mizraim."

One by one, people stood and spoke a litany of names. Finally, the man who had come in the wagon, the one Beerta had called "the eldest father" stood. "Abel," he said. He was the last, and the crowd remained silent while the horn blasted again and again.

"One blast for each one who's died," Beerta whispered.

When the horn had finished, the original speaker took his place on top of the table and gestured toward someone in the crowd. The eldest father came to the front.

"Eldest father," said the speaker, "today is a special day." He dropped to one knee. "We honor you and celebrate the day of your birth, along with the Day of Remembrance. Tell us the words from Yahweh."

The man stepped onto the table, surveyed the crowd, and then spoke. "Yahweh said to the serpent, 'From now on, you and the woman will be enemies, and your children and hers will be enemies. He will crush your head, and you will strike his heel.'" The man waited a moment for his words to sink in and then continued, "Because of rebellion, the beast now rules this Earth, the scepter now rests in his grip, and he and his kind have struck many heels, but it will not always be so. There is hope! Though the beast may strike us a thousand times, we will crush him!"

"Yes!" the crowd shouted. At the same moment, every fist pounded the tables once.

"Though the beast may strike us ten thousand times, we will crush him!"

"Yes!" The fists pounded again, twice this time.

"And the Earth will belong to humans once again!" the man shouted.

"Yes!" The fists pounded three times.

"Yahweh has decreed it, and so shall it be!"

The crowd erupted in a cheer, stomping their feet so hard that the ground shook. A chorus of pipes and lyres began to play, and the feast began.

Gramps, Jak, and Tess had shared plenty of Thanksgiving and Christmas meals before, but never had they seen so much food. Juicy corn on the cob dipped into melted salted butter or cheese, followed by the black beans that tasted like chicken, steaming pots of mashed potatoes and gravy, corn chowder, bread, peas-in-the-pod, fresh grapes and oranges, and dark apple pie topped with white cream that tasted like ice cream, except that it was much sweeter and softer and didn't melt. The whole time people leaned over their shoulders saying things like, "Won't you have another cob?" or "Certainly you can't be finished so soon," or "That mug is a-cryin' out for more!" Each time, their plates and mugs were filled to overflowing with whatever that person had in his hands.

It would have been wonderful except for the fact that Jak wasn't very hungry. His stomach still felt queasy and the thought of eating made him even more queasy. He didn't want to appear rude though, so he forced some mashed potatoes down his throat, but they felt like giant marbles rolling around in his gut. "What's wrong, Jak?" asked Beerta, "You haven't had a bit of food except for some mushed potato."

"You feeling okay?" asked Gramps.

"Yeah, I'm fine," said Jak, even though he really wasn't. He didn't want anyone to worry about him. "I'm just not that hungry." After that he pushed the food around on his plate to make it look like he was eating, and when he could, he began secretly transferring food from his plate to a spot of ground next to him where Macy sat eying his feast. She was more than happy to dispose of it, most often licking his fingers clean before he even had a chance to drop it on the ground.

After the meal was well under way, Nal stiffly got up from where he was sitting next to Jared and approached Jak and Tess. When she saw him coming, Tess swept her hair back over her shoulders and sat up a little straighter. He sat down cross-legged next to them, looking uncomfortable.

"Sorry 'bout what I said earlier," he finally said, "I mean, 'bout the clothes." His eyes shifted first one direction then another as he spoke.

Jak shook his head. "Don't worry about it. It's not a big deal."

"The thing is, I still think Enoch's alive, but my father won't hear of it. He says we have to move on, but I can't. I won't. It was a shock to see his clothes on you tonight, that's all."

There was an awkward silence, and Jak racked his brain for something to say. His eyes fell on the tremendous pile of brush. When he had seen it from the top of the hill, it didn't seem that large, but up close, it was humongous. It seemed odd that such a large pile of garbage was heaped right next to the roasting grounds.

"Why's that big pile of sticks here?" asked Jak.

Nal turned around and gazed at the pile. "Thorns," he said. "The plan in the beginnin' was that we would plant seeds and grow food without weeds gettin' in the way."

Jak immediately thought of the garden they had planted with Man and Woman.

"That would have been good," Nal continued, "But El cursed the ground, and now it seems like I spend most every day either pickin' weeds out of a garden or gettin' rid of thorns so we can plant one. Thorns and weeds are always growin' where they shouldn't. So we pile them up, and then, on Remembrance Day, we burn them."

"You're going to burn that whole pile?" asked Jak. A smile spread across his face in spite of the roiling in his stomach. He loved fire, and this would be like setting a small building ablaze.

"Yeah, tonight." Nal looked at the western horizon. "The sun has finally dropped all the way, which means the firing ceremony will begin any minute."

Jak's stomach flip-flopped, not because he was queasy, but because he was excited about lighting the stack on fire. He had never lit something this big on fire before and wondered how high the flames would flare.

The horn blasted again, and the laughter and conversation faded to silence.

"It's time," said Nal.

Jak clutched his stomach, this time because he *really* didn't feel so good. A tiny shock wave began to pulse from his heel. Then it hit him full blast—a wave of pain twisting its way through his veins. He dropped to the ground and began shaking. It felt like someone had set him on fire instead of the thorn pile. His breath came in ragged heaves. He heard someone shout his name, again felt the sharp sting of a hand across his face, and Tess's face came into focus.

He groaned. "Can't you find a different way of bringing me back besides slapping me?" said Jak, shaking slightly, but Tess didn't laugh. The pain wasn't as great, but he felt weak and nauseous. The alien presence in his blood was stronger than it had been before, as if the spider had grown and now sat lurking and vigilant for its next chance to take him down.

"This isn't funny, Jak," said Tess, "you're sick."

"Look at his eyes," whispered Nal. "They've just gone bloodshot. And his skin..."

"Shhh," his mother shushed him. "I'll take him home so he can rest."

"No," whispered Jak. "The fire... I want to see the fire."

"You need to rest, Jak" said Gramps.

"No!" said Jak, "I know what's happening to me." His eyes welled up with tears, but he blinked them back. "I know I'm going to go crazy in a day or so and then...and then...well, can't I at least see the fire?"

"The boy is right," said Jared. "Let him stay." Beerta looked as if she did not agree, but she held her tongue.

Jak turned on his side so he could see the pile of thorns. By this time, the eldest father had approached the pile. In his arms lay a lamb. It was then that Jak noticed an alcove nestled into the bottom of the pile of thorns, a hollow spot with a table. Suddenly, a knife glinted in the torchlight. The lamb bleated once and then went limp.

Jak perched a little higher on his elbows, not believing what he had just seen. The man had just killed the lamb, slit its throat wide open! "What is he doing?" asked Jak, trying to keep his body propped up. He still felt weak, but he wanted to see.

"He just killed the lamb," said Nal.

"I know that." Jak took a shallow breath. "But why?"

"Listen."

The man laid the lamb on the table, the blood pooling on the top and dripping over the edges. He lifted his face and his arms to the sky and called out, "Yahweh, from the sweat of our brow we offer to you a sacrifice in our place. We invited death into the world, and death will find us, but for today, place the pure blood of this lamb on us and put our poisoned blood upon him. Blot out the evil in our hearts that we have piled up like this pile of thorns. Burn the poison and the guilt away." He lowered his arms and stepped out of the alcove, leaving the dead lamb on the table.

The entire crowd waited, staring at the pile. No one coughed or sniffled or hardly even blinked. They just waited.

A minute passed, yet not one person stepped forward to light the fire. Quietly, they all just kept staring and waiting.

Jak was just about to ask Nal if perhaps he could light the fire when a small plume of smoke wisped out from the pile. It was followed by an orange tongue of flame that licked up the thorns until a fire fifty feet high roared into the air, consuming the lamb, the table, and the blood. But he had not seen anyone approach the pile. *Who had lit the fire?*

As if to answer his question, the entire crowd whispered, "Yahweh," and fell to their knees, bowing their faces to the ground.

At the same moment, an odd sensation swept through Jak. He tensed, waiting for the twisting pain to shoot up his leg and hit him once again, but it didn't come. Something else came instead: fresh air pushed up through his pores, leaving him feeling like a clean sheet blowing in a warm breeze.

He took a deep breath and sat up, stretching his arms and then his legs.

It was gone, the burning in his veins was gone! Jak had no idea how it had happened, but his head was clear, the marbles in his stomach had disappeared and he felt good again. His foot wasn't strong yet, and his heel still bore the angry red tooth tracks, but he could deal with that. *This is just as mysterious as the fire*, he thought. Evidently Yahweh had lit the fire, but had he done something to make Jak well too? Or was it just a coincidence?

The mountain of thorns began to cave in on itself and a few men walked the perimeter, pushing glowing embers back into the pile. The crowd relaxed and a general air of peace permeated the gathering as they began to return to their places.

Beerta smoothed the wrinkles from her dress and gave a halfhearted smile. "It is finished," she said quietly. "We are clean again." She wiped a tear away from her cheek and turned around. "Now we can get you home, Jak, and take care of you as best as we can until..." She paused. Jak wasn't there. "Jak?" She looked around and saw him seated at the mat, eating a piece of cornbread. "Jak," she said, shocked, "what are you doin'?"

"I'm starving." Jak's mouth was full of cornbread, and a few crumbs flew out of his mouth onto the ground as he spoke.

"But... the poison and the pain. What happened?"

He shrugged his shoulders. "I don't know. As soon as the fire got big, I felt better, and then I got really hungry."

She peered into his eyes. "The bloodshot is gone!" Then she felt his forehead. "And no fever either."

"Your color is better too," said Gramps.

"My color? What color was I before?"

"You were turnin' yellow," said Nal. "On the road to madness."

"Nal!" said Beerta.

"I'm just sayin' what's true!"

"Some things are better left unsaid," replied his mother.

"Strange," said Jared. "I've never heard of anyone getting better after being bitten by the black beast."

"I feel better," said Jak. "Honest, I do. Can I stay by the fire for a while?"

"Well, if you're feeling better you can," said Gramps, "but if you start feeling bad again, you'll have to lie down."

Now that Jak didn't have to worry about going mad, he could concentrate on finding someone in the village who might know something about Man and Woman. After all, there were at least 400 years of history to sort through. He was sure someone would know something.

A shrill whistle pierced the air.

"The musicians are ready," said Nal. "C'mon." He led Jak and Tess to the largest tree in the village, an old pine on the edge of the roasting grounds. The crowd had gathered under the tree around a stage upon which stood a troupe of musicians with drums and shells that hung like chimes.

The drums started first with a heavy thump, followed by the light and airy clattering of the shells. A tall, thin man with a pointy red beard began to sing...

The Promise is made,
The Promise is true.
Someday the Quelcher will come down to you.
And when that day comes,
then the serpent will die.
Crushed by the heel so the scepter can rise.

Let it rise, let it rise,
Rise like the sun at the serpent's demise.
So keep your eyes peeled and your ears open wide.
'Cause someday among us the Quelcher will rise.
Let him rise.

When the song was finished, the musicians made a sweeping bow, and the crowd burst into applause. The band began playing music again, and a space cleared in the field for dancing.

"What's a Quelcher?" asked Jak.

"Yeah," said Tess. "What was that all about?"

"Well," said Nal, "after the first man and woman ate the fruit, the serpent was in trouble for lyin' to the woman, so El made a promise. He said the serpent would strike the woman's child in the heel, but the child would crush the serpent's head. That's part of Remembrance Day, remembering that the Quelcher will come someday."

"So it's a person?" said Jak.

"Yep. He's the one who will come and crush the serpent's head."

"But first he'll get bitten in the heel?"

Nal nodded.

This sounded very familiar to Jak, but he had other things on his mind, so he pushed it aside.

"Nal, the eldest father, the guy with the birthday," said Jak, "can I talk to him?"

"I s'pose you could. How come?"

"Because I'm wondering what happened to a couple of people. I want to see if he's ever heard of them or maybe even met them."

"He'd be the right one to ask," said Nal. "He knows everyone both in this village and in the villages beyond."

"How old is he anyway?" said Tess.

"Today is his 500th birthday."

Jak just about fell over. "Are you serious? He's five hundred years old?"

"Of course," said Nal. "What's so strange about that?"

"Because where we come from, hardly anybody even makes it to one hundred years." Jak ran through the math in his head. Jared had said Scorch had been stealing children for almost 400 years, yet this man was 500 years old. He must've known Man and Woman. "When was he born?"

"When was he born?" Nal gave Jak a funny look. "In the beginning."

CHAPTER 31

Eve's Brainstorm

"What?" said Jak and Tess at the same time, their eyes popping wide in amazement. They only knew one person who had a birthday "in the beginning."

"Are you saying," said Jak, still reeling from the shock, "that the eldest father is Man, the very first man El made?"

"Of course he's the first man El made. His name is Adam."

"He's the one we wanted to find!" said Jak. He could hardly stand still. "Him and Woman. The woman with him in the wagon was Woman, right?"

"No, it was a chimpanzee." Nal rolled his eyes. "Of course it was a woman. Her name is Eve, and she was the first woman."

Jak and Tess couldn't believe it. After 500 years, Man and Woman were still alive.

"Can we go talk with him, right now?" said Jak.

"I'll go ask," said Nal. He ran over to where Beerta was in an animated conversation with a gaggle of women about the proper way to cook skunk weed.

"Do you think they'll remember us?" said Jak.

"I don't know," said Tess. "Five hundred years is a long time."

Nal ran back. "Yeah, she said it's fine, as long as I keep an eye on you, Jak."

They couldn't find Gramps, he was lost somewhere in the crowd, so just the three of them walked over to the table where Adam and Eve were seated. It was adorned with green, purple, and tan grasses, woven into square patterns and fastened around the table so that it covered the top and hung down over the sides. Next to Adam and Eve sat a man with a strong face and a light brown beard. Next to him was a woman with long dark brown hair pulled back into a wide ponytail, and two young children. On the other side of the table sat a sour-looking man with thick black eyebrows furrowed into a frown that matched his mouth. He sat alone.

As they approached the table, Adam saw them coming and his face lit up. "Nal!" Adam stood and slapped Nal on the shoulder. "You 'er becomin' a strappin' young man. You must've grown a foot since I saw you last."

"Hullo, Great Father." Nal couldn't hide his embarrassment or his pleasure at the comments. He shifted uncomfortably from foot to foot. "I have some guests from another village with me. They want to meet you."

Adam studied Jak's and Tess's faces while Nal talked. He concentrated hard, and then a smile cracked his face. "Jak and Tess!" he said, slapping them on the shoulder as well. "You made it! After five hundred years, you made it to a Remembrance Day. How appropriate since you were there in the beginning as well. It is good for you to remember. Eve..." He turned and touched his wife on the shoulder. She broke away from feeding one of the children, her hands covered with fragments of corn.

"Eve, this is—"

"Tess and Jak! It has been many years!" Her hazel-green eyes flashed with excitement, and she jumped up, slapping away the kernels of corn from her fingers, and hugged them both. She hadn't changed much. Her hair was still raven black with just a few streaks of gray to show her age, but her face was still as smooth and unwrinkled as the day they met her. "It seems like only yesterday we were together in the garden. How are you?"

She has that right, thought Jak, *just like yesterday.* But so much had happened in such a short time that it was hard to know where to begin.

Nal stood open-mouthed and dumbfounded. "You mean you know Great Father and Great Mother?"

Jak nodded. "Yep. We were together in the garden. After all the bad stuff happened, El sent us on a journey, but it's only taken us a couple of days to get here instead of five hundred years."

"Really?" said Adam. "How did he do that?"

"We don't know," said Jak. "He gave us a canoe and told us the follow the Scarlet Thread, so we did, and we ended up here."

"Ah, the Thread," said Adam wistfully. "You are following the Thread."

Jak nodded. "We paddled upstream above Split Falls till we came to a bigger river that forked into another river, and we followed that one down here."

"You have discovered the Tigris. It is a good river—full of fish who love to play tag with the otters," said Adam.

"But it is also dangerous," said the sour-looking man next to Adam. His black whiskers grew in uneven patches across his face. A birthmark the size of a quarter peeked through one of the holes in his right cheek, the kind of mark that if you stared at it long enough, it took the shape of a duck or a half-eaten candy bar. "That is where the black one always hides."

Adam lifted his eyebrows and nodded his head slowly. "True enough, Cain, but let's not talk about that right now."

Cain shook his head. "I'm just saying." He eyed Jak and Tess and then pressed a steaming mug to his lips.

"This is our oldest son Cain," said Adam, waving toward Cain. Then he waved his hand to the people sitting next to Eve. "And this is our son Seth and his wife Talia and their current young 'uns, Uriel and Yaresh. Sit and join us. There is plenty of room." He motioned for Cain to move over.

Cain grunted and grudgingly shifted to the end of the seat.

Jak, Tess, and Nal joined him.

"Let's see... where were we?," said Adam. "Yes, the Tigris River and fish and otters."

This was the first time they had seen Man and Woman with real clothes on. Adam wore a pair of loose-fitting blue breeches made of soft leather and a brown tunic wrapped with a wide leather belt, similar to what Guardian had worn. Eve wore a long tan dress with silver beads sewn in a starburst pattern on the chest and along the hems of the sleeves.

"I like your pants," said Tess.

"Ah, yes, pants," said Adam. "I took your original design and made a few modifications. Turned out quite nice, I think. Eve went a different route and made something she calls dressing."

"Dress, dear, not dressing," said Eve. "Dressing is what we put on lettuce and other leaves of the garden."

"Ah, yes, dress. Got it."

Jak's curiosity burned inside him, and he couldn't wait anymore. "What happened?" he blurted out. "Why did you eat the black cherries when El warned you not to."

Tess kicked Jak under the table and gave him a what-a-stupid-thing-to-ask-you-idiot look, but Jak didn't care. He had to know what happened the last day in the garden.

Adam nodded his head slow and long. "Ahhh, that is the question I have been asking myself for five hundred years. It is the Day of Remembrance, so let us remember." He closed his eyes and took a deep breath. "It's like this, Jak, and I'm not blaming anyone." He shot a guilty glance at Eve. "Truly, I've no one to blame but myself. I am only telling the facts. Remember the red leviathan?"

Jak and Tess nodded. "Of course."

"Did you know he could talk?"

"Jared said something about that," said Jak, "but I never heard him talk."

"He told Eve that El had given him the gift of speech that last night we watched the stars together, and that was why El came so late."

"He told me," said Eve, taking over the story, "that the reason El gave us the instruction about the Tree of Knowing was because he was stingy and did not want us to be like him. He said we would not die if we ate the fruit, but it instead would make us wise and we would know about evil, just like El. I became angry that El would hide such a good thing from us, so I plucked a black cherry and tasted it. It was even more powerful than the zingers, which made me believe even more that what Red said was true. So I picked another and took it to Adam."

"And I desperately wanted to know about evil," said Adam, "so I ate it too. That's when it all changed. The garden went quiet and cold, and suddenly we understood what you meant about being ashamed. We pulled our pants from our necks to our hips and ran into the woods to gather more leaves, but more importantly, to hide from El. We did not want him to see us like that.

"We hid for most of the day until the cool of the evening, when El normally came to see us. We heard him walking in the garden, and he called for us, wondering where we were, so I answered from our hiding place. I told him we were hiding because we were naked. And then he appeared as we had never seen him before. He was no longer a brilliant, radiant light. This time, he was more like a shiny man wrapped in rags. He said, 'Who told you you are naked? Did you eat from the tree I told you not to eat from?'"

"And then Adam blamed it on me," said Eve.

Adam rubbed his whiskers and stared at the ground.

"But I was no better," Eve continued. "I blamed it on Red."

"Then El doled out the curses," said Adam, looking up again.

"You mean the thorns?" said Jak.

"Yes. He cursed the ground, so instead of growing the seeds he gave us, it would grow thorns and thistles. But He also cursed Eve so that bearing children would be painful. It was supposed to be a blessed event, the bringing in of a new human, but now it is accompanied by agony."

"But what happened to Red and Scorch?" said Jak. "When we got there, Eve was crying, and then Red and Scorch both dropped to the ground. We watched Scorch change. Her legs disappeared, her mane scraped off, and her teeth turned into knives. What happened?"

"It is the curse of the serpent," said Adam quietly. "That is the name I have given him now that he has changed — serpent. We did not know at the time, but we know now that Red was no longer himself that day. He was something more. He had invited something into himself that fused with him, so he became something altogether different. We had desired to know evil, and after we ate of the fruit, we both knew evil in our hearts and saw it standing right before us. Red had become evil. We no longer ruled the Earth. Our rebellion handed the scepter to a new master."

"Lucifer," whispered Jak. He did not want to believe it, but he could not deny the truth. Their friend had betrayed them.

"Wait a second," said Tess. "Are you saying Red and Lucifer are the same?"

Adam nodded his head. "Yes."

"But that's impossible!" said Tess. "He's just a leviathan."

"Tess, remember what I told you about that morning?" said Jak. "Scorch and Red came through our camp, and he ignored me. I told you something was different about him."

"Very different," said Eve.

219

Adam continued, "El told Red that because he had deceived Eve, he would be cursed above all other animals. He would crawl on his belly forever, eating dust; and humans and serpents would hate one another."

"But what about Scorch?" said Jak. "She didn't do anything."

"They are of the same race and share the same fate," said Adam. "I am sorry, but evil has wrecked her too."

"But it isn't fair!" said Jak.

"I know," said Adam. He closed his eyes and rubbed his temple. "I failed as the ruler. It was up to me to rule wisely, and I failed. Every day for five hundred years, I have wished I could go back and throw the cherry into the woods or crush it beneath my toes, but I can't. Even though El had warned that death would follow, I insisted that my way was better than El's way, and now all of creation pays for my arrogance. Evil has devoured us." He looked away, bit his lip, and then focused on Jak once more. "I cannot do any more than to say I am sorry, and I am. I am truly sorry."

"But why did El curse the ground and curse birth too?"

"I think to remind us that we depend on him for everything. Our arrogance, now that we have the knowledge of good and evil, is so strong that it drives us away from El. He reminds us daily that food and life are gifts from his hand."

"It would have been a lot better if he had just written us a note," said Nal.

Adam smiled. "But he did give us something else, something good. He gave us the Promise. That's what Remembrance Day is for. In the midst of placing the curse on the red leviathan, El said, "From now on, you and the woman will be enemies, and your children and hers will be enemies. He will crush your head, and you will strike his heel.""

Jak's mind went back to the song the musicians had just sung. "You mean that thing about the Quelcher?"

Adam nodded. "It is the first thing I think of when I wake up and the last thing on my mind when I go to bed. It is a promise for the future, that someday someone will crush the serpent's head. Rule of the Earth will be given back to humans, and we will live in freedom and paradise alongside Yahweh once again."

"But how do you know it will happen?" said Jak. "I mean, El kicked you out of the garden, put a curse on the Earth, and makes you pull thorns in order to live. You can't even see him or talk with him. Remember how it was in the garden? He wouldn't even let us come near him."

"It will happen because Yahweh has decreed it," said Adam staunchly. "And so it shall come to pass."

"Part of it came to pass already," said Tess. "Scorch bit Jak in the heel in the garden and almost tore his foot off."

Eve's face turned gray. "You were bitten? Let me see."

Jak hoisted his leg onto a stool and pulled his pant leg up to his knee. It looked different than it had earlier in the day. The ankle bone was still soft, and the scarred tracks still dug deep into his skin, but instead of raw and red, the skin was white and firm. *That's interesting*, thought Jak. *Must've changed after the fire.*

Eve drew in a sharp breath and probed gently with her fingers. "Oh, Jak."

"The poison looked like it would claim 'im tonight, Great Mother," said Nal, "His eyes were bloodshot and his skin had yellowed, but he felt better after the fire."

"It is a blessing from El," she said. "No one has been bitten by the Black Serpent without going mad." She paused. "Adam, do you think it could be?"

Adam stroked his beard. "Perhaps, but he is so young. How could he be the one?"

"The one what?" said Jak, completely clueless.

"Since when does age matter?" said Eve, straightening and flashing an intense stare at Adam. "El handed creation over to us when we were but hours old. I am merely saying that it fits the Promise, and that Jak could be the one."

"The one what?!" repeated Jak.

"The Quelcher," said Adam, "the one who crushes the head of the serpent."

CHAPTER 32

The Thing about Cain

Jak was flabbergasted at the suggestion. He was only twelve, and the last time Scorch saw him, she almost ripped his foot off. Besides, even if he could crush her head, he wouldn't. "I don't think I'm any kind of Quelcher," he said.

"Then how did you heal so quickly?" said Eve.

"Back in the garden, Guardian gave me..." Jak was going to say "some leaves from the tree," but something else popped into his mind instead. "...some cards."

In all the excitement of finding Man and Woman and the pain of the poison, Jak had totally forgotten about the cards Guardian had given him. Suddenly, it became very important to get the cards out. He couldn't remember what the people looked like on the two cards with the red line. Maybe one of them was here and he would miss him if he wasn't careful. He rummaged in his bag.

"Perhaps you are not the Quelcher, but I cannot help but hope," said Adam. "Every time a report comes back that another has been bitten in the heel, I wonder if this is the one. I cannot uninvite death or evil into the Earth, but the serpents can die, and then we can rule the Earth once again."

Jak pulled the cards out. "Here... look at this." He spoke so loudly that people at the neighboring table stopped talking and looked at him.

Tess kicked him under the table again and gave him another shut-up-you-idiot look.

Jak bit his tongue, feeling foolish for the outburst, but Adam had to know about death and the book and the cards. He waited till the conversations around them resumed and then casually leaned in toward the middle of the table.

Adam and the others leaned in as well.

"I have something," Jak whispered, showing them the cards. "Guardian gave them to me. He said they'll give the book special power..."

Tess kicked him under the table again and gave him the same look, but he ignored her, although he did glance around to make sure no one suspicious was eavesdropping and lowered his voice even further. "...power to kill death and evil and get rid of Lucifer all at the same time. Even the people who have died will come back to life."

Nal, Adam and Eve stared at him, dumbfounded. "The book you had in the garden?" asked Adam.

Jak nodded. "But first, I have to follow the Scarlet Thread and find some of the people on the cards." He flipped through the deck until he found the man with the crow's feet around his eyes. "Do you know this man?"

Adam held the card up to the torchlight and shook his head. "No. Never seen 'im before"

"How about..." Jak found the second card, and was just about to give it to Adam when he stopped and held it up to Adam's face. They matched.

"It's you!" said Jak. "You're one of the people I'm supposed to find."

"Let me see that," said Tess. She took the card from Jak and compared it to Adam. "You're right! It is him."

"That's strange. I have seen many travelers following the Thread, but I have never seen any cards, certainly none with my face on them. How can my face be in two places at the same time?"

"It's not really you, just a picture of you," said Jak, "like a drawing."

Adam held out his hand. "Can I see it?"

Tess passed the card to Adam. As soon as his fingers touched it, the card popped and sputtered a shower of blue sparks. Adam dropped the card on the table, shaking the smoke from his fingers.

"Are you okay?" said Jak.

"Yes, I'm fine—just surprised is all."

"I'm sorry. I didn't know it was going to do that."

Adam stooped over the card without picking it up again. Eve and Seth crowded next to him to get a look too. "That's definitely you, Father," said Seth.

Adam fingered the end of his nose. "Is my nose really that big?"

"Your nose is fine," said Eve.

"My name and the Promise are here too."

"They are?" said Jak. He and Tess craned their necks to look at the card, both curious to see what the first card would say that could infuse power into the book. Sure enough, at the bottom of the card, words had formed in the black box.

Adam

El said to the serpent, "From now on, you and the woman will be enemies, and your children and hers will be enemies. He will crush your head, and you will strike his heel."

"So that's it?" said Tess, "That's what we came here for? A repeat of what we already heard?" She plunked back down in her seat and crossed her arms with a frown pasted to her mouth.

"What were you expectin'?" said Adam.

"Oh, I don't know, maybe a spell or a magic charm," said Tess.

"Girl," said Adam, "spells and charms are the traps of the evil one. He promises power and freedom through magic, but in the end, you belong to him." He glanced at Cain.

Cain wouldn't meet his gaze but looked back down to the ground.

"Forget it. It doesn't matter," said Tess.

Eve handed the card back to Jak.

He slipped it back into the little gunnysack with the other cards but then remembered that he was supposed to put the card in the book. He opened to the cloth page and slipped Adam's card in the first slot.

Immediately, a red thread began to sew itself across the top of the pocket.

Jak pulled his fingers back and watched till it was done. He could still see Adam's face peering through the cloth, but the card was now securely fastened in the page. Suddenly it occurred to him that there were three pockets in the book but only two Thread cards. Had he missed one?

"So that's the book that'll get rid of Lucifer, huh?" Cain hunched over the table and peered at the open book. His eyes looked hungry.

"Yeah," said Jak. "That's it."

He reached for the book, but Jak slapped it shut and put it back in the book bag before he could touch it. Jak wasn't too excited about passing the book around for show-n-tell.

Cain leaned back. "Better keep a good eye on it. Lucifer'd pay dearly to have a weapon like that."

I'm sure he would, thought Jak.

A pair of hands fastened onto Jak's shoulders and squeezed. He tried to stand up, but the hands were strong and kept him in his seat.

"Man and Woman," said a voice hovering over Jak's head.

Jak relaxed – it was Gramps.

"Happy birthday! Five hundred years is quite a milestone."

"Clarence, is that you? Adam stood and pumped Gramps's hand. "It is you! It is good to see you, my friend."

"I see you've got a touch of gray now," said Gramps. He pointed to Adam's hair.

"And you don't," said Adam, "What happened?"

"Fruit from the Tree of Life. I ate the whole thing that last evening we were together and woke up in the morning like this. I haven't felt this good in forty years. Are you folks going to be around for a while?"

"Yes, for two more days. Remembrance Day Celebrations always last three days," said Adam.

"Good, because I've got to steal these three away for a bit."

Jak had no idea why Gramps needed them, but he led the three of them away from the table in an easygoing brisk trot. Anyone watching them would not have known that anything was wrong, but Jak knew from the way Gramps's jaw was set that something was not right.

As soon as they got out of earshot of Adam's table, Tess exploded. "What were you doing back there, telling everybody and their brother about the cards and what we're doing? Don't you know when to keep your mouth shut?"

"It was just Man and Woman. We can trust them," he said.

226

"Is it really true, the things you said back there about getting rid of death and evil and Lucifer?" asked Nal. Jak nodded, but he was distracted by Tess's question.

"She's right, Jak. Do you know who else was at the table?" said Gramps.

"Well, Seth and his family...and Cain." Jak's face grew hot, and he felt sweat ringing the armpits of his shirt.

"Yes, Cain. He's the one I'm concerned about. You didn't tell him about the book, did you?"

If a big enough rock had been there, Jak would have crawled underneath it.

"Yes," said Tess. "He blabbed all about the book and the cards and what El told us to do, then he grabbed Cain's hand and asked him to come with us!"

"I did not!" said Jak.

"Maybe not, but it wouldn't have surprised me if you had! You shouldn't have told Cain anything about us at all. He gives me the creeps."

Gramps ran his hand over his forehead and down his face, smearing it into a cascade of wrinkles. "Jak, do you know who Cain is?"

"Yes. He's Adam and Eve's oldest son."

"They used to have another son named Abel," said Gramps.

That name rang a bell. Adam had stood and said it during the ceremony.

"Abel's dead, isn't he?" said Jak.

Nal nodded. "Yep, by Cain's hand." By this time, they had arrived back at Jared and Beerta's blanket.

Gramps motioned to Jared. "Jared, tell him about Cain."

"You didn't tell 'im anythin', did ya, Jak?" said Jared. "Your grandfather told us a bit about the book."

"Maybe a little," said Jak sheepishly.

Jared shook his head. "That can only come to no good. Cain is a wanderer, shunned by El from his own people because he kilt his brother Abel in a fit of rage."

"Why would he kill his brother?" asked Jak .

"Because El accepted Abel's offering but not Cain's. Yahweh wouldn't stand for Cain's attitude, so Cain had a temper tantrum, and a fit of pride and jealousy ended in a pool of blood. He used to be a fine farmer, but after the murder, El wouldn't let anything grow from Cain's labor. He forced Cain to wander the Earth and forage from the land. Adam lost track of him for a long time, till he showed up a few years ago at Remembrance Day, a sour-puss if I ever saw one. Took a lot of gall to show up here again. Most say he should've stayed away."

Beerta walked up and saw the expression on Jak's face. "What kinda stories are you fillin' the boy's head with now, Jared, son of Mahalalel? You aren't talking about the beast again, are you?"

"No. We're talkin' 'bout Mr. Sour-puss o'er there."

Beerta followed his gaze to Cain. "You best stay away from him, Jak. It could be nothin' but trouble if he finds out what you're up to."

Jak's cheeks flushed hot once again.

"Too late for that," said Tess. "Blabbermouth already told him everything."

"I didn't know," Jak stammered. "He was with Adam and Eve, and nobody told me I shouldn't have said anything."

"Well, can't be helped then," said Beerta, pursing her lips. "You'll have to keep a sharp eye out though. Some say Cain's with the Beelzin now—that he hooked up with 'em while he was wanderin' in the east. Other's say the black one bit him in a fight, but the poison is just takin' a long time to spread through his body."

"I'd say it landed in his face," said Nal.

"He keeps to himself," said Beerta, ignoring Nal's interruption, "so no one really knows what's goin' on inside his head."

"The Beelzin are what worries me," said Gramps.

"What's a Beelzin anyway?" said Jak. The first thing that came to his mind was a fat little yellow car with a rounded top, but he knew that wasn't right.

"The Beelzin are men and women devoted to serving Beelzebub," said Jared, revulsion spilling from every word. "Each is marked with an almost invisible brand on the wrist called a silver tongue, a snake circled around bitin' his own tail, the sign of Beelz. Some also 'ave a silver band cast in the same image embedded above the elbow. It's supposed to remind 'im that Beelz hears all, sees all, and knows all."

"Which is an out-and-out lie," said Beerta. "That snake can't hear, see, or know any more than the rest of us."

"So what do I do now?" said Jak. He wished the Scarlet Thread could take him backwards in time, too, so he could undo the past half-hour.

"What exactly did you tell Cain, son?" said Gramps.

"That El sent me on a journey with the book and I had to find the right people on the cards to give the book the power to get rid of Lucifer, death, and evil." Jak swallowed hard and wished the ground would open and swallow him up. "And there's one more thing."

"What is it, Jak?" asked Beerta in as comforting a voice as she could muster.

"He... he saw... I accidentally let him see the book. I... I didn't know."

No one said anything for a minute and only fidgeted as they thought about Jak's dilemma.

"Well," said Gramps, stroking his beard, "not much more you can add to that. You told him pretty much everything."

"We're all tired," said Beerta. "How 'bout if we sleep on it? There's nothing we can do about it tonight anyway."

Beerta and Nal led them through the village back to their house, where they laid out three shallow mattresses and blankets in the same room where Jak had put on Enoch's clothes.

Tess suddenly made a face and smacked her lips. "Do you realize we haven't brushed our teeth once since we've been gone?"

She was right. They hadn't needed to brush their teeth in the garden; their breath had always felt fresh. But now it felt like Jak's teeth were coated in mold.

"Oh dear," said Beerta. "Use this." She tore a small chunk from a dry white sponge and handed it to Tess. "It's the best you can do for cleaning yer teeth."

Tess hesitantly took the sponge and scraped it against her front teeth. "Wha' ith it?" she asked.

"Lamb's wool," said Beerta, handing her a cup of water.

"Ewww," Tess groaned, but she didn't stop until she had cleaned all her teeth. Then she grabbed the cup and ran outside. Jak and Gramps did the same thing with two other lamb's wool toothbrushes. When they had finally all settled in for the night, Beerta blew out an oil lamp that hung on the wall. "Goodnight. Sleep well." Then she swept quietly from the room back through the curtain.

Jak carefully lifted the book out of the bag and opened the cover. The words on the card glowed a faint red, and he read them again.

*El said to the serpent, "From now on, you and the woman will
be enemies, and your children and hers will be enemies. He will
crush your head, and you will strike his heel."*

It was true he had survived being struck in the heel, but there was no way
he could be the Quelcher, unless that was part of El's plan to get rid of death.
He wished El would show up and talk with him. He was tired of guessing
what El was up to. All he knew for sure was what El wrote on the first plaque:

The dead will live again, and the living will never die.

If he was ever going to see his grandmother again, he had to keep following
the Scarlet Thread.

Charred stumps were all that remained of the grove of cherry trees next
to the sea. Lucifer lazed in the cool of the water, gazing up at the stumps
and soaking up the chill of the sea. He was alone. The rest of the Lights
were creeping around the world of men, just as Lucifer had ordered, looking for opportunities to quietly twist human minds and pit them against
each other.

He did not like to pull back from perverting El's creation, but the body
of the leviathan required rest, and so he soaked in the sea. He was thinking
about a name he had heard a boy scream at him just before his human recruits
had rammed a lance through his heart. Beelzebub was the name, and Lucifer
liked it. It smacked of authority and fear and power, everything he craved.
Drool dripped down his fangs and sizzled into the water as he turned the
name over in his mind. He would still use Lucifer, of course, as his official
name, but Beelz would be a fitting second name for whenever he presided in
the beast's body.

He had grown accustomed to the unavoidable extra S whenever he
spoke through the beast's mouth and had discovered that it caused a
pleasing extra measure of discomfort whenever he spoke to the human
recruits. And if he ever needed to speak with authority and clarity, he

only needed to revert to his light form. All in all, his rule of the Earth was going well.

A pair of Lights, one putrescent orange and the other vomit yellow, careened across the sky and plowed into the water next to him, splashing water all over his face. "Most beautiful and beneficent Lucifer," one said.

He hated being disturbed during his afternoon nap and reluctantly opened one eye.

"What isss it?" he snapped. "You ssshould be out twissting humanss."

The tall vomit yellow Light pulled his dripping self together and spoke in a high, whiny voice that sounded like a whale was lying on top of him, "The boy—the man-child with the girl and the old man in the garden, the ones you told us about. Remember the boy?"

"Of courssse I remember. And I alssso remember you said you lossssst him, at Ssssplit Fallssss, five hundred yearsss ago."

"Not our fault," whined the Light, digging a hole in the sand with a spidery hand. "I have already told you that. That nasty Thread took him away. He had disappeared into a different time when we rounded the bend."

Red snorted a purple flame the size of a pencil out of his nose, expressing his disapproval once again. The search for the three other humans had proven futile, so they had had to remain content tormenting Man and Woman until they bore sons and daughters, who, in turn, bore sons and daughters. That's when the torment began to be satisfying. Prodding the humans into rage and deceit was like pushing a rock down a hill. Once they got going, they kept rolling on their own.

It wasn't long after that he noticed the Thread. At first, he thought the shimmering in the air was just a trick of the light or the leviathan's weak eyes, but it didn't go away, and, occasionally, it turned a deep shade of red for a moment before shimmering back to almost nothing.

Then came the Thread followers, the time-traveling explorers, both men and women, all carrying the wretched book they had received from the enemy. Supposedly they had been promised life forever if they stayed on the trail of this scarlet thread. Beelz didn't know how the enemy could promise life without death, for humans were destined to die. That fate was sealed for them the moment Man and Woman had eaten the black cherries.

But regardless of whether or not the enemy could truly offer life forever, the Thread followers were the special targets for torment. How many of them he had deceived into handing the book over to him and abandoning the path? Plenty. *Fools*, he thought, laughing to himself.

"Lucifer!" said the yellow Light.

Beelz's attention snapped back to the present. "What about the boy?" he growled.

"He's one of them," the Light spat out. "He is one of the Thread people." The orange pile of goo belched, and a brown cloud floated up Beelz's nostrils.

Beelz flared his nostrils, and his eyes narrowed to a slit. "What of it? You have ten sssecondsss."

The orange Light smacked at a bug on the surface of the shallows, splashing water into Beelz's face again while the yellow Light nervously continued. "Today is the human feast, that thing they call Remembrance Day. A Beelzin, one of Cain's boys, relayed a message about the boy. Appears he's got some sort of book."

"They all have booksss, you idiot."

"I know, but this one's different."

The orange pile of goo belched again, and Beelz spit out a plume of bright red flame, scorching him to a pile of ashes that wriggled toward the beach.

"How different?"

"The servant, the one with the four faces, told him, he did, to follow the Thread, and at the end, the book would.. it would... " The yellow Light stopped talking and scrunched down, sending a tiny wave into the sea.

"OUT WITH IT!" rasped Beelz.

"Alright, alright!" He scrunched down even further and blurted out the rest. "The book will get rid of death and evil and, and YOU — all three together! It will overpower us all! There. Now I have said it." When he had finished, he stayed still, as if expecting to be torched like the other Light, but Beelz sat transfixed, drool dribbling down his neck and mumbling to himself.

"But that iss not posssssible! That isss not the deal. When I ssstole the Earth from Man, it became mine forever. There issss no way to undo what hasss been done." *But what if there is?* he thought in horror. The news sat in his stomach like a pile of marsh worms. He suddenly arched up, the water rippling down his neck, and roared long and loud.

Lights began littering the horizon, a horde of giant gnats swarming from every direction, until the beach was flooded with dripping and oozing pillars of every shape and color.

Beelz squirmed and belched a plume of orange fire. "Hurry up! Every moment you ssslimeballsss wassste is lossst forever."

When they had finally assembled, Beelz ratcheted his mouth open to an unnatural size. A brilliant yellow beam shot into the sky and coalesced into beautiful columns of yellow flames.

"Lucifer! Lucifer!" the Lights roared as they bowed to the sand.

Lucifer gave a blinding flash, and the roar stopped. He twitched once and then bellowed, "FIND THE BOY!"

"What boy?" shouted a purplish Light.

"Show them," Lucifer instructed the putrescent yellow Light.

The Light morphed into a likeness of the boy.

A puke brown Light flickered and dripped a large splotch of goo on the ground. "Can we try to rip his tongue out when we do?"

"NO!" Lucifer's light pulsed. "If any limbs end up missing, you will be sucked dry and left to rot on the beach. You will immediately relay a message to me once he is found. He must be twisted and deceived as the Man and Woman until he willingly gives the book to me. Now get out and hunt him down. NOW!"

A fat green Light zoomed past Lucifer.

Lucifer slopped out a tentacle and caught him by the tail. "You!"

The green Light ripped his tail away and glared at Lucifer irritably. "What?"

Lucifer flared at him briefly. "Go to Cain in East Eden and personally instruct him to track the boy. He may be able to do what we cannot, that is, to follow him through time. He is to send word when he finds him so that I may devise a proper trap."

The green Light blinked once and slipped away.

CHAPTER 33
The Man with the Missing Finger

Jak jerked awake. Sweat soaked his shirt, and his blood was racing. He had been dreaming about Cain. In the dream, the murderer's hands were wrapped around Jak's throat, and he was dangling him over Split Falls, demanding that Jak give him the book and go home.

On his bed, Jak's fingers felt for the hard rectangle bound in his shirt; it was still there. He sighed in relief and sat up. He had to get some fresh air. Everyone else was still sleeping, so he tiptoed around the prone figures spread out on the mats to the doorway and stepped into the street.

The Thread still hung over the village like a fat floating electric wire, the end fluttering slightly in the breeze over the river, but it wasn't moving . Jak didn't know where to go, so he arbitrarily chose to go to the right. His t-shirt clung to his body like a wet fish, so he slipped the book out and pulled the shirt away to give his chest some air as he walked.

The sky was gelling into a thick red horizon, which cast a pinkish hue to the cobblestone street. The street was narrow and dipped down slightly as it zigged and zagged through the village. A handful of women in bright blues, oranges, and yellows joined Jak on the road with jars in their hands. Some had baskets on their heads full of fruit, bread, cloth, and other items. Most of them stopped at the market in the plaza and began setting up their wares, but a few continued down the street.

After about ten minutes, the road slipped out of the village, down a short flight of steps, and onto the riverbank. There, a group of women stood on the bank, gathering water, washing clothes, and chatting about the news of the morning. One woman stood above the rest at the top of the steps on a small platform, doing nothing except watching the water and holding a bell in her hands.

A light fog hung over the river, slowly steaming away as the sun's rays burned through it. Jak turned away from the women, headed upstream to a large rock warming itself in the sun, and sat down with the book on his lap. The sun felt good on his skin. He closed his eyes and soaked the sunshine into his face. The only darkness was inside his head.

What am I going to do about Cain? He kicked himself once more about giving the information so freely the night before. *What if Cain really is a Beelzin and ran to his Beelzin friends right after dinner, or worse, straight to Beelz?* If he had, then Jak knew right at that moment they were probably planning a way to get the book away from him, or something worse. "Something worse" had always meant him being killed, but the more he thought about it, he realized that the result would be the same no matter what happened: the book would not get to Megiddo, which meant that when he died he would stay dead and so would everybody else.

He also worried about the poison coursing through him. He felt fine this morning, but he wondered how long that would last. *The rest of the day? Two days?* Something had knocked it down last night, but it was still there, waiting.

His hands grew warmer and warmer in the sun until they became so hot it felt like he was holding a branding iron. He threw the book into his lap and opened his eyes. The book was smoking.

There were no flames—just fat billows of smoke puffing up. He danced the book on his lap, not sure what to do, but before he could decide, a strong gust of wind sprang up out of nowhere and blew the cover of the book open to the chapters he hadn't been able to read back at the bridge.

He hesitated. He had promised Tess he wouldn't open the book. Technically, though, he had kept his promise; the wind had opened the book, not him. He let his eyes glance at the pages.

It wasn't long before he realized it was the story of Adam and Eve. He saw the Promise that had appeared on the card and kept reading, the wind flipping the pages until Adam and Eve were kicked out of the garden, all the way through Cain killing Abel in a field. Then another gust of wind kicked up, and the pages rippled open to the middle of the book. One of the paragraphs glowed red, just like the Thread.

> Death had its hands around my throat;
> the terrors of the grave overtook me.
> I saw only trouble and sorrow.
> Then I called on the name of Yahweh:
> 'Please, Yahweh, save me!' How kind Yahweh is.

He thought about Cain's hands around his throat in his dream, and that same awful feeling wracked his insides. "The terrors of the grave" was a good way to put it.

Just as he was mulling over what he read, he heard a rustle in the reeds behind him. He slammed the book shut and whirled around, terrified that the Beelzin had arrived.

"Jak," said Nal, "I've been lookin' all over for you. What're you doin'?"

Jak breathed a sigh of relief. "You scared me. I needed some fresh air, so I went for a walk."

Nal jumped onto the rock next to him. "Gutsy comin' down to the river by yerself. Do you know why the woman on that platform holds the bell?"

"No."

Nal skipped a rock across the river. "She's watchin' for the Black Serpent, the one you called Scorch."

"What?" Jak sat up straight and pulled his legs up to the top of the rock.

"She's been seen 'ere before," said Nal. "When she took Enoch, it was just upriver a ways. If the bell lady sees any sign of the serpent, she'll ring the bell, and everyone'll clear out of the water. No one's ever rung it before, but still they watch, just in case."

That made Jak feel a little better, and he relaxed his legs again.

"I couldn't stop thinkin' 'bout what you said last night," said Nal, skipping another rock. "Does that mean that if Enoch is...I mean, if what my father says about him is true, that he'd come back to life?"

"That's what El wrote on the plaque," said Jak, "and that's what Guardian told me. It's hard to say if it's true or not, but look at my grandfather. He used to be wrinkled and gray, but now he's young again. I hope its true."

"Me too," said Nal. They sat together silently on the rock and watched the water swish by, one thinking about his grandmother, the other about his brother.

"I s'pose we should get goin'," said Nal, standing up. "Mum sent me to come and fetch you for breakfast. Are you 'ungry?'"

Jak wasn't sure how anybody could be hungry after last night. He hadn't eaten near as much as everyone else had, but his stomach still felt full. However, he wanted to be polite. "Uh, sure. A little, I guess."

"Good. Come on then. Everyone else is already eatin.'"

Jak wished he had brought the bag with him. He felt naked just carrying the book around out in the open.

When they got back to the house, he was greeted by a chorus of "Good morning, Jak."

Jared, Gramps, and Tess were sitting cross-legged on the floor, Macy was chewing a bone in the corner, and Beerta knelt by the fire filling a bowl.

"Come and get yer breakfast!" She thrust a two-pronged wooden fork into his hand and directed him to a mat on the floor in between Tess and Gramps.

Jak couldn't believe it. In the middle of the mat sat a bowl of hard-boiled eggs, a plate filled with toast, and a small trough of what looked like fried potatoes and onions. On his own mat sat a glass of grape juice, a pear cut to look like a bird, and a huge sticky bun. He stood there, transfixed. "This is as much of a feast as last night."

"Of course!" said Beerta, beaming. "You're a growin' boy." She slapped him on the back.

"It is soooo good, Jak," Tess said, her mouth full of food. She was halfway through her sticky bun, which had apparently put her in a good mood.

Jak inspected the bird-pear as he and Nal sat down. He wasn't sure if it was food or a decoration, so he speared a piece of toast.

"Jak," said Jared between bites, "I've been thinkin' about Cain." He swallowed, then continued. "First of all, we don't know for sure if Cain really is Beelzin or not. All we know is that he's a sour-puss who's interested in yer book. Second, we know he's a convicted killer who's been banished."

Such happy breakfast talk, Jak thought. *I can't wait to hear more.*

"Third," continued Jared, "if you lose that book, we're all in a heap of trouble, which means you hav' got to stay out of Cain's clutches, if indeed he's clutchin' after you. But for sure we know Beelz is either already after you or soon will be. Too bad about yer leg, 'cause it'd be better if you could move a bit faster than you can. You need someone who knows the difference between the good folk and the bad. I'd go along with you 'cept for my own bad leg. I'm a'feared I'd only slow you down worse."

Jak didn't hadn't noticed Jared's bad leg, but it made sense. Last night Jared had hung at the back of the pack, not far behind Jak. At the time, Jak thought he was just being polite. It had never occurred to him that Jared also had a hard time getting where he needed to go.

As soon as Jared had finished talking, Beerta stood up with her left hand on her hip, and wiped a wisp of hair behind her ear. She stared up to the sunlight streaming through the window at the top of the wall. The conversation turned to Cain and Abel and exactly what had happened in the field the day Abel died.

As they talked, Beerta continued staring out the window, rubbing one of the wooden forks. Suddenly she stopped polishing the fork and stepped toward Jared, interrupting the conversation. "Why don't you send Nal with 'im? Just till Jak gets to the end of our land. Maybe this Megiddo place is jus' o'er the border."

Both Tess and Nal stopped chewing.

"Yes, that's a great idea, Father!" said Nal, his voice full of excitement. "I can go and—"

Jared cut him off, "But Beerta, if he follows the Thread, he might ne'er make it back. You know what happens to people from the village if they follow the Thread."

She nodded her head. "I know, but if Jak doesn't make it to Megiddo, we'll all end up dead forever."

Nal spoke up again. "I can help protect Jak, Father. I can fight."

"I know you can, son. I've seen you trainin' with yer lance. Yer almost a man yerself and could probably take anyone in a fair fight." He looked at Nal square in the face, tears tugging at his eyes. "I just don't want ta lose you." He wiped his eyes with the back of his hand. "Clarence, what do you think?"

"We'd welcome any help we can get," said Gramps, "but it would be quite a sacrifice for you if he doesn't make it back."

Jared and Beerta gazed at each other silently for a moment until Jared broke away and slapped his hands together. "Alright. It's done then," said Jared. "Nal, take them as far as the eastern border, where the Pishon River cuts south. That's as far as you know anyhow, so if the Thread takes them further than that, say your goodbyes and try to get home. We'll trust that Yahweh who leads the Thread onward will lead you home as well. You should leave right away this mornin'. If the rumors about Cain are true, then every moment you stay here is one more moment Cain'll have to rally support from the other Beelzins."

Three sharp raps came on the wall next to the doorway.

Beerta pulled aside the curtain, revealing a short, fat man with a squat black-tasseled yellow fez on his head, and a crocodile smile showing two rows of perfect white teeth. A black beard graced his chin, and he was dressed in a yellow robe with a black sash, laced with silver and gold threads. "Good morning," he sang out, tipping his hat. "Is this where the Thread followers are staying?"

"Why, yes it is," said Beerta, "They're sittin' right here for breakfast."

"Ah good," said the man, " Might I have a word with them?"

Beerta flushed, realizing she had said too much.

"It's okay, Beerta," said Gramps, waving the man in.

"Come in," she said, bowing her head slightly.

"Thank you!" The stout man popped inside and wedged into the now cramped circle. He surveyed the group, nodding his head slowly, humming to himself and holding his hands with his fingers interlaced together. "My name is Rail Nettor," he said, still smiling the crocodile smile. "I come from a long and honorable line of Nettors from a valley in the south. I have been traveling on business and had the good fortune of attending the celebration last evening. I have traversed this valley many times, but never before have I seen the wondrous ribbon as I did last night."

"You saw it?" saw Jak.

"Briefly, m' boy, just a glimpse. I know it is indeed a rarity for one other than a Thread follower to see the Thread in all its wonder, but see it I did. Upon inquiry, I determined that you were the cause of the Thread. So I began to think, I did, about what it might be like to see where it goes. It's not every day when one happens upon a never-ending floating red thread. So I asked around to see where I might find you and ended up here."

Beerta handed a fork to the man while he was speaking.

He stabbed an egg and plugged it into his mouth. "Mmmm, exquisite cooking, ma'am." He swallowed and then stuffed an entire piece of toast in the gaping hole, smiling and nodding as he chewed.

Jak whispered to Tess, "I may eat a lot, but at least I don't eat like that."

Mr. Nettor swallowed what appeared to be the whole piece at once and smiled. "Let me get right to the point. I have a proposition for you. I am a dealer of cloth and clothing and sell nothing but the best. If I gave each of you, including your fine friends here, a brand new change of clothes, might I accompany you on your quest?

Gramps swallowed his last piece of toast and wiped his beard with a leaf napkin. "I'm not so sure you want to do that," said Gramps. "Apparently, once you travel into the future, you may not be able to get back."

"Pshaw. I don't care about that." He gulped down a glass of grape juice and plunked the glass back down on the table. "I may come from a long and honorable line, but it's been years since I've seen my family. I can just as well sell cloth in the future as sell it now."

"It's not safe to come with us either," said Gramps.

"Not safe?" said Mr. Nettor. "Why not?"

"Let's just say Beelz will be very interested in what we're doing."

A look of amusement crossed Mr. Nettor's face. "Oh, Beelz doesn't concern me one bit. If you ask me, he's just an overgrown lizard."

Jared sucked in his breath. "I don' think you've ever truly met 'im then."

"Oh yes I have! He's kind of like a dog. If you let him know you're afraid, he'll snap at you, but if you show him who the boss is, he'll run away like a bunny from a pack of wolves. In either case, I am not afraid. Certainly it couldn't hurt to have one more set of hands in case you happened upon an ill-favored visitor."

That was true. What could it hurt to have one more person come with them? Jak nodded at Gramps to show his approval.

"Well," said Gramps, "I guess it would be fine for you to join us, but you don't need to give us anything."

"Pshaw," said Mr. Nettor, swallowing a second cinnamon bun whole and wiping the sugar from his fat lips with the back of his hand. "It would be my pleasure. One of the perks of the business, you know."

Gramps folded the napkin and laid it back down on the mat. "Well, we're finishing up with breakfast and planning on heading out right away."

"Good, good," said Mr. Nettor. He heaved himself off the floor and smiled, his perfect white teeth shining in the sunlight. "I'll run along and get my things then."

Beerta opened the door and the fat little man bustled out, still smiling. Gramps stood and stretched, causing the muscles in his arms to bulge in a way Jak had never seen before on his grandfather.

Jak stood as well, chewing the head of the bird. He had finally decided it was part of breakfast and not just a decoration and had bitten into it just before Gramps announced it was time to go.

"Here," said Beerta said, handing Jak a bag. "Tisn't much—just some peanuts, bread, cheese, apples, and a bone."

"Tess," said Jak, "can you and Macy share the bone, or should we get another?"

She made a face at him and stood, rubbing her hands together to wipe off the last of the crumbs.

Beerta then gave a roll of blankets to Gramps. "This'll get you through the cold nights. I imagine you'll have a bit of sleepin' under the stars. And here's a bag of rocks for you."

"Rocks?" said Gramps, jingling the bag up and down.

"Jasper," she said. "We use it to trade. You will need to buy food and other items along the way."

Gramps stuffed the bag in his pocket. "Thank you."

Jak suddenly realized he was still in Enoch's clothes. "Beerta, do you have my pants?"

Beerta looked surprised. "Yer pants? I burnt them this morning."

Jak's jaw dropped. "You burned them?"

"Of course! They had been tainted by blood, so I had to."

"What?" Jak stammered. "What am I supposed to wear?"

Tess scolded him with her eyes. Obviously, he had stepped over some line of impoliteness again, but he didn't relish the thought of running around in pajamas the rest of the day.

"You can keep the clothes. They look nice on you, and I don't need them clutterin' up the house anymore." She took a deep breath and wiped the corners of her eyes.

They opened the door just in time to see Mr. Nettor in front of the house, sitting in a fancy wagon pulled by a pair of donkeys. The wooden bench where Mr. Nettor sat had carvings of birds spread over the back, and the seat was covered in thick sheepskin. Blue and white curtains hung on the sides and back, and a white curtain just behind the seat was tied with a satin sash to the side. Brilliantly colored fabric peeked out of the shelves on the wagon.

"Wow," said Tess. "Do we get to ride in that?"

"Of course, young lady. If you travel with me, we travel in style." Mr. Nettor climbed down and scratched the black donkey behind the ears. "This is Whitey." He reached to the other side and scratched the white donkey behind the ears. "And this is Blackey. I know... you're thinking they should be named the other way around, but I find it much more interesting this way. Hop on in." He helped Tess into the wagon. Gramps, Nal, and Jak climbed in right behind her.

The round man then went to the back of the wagon and opened a cabinet door that faced the rear. He pulled out a parcel tied with twine and huffed back toward the house.

"Ma'am, I have here the finest embroidered robe you'll find east of Eden." He held it out with both hands and bowed slightly.

"Thank you, Mr. Nettor," said Beerta, "but really, it isn't necessary."

"Oh, I insist. Just one slice of your toast was worth it all." He laid the parcel on the door stoop, smiled the crocodile smile while tipping his hat, and turned back to the wagon.

Macy stopped sniffing at the donkeys and jumped in next to Jak.

"You be careful." Beerta came close to the wagon, and grabbed Nal's hand. "Don't do anything foolish now, son. You're all we have left till Jak gets to where El's takin' him. This is a quiet leavin', so don't be yellin' to yer friends. Just lay low in the wagon till yer out of reach. And you, Jak," she said, grabbing his hand tight, "you hold the book close and don't give up. I want my Enoch back." Her lips quivered at the mention of Enoch's name. "Remember, Yahweh is yer protection and yer strength."

Jak looked at her in surprise. "That's the same thing Guardian told me," said Jak.

"Is it now?" said Beerta. "I s'pose that's 'cause it's the biggest hope we hold on to." She squeezed Jak's and Nal's hands at the same time.

"Will you tell Man and Woman... I mean, Adam and Eve goodbye for us?" asked Jak. "Tell them what happened and that we'll be back."

Beerta nodded. "Of course."

"Are we ready?" said Mr. Nettor.

"Yep, I guess so," said Gramps.

"Then we're off!" Mr. Nettor reached under the seat and pulled out a coiled rawhide whip. He cracked it in the air above the donkeys, and they started clip-clopping down the road toward the Thread.

He smiled at Tess when he saw her eyes go wide at the sight of the whip. "It's just for fun. I'd never hit them with it. Just the air."

Tess leaned over the side of the wagon and waved back to Beerta and Jared.

"El's blessing to you!" Beerta shouted after them. Both she and Jared held their palms out toward them, fingers stretched out. That's when Jak noticed that Jared only had four fingers on his right hand.

CHAPTER 34

The White Diamond

A bum leg, four fingers on his right hand, and a healthy dislike for Beelz and Scorch. There had to be more to the story, but now was not the right time for Jak to ask Nal about his father. As soon as they set out in the wagon, the Thread quivered and spurted across the river, out of sight through the trees.

"Where exactly are we headed, young Jak?" asked Mr. Nettor. The reins hung easily in his hands as they rumbled down the brown cobblestone.

"Just follow the Thread."

"And where is that?"

Jak had forgotten that he, Gramps, and Tess were the only ones who could see the Thread. "Right ahead of us." Jak pointed to where the Thread hung suspended over the river. "Over the river, straight into those trees on the other side."

"Right ahead of us?" said Tess. "I don't see it."

"You can't see it?" said Jak.

"I can't see it either, Jak," said Gramps.

A touch of panic washed through Jak at the realization that now he was the only one who could see the Thread.

"Maybe El hid it from everyone but you for a while," said Gramps. "Might be safer that way."

He hoped Gramps was right. "Head toward the path through the trees," Jak instructed Mr. Nettor, "and we'll be okay."

Once they were on track, Gramps and Mr. Nettor fell into conversation, and Jak sank down to a pillow behind the bench. He clutched the bag containing the book and the cards close to his chest.

"How far do you think it is to Megiddo?" he asked Nal.

Nal shrugged his shoulders. "I don' know. I never heard of it before, but it's at least a five-day journey to the Pishon River, maybe more, so I wouldn't be surprised if we run into it before then."

Nal's lance lay at his feet. It was about four feet long and had a dark wooden shaft with a leather strap tied through a hole in the end. Leather tongs wrapped a long pointed black rock that looked just as sharp as the knives back in Gramps's kitchen to the end of the shaft.

"Brace yourselves!" called Mr. Nettor. "We're coming to the river shallows. Blackey and Whitey have done this numerous times, so it won't be difficult, but it might get a little bumpy back there."

The steady roar of the river filled their ears, and the wagon lurched into the river bed.

"Steady now, Blackey." The whip cracked, and Jak winced. Even though Mr. Nettor had said he never hit the donkeys, Jak couldn't help but feel sorry for the donkeys when the whip snapped.

He lifted up the bottom of the blue fabric wall and peeked over the edge to the rushing water. It was dark brown, like root beer, with solid black rocks studding the riverbed and black streaks of minnows darting to and fro. The wheels of the wagon spun tiny streams of water into the air as they turned toward the opposite shore.

Suddenly the bell from the woman in the watchtower began ringing wildly, and women began screaming and rushing for the shore, abandoning dirty robes to float downstream.

Nal scooped up his lance and perched on the end of the wagon.

"She's here," whispered Nal.

"Who?" said Tess.

"The Black Serpent," said Nal. His eyes were wild, and his knuckles were white from holding the lance so tightly. "Hurry it up, Mr. Nettor! Get us out of the river!"

The whip cracked frantically, and Mr. Nettor shouted at the donkeys. "Hep, hep! Move along!"

Nal's eyes roved the shallow water upstream. The women downstream had thrashed out of the water and stood well above shore, pointing toward the wagon and shouting for them to get out of the water. A chorus of bells joined the watchtower bell as the alarm was raised all over the village. In a minute, armed men would line the shore.

A stone's throw upstream, something flashed in the water, and Jak and Nal both tensed. The wagon still had almost a quarter of the river to go.

Suddenly, a familiar high-pitched shriek scraped across their ears as something ripped through the fabric wall behind Jak.

Tess screamed as Jak and Nal whirled to find an enormous black head protruding into the wagon. Yellow eyes as big as saucers peered intently at Jak, and a low growl rumbled from the beast's scaly black throat.

This couldn't be her, thought Jak. *It is so ugly.* But then he saw the white diamond adorning the forehead and a shiver ran down his spine.

For a split second, the only thing that happened was that saliva dripped from Scorch's mouthful of crooked teeth and splattered on the floor.

"Get back!" shouted Nal, stabbing his lance toward her eyes, but Jak grabbed Nal's arm before the lance touched her.

"Wait," he whispered. He tuned out everything around him and began to stretch his hand toward Scorch's head. *She doesn't want to hurt us. She just wants me to pet her like I used to.* He reached for the familiar white spot. "Here, girl. It's okay. Nothing's going to hurt you."

Scorch didn't move.

He moved his hand slowly until it was poised an inch above the diamond. He could feel her hot breath on his arm.

"Jak," Nal whispered. "What're you doin'?"

Then Jak dropped one finger onto the white patch he had petted so many times before.

But as soon as the finger touched her scales, Scorch shrieked and lunged toward Jak, mashing her fangs together in a furious snap.

Jak dropped to the floor of the wagon as her head shot over him and ripped through the fabric wall on the other side of him.

She pulled back to strike again, but she pulled too hard, and her head slipped out of the wagon altogether.

Blackey and Whitey, fueled by pure terror, bolted up the embankment on the other side, the wagon tipping furiously in either direction as they tore down the road.

By this time, a swarm of men surrounded Scorch in the river with lances, scythes, and ox goads. They circled the beast, shouting and lunging time after time, trying to break through the armor of scales.

Scorch towered above her attackers, gnashing her teeth, hissing and roaring. A plume of blue flame erupted from her mouth, punching a hole in the group of men. She leapt through the hole and slipped under the surface, disappearing in a wake of white water upstream. Then the river was still.

Jak shuddered. This was no longer a question of whether or not Scorch's poison would kill him, because her teeth could rip him apart in the matter of a few seconds.

Tess huddled in the corner shaking, tears streaming down her face.

"Are you alright?" said Nal, crouching next to her and putting his hand on her shoulder.

She shook her head. "That is what she has become?"

Nal nodded. "Yeah—all teeth and rage. But we should be safe now. She stays close to water and almost never comes inland. That's why the village isn't built on the shore."

"Is that what happened to your father?" said Jak. "He only has four fingers on his right hand and walks with a limp like me. Was it Scorch?"

Nal stared at him for a moment, then looked away and shook his head. "No, twasn't Scorch. How's your leg today, Jak?"

Nal obviously didn't want to talk about it, so Jak didn't press any further.

Gramps swiveled around, sweat lining his face. "You guys okay back there?"

Jak nodded. "Yeah."

Mr. Nettor rustled under his seat and came up with a bag.

"I'd say surviving an encounter with the Black Serpent calls for a celebration. These are the finest dates east of Eden, straight from a tree handed down to me by my grandmother." He poured a handful out of the bag and distributed them. "We'll stop in a bit to fix the walls of the wagon, but for now, enjoy the dates."

Nal leaned back against the smooth wood of the wagon wall and chewed slowly. "The beast came the same way the day Enoch disappeared. One minute we was playin' in the field along the river, and the next the snake heaved out of the water and thrashed about and Enoch was gone. We never should've been there. The field's been left fallow for five years. Wildflowers are the only thing that grows there now, but no one is allowed to pick 'em. A living gravestone for Enoch is what my father calls 'em. I think of 'em more as an invitation to go lookin', and every spring the invitation comes again. I've never had the chance to go till now."

"Till now?" said Tess. "I thought you were taking us to Megiddo."

Nal shifted uncomfortably on his pillow. "I am. I just figgered that along the way I could keep an eye out for Enoch." He coughed. "So, Jak, who 'er we lookin' for now?"

Gramps turned around. "Good question, Nal, I've been wondering the same thing."

Jak dug into the book bag and pulled out the Thread card with the laughing man on it. "We're looking for him." He passed the card to Nal, who inspected it carefully for a moment before handing it to Gramps.

"I've never seen 'im before," said Nal.

Gramps took the card and looked at it with Mr. Nettor.

"No, can't say I've seen him either," said Mr. Nettor, "but I'll let you know the second I do."

One hundred yards up stream, unseen by any in the wagon, a hooded figure in a brown tunic splashed across the river and trotted in the same direction as the wagon.

CHAPTER 35
The Wandering Murderer

"Follow him," the hooded figure had been ordered. "Track the boy and send the information back to Beelz."

Cain threw back his hood and let the wind blow through his hair as he watched the wagon lumber over a slight rise on the trail. He was sick of taking orders from the slobbering red beast, yet he had been doing it for over 400 years. This order was almost like a death sentence because there was no guarantee that he would ever be able to get back to his own time. Marching through time by following the Thread was a one-way ticket.

"Not that it would make much difference," he snorted. Even though he had founded a city and had a wife and children, he was still a wanderer, just like Yahweh had told him he would be. Murdering his brother had undone him. So, yes, he would follow the boy. It wouldn't be too difficult to track him through time if he followed closely enough. As for reporting back to Beelz though, maybe he would and maybe he wouldn't.

He cloaked his head in the hood once again, grabbed his lance firmly in the middle of the shaft, and took off at a slight trot after the wagon.

CHAPTER 36
A Funeral Kidnapping

They spent two full days traveling east. The Thread did not slow down or speed up but kept at a steady pace above the road, if you could rightly call it a road. It was more of a path through the grass with enough room for two pairs of wagon wheels to roll through.

Often they passed groups of people, but no one knew the man on the card and no one had heard of Megiddo. More often than not, Mr. Nettor would say, "Watch yourself now. There's no telling what this one will do. Look at his eyes. They're shifty," or "See his hands, how they're close to his knife?"

At one point, a couple of young men even climbed into the wagon next to Mr. Nettor when Gramps was in the back taking a nap and began to push him off the wagon. They didn't realize he was not alone and quickly jumped down again when Nal pricked them with his lance. They laughed when they hit the ground and said it had been a joke, but Mr. Nettor didn't think it was very funny.

Right after the two intruders left, Jak noticed a man quite a ways behind them buying food from a woman at a farm. He had a dark brown tunic with a hood that protected his face from the sun, and he carried a lance similar to Nal's, except it had an ax blade on one side of the tip too. He had seen the same man yesterday, Jak was sure of it. "Tess," said Jak quietly. He pointed through the back of the wagon. "Do you recognize that man?"

"The bald guy?"

"No, beyond him—the one talking to that woman back at that farm."

"I can't even see his face, Jak. His hood is up."

"I know, but the rest of him... does he look familiar?"

She paused and stared at the man. "No. Who do you think he is?"

"I don't know. I could have sworn I saw him yesterday."

"There're lots of brown tunics with hoods, Jak," said Nal. "T'was probably somebody else you saw."

"Yeah, I guess so." But Jak didn't really guess so.

To pass the time, Nal showed Jak all he could in the confines of the wagon and in the dark of the campsite at night about fighting with a lance. Since Jak didn't have a lance, they cut off a section of branch from an oak tree and used Gramps's knife to shave the end into a dull point.

He did the best he could with one good leg to follow the footwork and jabbing strokes, but he was no match for Nal's speed and accuracy. If his leg had been better, he was confident he could at least feint away from an attacking lance, but it wasn't, so the best he could do was drop to the ground, which never put him in a good position. His muscles were sore from the sparring, but it felt good learning how to defend himself.

They also passed the time by listening to Mr. Nettor's tales of the fabric trade, how he would buy sun-yellow shades of fabric from the sulfur-rich lands in the south and then journey west to the sea to trade for the more luxuriant purples made from seashells. Then he would come back north and east, selling both purple and yellow fabric and buying the heavy wool blankets from the rich grazing lands of the north to sell in both south and west.

At lunchtime of the third day, after a particularly hard morning of dealing with cranky people on the road, the Thread led them through a village festooned with large woven banners dyed in a weak rainbow of colors and tied to trees and houses.

"It's a harvest festival. Looks like they used vegetable dyes in their banner instead of the good stuff," said Mr. Nettor, "but as long as the dinner is cooked, that's alright with me. This is my favorite time of the year. Look at all the food!"

Every house was festooned with squash and corn and an assortment of other foods recently harvested from the fields, and the main thoroughfare was crowded with people bustling about getting ready for the festival.

But in spite of the festivities, something didn't look right.

"How come everybody's carrying lances and bows and arrows?" said Jak. "You can't harvest anything with an arrow."

"Hmmmm, good question, my boy. I hadn't noticed that," said Mr. Nettor. "Excuse me, sir," Mr. Nettor said to a man passing the wagon with a humongous skin stuffed with bright red-feathered arrows. "Is not the harvest festival to be celebrated soon?"

The man nodded. "Yes, 'twas s'posed to be. We had all the fixin's for it, everything set, the games and the cakes and the bread, all set aside an' ready. But last night, those cursed Kanites dropped down silent as vultures and stole all our beer, just loaded the skins on camels and took off. Can't have a harvest festival without beer, so we're goin' to get it back, and we're goin' to teach them a lesson at the same time. Instead of a harvest festival, we're going to have ourselves a war." His eyes lit up and he cracked a toothy grin, except he didn't have much for teeth beyond a few crooked yellow stumps. "Plenty of killin'. Be more fun than a harvest festival anyway." He shuffled away cackling to himself.

Tess shuddered. "Aren't there any normal people around here? I don't think we've seen one normal person all day. Everyone is either angry or trying to steal something."

"Depends on what you call normal, young lady," said Mr. Nettor. He popped a fig into his mouth and chewed, smacking loudly. "In my travels it seems that everyone is angry and trying to steal something. That's just the way people are."

"I say we leave this place," said Gramps. "It's too crazy. I wouldn't be surprised if someone gets the bright idea of ransacking your wagon to make new war uniforms."

"But I haven't asked anyone yet about the card," said Jak.

"Ask him," said Gramps, pointing to a wild-haired boy running past. He whistled, and the boy stopped and squinted back at them.

Jak leaned forward past Gramps and held the card over the edge. "Hey, have you seen this man?"

The boy pinched the card between a grubby finger and thumb. "Depends. How much you paying?"

"Paying?" said Jak, taken aback. "I'm not paying anything. I'm just asking."

The boy shook his head quickly and let go of the card. "Then I haven't seen him."

Jak hadn't anticipated it being this difficult to get information. The only thing they had of any value was the jasper Beerta had given them, but if he had to pay every single person he asked about the laughing man, he would run out of jasper. On the other hand, it didn't matter if he had a bag of rocks or not. It was more important to find the man as soon as possible. He dug out a shiny pink rock the size of a raisin and held it up. "I'll give you this for information about the man."

The boy greedily took the rock and turned it around in his fingers. "Deal. I haven't seen him." Then he sprinted away from the wagon and disappeared around the corner of a house.

"Wait!" called Jak, but the boy was gone. Jak looked back at Gramps. "He stole the rock!"

"No, you asked for information, and he gave the information he had," said Gramps. "Next time say you'll pay if someone can lead you to the man on the card. Don't feel too bad though," said Gramps, winking at him. "I didn't expect him to do that either."

They pulled away from the village, a rock poorer, but a rock wiser as well. Within an hour, they came to another village, larger than the first and minus the bustle. Large torches marked both sides of the entrance to the village, flickering with orange flames, but no one was there. The village was as empty as a ghost town; it even sounded like a ghost town. A wail rose and fell like the wind, and not just one voice, but a chorus of voices accompanied by the beating of a drum and the smell of smoke. It reminded Jak of Remembrance Day when the people listed the names of the dead.

The further they rode into the cluster of houses, the louder the wail and the thicker the smoke. Past the last house they saw a hundred or more people in a field dressed in black capes and circled around a wooden structure as tall as a man. It was engulfed in flames.

"It's a funeral pyre," whispered Mr. Nettor. "Look up top at that black cloth. Strange though. I don't see the body."

A large figure broke away from the rest and hurried away from the pyre toward the wagon. His hair was woven into black braids and thrown into a wild pile over his shoulders.

"What do you want?" he said in a low, rough voice. "Can you not see we are in the midst of a passing?" He suddenly stopped speaking and stared at Jak. "Is this some sort of joke?"

"No," said Gramps. "We did not mean to intrude. We are only passing through."

"Who is this boy?" The man thrust a dirty finger toward Jak.

"He is my grandson. Why?"

"Liar!" The man's eyes narrowed. "He is the spirit of the boy death stole from our village. Give him to me."

"Now wait a second here," said Gramps. "I'm sorry for your loss, but the boy belongs to us. His name is Jak Hamelton, and he's my grandson."

"No! He is the one come back from the dead!" The man stabbed his hand out, grabbed Jak's arm and started tugging him over the side.

Nal grabbed his other hand and pulled the other direction.

"Let go of me!" Jak shouted.

Tess picked up Jak's sparring lance and rapped the man in the knuckles. He yelped and let go.

As soon as Jak's arm was free, Tess yanked him behind a curtain.

The other people in the mourning party turned, and a group of men ran to the wagon, surrounding it. One of the men with a crown of green leaves and covered with a purple-fringed black cape approached. "Who dares interrupt a passing?" he demanded. "Did you not see the flares?"

Gramps stood his ground. "We are sorry to intrude. We are travelers and did not know what the flares meant."

"The boy! Look at the boy in the wagon!" the first man spat out. "He has come back. Shale has returned to us from the teeth of the Black Serpent."

The man with the leaves in his hair nodded to two men next to him, and they ripped away the blue fabric covering the wagon, exposing Jak's hiding place.

"See his face?" the first man said, pointing a grubby finger once again at Jak.

The leaf hair man nodded. "It is he! His body has returned to us alive." He turned to the other men and nodded again. "Take him."

"No!" shouted Gramps.

But it was too late. One man grabbed Nal from behind, preventing him from using his lance. Two others grabbed Blackey's and Whitey's halters and held them still while two more boarded the wagon and grabbed Jak's hands and feet.

"Wait!" Jak shouted as he struggled against them. "I'm not who you think I am. I am Jak Hamelton from Grantsburg, Wisconsin. Leave me alone!"

But it did no good, and they tossed him over the side like a sack of potatoes. He hit the ground on his side, knocking the wind out of him. He struggled to breathe and to stand at the same time, hoping to run, but two pair of arms locked him up tight while another hand clamped over his mouth.

"Take the others to the hole," the leaf man said with disdain.

Immediately, the two men holding the halters jerked the wagon toward a shack at the edge of the field.

The man with the leaf crown hurried Jak to the largest house in the village. It arched twice as high as any of the other houses with a peak gilded with bleached white bone. A black wooden door swung open silently as they climbed the steps to the threshold. Inside the house, upon each wall, hung a raft of oil lamps, flickering enough light to reveal brown-sugar colored wood paneling covering the interior.

A large woman rushed through the door and crushed Jak in her arms, wailing loudly. She was followed by a hulking hairy bald man, a spindly man with ragged black hair, and an equally ragged woman.

"Shale, you have returned," she said, sniffling.

Jak could hardly breathe, she wrapped him up so tight. The two breaths he was able to suck in he almost wished he could give back; she stank like a dead buffalo.

She yanked his head back by pulling the small hairs at the nape of his neck, and stared at him with bulbous eyes that would have looked quite nice on an iguana. "Your antics by the river have almost cost your mummy a year's worth of olive oil. Naughty, naughty boy. You are NOT allowed to go near the river again. Do you hear me?" She shook him. "We need you at the sacrifice tomorrow."

"Where have you put my friends?" said Jak, trying to talk using as little air as possible so he wouldn't have to breath buffalo woman's stench again.

"We are your friends," said the leaf-crowned man coldly, "your family, you belong with us. Tomorrow is a very special day. Here... drink this. It will make you feel better." He handed Jak a cup with steaming brown liquid in it that smelled like the chamomile tea his grandmother used to make before he went to bed.

Jak took a sip. It was definitely chamomile, with a touch of mint that sizzled on his tongue. "Where have you put the people who came with me in the wagon?" he asked again.

"They have been taken care of," the man said, smiling as if an invisible puppeteer had pulled the strings on each corner of his mouth. "You do not need to concern yourself with them. Tonight is a celebration. You have come back from the dead to help your people. You are to be honored above all others."

The first thing that came to Jak's mind was the Quelcher Adam had talked about. "I'm not the Quelcher, if that's what you're thinking."

"The Quelcher?" said the man, still smiling the plastic smile. "My boy, the Quelcher is a legend of the fathers fit only for old women and their cats. You are a real flesh-and-blood hero, ten times more of a hero than the fabled Quelcher could ever be."

"What did I do?" said Jak. The room was beginning to spin, and he had a hard time focusing on the man. He was vaguely aware of his clothes being removed and a fresh set of clothing being pushed and pulled over him. Someone kept daubing his face with something wet and warm.

"It is not what you have done, but what you *will* do. You will save your people from starvation. Have you forgotten the hordes of locusts stripping the crops and the orchards? Three years in a row the scavengers have left us devastated. Yahweh's anger must be appeased."

Yahweh? The name twirled around in his mind like a butterfly that refused to be caught. *What does Yahweh have to do with locusts?*

One of the attendants approached the leaf-crowned man, bowed, and then whispered into his ear.

He frowned. "It does not matter if his heel has been torn to shreds. The Shale among us now is the same as the one who left us. Yahweh has prepared him through an ordeal such that the sacrifice is more pure than we ever could have hoped."

The buffalo woman with the hefty bald man skulking behind her squinted her eyes and hissed, "What is it? He is still acceptable, is he not?"

Even through the haze of whatever was in the chamomile tea, Jak caught the words "sacrifice" and "he" in the same conversation. He had a vivid recollection of Adam slitting the throat of the lamb, and all of a sudden the room became very clear. He saw every movement, heard every word. He must have misheard what they said.

The servant propelled Jak forward until he stood directly in front of the leaf-crowned man.

"Father of the boy," said the man, "step forward with your mate."

The spindly man with ragged hair stepped in front of the priest along with the ragged woman.

"Mother of the boy, step forward with your mate."

The buffalo woman stepped forward with the hairy bald man.

"You offer a great gift to Yahweh," the leaf man said, "and to your people, and will be greatly rewarded for your generosity. The crops of your people will flourish, but yours will flourish seven-fold. The orchards will bloom and produce fruit, but yours will produce ten-fold."

"And the olive oil?" the woman crooned

"Yes, yes, a year's supply of olive oil from my own priestly portion will be yours."

They knelt in front of the priest with open hands and together shoved Jak forward into the priest's open arms.

The priest put both hands on Jak's shoulders.

"The village accepts your gift as the morning sacrifice."

"I do not trusst Cain," said Beelz. He had wrapped himself around a dead tree near the upper headwaters of the Tigris River and hung fifteen feet in the air. The heads of the Beelzin—Ramath from the north, Irtil from the west, Grunert from the east, and Limn from the south—had gathered along with the Council of Lights in a washed-out grotto filled with mosquitoes and snakes. The humans kept their knives at the ready just in case a snake got too friendly, and they kept slapping themselves as the mosquitoes dug into fresh flesh. Slapping oneself while holding an unsheathed knife is risky business, and each of them sported red slashes where they had accidentally stabbed themselves. This was all very entertaining for Beelz, which is one reason he had called for the meeting to be held there.

Irtil stood, bowed his head and said, "Most Malevolent Majesty, we have already put a plan in place, if you would but be patient, I am certain it would—"

"It iss not enough," Beelz snapped. "We cannot rely on two-faced toadiess to ssucccceed. We have not reccceived any information and it hass already been two dayss. We need another plan. The only advantage we have right now iss time. Every minute of the boy'ss time repressentss hourss and monthss of our own, however, it isss alssso our biggesst dissadvantage becausse it iss difficult to pinpoint exactly where he iss. Sso who hass an idea?"

No one responded.

"Come now! There iss great reward in sspeaking if your plan workss, and if it doessn't, I'll only give you half the punissshment you desserve."

This bit of encouragement loosened the mood, and a hum of conversation began among the humans and the Lights.

A flat voice from a skinny oil-blue Light spoke up from the back. "Why don't we just kidnap him and sit on him till he gives us the book?" A number of Lights voiced their agreement with this plan until Beelz snorted a red flame into the air and silenced them.

"You are ignorant and sstupid, Ammi. We are going for ssubtle. We want the boy to believe we are hiss friendss. There may come a point when we need some more forccceful ideass, but not yet."

Stul emitted a dark purple cloud of gas and then spoke articulately. "What about the female?"

"To which female are you referring, Sstul?"

"Yours."

Beelzebub eyes glowed red, and his mouth opened. Lucifer burst out of the leviathan's body in a brilliant flash of yellow and hovered above them, an octopus of light. "I do not use the females as some do. The women are toys for the weak and stupid among us."

Stul's fat round form twisted into the perfect representation of a man, muscular, with flawless brown skin, long braided black hair, and seductive brown eyes. "Perhaps you should get one, Lucius," said Stul, smirking through two rows of perfect white teeth. "I have heard the pleasures of a human female are many. It might calm your nerves." At this, a dark laughter of agreement rippled through the Council of Lights.

"However…" Stul's human form inflated, the legs, neck and arms swelling grotesquely like an overinflated plastic doll until they disappeared entirely and the round purple form of Stul emerged again. "I am not referring to a female human, but to the female serpent."

"What of her?" Lucifer coiled one glimmering yellow tentacle above the Beelzin lords, making them sweat profusely.

"From what I hear, she is pursuing the boy as well, for her own reasons, and she apparently has no difficulty hunting through time. My sources tell me she almost caught him where the Tigris flows past East Eden. Perhaps we can twist her so that she will not eat him until after we have a chance to rescue him from her jaws. Of course, the rescue would involve extracting the book first. Then she can feed freely."

Lucifer considered Stul's suggestion for a few moments and then sucked himself back into the leviathan's body with a snort. Beelz's eyes glowed red again and he spurted red sparks from his nose. "I like it. Capture the beassst. Devissse a potion to make her pliable, and then I will twissst her tiny mind until ssshe sssubmitsss."

The hole was pitch black and damp.

Tess felt something crawl across her hand and flung it at the wall.

"Hey, what'd you throw at me?" said Nal.

"Sorry," she said, "I was trying to get rid of a spider."

The men had crowded them into a tiny hut and then forced them to climb down a rope ladder to the bottom. It must have been a dried-out well and was not designed for four people, especially if one of them was as large as Mr. Nettor, so they squeezed together like sardines. Tess didn't mind squeezing next to her grandfather, and especially not next to Nal, but Mr. Nettor was like a living bowling ball.

The first thing she had tried to do was scale the wall, but they had been rubbed so smooth that she couldn't even lean against the wall without slipping.

"What do you think they did with Jak?" said Tess, looking for the umpteenth time at the slight gray outline that marked the top of the hole.

"I'm sure he's getting the royal treatment. After all, he just came back from the dead," said Gramps. "They're probably throwing him a party."

"Lucky him. How long do you think we'll have to stay down here?" said Tess. It was bad enough being stuck in the hole, but Tess's bladder was beginning to send her subtle signals that she needed to find a bathroom.

The door of the hut above them creaked open, and a shaft of light lit up the hole.

"Sumthin' to eat," said the guard.

"Finally!" said Mr. Nettor, his voice trembling. "My stomach has been growling for an hour."

Four pieces of stale bread landed on Mr. Nettor's head.

"Guard!" shouted Gramps, but the door slammed shut again.

"How many rocks are left in that bag?" asked Tess.

Mr. Nettor munched on the stale bread like a giant mouse next to Tess's ear.

"Why?" said Nal.

"Maybe we can pay the guard to let us out."

"Anybody not want their bread?" Mr. Nettor asked, his voice brimming with hope.

"Is food all you can think about right now?" snapped Tess. "We're in the middle of a crisis here."

"The rocks are in the wagon," said Gramps.

"Along with all my fabric," said Mr. Nettor.

"No one will miss a bunch of travelers if they let us die," said Gramps. "There's no way they'll strike a deal. We don't have anything to bargain with."

Tess slumped against the wall, tears stinging her eyes and wishing she hadn't left the only remaining black cherry in Mr. Nettor's wagon. If there was ever a time to take a bite, now was it.

CHAPTER 37

Dawning of the Day of Sacrifice

Jak dumped the rest of the tea out on the floor slowly over the rest of the night so the priest would think he was drinking it. The wide double doors of the house had been flung open, and the whole town flowed through. He had been brought every delicacy the town had: dancing girls, a foot rub, flowers for his hair, exotic food. Some of the foods he had seen at the Remembrance Day feast, but there were several concoctions he had never seen before. Any other time he would have loved to dive in and eat like it was the last day of his life, but now that it really *was* his last day of life, his appetite had left him.

He wondered if El knew what was going on. Guardian's words flew back to his mind: *Yahweh is my protection and my strength.* Jak sent out a telepathic message just in case Yahweh was in the neighborhood and could read his mind. He didn't know what to say, so he just mumbled whatever came to his mind. *Yahweh, I'm in trouble. Gonna be sacrificed tomorrow just like that lamb on Remembrance Day. Send help.* He hesitated, wondering if he needed to sign off, like in a letter — it couldn't hurt. *Sincerely, Jak Hamelton.*

He didn't know what he was expecting—maybe a flash of lightning or a horse to gallop through the doors and take him away, but nothing happened.

Jak wasn't surprised. "Yahweh is my protection and my strength," was a useless pile of words. Even if Yahweh did hear him, Jak couldn't think of one good reason why he would come to help him. Certainly, El had better things to do.

The party went till late in the night. Jak emptied at least three glasses of tea on the floor, making sure to keep as blank a stare on his face as he could. He got a lot of practice at blank stares in his sixth-grade English class, so it wasn't that hard. The hard part was keeping his eyes open. It must have been three o'clock in the morning before the two doors finally banged shut and Jak was hustled through an adjoining door into a bedroom.

He was so tired he hardly noticed the straw pushing into his back or the cold draft crawling along the floor. Even though he knew this was the last night of his life, his eyes closed shut, and he fell asleep.

Jak woke with a large hand clamped over his mouth and a figure stooped over his bed—a large figure that smelled like the wind. A huge head came near his. "Shhh! Yahweh sent me to give you this. It's all you need."

The figure thrust a stick into Jak's hand and abruptly disappeared at the same moment the door to the bedroom creaked open. A guard poked his head in the door and shone a lamplight into the room. Jak lay perfectly still, pretending to be asleep.

The door clicked shut again and Jak sat up, swung his feet onto the cold floor, and shivered.

Guardian had been there, and, from the knots that ran along the stick, Jak knew he was holding his sparring stick. But what was he supposed to do with it? *Does El expect me to knock the guards over the head and then limp away?* There was only one way out of the room, and that was the door he had come through. There weren't any windows or back doors. He felt the floor with his toes, hoping to find the sandals Beerta had given him, but the only thing he found was the book bag; at least they hadn't taken the book. But in his search for shoes, he also discovered something else: the source of the draft.

It was a chink in the wall, actually more than a chink. He could see a bit of gray light through the hole - dawn was coming fast. He had to get out of there as soon as possible. People would probably sleep a little later than normal because of the party, but once the sun was full up, it would be time for the sacrifice, and the last thing he wanted to do was end up like that lamb.

He poked his stick into the chink and rattled it around. Part of the wall fell off in chunks. He rattled it around again as quietly as he could, and more chunks fell off. He kept poking, and soon a hole formed at the base of the wall. It wasn't a big hole, but it was ample enough for a twelve-year-old boy to slip through. His only dilemma was if the guard poked his head in again to check on him and found him gone.

He looked around the room. There was just enough light to make out the form of a pitcher of water. He dumped the water on the floor and put the pitcher on the pillow, the bottom toward the head. Then he pulled the blankets up over the pitcher and fluffed them to look like a body. It wasn't perfect, but it would have to do.

Jak then scooted headfirst through the hole, checking to make sure no one was on the other side. The back of the room faced an alley, and it was empty. He pulled himself all the way through and stood up. *Now, where did they put Gramps and the others?*

Something moved near the corner, and Jak flattened himself next to the wall. A small shadow darted straight toward Jak, wagging her tail and licking his hand.

Jak bent down and rubbed her ears. "Macy? Good girl! Have you been waiting for me all night? Where are Gramps and Tess?"

She turned and trotted down the alley, occasionally stopping and turning to see if Jak was still following. She led him straight toward a little hut not far from the field, stopped by a tree, gave a quiet whine, and gazed at the hut.

It was easy to see why she stopped - an armed guard stood in front of the hut. The sky suddenly softened to a light pink, and a rooster crowed. The day had begun.

Sweat broke out on Jak's forehead. He had to think of something fast or he'd be in trouble.

The cards! That's it! thought Jak. *I need the cards!* He hadn't asked anyone yet about the laughing man. He dug in the bag, pulled out the gunny sack, and found the right card. Then he strode in full view of the guard straight toward the hut.

The guard stiffened. "Shale, what're you doing out? You're s'posed to be in seclusion at the priest's house."

"I was there all night, but he said I could take a last morning walk before the sacrifice. Can you help me with something?"

"What is it?" said the guard cautiously.

"Have you seen this man before?"

The guard took the card and scrutinized it in the early-morning light.

It was now or never. Jak swung his lance as hard as he could, just the way Nal had showed him, and cracked the guard over the head. Once the guard had crumpled to the ground, Jak picked up the card and said, "I'll take that as a no." He swung open the door and realized just in time that most of the floor was really a hole. "Gramps? You down there?"

"Jak? Is that you?"

"Yeah, and we've got to get out of here! They're going to kill me."

"Kill you?" said Tess. "I thought you were…"

"Throw the ladder down," interrupted Gramps, "the rope one near the door."

Jak pulled the ladder from a hook and tossed it down the hole.

Tess came up first and disappeared behind the trees. It took the full strength of both Gramps and Nal to get Mr. Nettor up the ladder.

"As soon as we get back to the wagon," said Nal, heaving with all his might to push Mr. Nettor's ample rear end higher, "we're switching your snack bag with the donkey feed. Some carrots would do you good."

By the time they all made it to the top, the guard was beginning to stir. Jak considered whacking him over the head again, but he didn't have the heart to do it.

"They took the wagon over this way," said Mr. Nettor, pointing across the field.

They padded to the other side of the field to the end of the village. Sure enough, the wagon sat outside a stable.

"We're going to have to pull it," whispered Mr. Nettor. "It'll make too much noise to hook the donkeys up right now."

Gramps nodded his head. "You get the animals and we'll start pulling." Gramps and Nal grabbed the tongs of the wagon and began heaving it toward the sunrise.

Mr. Nettor caught up with them at a bend in the path, just out of sight of the village with Blackey and Whitey. "Help me," he puffed. "And hurry! I heard shouting in the village."

They slipped the harnesses over the donkeys as fast as they could and made their escape into the rising sun.

A long, dark form slid through the deepest corners of the river, hunting. Scorch's head darted through the water and snatched a river rat from the mud. She chewed slowly, squeezing every bit of flavor from the hide, but it didn't satisfy her; a rat was not the meal she was seeking. The serpent continued nosing her way through the water. Her primitive brain knew only one instinct. She was always on the move, always hunting, always licking the air with her tongue, straining for the smell of the boy. She had collected many, but none were him, none tasted of the same sweat and blood.

It was a lot harder than it used to be now that she was older and larger. Every year her neck and tail grew several inches in length, and she had to rely more and more on either the swimming or slithering to get where she wanted to go. To make things even more difficult, her flippers were almost useless on land.

She raised her head above the surface of the water and flicked her tongue, tasting the air for the telltale odor. Suddenly, she stopped swimming and flicked her tongue again; excitement began racing through her veins at the aroma. She twisted her coils, thrashing her great bulk in the other direction, and slithered back downstream.

Maybe today would be the day.

Cain's eyelids blinked open and drank in the sunlight that was just beginning to seep over the horizon. The wagon had never come out of the village last night, so he had bedded down on a rise with a clear view overlooking the village.

He wiped the sweat from his face with his robe.

The memory came in his dreams almost every night now: El standing before him, a burlap-sack-skinned man, tiny shafts of light bursting through the cracks and hitting him straight in the heart, saying the same words each time, "Sin is crouching at the door, and its desire is for you, but you must master it...master it...master it..."

But instead of mastering it, Cain had opened the door wide and embraced the rage against his brother. "Come out to see the freshly formed heads of grain," he had said to entice Abel deep into the fields.

Two pair of feet headed into the crops, but only one pair headed out, accompanied by a lance wet with blood. It stained the wood so deeply that it still showed red after a thousand washings in the river.

He could never trust El like his brother had, especially not now. The blood of many was on his hands. Death could not be undone, and 400 years of guilt was ripping him apart.

He rose and wrapped the robe around his shoulders, cinching it tight around his waist. Then he stopped and sniffed the air, his eyes darting in all directions. Being a wanderer for the past four centuries had sharpened his nose, and he knew the smell that now wafted from the river. He had smelled it several times before, each time right before the Black Serpent attacked.

He hesitated and laced his sandals slowly, thinking of the boy with the book and the murders that could not be undone. *Or can they? Can death really be undone?* He squinted his eyes against the sun as the thought tumbled around in his head. Then he stood and quickly melted into the morning, taking a path he knew like the back of his hand.

CHAPTER 38

The Stinky Card

They didn't let Blackey and Whitey stop running till almost lunchtime. During the trip, Jak told them what had happened.

"They were going to sacrifice you?" said Tess, turning over the pillows in the back of the wagon. "But didn't we get there during this kid's funeral? Why would they kill someone who just returned from the dead?"

"They said something about locust plagues destroying their food for the past three years and needing to appease Yahweh. I guess the reason they were so sad at the funeral had nothing to do with the boy dying and more to do with the fact that their sacrifice had been taken from them."

"And you look just like him," said Mr. Nettor. "Strange...strange indeed. Good thing you found a way to escape."

Tess continued to lift up objects in the back of the wagon and then set them back down.

"That's the part I don't understand," said Jak. "How did Guardian know where I was when all I did was send some kind of telepathic message to El?"

"Coincidence, my boy—a fortuitous coincidence."

"Coincidence, my eye," said Gramps. "That was no coincidence. Yahweh must've heard him and sent Guardian to help him."

"Perhaps," said Nettor. "Believe what you will."

"No matter what happened back there," said Nal, "the Black Serpent is the one who took the other boy. I've been thinkin' about it, and I don't think it's a coincidence that the beast took a boy who looked like Jak. All the children the beast stole from our village were boys who looked a lot like Jak too. Remember Enoch's clothes? They fit you almost perfectly." He paused for a moment. "I think she's huntin' for you."

"Me?" said Jak, surprised. "But why?"

Nal nodded his head. "You were her friend in the garden before Adam and Eve ate the fruit of the Knowing Tree, right?"

Jak nodded his head.

"And the first thing she did after she changed was to attack you, right?"

Jak nodded his head again.

"I'm sorry to say it, but somethin's gone funny in her head. She's after you."

Jak stared at Nal in disbelief. First Lucifer was after him, then Cain, and now Scorch. He was never going to make it to Megiddo.

Tess finally stopped her inspection of the back of the wagon and put her hands on her hips. "Has anybody seen the black cherry? I put it on this shelf yesterday morning before I sat down, and now I can't find it."

Mr. Nettor's eyebrows raised. "Uh, a black cherry?"

"Yeah, it was right here," she said, pointing to the shelf.

The little man rubbed his chin. "Just one cherry sitting by itself?" He looked away with a guilty expression on his face. "I believe I ate it," he said quietly.

"You ate it?" said Tess, the shock spreading all the way to her ears.

"I'm so sorry. I had no idea it was yours. I thought one of those blaggards back in the village left it in the wagon. I'll get you another, my dear, I promise. We can easily find cherries in any market."

Tess deflated onto a pillow. "Not cherries like that one," she said just loud enough that Jak could hear her. She sat silently looking out the back of the wagon as Gramps explained to Mr. Nettor what was so special about that particular cherry.

Jak was sorry to see Tess so out of sorts now that her only method of escape had disappeared, but he was secretly glad the black cherry was gone.

Now there was no question, the only way home was to follow the Thread to the end, the place where El said the dead would come back to life, the place where they would find Gramma Josie.

A little before noon, a large black object loomed into view like a gigantic black wart on the horizon.

"Aha!" said Mr. Nettor, waving his hand gleefully at the object. "The Grand Dome of Urchetaal! I thought we were getting near it. I have a friend here, and soon we shall be dining on the finest fruits of the bush—delectable, delightful, delicious!" He smacked his lips together, dribbling a bit of spittle down his double chin.

But as they moved ahead, no houses came into view. All they encountered were mounds of rubble blackened with soot, strewn like cow dung across the flat land. Nothing stirred as they picked their way through the debris. It was as quiet and still as a graveyard. But even among all that destruction, the most disturbing part of the landscape was the dome itself.

The dome stood guard over the land, a quiet giant black rock, rough and jagged with deep crevices and cracks in the face like a small mountain. A weathered brown rope draped around the rock from top to bottom like Christmas tree garland, and hanging from the rope were skulls—hundreds upon hundreds of human skulls.

Mr. Nettor pulled Blackey and Whitey up short in front of the dome and bounced down from the seat.

"No!" he cried in disbelief, his face contorted with grief. "I was just here a fortnight ago, and the land was bursting with life." He raised his arms and waved in front of the dome. "The market was here, and people were selling baskets and baskets and baskets of the fabled urche berry, along with purple cloth, dyed with the juice of the urche berry. There were urche berry pie, corn fritters, apple prisquet, and peach hepples. What has happened?"

"Rail," said Gramps, putting his hand on the little man's shoulder, "it's been a long time. The bones are bleached white. Remember, we're on the Thread's path now, so it might have been several hundred years since you've been here."

Mr. Nettor wiped a tear from his face with his handkerchief. "The passage of time should not have affected Urchetaal. It was boasted to be a city that would last until the end of... oh!" Mr. Nettor caught his breath, and his hand flew to his mouth as he stumbled over to the rock.

On one of the lowest strands of garland hung a skull with a large gold front tooth. It caught the rays of the sun and played them back across the road.

Mr. Nettor reached up to the skull, but stopped an inch before the gold tooth, staring and sputtering.

"Balliah," he said. "This is him, my friend I told you about. I would recognize his gold tooth anywhere." He went silent and pulled his hand away.

They didn't stay long in the dismal place. By mid-afternoon, the Thread had led them to a wide river that cut directly south. Boulders lined the banks on both sides, but each side was distinctly different than the other: on the east side of the river, fields of golden grass stretched into the distance; while on the west side by the wagon, trees edged their way all the way up to the boulders.

Mr. Nettor pulled the wagon up to a shady spot under some oaks, and they got out to stretch their legs. No one had said much since they left Urchetaal. Mr. Nettor still looked like he was in shock, and it didn't seem right to talk about the weather, so it was best not to say anything at all.

The heat of the sun was ferocious, so Jak limped down to the riverbank to fill the water skins. The cool sand in the shallow of the river felt good in between his toes. The poison had stayed at bay ever since the Remembrance Day fire, but today, his foot was beginning to twinge.

Nal jumped down from the tree he had climbed and ran down to the river. "What're you doin' gettin' water? You have a hard enough time getting' yerself where you need to go."

Jak laughed. "I'm not dead; I just have a hard time walking." As hard as it was for him to get around, he hated being treated like a cripple, so he did as much as he could for himself. "Is this the Pishon?"

"No," answered Nal. "The Pishon is much wider than this, so wide you'd have to ferry across. This probably feeds into the Pishon at some point downstream though." Nal dipped a skin under the water until it was fat and full, then heaved it onto the bank and tied it shut with the leather tongs. He paused before filling another skin. "You know the man you asked about the other day, the one with the brown tunic?"

"Yeah." Jak opened the mouth of a skin wide and watched the water swirl inside with a gurgle.

Nal dipped the next skin in the water, and it immediately began to swell. "I saw 'im yesterday when you were sleepin'."

Jak stopped filling the skin and stood up. "You did? Where?"

Macy growled and trotted back and forth on the shore, evidently smelling a muskrat or a skunk.

"He was headin' the same direction we were, but he hurried into the woods before I could get a good look at 'im.'"

"That makes three times in three days we've seen him," said Jak. "It has to be Cain. Who else would be following us?" He dipped the skin back under the surface, lost in thought, unaware of the ripples that had surfaced upstream.

Suddenly, a long black body exploded out of the water and launched itself straight toward the shallows where Jak stood.

Macy dove into the river in front of Jak, barking while the creature crashed down into the water, sending a spray twenty feet in the air.

Stunned, Jak dropped the skin and stumbled toward the shore while the beast writhed, half-swimming, half-slithering through the shallow water toward Jak.

But before Jak had even gotten onto the bank, a barrage of nets shot across the river from the opposite bank. A mob of men charged into the water, shouting and throwing ropes and more nets around the beast.

Nal grabbed Jak's arm. "C'mon!"

They scrambled up the bank and watched from the safety of the trees. There had to be at least one hundred men in the water wrapped around Scorch's body, pressing her into the sand of the shallows. Scorch twisted and fought with all of her strength, tossing men around like beanbags, but every man she tossed was quickly replaced by two more men from the bank. The battle raged on for almost ten minutes until the men finally managed to weigh the beast down. Drops of yellow drool spilled down her fangs, and her eyes darted wildly. A swarthy man in a white turban and a victorious grin strode confidently through the water, chuckling to himself, and strapped an iron muzzle to her face. As soon as the muzzle was in place, Scorch went strangely limp, as if her will to struggle had been sucked away.

"Haul him up, boys!" the turbaned man called.

The men hauled Scorch to the other side of the river, rolled her up the bank, and loaded her onto a long cart. The tip of her snout touched the front of the cart, and the tip of her tail dripped over the back. A team of ten donkeys shied nervously at the front as the great serpent was heaved into the cart behind them.

Only then did Macy clamber up the bank and shake the water from her fur.

Tess and Gramps ran down to where Jak and Nal stood on the bank. Mr. Nettor waddled behind as quickly as he could.

"What happened? What's going on?" asked Tess. Her hair was wound around her head in a tangled mess from running, and she quickly brushed it behind her ears.

Nal pointed to the other shore. "The beast almost ate Jak for lunch!"

"She was this close to us?" Gramps shook his head, breathless from the sprint. "Where'd the men come from?"

Jak shrugged his shoulders. "Don't know. As soon as Scorch came, they were there—like they knew she was going to show up. But I didn't see them until I saw her."

"Lucky for you, Jak," said Mr. Nettor, leaning on his knees and panting heavily.

"Red doesn't travel with her, does he?" asked Jak.

"You mean Beelz?" asked Nal.

"Yeah, him."

"Not that I know of. They've never been seen together, but I s'pose he could be around somewhere."

As they watched the cart creak east, the Thread floated across the river and followed the same path the men had taken.

Jak took a deep breath. "The Thread just crossed the river, so let's follow it right away, while I can still see Scorch strapped to that wagon."

They hurried back up to the wagon, repacked their supplies, and creaked toward the river.

Blackey's and Whitey's ears flicked, and they danced forward and backwards as they got close to the water. Macy growled again; the scent of the serpent must've hung strong in the air, because the donkeys and the dog didn't want to go in. Mr. Nettor flicked his whip several times, and the stubborn animals finally cantered into the water.

All eyes watched both sides of the river. They knew if Beelz showed up, they were doomed. The donkeys made a quick trip of it, pulling them up and out soon after entering. They shook themselves on the other side, shedding the water from their hides and flicking their ears.

The Scorch processional was barely in sight. For such a large cavalcade, they made good time.

On one hand, it made Jak feel good to know that Scorch had been captured and lay strapped to the wagon ahead of them, but on the other, he couldn't help feeling sorry for her. She hadn't asked to become what she was any more than he had.

Soon a white wall and a mammoth gate came into view. The wall sprawled across the plain and crawled into the hills in the north. Above the wall, a few rooftops peeked out. The processional had stopped outside the city, but the Thread dipped through the gate and entered.

"We're supposed to go inside," said Jak, "That's where the Thread went."

When they made it to the gate, the procession had not moved an inch. A gaggle of curious onlookers kept a healthy distance between themselves and the wagon with the long black load.

"Do you think it's safe to go past her?" asked Jak nervously. He didn't want to look at her, but he couldn't help himself.

Scorch lay still as a stone, her eyes wide open and her skin drying in the sun. She almost looked dead already.

"Only one way to find out, m' boy," said Mr. Nettor. He clicked to the donkeys, and they trotted past the wagon, but as soon as they passed the cart, Scorch's tongue flickered, and she jerked. The man at her head pressed his thumb into the harness near the forehead, and she calmed down again. And then they were through the gate, safe.

Jak's body relaxed, but his mind was buzzing. *What are they going to do to her? Kill her? It's not like somebody can keep her as a pet. But if the promise about the Quelcher is true, they won't be able to kill her anyway.* At least he didn't think they would. *That's the Quelcher's job, right?*

The Thread made it as far as the marketplace and then stopped. The market was crowded with people, wagons, and donkeys. Strings of fat white onions and purple and green grapes hung in the market stalls. Below them were baskets of oranges, pomegranates, bananas, green peppers, flowers, brightly colored tunics, pants, and robes, but no one was shopping. Instead, everyone stood silent and fidgeting, their eyes glued to the same turbaned man from the river who was now standing on top of a rough wooden stage.

Next to him stood a line of wilting wide-eyed children of various ages— from a four-year-old little boy with an intense cowlick to a girl about Jak's age with big brown eyes. They were clothed in ill-fitting robes that either trailed on the wooden slats behind them or stopped just short of their ankles, and their skin looked as if a week's worth of dirt had recently been scrubbed away.

At first, Jak thought they were a part of a theater performance in the market, but then he noticed a light black chain that connected black manacles around each of their ankles.

He choked back a cry, realizing that they were slaves and that the turbaned man must have interrupted a slave auction.

"Tomorrow," shouted the man, waving one arm in the air, "the fights will be better than ever. Ten young leviathans against the biggest, baddest beast east of Eden!"

"Is it the one?" shouted a woman holding a little boy who was sucking his thumb.

The man ignored her. "Never before have you seen such strength and cunning. And the teeth!" The man's eyes widened, and he exaggerated the size with both hands. "The teeth of this wretched beast are like shards of hardened glass."

"But is it the child-stealer?" called another woman.

He ignored her as well. "As long as three carts put together and as thick as a man! 'Twill be a fight to remember, that's for sure!"

The crowd was growing impatient, and several people shouted at the same time, "Is it the Black Serpent? Tell us!"

The man grinned and shushed the crowd with his hands. "Judge for yourselves, but keep quiet or you may arouse his fury." He winked and signaled someone at the gate, and the cart eked through the archway. The crowd stopped breathing.

As eager as they had been to know the identity of the beast, none ventured close to the wagon. They chose instead to press themselves as far as they could to the edges of the market, craning their necks to see the fabled serpent.

"Take 'im to the pools!" the turbaned man called out. "Give 'im a good rest 'fore the games begin." When the cart had disappeared up the street, the man stood with his hands extended out to the sky. "Tomorrow at noon shall be the most memorable fight of all time! Come early to place your bets, my friends. Will 'e live or will 'e die?" And then he jumped down from the wagon.

The buzz of the crowd could be felt, a tangible tingle in the air.

"Hold on," said Jak. "I have to see what's going to happen." He climbed down from the wagon and hobbled over to where the turbaned man was having a quiet conversation with another man who was smoking a long black pipe.

"How'd you catch 'im?" asked the smoker, blowing out a long ribbon of gray smoke.

"I got a tip. A man came in this mornin' and asked me if I'd like to catch the Black Serpent. I told 'im of course I would. There're plenty a little serpents 'round for fightin', but the Black Serpent is every matcher's dream. So he tells me to wait by the shallows today 'cause the beast'd be showin' up. Sure enough, 'e did! 'e's a big un, ain't 'e?"

The smoker nodded his head. "A beaut'! There'll be good money in 'im."

Jak tugged on the turbaned man's sleeve.

He looked down and inspected Jak like he was a cockroach. "What do you want, boy?"

"What are you going to do with her?"

"Her? Who're you talkin' about?" He spat on the ground, almost hitting Jak's foot.

"The Black Serpent is a her," said Jak, "not a him."

The two men looked at each other and broke into laughter. "And how would you know that, boy?" said the turbaned man, wiping his eyes on his sleeve. "Have you been peekin' at her when you shouldn't a been?" He laughed again before his sour demeanor returned. "Male or female makes no difference to me as long as the crowd likes 'im. A happy crowd buys more beer and makes more bets. The beast just needs some jabs to the head to get 'im riled up to give a good show. Gonna fight 'im against ten smaller serpents, I am. The Black Serpent 'as stolen boys far and wide, and plenty'll show up to watch 'im fight."

"But she'll die! She can't fight that many."

The man looked at Jak with a puzzled expression. "Don't matter to me if 'e lives or dies, as long as I end up with more money in my pocket." With that, he turned on his heel and strode off in a huff.

Jak stood there, a storm brewing in his stomach, but there was nothing he could do.

The Thread hadn't moved from the market, and nightfall was soon approaching, so they found a nearby inn where they could stay the night. "My treat," Mr. Nettor said as they approached the inn. "We've been camping out too many nights for my liking." As soon as they were settled, he went back down to the market to get some food for dinner, also his treat.

Jak lay on the bed with Macy's head resting on his lap. He couldn't stop thinking about the slave children. How had things gotten so bad since the garden? Everyplace they'd been since leaving East Eden had been contaminated with violence and evil; the goodness of the garden was completely gone.

He took the book and the cards out of the bag and stared at them, the weapons that supposedly could restore paradise.

"You're not going to read it, right?" said Tess, arching an eyebrow at him.

He hadn't told her about reading the book back in Eden or in East Eden, and he wasn't going to tell her now either.

"No. I'm just looking at the cards." It was true, because that's what he was doing, but his mind was really churning over what to do about Scorch. He began mindlessly shuffling through the cards. The first was a picture of a round-faced man playing a pipe, followed by a farmer with a rope leading a couple of cows.

Nal and Tess sat at the only table in the room playing a stick game that Nal called "Stinkers."

Gramps sat by the window, watching the crowd below. He looked a little bit more like his old self now. Some wrinkles had crept back into his forehead, and gray hair had begun to overtake the brown near his ears.

"You're getting gray again, Gramps," said Jak. He flipped over a card of a barrel-chested man with arms as thick as Jak's leg, pouring hot metal into a mold.

"I figgered as much," said Gramps, stretching a few strands out to check if he could see them. "I don't feel as strong as I did when we left the garden. Every now and then, my heart skips a beat. Makes me think about death all over again. I can't help wondering about your grandmother, what it'll be like to be with her again." He sighed and leaned heavily against the windowsill. "The Tree of Life is quite a discovery, Jak. Men have been searching for something like it for thousands of years. But we actually found it. We had it in our fingers and even tasted it for just a moment, but now it's gone."

Jak flipped over a card of a man in a green robe holding a sheaf of wheat. "Gramps, do you think Scorch could ever change back to the way she was?"

"Change back?"

"Yeah. I don't mean her body, but her mind... so she's nice again."

Gramps stared out the window and stroked his beard. "Well, I don't know. It'd have to be something pretty powerful to bring her back—maybe even something from the garden itself. Too bad we don't have any of that fruit."

Jak flipped over a card of the Tree of Life and a zing spun up his spine. He *did* have something from the garden! He dug in the bag and pulled out the zinger seed. It still had some dirt on it from when he had tried to plant it in the riverbank at the top of Split Falls. He brushed the dirt away and held it aloft. "Something like this?"

Gramps turned his head away from the last rays of the setting sun to look. When he saw what Jak was holding, his jaw dropped. "Where'd you get that?"

"From the very first zinger I ate. It ended up in the bag, and I've had it ever since."

"Tempted to gnaw on it myself," said Gramps, turning the seed around in his fingers to inspect it. "But I won't."

"You stink!" shouted Tess.

Nal groaned.

"So do you, Tess," Gramps replied.

She made a face. "I was talking to Nal, not you. We're playing a game."

"So you think that if Scorch ate it," said Jak, "it might change her?"

"I don't know, son. You never know what'll happen with the Tree of Life. Maybe something will happen, or maybe nothing at all. You'd never get close enough to her to try anyway. She'd kill you, Jak. She's not your pet anymore, I'm afraid. You know that, right?"

Jak nodded his head. "Yeah, I know." He flipped over another card. This one pictured a man with a straight nose and a grin – a man Jak had seen before. A tiny shower of sparks sputtered, sending an acrid odor into the air and etching a name into the bottom of the card.

"What?" roared Beelz, belching a plume of purple fire.

A trio of Lights stood resolutely before the serpent, dripping onto the rocks on the beach as they bore the brunt of Beelz's outburst.

"What do you mean sssomebody elssse captured the female ssserpent before you could? You incompetent foolsss!" Beelz slithered on the rocks around the Lights, scraping deep ruts in the ground with the scales on his belly. "How hard iss it to trap a sssilly little ssserpent? Mussst I do everything myssself?"

"Perhaps you should, Most Marvelous Moron," one of the Lights retorted. "Then you could taste for yourself how easy it is *not* to accomplish some of the odious chores you put us to."

"Yes," chimed in a second. "It is most difficult to determine the where and the when of her arrival. We were almost upon her when the humans caught her."

"We were almossst upon her when the humanss caught her," mimicked Beelz. "Excussess! Nothing but lame excussess. How isss it the inssipid humanss could capture her and you could not?"

"We do not know," the squeaky voice of the third answered, "but we do know where they have taken her."

"Then why didn't you begin with that information, you fool? Where iss ssshe?"

"They have taken her to the pools at Enoch."

Beelz raised his head ten feet in the air, his eyelids blinking sideways against the wind blowing off the ocean. "Well, then, your work isss half-done. Sssend the Beelzin tonight to inject the potion through the diamond and free her to ressume her hunt for the boy." He rasped a laugh. "Or ssshould I say, *my* hunt for the boy."

CHAPTER 39

Squish and Burgers

ᘿ

"Ew, Jak!" said Tess, wrinkling her nose. "You really do stink."

"No I don't! It's the card. Come and look. As soon as I touched it, those sparks flew again and a name showed up."

"The laughing-man card?" said Tess, getting up out of her seat.

"No, a different one. It's a picture of Seth. Remember Seth? Adam and Eve's son?"

Everyone crowded around Jak and looked at the card in Jak's hand. "SETH" was now etched in the black box at the bottom.

"How come this card did something but none of the others did?" said Tess.

"Have you touched all the cards tonight?" asked Gramps, flipping through the rest of the deck.

"Not yet," said Jak. He picked up the next card without even looking at it. As soon as he touched it, the sparks flew, etching "C-A-I-N" into the box. "Cain!" said Jak.

"Yep, that's definitely Cain," said Nal. "Same sour-puss face he's 'ad for years."

Suddenly, Jak's brain clicked, and his stomach flip-flopped. "Nal, the man following us is Cain. I just know it."

"What makes you so sure?" said Nal.

"Look at the tunic on the card. It's the same tree-bark brown as the one the man is wearing, and I just remembered where I saw the axe-head lance. I saw it on Remembrance Day, leaning against the table next to Cain. I'm positive it's him."

Gramps took in a deep breath. "Well, that's what we feared from the beginning, so it's not much of a surprise."

"True," said Jak, "but what do we do?"

Just then, the sound of heavy footsteps came thudding up the stairs and a hand lightly pounded the door. "Anybody home?" a familiar voice called from the other side of the door.

Nal unbarred the door and swung it open. "Come on in, Mr. Nettor."

Mr. Nettor rolled in with a huge crocodile smile on his face. "Pack your things. I have a surprise for you."

"But we just got here," said Tess.

"Ah, I know, but I discovered a friend of a friend of a friend here in the city. He lives not far from the market, and he's invited us to stay in his home, a very nice home if I do say so myself. I think you'll find it much to your liking, young lady."

Mr. Nettor was right. A servant in a starch-white robe opened the double-door gate that hung in an archway of the wall that surrounded the house. He bowed his head. "Come in. Master Lamech is expecting you. Your wagon and donkeys have already been seen to."

"Thank you, m'boy," said Mr. Nettor, and he led them through the gate into a very busy open courtyard.

Surrounded by a ring of palm trees, a group of small children splashed in a pool along with a family of otters. Older children played in the courtyard; one was riding a tiger and another a gorilla while the rest chased them around the yard followed by a pack of monkeys.

Their mothers chatted in the shade while cutting up a variety of fruits and vegetables, occasionally shouting at one or another of the children. Smoke and a loud clanging came through an archway on one side of the courtyard, while on the other side the sound of music being played on stringed instrument came through another archway. Men milled about, making their way through each of the archways talking and laughing.

A small tower jutted up at each corner of the complex, and everything seemed clean, whitewashed bone white.

A man in a green sash and a white robe walked out of a doorway with his arms extended. When the women on the other side of the pool saw him, two of them got up and hurried to his side.

"Ah, my dearest Rail! Welcome!" He kissed Mr. Nettor on both cheeks and then turned his attention to the rest of them, bowing a sweeping bow. "My name is Lamech." He put his arms around both women. "This is my wife Adah." He gestured with his head toward the plump woman on his left. "And my wife Zillah." He nodded toward the taller woman on his right. Both women nodded and smiled along with Lamech as he spread his arms wide. "Welcome to our home!"

Lamech's hair was black as crow feathers, swept back so it just touched his shoulders. A long white scar jagged from his right temple down across his cheek and ended just before his lips, making it look like he wore a mask over his face.

"This is Clarence Thompson," said Mr. Nettor, pointing to Gramps.

Gramps stuck out his hand, but Lamech ignored it and instead grabbed Gramps's neck, brought his face to Gramps's, and kissed him on both cheeks. "Welcome, Clarence!"

Gramps sputtered, "Uh, thank you."

"And this is Jak, Tess, and Nal." said Mr. Nettor. Macy poked her head out from behind Jak. "And Macy," he added.

"Welcome! Welcome to Enoch. Friends of Rail's are friends of ours!"

The blood drained from Nal's face. "Did you say Enoch?"

"Yes," said Lamech. "That is the name of this city."

"How did it get its name?"

"It was the name of the firstborn son of the man who founded the city. The son lives on the west hill by the pools."

"Oh." His face fell, and he said nothing more.

"Is something wrong?" asked Lamech, cocking one eyebrow.

"It's just that I'm looking for my brother. He was lost five years ago. The Black Serpent took him. His name is also Enoch."

Lamech shook his head. "I'm sorry to tell you this, son, but if the Black Serpent took him, I'm afraid your brother is no more." Nal did not reply.

"I asked Lamech about Urchetaal," said Mr. Nettor. "He said it has been abandoned for fifty years."

"Fifty years?" said Gramps. "What year is it right now anyway?"

"It has been 749 years since Yahweh drew Adam from the dirt," said Lamech.

"Wow! The Thread has taken us through 249 years since Thursday," said Jak.

Lamech smiled. "The Thread will do that, I hear." He led them to a table on the other side of the pool and they sat down. Another servant appeared with glasses and poured a smoky white liquid that smelled like coconut milk.

"Urchetaal was a marvelous place," said Lamech wistfully, setting his glass down and wiping his beard with a cloth. "It was destroyed by the Nephilim, you know."

"What's a Nephilim?" asked Jak.

"Nephilim is the name we give to the giant folk."

"Giants?" said Jak and Tess at the same time.

"You don't mean *real* giants," said Tess, "like the 'fe, fi, fo, fum, I smell the blood of an Englishman' kind of giant, right?"

"I am not sure what that kind of giant is. I'm talking about a giant as in an exceptionally large human being."

"How big are they?" asked Jak.

"Oh, nine or ten feet tall. Some have six fingers on each hand. They are not a bad-looking lot, just big."

Gramps gave a low whistle. "So you're saying real giants called the Nephilim live around here?"

"Mostly in the mountains, but many live in the flatlands as well."

"What happened to Urchetaal?" asked Nal.

"Stupidity." Lamech took another swig and wiped his beard once again. "Urchetaal was a thriving village for many years. The soil in that region is just right for a special berry called urche, hence the town's name of Urchetaal. Have you tasted urche yet?"

None of them had ever even heard of it except Mr. Nettor.

"You really must try some before you leave. It's a dark berry grown on vines that explodes in your mouth and sends a sweetness of the sort no other berry can even hope for. Quite tasty, I must say! The prosperity of Urchetaal grew as easily as the berry did. People would come from miles to buy berries, including the giants. And, being so large, they always bought a great deal, which made it very tempting for one of the Urchetaal elders to skew his scales."

"Skew his scales?" asked Tess.

"Yes. The man sabotaged the scales so they read incorrectly. When the giants bought a pound of urche, he really only gave them three quarters of a pound. That isn't so bad if you're only buying a pound, but these giants bought hundreds of pounds every harvest season. No one knows how many years the elder tricked the giants, but when the giants found out, they stormed the village, and...well, you saw the result. It was a very graphic signal to the rest of the world that it is unwise to swindle a giant."

"But where did the giants come from?" asked Nal. "I thought everyone descended from Adam and Eve, but they're not *that* tall."

"That's the strange part," said Lamech, nodding his head. "The mothers are normal human women, but the fathers are altogether different. They're hardly even flesh and blood. It's more like they're made out of light. Some think they're not even from this world, yet they have a hearty appetite for flesh and blood."

"They eat people?" said Jak.

"No, no, no, not that. They have a hearty appetite for flesh-and-blood *beauty*. If a town has an exceptionally beautiful girl, it is almost certain she will be taken by the Lights as a wife. It's so bad that sometimes a father will mutilate his own daughter's face to keep her strength in the village. These creatures take whomever they please without offering any sort of dowry. The girls never last long though."

"Because the Lights eat them?" said Jak.

"No. I already told you they don't eat people. The girls don't last long because of the babies. I'm told that the first of the Nephilim, Anak, weighed twenty-five pounds at birth. The women are the same size as you and me. Most die in childbirth with their first giant baby, which means that the Lights are constantly on the prowl for new beautiful girls."

At this point, Lamech glanced long and hard at Tess without speaking. "I don't mean to be forward, Clarence, but your granddaughter may be at risk in this part of the country. Many fathers try to keep their girls plain in case the Lights show up. You never know when they will come. They just appear, like the mist. Is there any way we could make her—oh, how shall I say it—ugly?"

"I suppose we could cut her hair," Gramps said, lifting a lock of Tess's hair.

"No way!" said Tess, jerking it out of his hand. "I've been working for two years to grow my hair out. There is no way you're cutting my hair."

"But what about the Lights?"

"I'll scratch their eyes out before I let one of them take me."

Jak had no problem visualizing this.

"Well, think about it," said Lamech. "In the meantime, my home is your home." He looked at the sun. "It is getting late. I have some business to attend to with my field workers. Harvest is a busy season, but I will see you at dinner tonight. My servants will show you to your rooms. "

Jak, Nal, Mr. Nettor, and Gramps shared a room right next to Tess and a few other young women. Gramps and Mr. Nettor were already snoring, but Jak and Nal lay on their beds in the dark, listening to the nighttime sounds of the houses around them.

Jak's belly was full of roasted squash and apple pie. He had initially balked at the roasted squash, for the very word "squash" made him feel queasy. His mother knew this so whenever she made squash, she always called it "squish," and Jak would close his eyes and plug his nose as he stuffed the required spoonful into his mouth. Then he would quickly wash it down with a glass of milk and forkfuls of meatloaf or whatever else they were having for dinner. But the squash Lamech served wasn't that bad; it was kind of like a squishy orange hamburger.

Dinner had been quite an event, not unlike the Remembrance Day feast. There were all sorts of vegetables and fruits and beans and breads, but no meat—not a chicken leg or slice of roast beef in sight. It seemed odd because there were plenty of animals around. Entire flocks of sheep and goats wandered around the wagon as they followed the Thread, and Jak was certain someone somewhere must have discovered that eating meat was a good thing.

"Nal, doesn't anybody around here eat meat?" said Jak.

"Eat meat?" said Nal, as if the thought had never even occurred to him before. "You mean flesh, like muscles and skin? Are you serious?" He scrunched up his face like it was the most disgusting thing he'd ever heard.

"Yes, I'm serious."

"And where would we get this flesh? From dead people?"

"I don't mean people meat!" Jak had a sudden thought of chewing someone else's fingernails and almost gagged. "That would be gross. I don't think that's even legal. I mean animal meat. You know, like sheep, cows, pigs."

"And why would we eat this meat?" said Nal, confused. "El has given us plenty to eat without having to kill an animal."

"Because it's filling, it makes you strong, and it tastes good. There's nothing like a good burger."

"What's a burger?"

"A burger is the greatest invention since baseball. Mmmm... loaded up with pickles and cheese and ketchup and a pile of fries and..." But then he remembered Nal didn't know what a burger was, so he would have to start from the beginning. "It all starts with the cow, because burgers come from cows. The meat man must run the cow meat through some kind of grinder because it comes out in strings, like Play Dough run through the masher thingy. I'm pretty sure cow meat isn't stringy naturally. Otherwise, cows would wobble, and I've never seen a wobbling cow." Jak stopped, suddenly feeling like he was talking to the wall. "Nal, are you awake?"

Steady breathing was the only answer he got, which meant he would have to resume his hamburger monologue the next day. Maybe he could even convince them to try it. He lay on his bed thinking about how the meat man made hamburger, and then his thoughts drifted to his hamburger heel right after Scorch had ripped his leg apart. *Scorch.*

She was there, somewhere in the dark. The man with the white turban had said she was at the pools. *At least she's wet. She'll like that,* Jak thought.

He pulled the seed from his bag and held it up to the half-moon hanging in the window. *Maybe Gramps was right. Maybe this is exactly what she needs to get well, a seed from the fruit of the Tree of Life. But how could anybody get close enough to her without getting eaten first?*

Jak sat up as if he'd been hit by lightning. *The muzzle!* The turbaned man had put a muzzle on her, and she was probably still wearing it. There was something about the muzzle that had calmed her down. Knowing this was the only chance he was going to get, he rolled out of bed, slung the book bag around his neck, grabbed his sparring stick, and slipped out the door. Now all he had to do was find the pools.

CHAPTER 40

A Trio of Helpful Giants

A few torches flickered in the courtyard, but other than that, the yard was lit only by the moon. It was harder to get out of the housing complex than Jak thought it would be. He first tried the big gate, but it was guarded by a servant. He wasn't armed, but Jak wasn't going to whack him on the head to escape; he needed a quiet exit. Jak turned around without the guard seeing him and tiptoed in the other direction. On the other side of the complex, Jak discovered a single door that looked like it led outside, but it was barred with solid piece of lumber that was so heavy he could hardly lift it. That wasn't going to work either.

The door had a window cut into it that was covered with a wooden shutter. He reached up with the stick and flicked it open. The hole wasn't very big, but it looked big enough for him to squeeze through. He climbed up on top of the bar and peeked out. An alleyway ran on the other side. *Perfect.*

Jak dropped the stick through the window. It clattered on the cobblestones so loudly that Jak crouched down, hoping no one had noticed. When no one came to investigate, he squeezed through the window and dropped to the street, landing solidly on his left foot. Then he reached back through the window with the stick and tried to close the shutter, but he couldn't do it. There wasn't anything to latch onto, so he just left it open. He hoped it would go unnoticed, and besides that, he needed a way back in.

He hadn't taken more than two steps when a voice froze him in his tracks.

"Hey there! Ya wouldn' 'appen ta hev a shek'l on ya, wud ya?" A man staggered toward Jak with one hand on the wall to support himself. "'Just one's all I need." He hiccupped. "One tiny li'l shek'l so's I c'n git flow'rs for the bride. I'm goin' to a weddin' at the tav'rn, an' I can't show up without a presn't now, c'n I?" He swayed back and forth in the alley, alcohol reeking from every pore in his body.

"Um, no, I don't," said Jak. He started backing up. "Sorry."

"Hey, where're ya goin', ya lil' twerp?" The man grabbed for Jak's arm, but Jak turned around and ran as quickly as his bad leg allowed around the corner.

He didn't stop until he was well past the market place. The Thread still hung over the middle of the market, glowing a soft red; Jak made a mental note to ask Lamech first thing in the morning about the laughing-man card. There hadn't been an opportunity at dinner, but he had to make an opportunity at breakfast.

Lamech had told them Enoch lived on the west hill by the pools, which meant Jak had to go up the hill to find the pools.

Just then, he heard loud shouts coming from an alley. A man carrying a gunny sack shot out of the alley to the right and ran past Jak toward the market. A second later, three more men ran out of the alley shouting, "Thief! Stop him!"

Jak pressed himself against the wall as the men ran past, hoping his small size made him invisible. His head was turned sideways so that his right ear was pressed into the stone wall. He could hear a child crying on the other side. He really had to find the pools, but he couldn't tear himself away from the pitiful sound on the other side of the wall. *Who is it, and why are they crying?*

Jak turned around and saw a closed door set back into the wall behind him. A man slumped on the ground next to the door, snoring quietly. *Maybe there's a window in the alley.* Jak slunk into the alley. Sure enough, there was a barred window just above his head.

"But there's nothing we can do," whimpered a little boy. "We're gonna get sold, just like Mum 'n Dad. We'll prob'ly never see each other agin."

Jak caught his breath. It was the slave children he had seen on the wagon in the market.

"Hush, Rispah. Yahweh will help us."

"But tomorrow—"

"Shhh," repeated the girl. "Just go to sleep."

Jak couldn't stand it any longer. He found a log from a pile of wood stacked in the alley and set it up so he could stand on it. "Pssst," he hissed.

There was silence.

"Psst! It's okay. I want to help you."

"Where are you?" the girl asked.

"Up here, in the window."

Suddenly the dirty face of the brown-eyed girl was in front of his.

"Who are you?" she asked.

"I saw you today in the market. Are you slaves?"

The girl nodded. "We're to be sold tomorrow morning. Can you get us out of here?"

"I...I hope so," he said, but he had no idea of what to do.

"Is the man still guarding the door?"

"Kind of. He's sleeping."

"He had a key with him when he locked us in here. Did you see it?"

"No, but I can look." Jak sounded a lot braver than he felt, but he hopped down from the log and peeked around the corner.

The man was still sleeping. And no one was coming from either direction.

Jak nonchalantly walked back out of the alley until he was next to the man and then sat on the stoop like he was supposed to be there.

Still, the guard slept. Now that Jak was next to him he figured out why the man was in such a deep stupor. The sickening smell of old alcohol oozed from his breath and hung in the air like bad gas with no place to go. A knife and a horn rested in the guard's lap, and around his neck hung a large iron key.

Jak rubbed his chin, trying to figure out what to do. He was sure he'd never be able to get the key off the man's neck, not without waking him up, even if he was drunk. He touched the string that held the key. It was leather, too tough to rip or pull loose. *If only I had Gramps's knife, then I could just slit the leather and...wait a second!* He slowly reached for the guard's knife, nestled underneath one of his hands. Jak lifted one of the guard's fingers at a time until he was able to slide the blade free.

293

The man shifted positions and yawned but then settled back against the wall in a different position.

Jak sat perfectly still until the man stopped moving and then slowly brought the knife to the leather and gave one quick slice. The key dropped onto the man's chest, and the man's eyes opened.

"I think the pig'll win," he slurred. Then his eyes closed, and his head thumped back against the wall.

Jak slipped the key into the lock and turned until he heard a solid *click*. Then he pushed against the door, and the door creaked inward. He bit his tongue until the creaking stopped. The open space was just wide enough for him to slip his head in.

The room was full of children, the same children he had seen that morning on the slave wagon.

The brown-eyed girl jumped up. "C'mon!" she whispered to the others, herding them into a line. "Yahweh has sent help!" She led them silently, single-file, out the door and into the alley.

Jak closed the door behind them and ran after the children.

They were huddled under the window, waiting for him.

"Thank you," said the girl. "You saved our lives."

"Where are you going to go?"

"To the east gate. From there, we can find our way home." She hugged him. "G'bye."

The other children gave him a quick hug, and then she led them down the alley where they disappeared into the shadows.

Jak gulped and realized he was still holding the key. He dropped it behind the log and, after checking both ways, sauntered back into the street. He had to get out of there before he got caught, but he was glad he had stopped. He couldn't imagine getting torn away from his family and forced into slavery.

The road began to slant uphill, which seemed like the right direction. Hopefully, he would find somebody who could tell him where the pools were.

A lazy chorus of voices accompanied by the plinking of some stringed instrument floated out a well-lit doorway and down the street. Two men and a woman, arm in arm, ducked through the doorway, still singing, and stumbled down the street toward him.

Jak caught his breath. He hadn't noticed at first because all three were the same size, but it was obvious that their heads stood well above the roofs of some of the houses. *Giants.* Jak was so shocked that he forgot he was standing in the middle of the street, directly in the path of these enormous people. He stood with his mouth open, looking up until the giants were right in front of him. *What had Lamech called them? Nephilim?*

"Get out of the way, lad," one of the men said in a thick voice, "unless you wish to join our trio and make it a quartet."

"Ohhh, that would be a nice addition," said the woman, winking at Jak. Her voice was almost as deep as the man's. She held out her hand, and Jak recoiled. She had six fingers, each as thick as his wrist. "Oh, look at that! I don't think he's seen the likes of us before, have you?"

"No, ma'am," said Jak politely, shaking his head.

"He has manners," said the second man.

"Yes, sir," said Jak.

"I like that. Being called 'sir' is a nice change from 'freak,' wouldn't you say?"

"Yes, sir." Jak couldn't imagine anyone in their right mind calling the giants names. Certainly they could sit on anyone they didn't like and squish them flat as a pancake.

"What're you doing out so late, lad?" asked the first.

Jak's head spun. He hadn't prepared a story since he didn't think that he would need one so late at night, so he said the first thing that came to his mind. "Um, my father told me to get a good seat at the pools for the match tomorrow, so I'm heading up right now."

"That's the ticket!" said the second man. "The early bird gets the worm."

"That's why we're in town too," said the woman. "We just got in tonight from the hills. The bird couriers sent a message that this is supposed to be the biggest match ever. Did you hear that they caught the Black Serpent?"

"Yes, ma'am. That's why my father sent me so early, but I forgot how to get there. Do you know the way?"

"Oh, that's simple. You can't miss it," said the first giant. He turned halfway and pointed up the hill. "Just head straight up the hill till you can't go no more. They're at the very top, a round rock amphitheater. If you want to get splashed, sit near the front, but be careful, because sometimes a person in the front gets a bite taken out of him by one of the bigger serpents who slips over the edge, and I've heard the Black Serpent is the biggest of all of 'em. The smell of human flesh is hard for them to resist."

"That's right," said the second man. "Hard to resist."

The woman let loose a yawn and took both of her partners' arms again. "Well, it was nice talking with you, lad, but we must be off ourselves. High noon isn't far away, and we've got to get some sleep so we can get some good seats ourselves."

They started singing again and continued their stumble down the street.

Jak fingered the seed in the bag and hurried up the hill. His story had worked. Hopefully no one would become suspicious and follow him. Immediately the words *"Yahweh is my protection and my strength"* ran through his mind. He didn't know what El would think about his nighttime expedition, but it wouldn't hurt to send him another message, especially since the last one seemed to work.

He whispered the message this time as well as sending it by telepathy. "Hi again, Mr. Yahweh. It's me, Jak. I'm going to see if I can help Scorch with this seed from the Tree of Life, and it's kind of creepy out here in the dark, so I was just wondering if you could help me out." He hoped it wouldn't be too much, but they needed as much help as he did, so he decided to add one more request. "Can you help those kids too?" *There. That ought to do it.*

The giant's information was correct. The amphitheater was impossible to miss since it crowned the hill. Jak climbed the steep stairs that snaked up the side and stood at the very top. From there he could see for miles in the moonlight across the flatlands. It was strange to think that just a week earlier, the main thing on his mind had been how to find the perimeter of a triangle. Now his biggest concern was getting to Megiddo with the book to get rid of death, Beelz, and evil—and to avoid getting eaten by Scorch in the process. He hoped that last part would change tonight and maybe Scorch would come with them. He knew she would be good protection against Beelzebub if he could get her back to her normal self.

The other side of the amphitheater angled sharply down to a flat black body of water in the middle. The reflection of the moon wavered in a wake of ripples. He wondered if something was already swimming in the water. As if in answer to his question, a neck and head reared out of the water and shot a small blue flame into the air, but the head was much too small to be Scorch's.

He carefully picked his way down the bleachers. They had been hewn out of the rock and were separated from the pool by at least ten feet, but if he somehow tumbled into the water, no one would ever know where he went. He was sure his bones would be picked clean in a matter of minutes.

At the bottom of the bleachers, ten channels stretched from underneath the bleachers and connected to the pool. The head of each channel was blocked off from the pool by a barred gate that occasionally clanged as if something had rammed into it—something like an angry leviathan eager to break free.

He walked down a low corridor that sloped down under the bleachers and came to a gate that was locked with a heavy chain. It was obviously intended to keep out adults and not kids, because he easily climbed through the bars and continued down the corridor. Every twenty feet, a moonbeam strayed in through what must have been garbage chutes, because large piles of rotting banana peels and peanut shells lay in the tunnel beneath them. The piles stank, and Jak plugged his nose as he went by.

The path leveled off, and he came to an arched window on the side of the corridor blocked by thick iron bars. On the other side of the window lay a rock shelf that sloped off into a channel of water.

Suddenly, a fanged mouth shot out of the water, shrieking and slamming into the iron bars next to Jak.

Jak fell back to the rock wall of the corridor, shaking. He hoped the bars were strong enough to keep the beast contained in the channel.

The leviathan gnawed at the iron, green saliva dribbling onto the rock as its body writhed, trying to break through the bars to get at Jak, but the bars held firm.

Jak took a deep breath, wiped the sweat off his face, and hurried on to a second window, also barred with iron and leading to a channel. But the swirls in the channel were too small for Scorch, so he kept going until he had passed a total of nine chambers in all, each blocked by the iron bars and each containing a smaller leviathan.

The corridor came to a dead end at the tenth chamber. *This must be the one.*

He thrust his hand into the bag to reassure himself with the hard, smooth edges of the zinger seed. He was half-inclined to go back the way he came and climb into bed as if he had never ventured out in the first place, but he had to know if he could save her. He hoped the muzzle was still on, so she wouldn't bite him if the seed didn't help her.

The channel lay still for a moment, but then the water swirled and a huge black head reared. The water ran down the scales like a waterfall as the head rested itself on the rock shelf on the other side of the iron bars. A low moan escaped the creature's throat.

It was her. The chains of the muzzle rattled and clinked on the rock as she settled herself.

Jak's heart rattled and clinked as well, pounding so hard his chest hurt. He took a deep breath and slipped through the bars.

CHAPTER 41

How to Avoid Getting Eaten by a Serpent

He approached Scorch slowly. It was hard to believe that Man and Woman's rebellion had twisted such a beautiful creature into this ugly bulk of rough scales and teeth. If only they had left the Tree of Knowing Good and Evil alone, then evil never would have invaded, and the world wouldn't be such a mess. But it was too late now, and there was no way to undo what they had done.

He felt a tingling sensation against his side, so he reached into the bag again. The book was burning hot, and the thought entered his mind that there *was* a way to undo Man and Woman's rebellion and that that was the whole reason he was there. *Maybe I really am the Quelcher. Maybe I'll crush the evil right out of Scorch with the seed.*

"Hey, girl," said Jak softly. "It's me."

She opened one eye and stared at him lazily, as if she was drugged, but she didn't move.

He kept moving toward her, talking in a low, soothing voice. "I know you've had a rough time the past 750 years, but I think I have a way to help you."

She still didn't move – just kept watching him with one cloudy, unblinking yellow eye.

A narrow chasm, about six feet deep and a foot wide, separated Jak from Scorch. He would have to jump to get to her, so he pushed off with his left foot and quickly brought it forward so he could land on the same foot, but he tripped as he landed and his hand slapped against Scorch's face.

Still, she did not move. The muzzle was locked around the back of her head, forcing her jaws shut so tight that he wasn't sure if the seed would even fit in between her teeth. A solid metal stud at the top of the muzzle pressed so firmly into the diamond on her forehead that it was forcing a dent into the delicate white scales.

Jak rubbed his fingers over the white scales that he could touch, and a rumble climbed up Scorch's throat, vibrating the entire shelf.

She's purring, thought Jak. *Maybe she's remembering what it was like in the garden.* He ran his other hand around the top of the muzzle, trying to figure out if there was a way to loosen it so the stud didn't dig into her forehead so much. If he pulled hard enough, he was able to pull the stud away from the diamond, but as soon as he let go, it dug into her head once again.

Jak picked up a rock the size of a grape and stuffed it in between the muzzle and the tougher black scales around the diamond. This time, when he let go, the stud hung suspended a fraction of an inch away.

"There. That's better." He rubbed the white spot directly now.

Scorch closed her eyes, and the purr deepened.

"I brought you something," he said, holding the seed in front of her. "A seed from a zinger. I think it might help you, but I have to stuff it into your mouth."

It was like she knew exactly what he wanted because she bared her lips, further revealing two rows of teeth, the same teeth that had wrapped around his foot in Eden.

He shook the memory out of his head. He didn't want to think about that. He bent down and found a gap between two of the smaller teeth and shoved the seed in her mouth. "Swallow that and we'll see what happens."

Her tongue flickered out, licked the air next to Jak, and disappeared back into her mouth. Then it flickered out again, this time touching his hand. Her eyes burst open, no longer clouded, but clear, and her purr changed to a growl. She jerked her head off the shelf and smashed it against the rock walls of the chamber, shattering the muzzle lock and sending pieces of the broken muzzle plunging into the water.

It all happened so fast that Jak didn't have time to jump behind the safety of the iron bars.

Scorch's head shot like a bullet toward Jak, her mouth open and drooling a greenish-yellow ooze.

Jak frantically scrambled backwards, but he forgot about the chasm, and it's a good thing he did, because he tumbled over the edge just in time for Scorch's teeth to miss his head.

His face scraped against the edges of the rock until his body wedged sideways in a narrow spot near the bottom, leaving only his left arm free and dangling underneath toward the rock bottom.

He lay there for half a second, dazed and thinking he never should have come. His only chance was that Scorch would be confused about where he went.

At that moment, his heel twinged, and the ache—that same deep ache that had taken over in East Eden—swept up his leg.

No, not now! He willed the feeling to go back into his heel, but it didn't. Instead, the pain rocketed through his whole body.

He gasped and tried to curl up into a ball, but he couldn't move because his legs were pinned in between the rocks. Jak closed his eyes and tried to control his breathing, hoping it would lessen the pain. Deep breath in, let it out. Deep breath in, let it out.

Something warm and slimy dripped on his forehead.

He opened his eyes and saw a string of slime hanging from a long black forked tongue waving in the air above him.

She had found him.

The tongue slurped back up, and one yellow eye peered down into the crack. Then Scorch screeched and started scrabbling at the chasm with her teeth, but the hole was much too narrow for her head.

In a fit of frustration, she began ramming her face against the rocks like a giant hammer, trying to break them apart. The wall on Jak's right gave a sickening crack, but it didn't move. Scorch screeched again and let loose a torrent of fire into the crack, engulfing Jak's whole body in flames.

He gasped and turned his head to the side. The heat was unbearable. His skin felt like crackling bacon, and the pungent odor of burning flesh wafted up his nose.

"Yahweh!" he screamed. "Help me!"

The flames abruptly vanished.

The last thing Jak remembered was hearing Scorch screech and the iron bars of the chamber snapping. Then everything went black.

CHAPTER 42

The Unhappy Bald Giant

Jak felt a warm blanket on top of him and something wet pressing against his face. He tried to open his eyes but found that only his left eye would obey. As the light slowly faded into focus, a pair of paws scratched at the floor next to the bed, and he heard a familiar whine.

"Ah, you're back," said a woman's voice, low and rough. "You're a very lucky boy."

"Where am I?" he groaned. His mouth felt glued shut.

"You're back at Lamech's house, but it's a wonder he don't turn you out."

Jak turned his head to get a better look at the woman. But as soon as he did, the skin of his face crackled and it all came rushing back – Scorch, the crevice, the flame and the burning. The familiar throb hummed in his heel again, but it was nowhere near what it had been in the chasm.

A fat old woman with a pile of gray hair gathered in a bun knelt by his side and poured the contents of a pitcher over his head. Something wet and warm oozed over down his forehead.

"Don't move or you'll tear the bandages off your face and hand. You've already done enough damage both to yourself and to..." She stopped before finishing her sentence, narrowed her eyes at him, and put the pitcher next to a basin on the floor next to the bed.

"To what?" Jak mumbled. "What happened?" He tried to touch his face with his right hand, but he could hardly move it. It was numb—not only his hand, but the whole right side of his body was numb down to his waist. He looked down and discovered that his hand, chest, and waist were totally wrapped in bandages.

His left hand worked, though, so he raised it to his face and discovered his head was also wrapped in bandages. He wondered how much of him had burned and why his right side was completely numb, but he was afraid to ask.

The woman stood and shuffled out the door without answering his question about what happened.

"Jak?" Gramps peeked his head through the doorway and then came into the room followed by Tess. He ran his hand over his beard as he inspected Jak's new appearance. "You got hit hard up there. Glad Nal found you."

Tess wasn't nearly so calm. Her eyes were puffy, her face was red and she lit into him right away. "What were you thinking, Jak Hamelton? You're already a cripple, you know Scorch is hunting you, and..." She lowered her voice. "And supposedly you're on a mission from El to get rid of death once and for all. You'd think even one of those things would be enough to keep you from visiting a deranged thirty-foot killer snake by yourself in the middle of the night. Do you want us to think you're brave? Well, for your information, I don't! You're an idiot."

She sniffled and, finding nothing resembling a handkerchief in the room, wiped her nose with the bed sheet before she went on with her rant. "I don't really want to be here. Do you understand that? I want to go home, but I can't. I'm stuck here with you and Gramps and this ridiculous dream that maybe Gramma will come back to life, as long as you get to Megiddo with the book. And I want it to happen, Jak. I really do. That's the only thing that keeps me from going crazy. I saw what the zingers did for Gramps, so maybe the plaque back by the sea is right. Maybe the dead will live again. But I don't think I can keep going if you continue doing stupid things that might get you killed. Did you even ask Lamech about the card yet?"

Jak hated it when she went on a rampage, especially because most often it meant he had done something wrong. "No. I was going to do it at breakfast."

"You should have done it right away," said Tess, "as soon as we got here. You act like we have all the time in the world. Well, we don't. Just because we skip hundreds of years each day doesn't mean *we* stay young. I'm almost fifteen, and I'm not spending the next umpteen years chasing this stupid thread." She sat down on the floor hard, crossed her arms, and stared at the wall.

Jak was speechless, but he knew his cousin was right. He hadn't thought at all about how Tess—or anyone else, for that matter—felt about the whole journey.

"I'm sorry," he said. His lips hurt when he talked, but he had to say something. "I just thought I could... I thought it would be my only chance to help her."

Tess turned back to the bed. "How could you help her, Jak? It's not like you're a snake psychotherapist."

"I had a seed." Jak stopped and took a breath. "A seed from a zinger... ended up in the bag. Gramps thought if she ate it she might get better."

She whirled around and faced Gramps, her mouth and eyes open wide in shock. "*You* helped him with this?" she demanded.

Gramps's eyebrows shot up in defense. "I did not. We were only talking about possibilities. I never said anything about going to the pools."

"I can't believe this!" said Tess. "You told him to give the seed to Scorch."

"I did no such thing!" Gramps insisted.

"But giving him the idea is the same as telling him to go."

Jak painfully pushed himself up with his left hand. "He didn't tell me to go," he said, trying not to move his lips. "It was all my idea. I didn't wake anyone up because I thought they would make me stay here."

"Which is exactly what I would have told you," said Gramps, relaxing a bit. "But there's nothing we can do about it now. You've made a mess of things around here, though, that's for sure."

Jak lay back down. "What happened to Scorch?"

"The right question to ask," said a silky voice belonging to Lamech, "is what happened to Enoch." He swept into the room with a grim smile on his face, his white robe flowing behind him like a train. "Enoch is pounding on my door, armed to the teeth, ready to hang a certain boy by the neck for destroying the single most important day of the year."

He sat cross-legged on a fat red pillow next to Jak's bed. "This was the most anticipated match ever. Ten serpents against the fabled, child-stealing

Black Serpent of legend that has terrorized Adam's descendants for 750 years. Not only did you wreck the holiday, but you also managed to release the serpent back to the wild after it had finally been captured and put in the pools."

Lamech leaned forward. "Do you have any idea what this means, Jak?"

"No," he said quietly.

"Did you tamper with the muzzle?" Lamech asked.

"No." He thought about correcting Lamech and telling him Scorch was a girl, but he decided that would take too much energy. "I just put a rock in between the muzzle and her forehead so I could rub the diamond. She likes that. It usually calms her down."

"That's called tampering." Lamech sat straight again, his eyes narrowing into slits at first and then softening. "The muzzle was designed by my son, Tubal-Cain, an iron smith and student of serpents, designed for the very purpose of pressing into the diamond. It causes the beast to submit so that even a child can lead him. Which, evidently, is exactly what happened. After you tampered with the muzzle, he pounded through two-inch thick iron bars, which had also been forged by my son Tubal-Cain, and slithered down into the city. Do you have any idea what kind of damage a thirty-foot long serpent causes?"

Jak just stared at Lamech, hardly breathing.

Lamech continued, waving his arms in the air as he talked. "Entire buildings fall down, donkeys run wild, and carts end up smashed into pieces. You're lucky no one was seriously hurt. If he had slid down the hill during the day, there would have been a grand stampede, not to mention the possibility of another child stolen. For that matter, an entire group of slave children disappeared last night as well. You wouldn't know anything about that, would you?"

Before Jak could think of a suitable answer that wouldn't get him in more trouble, Lamech continued.

"You were very lucky, Jak, very lucky. Half the town wants to hang you, and the other half wants to slit your throat. A few old women are ready to crown you as the Quelcher, convinced that only the Quelcher would be brave enough to crawl into the den of the serpent, but I'm not sure whether it was bravery or foolishness. It was probably a mixture of both." He placed a hand on Jak's arm in a sudden gesture of warmth. "How are you feeling?"

After all the information Lamech had just poured into him, Jak didn't feel very well. His head throbbed, his heel ached, and his stomach felt like he'd swallowed a two-ton iron ball.

"Okay, I guess." He tried to sit up. He had to get the cards out of the bag and ask Lamech about the laughing-man card. But as soon as he leaned over, the room began to spin, and he dropped back to the bed.

"I can see that is not entirely true." Lamech patted him on the shoulder. "I will tell the council they will have to wait to question you about the disruption of the pool matches. Since you are my guest and since you are recovering, you have a certain level of protection, however, if they find you guilty of serious wrongdoing, there is nothing I can do. I am sorry. I will check back later in the day to see how you are feeling. The servants will keep you well covered with perim juice. It will numb the pain so you can rest. It is a bit inconvenient because of the paralysis, but it is well worth it. Perhaps Yahweh or another power will grant you a speedy recovery." He patted Jak's arm again, rose to his feet, and headed out.

"Wait," said Jak as loud as he could.

Lamech stopped and turned around.

He forced himself up again, pulled the deck from the bag, and held up the card with the laughing man on it. "Do you know this man?"

Lamech gave it a quick glance and shook his head. "No, I've never seen him before." Then he spun and swept out the door.

Tess rubbed her hand across her forehead and shook her head. "I can't believe you asked him that right now."

"But you're the one who said I took too long," Jak mumbled, gently reclining back down on the bed and closing his eyes.

"Yeah, but there is something called tact that you obviously know nothing about."

She's impossible, thought Jak, but he didn't say so because he was in no mood to get in an argument with the Queen of Debate.

Nal burst through the door. "He's awake?"

Jak opened his one good eye again. "Hi, Nal."

"You're crazy," said Nal, striding toward Jak's bed, "crawling in with Scorch like that. Why'd you do it?"

"You rest," said Gramps to Jak, "I'll fill Nal in."

Jak winced when Gramps got to the part about the seed, and wished he had chosen to stay in bed the previous night.

"I don't think it worked," said Nal. "I just overheard three of the Nephilim talking about you. They said they saw you outside the Happy Hollows

Tavern on your way up the hill. You told them your father had sent you to get a good seat."

"You told them that?" said Gramps.

"I had to say something to get to the pools."

"Anyway," said Nal, "they were in the market singing up a storm with a bunch of other drunks when they heard a terrible roar and racket coming down the hill. It was too dark to tell what was going on. Except for the occasional burst of flame, they couldn't see anything. Then a building fell over and a bunch of people came screaming down the hill with the Black Serpent slithering not far behind. The Nephilim, big as they are, weren't quite so afraid as normal folk, so they stayed in the market and tried to corner her, but they couldn't. Every time they came close to trapping her, she blew flames at them — singed the hair off one of the giants. He's bald as a watermelon now with burns all over his scalp. They're furious, said they would've squashed you like a bug if they knew you were going to let her go like that."

"So…the seed didn't work," mumbled Jak with disappointment.

"Duh," said Tess.

"I heard," Nal continued, "that the men who take bets for the matches are takin' bets on whether or not you'll live to the end of the week. People are boilin' mad at you."

"How'd you find me?" said Jak.

"Macy," said Nal.

At the sound of her name, Macy poked her head up from where she was sleeping next to the bed and wagged her tail.

"As soon as she heard the battle in the market, she started pawing at the little door in the back, so one of Lamech's servants and I followed her up the hill to the pools. She led us straight to the hole. You were a burnt-up mess, but we finally got you out. He carried you back all the way by himself. I thought you were a goner for sure."

Jak scratched the little dog's ears. "Good girl, Macy. What was the servant's name?"

"I don' know. I'd never seen 'im before. He's a tall, thick fellow with messy black hair and black eyes. We found this in the crevice next to you. He washed all the serpent spit off, so it should be clean." He handed Jak a small brown object.

"The seed!" Jak took the seed from Nal. "It must've fallen out of her mouth." He was going to add "when she was trying to eat me," but decided not to since Tess was sitting next to him. "Thanks... for the seed and for getting me out of there."

Nal's face flushed slight pink. "It was nothin'. It had to be done."

"Where's Mr. Nettor?" said Jak.

"Oh, he's out making hay while the sun shines," said Gramps. "He said so many people are in the market right now because of the canceled pool matches that he'll make a fortune selling 250-year-old fabric."

At least somebody's happy, thought Jak. He closed his eyes. He couldn't remember the last time he'd felt so tired.

"You need to rest," said Gramps, standing up. Tess and Nal stood with Gramps, but Gramps didn't move, he only stood there stroking his beard like he was deep in thought. "This is serious, Jak. People are angry—almost angry enough to storm Lamech's gates to get to you. You're safe for at least a few days as long as you stay here and recuperate. After that, though, I don't know what'll happen."

Jak sighed and once again wished the Thread could take him back in time so he could fix all this.

CHAPTER 43
Charms & Candles

The next few days were a blur of pain and dizziness. He could only use the perim juice for pain the first day. After that, the servant woman told him it would get in the way of proper healing. Instead, she rubbed a different sort of gel into the burns, something that was supposed to cool the burn.

But most of the time, the right side of his body burned like the fire was still on him. Plus, he had a blinding headache, and his heel hurt so bad that all he could do was lie in bed and think about it.

What is up with my heel anyway? he wondered. Remembrance Day had taken much of the pain away the first time, and he had hoped it would keep getting better. Apparently that was not the case. *But does this mean I'm going to go crazy?* He stretched the skin on his belly, looking for yellow spots, but it didn't look any different to him.

Nal, Tess, and Gramps decided they would take turns spending the days with Jak, while the other two cut and bound wheat in Lamech's fields. It was a nice change for them to get out and stretch their muscles after so many days cooped up in the wagon. Mr. Nettor opted to continue doing a little business in the city. He had discovered the women in the city loved a certain chartreuse veil that he had in abundance, and he couldn't let such a profitable opportunity slip by.

As soon as the sun came up on the fourth day after visiting Scorch, Jak was awakened by a familiar smell. He pushed himself up to his elbows but sank back down right away, his head pounding. It was the same odor he had smelled back in East Eden when he had sat on the rocks. He pulled the book out of the bag carefully with his thumb and finger. It was hot and smoking. A wind swept through the window, cleared the smoke away, and rippled through the pages until a sentence glowed red.

> **Death had its hands around my throat;**
> the terrors of the grave overtook me.
> I saw only trouble and sorrow,
> then I called on the name of Yahweh.
> "Please, Yahweh, save me!"
> How kind Yahweh is!
> How good he is!

Jak had no idea who the writer of the words was, but it occurred to him that he should send another message to Yahweh. He didn't know exactly what to say, but he did the best he could. "Yahweh, if you can hear me," he began, "I need help again. I got into a scrape with Scorch and messed up my head and my right hand and, well, pretty much the entire right side of my body is burned. Will you please somehow send me a leaf from the Tree of Life?" Jak knew Guardian had said there would be no more gifts from the tree, but he figured it didn't hurt to ask.

Gramps and Nal left for the fields right after breakfast, but Tess stayed with him. She sat on the floor next to him, hugging her knees to her chest. "So, what do you want to do?" she asked.

Jak gave a weak smile. "Play football."

"Well, I'm sorry," she said, sounding a lot like his mother again, "but because of your recent extracurricular activities, that's not on the agenda for today."

"What is?"

"Mostly sleeping and lying around for you. I might go shopping while you nap." She jingled the bag of jasper.

"Sounds like fun."

A knock came at the door, and it creaked open a crack. "Hello? Anybody home?" rang out a melodic voice.

"Come on in," said Tess.

The door pushed open, and the plump form of Adah, Lamech's first wife, strode in.

"Good morning, Jak," she sang as she put a basket on the table and then peeled back the bandage over his temple, still humming to herself. "No surprises here. The burn is still raw and ugly." She carefully removed it, replaced it with a fresh bandage, and then shut the door and shutters.

It felt good on his one working eye to have the light dimmed, and he wondered why he hadn't asked for the shutter to be closed four days ago.

"Today we begin your healing," she said matter-of-factly.

Jak was confused. After all, they'd been slathering him with all kinds of concoctions for days. "What do you mean *begin* my healing?"

She pulled a corked bottle, a bouquet of lavender, and a black candle from the basket and placed them on the table. "Your escape from the Black Serpent shows you have great luck. Your luck continues in that it is the strongest time of the month for healing. The world is full of healing energy during a half-moon. We need you to get well, young man, so I am going to draw in as much healing energy as we can."

She drew a circle in the dirt floor with a stick, then put the candle and flowers in the circle with her, lighting the candle with a chunk of burning coal held in a clay pot. "The Lights give us much wisdom and knowledge about the energy in the world around us and how we can direct it."

"I thought Lamech said the Lights steal brides," said Jak.

Adah looked at him thoughtfully. "I prefer to think of it as a trade. They give us wisdom, and we give them wives in return. Now, give me your burned hand."

Jak hesitated, uncertain of what she was going to do, but then he held out his hand as she instructed.

She sat down in the circle, took his hand, closed her eyes, and began to mumble under her breath, touching the various items in the circle with her.

Jak couldn't tell what she was saying; he could only catch a few words here and there.

The whole time Tess sat in the corner, mesmerized.

Finally Adah released his hand and stood up. She tied a stalk of lavender around his wrist and instructed, "Leave this on until I come back tomorrow morning. I charmed it for healing before I came.

"And you learned this from the Lights?" said Jak.

"Yes, this and much more. The Lights are very wise." She repacked the candle and flowers and rubbed out the circle with a straw broom. "You must rest now. Healing takes much energy."

Jak was very confused. Adam had said charms were traps of Lucifer, yet Adah had just given him a charmed bracelet that was supposed to help heal him. Obviously, she thought charms were just fine. He wondered if anything else had changed. "Adah?" he said.

She stopped. "Yes?"

"What do you know about the Promise?"

"You mean the Promise Adam and Eve received from El?"

"Yeah."

"Well, I think it's a wonderful idea, however, I don't think things are as bad as Adam thinks they are."

"Is he still alive?"

"The last I heard, yes, although he's beginning to slow down. He's almost 750 years old, you know, and still convinced the red beast, this Beelzebub creature, stole something from him. But if you ask me, I can't help but wonder if something's not right with Adam's head. The red beast hasn't been seen for ages. I think it's a legend. Like most legends, I'm sure some reality is at the root of it, but it's been pulled and stretched until it is no longer believable."

"But we saw him. We were friends at one time, until he went bad."

"See? That's the reality I was talking about. But to say that a single creature could steal the Earth from Adam is... well, it's hard to believe."

"What about evil and death?"

"Like I said, I don't think things are as bad as Adam makes them out to be. Yes, there are some bad things that happen in life, like the drought fifty years ago. It lasted for ten years, and many people died, but the Lights were angry, and it took a while for them to cool down. Once the appropriate sacrifices were made, the Lights blessed us with the evening mist to water the crops again." She smiled like she was reciting nursery rhymes to a three-year-old. "Do you have any more questions?"

Jak was still processing what she had just said about the Lights blessing them with the morning mist. As far as he knew, the mist was sent by El. "What do you think about El?"

"El? Hmmm. Well, I think the whole idea of a being like El is a little much, if you ask me. Adam would have us all believe he is the one who orders Sun to run his course through the sky, and Moon to grow fat with pregnancy and then skinny with the birth of a new month—even for the ground to push up the seedlings to a full harvest. But I have a hard time believing just one being could do all that. He probably has a root in reality as well, just like the red beast, but I don't know much about him beyond that. That is why the Lights are so helpful. They instruct us in what is true. The Light of the Harvest sends the evening mist and makes the grain grow. She is the one who was so angry years ago. We became selfish and had neglected to give her the best of our young ones. When we resumed the annual sacrifices, the evening mists came again. The Light of Protection teaches our men how to fight and make weapons and then watches over us in war. Without him, Enoch would have fallen long ago."

She smiled again. "Are we finished with the questions?"

"I guess so. For now anyway," answered Jak.

"You get some sleep now. I'll see you tomorrow."

When the door closed, Tess almost leapt off the floor. "That was amazing! She knew just what to do to make you better."

"Amazing? I thought it was weird, everything she said about the Lights, and the candle and this charm thing."

"Well, you won't feel that way when you're healed."

He yawned. "I think I need to sleep now."

"Good. Sleep will help. I'm going to go out to the plaza for a while."

Jak wasn't really as tired as he let on. The truth was, he just needed to be alone to think. He wished the book would open again to the paragraph he had read that morning about calling on the name of Yahweh. Adah didn't even believe in Yahweh; she thought Adam was a crazy old coot, cracked in the head.

Mr. Nettor came back earlier than anyone else, humming to himself as if had just had the best day of his life. "Ah, Jak, m'boy," he said, "The women here sure love the fabric! I'll be a rich man because of your little escapade."

Macy got up and sniffed the smells of the marketplace that wafted from his robe.

He laughed and patted the dog on the head, but then his voice grew serious. "Although I am sad about your accident. How're you feeling?"

Jak stopped staring at the dinosaur-shaped spot in the ceiling and turned to give him a dull stare. "Terrible."

Mr. Nettor plopped himself onto the pillow next to him and popped a date into his mouth. "You know, I've been meaning to tell you this, but it seems that following the Thread is a dangerous prospect for you. Have you thought at all about hanging it up?" He licked a sticky finger as he waited for Jak to respond.

"Hanging it up?" said Jak.

"Yes, you know—turning the book in and going home. Scorch won't be there to harass you, this Beelz fellow won't be after you anymore, and neither will Cain. You'll be free to be a boy again, no worries." He smiled the crocodile smile and popped another date in his mouth.

"But it's my grandmother's book. I could never just give it away."

Mr. Nettor rolled his eyes toward the ceiling and thought for a second. "Well, maybe you could go home without turning the book in."

"How would I do that?"

"Oh, I know a fellow in a little town north of here who recycles old books, and I'm sure he could think of a way."

Mr. Nettor had a point. It would be wonderful to go home and be a normal kid again—to get a burger, watch a movie, and forget about this crazy journey to Megiddo. The book began to tingle on his chest, and a pang ramrodded through his head and his heel at the same time, reminding him that if he went home, nothing would change. Pain was everywhere, evil was everywhere, and death could not be avoided—unless he stayed where he was and kept following the Thread.

"No, I'm going to stay," he said quietly, turning to stare at the spot again.

"Alright," said Mr. Nettor, heaving himself up from the pillow. "Just trying to help. Let me know if you change your mind."

Nal stayed with him the next day, and so did the pain in his head and foot. Adah stopped by again in the morning and repeated everything she had done the day before, including tying a fresh lavender stalk to his arm, but Jak felt worse now than before she had come.

316

"What's that for?" said Nal after she left.

Jak held up his arm. "This? It's a healing charm, supposedly."

"A healin' charm?" Nal looked troubled. "Why'd she give you that?"

"She thinks it will heal me. Adah showed up yesterday and did all the same things she did today. She doesn't think much of El. She says he's kind of like a fable, just a made-up fairytale."

"Whenever I got hurt as a kid," said Nal, "mum asked El to heal me. And when Enoch was taken, I would hear her crying at night, pleadin' with El to bring him back. She didn't ask much from El after that. She still went to Remembrance Day and all that, but it was like part of her vanished when Enoch was taken away. My father says it's all the fault of Beelzebub and evil messin' up the Earth."

There was silence between them for a moment until Jak decided that the right moment had finally come. "Nal?"

"Yeah?"

"How come your father only has four fingers on his right hand and walks with a limp?"

Nal didn't say anything for a minute, and Jak thought he was going to change the subject like the last time he asked, but he didn't.

"Remember when you first came to East Eden and my father was so suspicious of your grandfather being a Beelzin?"

Jak nodded.

"The reason he was so suspicious, and the reason my father hates the Beelzin so much is because my father..." He paused again and cringed like it was hard for him to blurt it out. "My father used to be a Beelzin."

CHAPTER 44
A Powerful Cup of Tea

"What?" said Jak. He sat up so fast that the blood didn't have time to catch up to his head and he got dizzy. "He was a Beelzin?"

Nal nodded. "If you look at his wrist, you can still see the mark of the beast. He's burned it out with a branding iron several times, but the tail of the serpent still shows through a little.

Nal settled back on a cushion next to Jak's bed. "It's like this. One of Cain's great grandsons, Mehujael, and my father were friends when they were boys. Mehujael's father Irad had come to live in East Eden for business reasons for a year and then they moved back home, but my father never forgot Mehujael. He was a little older than my father, and my father idolized him like a big brother. One day, when they had both grown to manhood, Mehujael came back. He was strong and handsome and confident, and my father looked up to him even more. What he didn't know was that Mehujael had just become a Beelzin and had come to recruit him. My father traveled for a couple of years with Mehujael on business, and, without hardly even knowing it, he joined them.

"He isn't proud of his past, so he hardly ever speaks of it, but I do know that he helped start a riot in a village not far from East Eden over planting rights in a certain field. Ten men died in the riot."

Nal bit his lip and looked out the window. "After that, he was a part of a ring of thieves for a while. They broke into peoples' homes at night while they were sleepin', bound their mouths, hands, and legs, and then robbed them while they watched. After that, they beat them until they passed out from the pain.

"One night they were drunk and broke into a house and did their normal routine, but as my father was tyin' up the woman, he realized it was his younger sister. He had a mask on, so she didn't know it was him, but as soon as he recognized her, he ran out of the house. That was the day he quit. Yahweh pierced his heart with guilt, and my dad worked for years to pay back everything he stole four times over, but he could never wipe away the memories of the awful things he had done."

Nal got up and started pacing. It was evident he did not enjoy telling the story, and Jak could see why he had changed the subject before.

"But the Beelzin," said Nal, "weren't happy about him runnin' away and threatened him almost every day—a dead goat in his garden, blood painted on the wall of his house, and many other warnin's. A year after he quit, he was out watchin' a flock of sheep, and a gang of Beelzin cornered him in a valley and beat him almost to death. His knee got smashed with a cudgel, and he's walked with a limp ever since.

"Mum helped take care of him while he was laid up, and they fell in love. So after he healed, they married and began havin' children, one of which was a little girl born about thirty years before I was. Her name was Abigail. They tell me she had raven-black hair and a quick smile that made my father laugh — those were the days he used to laugh. He loved her very much. One day when she was four years old she disappeared, just like Enoch, except it wasn't the Black Serpent who took her.

"Father and Mum were desperate, and they searched everywhere for Abigail. Eventually my father found her in the woods, torn apart in the fashion of Beelzebub and the Beelzin. A wild boar was there, too, feeding on her remains, and my father attacked him with his bare hands. He killed the boar, but the boar took his finger."

Tears filled Nal's eyes as he finished. "So that's why my father has four fingers and walks with a limp."

A warm breeze blew through the room. The sounds of market haggling drifted through the window with it and settled on the table like dust.

"I hate Beelzebub," said Jak, rage boiling inside him over Nal's story, over what had happened in the garden and over the death of his grandmother. "And I hate evil and I hate death."

That night, Jak slept fitfully, the same dream playing over and over in his head. In the dream, he was lying in bed, and El walked through the door, so bright that Jak couldn't even look at him. Seven burning black candles and seven stalks of lavender stood in the circle Adah had drawn on the floor. The heat and light from El grew steadily stronger until, just like when he had sneaked into the garden, Jak could hardly breathe. Then the circle, candles and lavender burst into flames, burned to ash, and a strong wind blew them away through the doorway. After that El disappeared.

When Jak woke up, he was almost as tired as when he had gone to bed. He still had a headache, his heel still throbbed, and in addition to that, the burns were beginning to hurt too. It looked like it was going to be another fun day.

It was Gramps's turn to stay with him, so he told him about the dream as soon as Nal left for the field and Mr. Nettor left for the market.

"The dream doesn't surprise me one bit," said Gramps. "There's just something wrong about this whole candles and charms thing. The Lights don't control the evening mist or the crops or any of that. That was El's doing long before they showed up."

He crossed his legs together and leaned in toward Jak's bed. "Do you remember what Guardian told you about El, that you'd get to meet him along the way, just in ways you don't expect? This sounds like one of those ways, and I don't think he likes what Adah is doing one bit." He paused. "You want me to take that lavender off your wrist?"

Adah was not going to be happy if he took it off, but if he left it on, *he* was not going to be happy. Jak nodded.

Gramps took out the Swiss Army knife, sliced the bracelet, and let it fall to the dirt. He was putting the knife away when Adah knocked and poked her head into the doorway.

"Good morning, Jak," she sang out. "And how are you feeling today?"

"A lot better than yesterday." He still had a headache, the burns still stung, and his foot still hurt, but something dark had fallen away from his soul the same moment the bracelet hit the floor.

She stopped before unloading her basket on the table, transfixed by his wrist. "Where's the lavender charm I gave you yesterday?"

"I took it off."

"Took it off?" She put the basket on the table and knelt down to his level on the floor. "But Jak, dear, we need you to get better. If you take the charm off, you won't be able to harness the healing energy of the Earth."

He shrugged. "I don't really want to harness the healing energy of the Earth."

"But, Jak, don't you want to get better?" Her lower lip jutted out in a fake pout, and once again she took on the voice of a preschool teacher reprimanding a three-year-old.

"Of course I want to get better, but I don't think a charm is what I need."

She leaned her rear end back until she was sitting on her heels. "Okay. Do you want me to leave a black candle with you instead? It would be almost as strong as the charm."

"No. I don't want any of it," said Jak. "No charms, no candles, no lavender, none of it."

"Really?" said Adah, shocked. "Well, I certainly won't force you to do something you don't want to do, even though I do think it would be best for you." She pursed her lips together and lightly tapped the table. "You will at least rest, though, right?"

Jak nodded his head. "Yes. I'll rest."

"Good." She squeezed his hand, opened her basket and took out two cups. "How about a cup of tea? It's not a potion or anything like that, merely tea. Tea is acceptable, right?"

Jak nodded again.

"Good. Clarence, I brought some for you as well."

She unloaded a kettle from her basket and poured two cups of tea. A curl of steam escaped from the spout as she put it on the table. "Have a nice rest." She forced a plastic smile and stepped out the doorway.

As soon as she was gone, Gramps chuckled. "I don't think she's very happy with you, son, but it was fun to watch her face when you told her what you did. I'm glad you didn't turn down the tea though. It smells wonderful." He gave one cup to Jak, and took a swig from his own.

"What do you think my mom is doing right now?" said Jak.

"She's probably working her fingers to the bone, like she normally does."

"Do you think she even knows we're gone?"

"I don't know. The Thread's funny about time, so maybe it'll plunk us straight back in the basement trying to catch that confounded gerbil." He took another sip. "Say, where'd you put that seed? I wanna take a look at it."

"It's here, in the bag." Jak dug the seed out and handed it to Gramps.

Gramps turned it over in his hands, inspecting it like he would a spark plug from his truck. A brown stain traced around the edges where the seed was thinnest. Gramps tried to scrape it off, but the stain remained. "Got a little dirty. Kind of reminds me of the whole rebellion. At first things were good, then the rebellion, and—bam!—evil took over and stained it all up."

He handed the seed back to Jak, but it slipped in the hand-off and landed on the floor, sending a small splinter spinning off the edge of the seed.

Macy woofed and nosed at the broken piece.

Gramps picked up both the seed and the sliver and gave them to Jak. "Wups."

"That's alright," said Jak. "It's just a little chunk." He flicked it back on the floor and put the seed back in the bag.

"Hold on. Don't throw that away quite so fast." Gramps bent over and picked the sliver off the floor. "There might be something in this chunk that'll help you."

"Didn't help Scorch."

"It fell out of her mouth before she had a chance to swallow it. Here. Why don't you take it like a pill with the tea and let's see what happens? If it doesn't do anything, you haven't lost anything, but if it does... well, we'll see."

It was true he had nothing to lose, so Jak swallowed the sliver and waited. The zingers back in the garden had zinged him as soon as he ate them, but he felt nothing from the sliver. If it was going to help him, it was going to be a very, very slow process.

"Well?" said Gramps.

"Nothing."

Gramps frowned. "Oh well. At least we tried." He drained his cup and yawned. "I think it's time for a nap." Gramps stretched out on his bed and was asleep in minutes. So was Jak.

Jak woke with an insistent buzz permeating his chest as if he had swallowed a ringing alarm clock. He put his hand on his chest and felt the hard rectangle of the book; it was tingling again. He sat up, expecting his head to swim with dizziness, but, for the first time in a week he felt well. There was no dizziness, no pain, and no burning. Jak unwrapped the bandage on his hand and was greeted by healthy pink skin. The seed had worked!

He squeezed his fingers underneath the bandage on his face and felt the skin. It felt smooth and didn't hurt when he touched it. With trembling hands, he unwrapped the bandage from his head, chest, and waist. New skin had replaced the burned skin. "Gramps!" he cried out. "Wake up!"

But Gramps didn't answer.

"Gramps?" Jak shook him, but still he didn't answer. *Wow,* thought Jak. *He must really be tired.*

The sun shone through the cracks in the shutter, which meant it was the middle of the afternoon. His legs felt cramped, like they needed a good stretch, so he decided to put on the breeches and sandals that had been laid out for him and go for a walk.

He stood up, half-hoping to be able to walk normally, but he couldn't. His right foot still hurt and didn't work right, but at least the rest of him felt well.

It felt strange to be up, and he stood there for a moment swaying gently from side to side before trying to walk, but he soon got his bearings and headed outside. The sun felt good on his skin; he closed his eyes and drank it in.

Just a few men were milling around the music shop, but no one else was out. He assumed most were taking naps or doing inside work out of reach of the afternoon heat. Jak strolled past the little door he had climbed out of just six nights previous. It seemed like it had been ages ago, but he knew no one had forgotten. The council was only biding their time until he was well, and since he was up and out strolling right now, that meant they would probably hold court the next day.

He wondered what they would do to him. He didn't think they would hang him for an offense like setting Scorch free, but they were pretty mad.

As he walked past a shuttered window, two voices penetrated through the wood. One of the voices belonged to Lamech, but the other was one Jak did not recognize.

"The boy is here?" the unfamiliar voice said.

Jak stopped, frozen. They were talking about him.

"He is," said Lamech, "but he is sleeping right now. I had Adah give both the boy and his grandfather an especially potent tea. They'll be out till late afternoon. Healing takes a lot of rest, you know." Lamech chuckled.

Jak's ears perked up even more at the mention of the tea. No wonder he hadn't been able to wake Gramps up. *But why would Lamech want us to sleep through the afternoon?*

"Is he alright?" the second voice asked.

"No. He's badly burned. The beast scorched the right side of his face and chest. Hopefully he will be in condition to travel by the time the caravan arrives in two days, but if he isn't, I have a few tricks up my sleeve."

"And the girl?"

"She is in the fields working with the other boy. They said they wanted to do something besides sit in a wagon, so I told them it would be okay to spend their days with the harvesters. Isn't that ironic? She makes me money even in the few days before the caravan comes!"

Caravan? Jak didn't like the tone in Lamech's voice. It had changed from the caring host to an evil snake ready to strike. Jak carefully crept toward the shutter and peeked through a crack to get a look at who Lamech was scheming with.

Lamech sat on one side of a table with a clay tablet laid before him and a wooden stylus in his fingers. He was pressing a series of symbols into the clay as he talked. The other man sat directly across from Lamech. His hood was thrown back over his brown tunic, revealing thick black eyebrows and a sour expression on his face.

Cain!

Jak dropped down underneath the window. He couldn't believe Cain was there. *Why is he talking with Lamech? How did he find us? And why did he ask about Tess?*

"Who are you selling her to?" said Cain.

Jak almost cried out. *Selling her? Is that what Lamech and Cain are up to? Selling Tess as a slave?* His hands began to tremble. It was bad enough to have Cain after them; at least he knew Cain was the bad guy. But Lamech had taken them in, eaten with them, and laughed at his jokes. But the truth was that he was a two-faced scumbag, just waiting for the chance to trade them for cash.

"Quality goods require a qualified purchaser."

"So you are going to the Lights?"

"But of course, my friend. Who else would pay top dollar for such a pretty thing as the girl?"

"Hmm," Cain said. "Which Light wants to buy her?"

"Ness. He would like a younger girl to replace his previous women. Won't that be nice? Ness and Tess will make a fine couple."

It was all Jak could do to keep himself from jumping up and choking Lamech to death, but he forced himself to lie still.

"And what of the boy?"

"I told Ness he would make an excellent chamber pot scrubber and that he would be a fool not to bid on him." Lamech laughed. "But the boy must remain veiled until the bidding is completed. Scarred children do not bring quite as high a price."

"What about Beelz?" said Cain. "Has he not said he wants the boy?"

"Beelz wants the *book*. With the book in his possession, his rule of the Earth will never end. But the boy is nothing. There is no reason not to make a little profit from him."

"How will you get the book?"

"I find it amazing how sharp these new iron knives are that Tubal-Cain has made. I don't think it would take much to slice off his grandfather's tongue, do you?"

"Beelz said not to use force."

"Beelz does not need to know."

Cain grunted. "Alright. It's your head that will roll, not mine. As agreed, I will pick up the children in two days and deliver them to the auction. As to our other business, I am ready to take the weapons as well. Tomorrow, I will send an empty wagon. Place the iron spear tips, lance heads, and the new weapon... what do you call them?"

"Swords," answered Lamech.

"Yes, swords. Place them all on the floor and cover them well with hay. Do not skimp on me this time, Lamech, or I will descend upon your house like a flock of vultures."

"Do not threaten me, Great Father, for there is no need. The last incident was a mistake, I assure you. I am a businessman. Cheating my customers is not profitable."

Cain grunted again. "I have heard otherwise."

"Really? Then to show my good faith, here are the thirty pieces of silver you are promised for delivering the girl and boy to the auction for me. I give it to you two days early." A bag of coins landed with a jingle on the table.

"What will you do with the grandfather and the other boy?" asked Cain.

"They are doing such a fine job in the fields that I think I shall keep them. A whip may encourage even further productivity. Now, take your money and be on your way. The hour grows late, and there is much to accomplish in two days' time."

The two chairs skidded backwards across the floor.

Jak shot up and scooted away along the wall. He had to find someplace to hide. He pushed open the first door he came to but kept it open enough to peek out the crack.

Cain walked briskly through the plaza and disappeared through the main gate, but Lamech stayed in the ledger room.

Jak couldn't believe Lamech was going to sell Tess to a Light as a wife, put him up for auction at the slave market, and force Gramps and Nal to work in the fields. This was almost worse than when he had been mistaken for Shale because there was no way to escape. Lamech had told him the doors were guarded twenty-four hours a day to protect him, but the truth was that the guards were there to keep Jak from getting *out*.

"Jak! You're up!" a voice rang out.

Jak whirled around to find Adah right behind him, her hands covered in flour up to the elbows.

The blood rushed to his face. "Ah, yes. I'm feeling much better after my nap."

"Yes, you are." She inspected his face, right arm and chest, making little "tsk" sounds the whole time. "My, my! Those charms paid off, didn't they?"

Jak didn't respond. He was trying to think of a reason that would explain why he had come through this door. The smell of fresh-baked bread gave him the answer he needed.

"I...I'm hungry and thought I'd come over and see if there was any bread. It sure smells good."

"You're in luck," said Adah. "I have just pulled a flatbread off the cooking stone. Here. You sit down and have a bite to eat." She gestured to a woven mat on the floor, so Jak sat.

His stomach grumbled. He had told the truth, for he was hungry, but at the same time, he didn't feel like eating. He wondered if Adah knew what was going on. The conversations of the past few days ran through his mind – she said she and Lamech needed him to be well. Of course she knew what was going on, that's why she was so concerned about him healing! The realization hit him so hard he almost stopped breathing. He was being groomed for sale the whole time.

"Here, Jak. Take two of these and this as well." She handed him two pieces of flatbread and some sort of dried husk that smelled like beef jerky. "The bread and beans will give you some color in your face and put some meat on your bones. Won't that be nice?"

"Yes," he said. "That would be great." He could not fathom how she could smile at him like that, knowing he was going to be sold as a slave in two days. He forced himself to swallow a chunk of bread so his tongue wouldn't accidentally say something he would regret.

The door creaked open again, and this time Lamech stepped through. "Jak!" A pleasant smile lit his face. "It is good to see you up and around. Are you feeling better?"

Jak nodded, his mouth full of bread and his gut full of adrenaline. Of all the rooms he could have ducked into, he had to choose the one where the Fox and one of the Mrs. Foxes were having lunch.

Lamech came closer and inspected Jak's wounds. "Amazing. It's almost as if you were never burned in the first place!"

"It was the charms, Lamech. I told you they would work," said Adah.

"Very impressive!" he said, sitting down next to Jak, his green robe swooshing along the floor. "Where's Zillah?"

"She went to the market to get some more oil," said Adah. "When she came back yesterday, Jak, she said your friend Nettor is making quite a stir in the market with his fabrics. Everybody wants some."

"Oh," said Jak. He didn't know what else to say. How was he supposed to make small talk with people who would soon be selling him into slavery? "So," said Jak, "how'd you get that scar?" Tess probably would have kicked him for asking, but it was all he could think of.

"Ah, the scar." Lamech ran his hand from his temple to the corner of his lips. "This happened a long time ago. I was coming back from delivering a shipment of wool to a buyer's house and was attacked along the road by a young man hoping to relieve me of my purse. He scraped a knife across my head, trying to kill me, but I was able to drive the wagon into a tree and knock him off. Then I jumped down from the wagon and crushed his head with a rock. Tisn't pretty to talk about, but I was fighting for my life."

"Oh," said Jak, at a loss for words once again, except now it was worse because it felt like he was supposed to feel sorry for Lamech. He couldn't stand being in that little room with these two snakes any longer. He needed to get out now, so he picked up the one remaining flatbread and the jerky. "Well, I think I'm going to go back to my room and rest a little more. I'll see you later."

"Don't be afraid to come back and get some more if you're still hungry, dear," said Adah.

Jak pushed the door open and thought, *Yeah, right, so you can fatten me up some more.* He hobbled back across the plaza and burst into his room. "Gramps, wake up!"

Gramps snorted. "Huh? Wh-what?"

He shook his grandfather's arm, glad he was finally awake. "Wake up. We have to talk."

"About what?" He rubbed the sleep from his eyes.

Jak shut the door and whispered, "About Lamech and Adah." He told Gramps what he had discovered.

When he was finished, Gramps sat on the bed, shocked. "Unbelievable! The evil just doesn't stop. So we have two days before the caravan comes?"

"Yep. Just two days."

"Hmmm. And now that you're feeling better, I bet the council's going to want to meet around that time as well," said Gramps. "Well, let's see. All we have to do is get past the guards at the doors without Lamech finding out and then make our way through angry crowds who would love to kill you. Shouldn't be too hard."

"Yeah, not hard at all," said Jak. It sounded like the plot of a comedy adventure movie, but there was nothing funny about the predicament they were in. He flopped back on his bed roll on the floor. "What are we going to do?" When his head hit the bed, something crinkled under his pillow. He lifted it up and found a thin piece of gray tree bark underneath with black charcoal writing on one side.

"Was someone in our room before I came back?" he asked.

"Beats me," said Gramps. "That tea knocked me out cold. What is that?"

"It's a note. It says, 'Danger. Lamech sell you as slaves. Hide hay wagon tomorrow morning.'"

"That's got to be Cain's wagon," said Gramps.

"That doesn't make any sense," said Jak. "Cain is the one taking us to the auction. His wagon is the last place I'd want to hide. Besides, who would send me a note about escaping? Maybe it's a trap."

"Hard to believe it's a trap since we're already in one. Maybe it was one of the servants who knows what's going on. Somebody besides Lamech has got to be privy to the slave and sword sales."

Jak snapped his fingers. "It's that servant who helped Nal carry me back! It has to be him. Maybe he's driving the wagon for Cain."

Gramps ran his fingers over his graying mustache "Maybe so. It might work, too, because tomorrow is Tess's turn to stay home with you. Nal and I could go to the fields while the two of you hide. We could meet you somewhere later."

"What about Mr. Nettor?"

Suddenly, voices filled the plaza. The workday had drawn to a close, and people were returning from both the market and the fields.

The door opened, and Mr. Nettor waddled in with Nal and Tess close behind.

"Good evening, young Jak," said Mr. Nettor, slapping a full bag of coins on the table. "You are looking well."

"I'll say," said Nal. "Your face is all better!"

"Yes," said Jak sternly, "but we have to talk." He shut the door and gave them the quick story of how he had gotten better, and then told them what he had overheard.

"Shocking. Absolutely shocking," said Mr. Nettor. "You're certain that's what he said?"

Jak nodded his head.

"Whoa, there, Tess," said Nal, sticking his hand out to block Tess from leaving the room. She had grabbed his lance and was headed out the door. "Where do you think you're goin'?"

"Where do you think?" She glared at him.

"Tess, it won't do any good to fight Lamech," said Gramps. "We have to escape."

"Escape to where?" she demanded. "We'll never be able to get out of here. You heard Jak. The wagon belongs to Cain."

"But how else will you be able to get out of the courtyard?" asked Nal. "It won't be hard for Clarence and me to walk away from the field. We're just helpin' out there anyway. We could even say we're takin' a short break to run to the market."

"But where will we meet?" said Tess. "We don't know the city."

"The east gate," said Mr. Nettor. "Everyone meet at the east gate. I'll take Macy with me in the morning and set up shop in the eastern market. There is a hedge by the palm trees at the gate that you can hide behind."

No one slept very well that night except Mr. Nettor; his snoring could have kept up an entire room of narcoleptics, but his snoring wasn't the problem for Jak. Death was.

He kept thinking about Mr. Nettor's offer. It was becoming increasingly tempting to go home. If he left, Beelz wouldn't be after him anymore, Lamech couldn't sell them as slaves, and there wouldn't be an entire city ready to slit his throat. But the problem was that no matter where he went, death would not go away. *Death, death, death, fueled by evil, evil, evil. Stupid Tree of Knowing Good and Evil.*

But it wasn't the tree's fault. It was Adam's and Eve's. But then again, Jak was sure if they hadn't eaten it, somebody else probably would have.

Morning finally came. Nal, Gramps, and Mr. Nettor left right after breakfast, and Jak and Tess anxiously waited for the wagon to show up. They didn't have to wait long.

Almost as soon as the last group of workers left, someone whistled and a whip cracked. The big double-door gate swung inward, and an empty wagon pulled by a team of donkeys rolled into the courtyard, straight to a door not far from Jak's room, with a familiar figure holding the reins.

Cain was back.

CHAPTER 45

Dust Storm

Tess panicked. "I thought Cain was sending someone to drive for him. Now what do we do? If he sees us, we're dead."

Cain jumped down from the seat. A cadre of Lamech's servants met him with bundles wrapped in burlap. Cain peeled back the covering from one of the bundles, revealing the sharp edge of a blade. He tested it with his finger, nodded his head, and pulled the tarp back from the top of the wagon.

Lamech's servants hurried to load the burlap bundles into the bed of the wagon and then went back for more. At least twenty bundles made it into the wagon, enough weapons to outfit a small army. When they finished loading the bundles, they opened the stable door and began tossing hay into the bed. They didn't stop until it piled well above the driver's seat. Then the entire troop, including Cain, walked back to the arsenal room, leaving the plaza deserted and empty.

"Now! We have to leave right now," said Jak, opening the door.

"Are you crazy? He'll be back out in a second."

"But we can't stay here... unless you want to be the next Mrs. Light. How would you like that?"

Tess needed no further convincing. She pushed him aside and hurried out, with Jak right behind her. They crawled over the edge of the wagon and burrowed through the hay until they lay right on top of the burlap bundles.

A door slammed shut, and footsteps crunched across the plaza.

Jak tried to get comfortable, but a sharp point poked through the bundle under Jak and began jabbing him in the back. He shifted and shimmied, trying to move his body away.

The footsteps were almost right at the wagon now.

Tess punched her cousin, and he stopped moving, but the point still dug into his back. He mouthed a silent scream and then almost fell into a coughing fit when hay fell into his mouth. It would be a miracle if they weren't discovered.

The footsteps stopped, and the wagon tilted sideways as the driver climbed up into the seat. A whip cracked, and the cart jumped forward. The gate creaked open, and the two stowaways felt the wagon transition from the dirt of the plaza to the cobblestone of the street. They were out.

Nal put his scythe down and wiped the sweat from his forehead. The curved knife sure made harvesting easier. He wished they had some like that back at his house, but they didn't have any of this hard shiny substance the workers called iron. All Nal had ever used was a sharp rock and a beating stick. The harvesters said it was all made by Tubal-Cain, Lamech's son. He wondered if Jak and Tess had made their escape yet.

Gramps stopped swinging as well and walked over to Nal. "Well, I think it's time to head to the market. What do you think?"

Nal nodded. "Yes, I think that's a great idea."

Gramps approached the supervisor, who was engrossed in sharpening a scythe with a gritty gray stone. "We're going to do a little sightseeing today. Maybe go up to see the pools. Heard so much about them, but never actually gone to see what they look like. We'll be back after lunch."

The supervisor never even looked up; he only grunted and nodded his head. Nal and Gramps left the field in the direction of the pools, then circled around and headed toward the east gate.

⤜⤛

The click-clacking bumps of the road helped Jak wriggle free from the tip of the sword. He pushed some hay underneath him to provide some padding and then reached back to feel the skin where he had been pricked. He didn't want to bleed all over the swords and leave a trail for Cain to follow. The cut wasn't too bad, just a little damp. As soon as they got off the wagon, he'd have Tess check it. *But how are we going to get out without getting caught?*

The wagon stopped, and the driver creaked out of the seat, causing the wagon to sway back and forth as he stepped off.

"Cain!" a heavy voice boomed. "Hey, everyone, look who's here!"

"Great Father!" shouted another voice. "Come 'n have a drink."

"Yes, a drink!"

"You think I'd stoop low enough to drink with the likes of you?" said Cain with disdain.

There was silence.

"Yes?" the second voice said with uncertainty.

"Hah!" Cain snorted. "You're right."

Laughter broke out as Cain's feet clomped off the cobblestone. A chorus of voices shouted Cain's name, and a door clanked shut amidst the clinking of cups.

"He's gone. Let's go," said Jak.

They peeked through the hay over the side of the wagon. They were parked along a wall, so they scrambled over the edge where they couldn't be seen and melted into the crowd.

"Are you sure this is the right way?" asked Tess, constantly looking over her shoulder to see if Cain or anyone else was following them.

"Yep," said Jak. "The market is over there, and Mr. Nettor said the gate is just beyond it."

"But how do you know?"

He pointed up. "The Thread is right above us."

"It is?" She squinted up and tilted her head in various positions, trying to catch a glimpse of the Thread, but it was no use. "I can't see it. When did that show up?"

"Right after we got out of the wagon, I saw it come around the corner. It's got to be headed out of town."

They pressed forward, blending into the shadows wherever they could until they heard the hawking of buyers and sellers in the East Market. They broke into a large plaza just like the one on the other side of the city. Vendors and buyers lined each side of the street, haggling over the price of a string of beads or a young lamb. It was the perfect place to wait without anyone noticing.

"Do you see Mr. Nettor?" asked Tess.

"No, not yet," said Jak. "Let's go over by the palms." They chose a spot behind the bushes in the shadow of one of the palms next to the gate and sat down, Tess twirling her hair around one finger and Jak chewing his lip, knowing that every minute that ticked by was one more minute for Lamech to discover they had disappeared.

Within a half-hour, Gramps and Nal made their way through the maze of booths and spotted Jak and Tess behind the bushes. "Did you see the Thread?" said Gramps, sitting down next to them. Jak nodded.

"Me too," said Gramps, "just for a moment. Good thing because we didn't know exactly where the east gate was. The Thread led us straight here. I guess El is ready for us to move on as well. No sign of Nettor?"

No sooner were the words out of his mouth than Blackey and Whitey appeared with the familiar blue and white wagon picking its way through the crowd.

Mr. Nettor drove straight up to the gate, in between palms and the crowd. Then he discreetly peered into the bushes and whispered, "Hop in. The longer I sit here, the sooner a crowd will gather and want to buy fabric."

They didn't need anymore prompting than that, and climbed single-file into the wagon. Jak and Tess huddled in the back out of sight under the wagon cover while Mr. Nettor clicked Blackey and Whitey through the gate.

"Are you headed out, fabric man?" one of the gate guards called.

"Yes I am, my good man. Business has been so good even with the unfortunate loss of the Black Serpent that I've plum run out of cloth. I'll be back though! The gold and silver coins of Enoch call my name."

The guard laughed and waved them on through.

Mr. Nettor gave Blackey and Whitey their heads, and they bounced down the road, the Thread continuing to zoom ahead of them.

"See it, Mr. Nettor?" said Jak.

"See what, my boy?"

"The Thread. It's right there ahead of you."

"Hmmm. Nope. I don't see a thing." Mr. Nettor shaded his eyes and peered into the air ahead. "Wait! Yes, there it is! It just glimmered into view. See? That's what I mean, boy. The Thread could be hanging right above our heads, and most people don't even know it. They just continue on with life as normal. But it's those few moments of sight that always made me wonder."

The wagon rolled down the path leaving a plume of dust in its wake. Their escape could not have gone any better, and finally, Jak felt like he could breathe easy once again.

Suddenly, bells from the city began to peal behind them. The road was flat and straight, so they could still see the gate a half-mile back. It buzzed with activity. Men armed with scythes, spears, and clubs poured through on foot and on donkeys and began streaming down the road behind them like ants to a picnic.

"What's going on back there?" said Mr. Nettor.

"Lamech must've discovered we're gone!" shouted Jak. "The whole city is coming after us!"

"We've gotta get a move on, Rail," said Gramps.

Mr. Nettor cracked the whip above Blackey and Whitey, and the wagon surged ahead. "Come on, boys! If we ever needed speed, now's the time."

The men on donkeys shot along the road at least twice as fast as the wagon, shouting and waving their weapons. The man in front wore a familiar brown tunic and was thrusting a familiar ax-headed lance into the air.

Suddenly, an arrow thumped into the back gate of the wagon, nailing Jak's sleeve to the wood. He struggled to pull out the arrow, but it snapped in half. He slid his sleeve over the broken shaft to free himself.

"Hurry, Mr. Nettor! They're catching up," said Tess.

"And Cain is at the head of the pack!" said Jak.

Mr. Nettor wiped his brow with his handkerchief. "I'm sorry, but this is as fast as we can go."

Cain's donkey pulled ahead of the other men; he was less than a stone's throw away.

Jak was sure that in a few moments' time, they would be captured and sold into slavery—or worse. Suddenly, the words from the book entered into his head.

Death had its hands around my throat; the terrors of the grave overtook me. I saw only trouble and sorrow. Then I called on the name of Yahweh: 'Please, Yahweh, save me!' How kind Yahweh is.

Jak wasn't sure that Yahweh had helped him in the past or not, but he had nothing to lose, so he closed his eyes and concentrated as hard as he could. *"Yahweh, I hate to be a bother, but we need help again. So if it isn't too much trouble, DO SOMETHING."*

A loud spurt blew up behind them, and Jak opened his eyes. The Thread shimmered and shook, sending a thick cloud of swirling red dust in between the men and the wagon until the men could no longer be seen. Even the shouting faded. The only thing they could hear was the steady gallop of Blackey's and Whitey's hooves along with the wagon wheels rumbling down the road.

Wind swept the cloud away, revealing the city still behind them and the gate still open, but the men were gone.

"Where'd they go?" said Tess.

"Doesn't matter, as long as they're gone," said Gramps.

"Gone?" said Mr. Nettor, trying to crank his head to see. "How can that be? They were just there."

"Not anymore," said Nal. He laid his lance back down underneath the seat. "The Thread sent a dust storm, and they disappeared."

Mr. Nettor slowed the donkeys down to a trot and turned all the way around to see for himself.

"Well, I'll be! How strange. They're all gone." He wiped his forehead again with the handkerchief. "That Thread of yours does the strangest things, m'boy!"

"I think it's El, not the Thread," said Gramps.

"Whatever it is, I'd say this calls for a celebration." Mr. Nettor dug a well-worn cloth bag out from under his seat. "Dates, anyone?"

The road curved toward the south, and the hills along the eastern side gradually grew into mountains, covered from top to bottom with tall trees that spread long, bushy fingers into the sky. Each branch was covered with several barrel-like cones and hundreds of clusters of needles that looked like skimpy sea anemones. The air was intoxicating with the fresh perfume of pine.

Jak kept changing positions on his pillow, but he couldn't get comfortable because the book would not stop tingling. It didn't hurt, per se, but it gave a constant light tingle. Finally he took the bag off and laid it next to him. Guardian had never said anything about how irritating the book would be. The gentle sway of the wagon mesmerized him and he yawned. In a few minutes, his head slid onto his chest, and he was asleep.

As soon as the red dust began spraying, Cain's donkey stumbled and sent Cain flying into the air. He flipped over the donkey's head and landed hard on his back with the wind knocked out of him. The dust stung his eyes and plugged his nose until he could hardly breathe. He pulled his hood down and buried his face in his tunic, taking carefully measured breaths while the dust swarmed over his head.

It didn't last long—only a few minutes—but when the dust cleared and he stood up again, everyone was gone. The road leading back to Enoch was clear of the swarm of men, and the road ahead was vacant; the wagon was gone, nowhere in sight.

He peeled off the tunic and slapped it against a tree, sending great plumes of red dust floating away in the breeze.

The anger in the city of Enoch toward Jak had been so strong that Cain could taste it. He knew that if he didn't get to the wagon before the mob, they would rip the boy apart, and Cain could not allow that. The boy was too valuable.

The back of his throat tickled; it was covered with the red dust. He coughed and spat on the ground. He had been caught in a time storm, he was sure of it, which meant he had been transported somewhere between the time the boy had left Enoch and wherever the boy was now, but he had no way of knowing how much time lay between him and the boy. It could be a few months or a few years, maybe even decades or centuries.

Cain creased his forehead with his fingers, trying to decide what to do. He could go back to Enoch and see what time he was now in, but that wouldn't do any good because he still wouldn't know where the boy was.

While he was weighing his options, something moved beyond the tree, and Cain swung his lance in front of him.

His donkey brayed as it moved to rip up a new chunk of grass.

Cain relaxed. The donkey had been carried there, too, and that was just as well. The animal would be useful.

"C'mon, donkey," Cain said to the animal. "Let's go find the boy."

PART THREE
CLEANSING

CHAPTER 46

The Crazy Boat-Builder

Thud. Thud. Thud.

A steady pounding startled Jak awake. He lifted the flap and peeked out. The hammering came from somewhere through the trees, along with laughter and shouting. Just before the spot where the Thread and the road took an abrupt right turn and plunged down the hill, a crooked sign hung on a tree. In sloppy yellow paint, it read "Fool's Point." Underneath, in smaller letters, it read, "Caution: Boat Construction."

Now that they were out of the trees, he could see a crowd of men and women drinking from large cups, laughing and jostling with each other while they pointed to something in the valley.

"What do you think is going on?" said Tess.

"Somebody's building a boat, I guess," said Gramps, stating the obvious.

A man staggered to the top of a boulder in the middle of the crowd, raised his arms in the air and began to shout in a drunken drawl. "Are ya ready? Les' sing it a'gin."

The crowd shouted their approval as the man began to chant:

The crazy old man [and the crowd shouted back: *the crazy old man*]
Got himself a tool [*got himself a tool*]
He hammers on the hill [*hammers on the hill*]
He's a crazy old fool [*crazy old fool*]

Then the man fell backwards off the rock, laughing hysterically. A couple of his friends caught him and placed him safely on the ground, but a moment later, he climbed back on and they did it all over again.

Gramps shook his head and frowned. "What a bunch of drunks."

"Well, whoever the old man in the song in, they obviously think he's crazy," said Mr. Nettor. "Maybe they're right." They passed the sign and began the descent into a valley.

Jak looked down to the right and shuddered at the sheer drop. One wrong move, and the wagon would plummet 100 feet to the rocks below. He tried not to think about it.

"How big d'you suppose the boat is?" asked Nal. "The biggest boat I've seen was a ten-man river boat. We use it for fishing upstream. Do you think this boat's bigger than that?"

"Well, if it is, no wonder they think he's crazy," said Mr. Nettor. "There's no water around here for miles and miles, not for a big boat. Maybe on the Euphrates, but here? Not a chance."

At the bottom of the hill, the road veered into the valley, and they finally had the chance to turn around and get a glimpse of the boat that had been advertised on the sign at the top of the hill.

Jak had anticipated a large canoe, or maybe a small yacht-like vessel, but what they saw when they turned around was beyond his wildest expectations.

"*That's* the boat?" he said.

⁂

"Report!" Beelz laid his head on a rock and propped his mouth open wide so the light of Lucifer could pour out. A crew of Lights almost as tall as Lucifer himself arranged itself haphazardly in front of him, creating a palette of disgusting colors and smells. "What is the current status of the female leviathan?"

The tallest of the Lights, a putrescent green glimmery kind of light dripping a yellowish snot that smelled like dirty socks, bowed slightly. "Master of all Deception, the Beelzin were too late in Enoch. The boy unexpectedly went to the pools and released her."

"He let her go?" Lucifer burned a deeper shade of yellow. "Fool! Doesn't he know she is trying to eat him?"

"Apparently not, although the Beelzin themselves had to run for their lives as they were in the pool chambers when it occurred."

"Did they escape?"

"Yes, unscathed."

"Pity. Often those who fail in their assignments incur their own punishment. Where is the boy now?"

A pale pumpkin-orange Light pulsed and bowed. "Lord Lecher, we pursue him even now across the sands of time and the landscapes of tree-covered mountains that reach to the sky filled with—"

Lucifer smacked him across the head with a tentacle, stunning him to silence. "Cut out the word waterfall and just give me the facts."

The burnt orange Light sighed and continued. "We don't know."

"WHAT? You don't know? He was right there in the chambers. Did not the Beelzin have the presence of mind to follow him?"

"It was not that easy, my Lord. The boy disappeared. We do know that the boy's dog found him, and he was taken to Lamech's house."

"Lamech? In Nod?"

"Yes, my Lord, the city of Enoch to be specific."

Lucifer paced in the air. "This should not be a difficult thing then. Lamech will certainly keep him for me while we make a plan to retrieve the book."

The Light flittered and pulsed for a moment and then quietly said, "The boy is no longer there."

Lucifer did not flare into a rage as all the Lights expected him to. Instead, he took a deep breath. "Help me understand how a little boy can escape the Beelzin twice in the space of four days."

"No one knows, my Lord. As soon as his room was discovered empty, Lamech sent out his men, and they found the wagon headed east. They pursued, but the wagon disappeared in a Thread storm."

"Blasted Yahweh and his blasted Thread. So we do not know which time he is in?"

"That is correct, sir, but we do have some good news."

"What is it?" snapped Lucifer.

"The Black Serpent has been recovered."

"Why didn't you say that in the beginning, numbskull. Has her programming begun?"

A pale blue Light shimmered and glided forward. "Yes, my Lord. The potion along with some torture has made her most compliant. It was quite amusing to watch her writhe when the Beelzin drove the glowing spikes in between her scales."

"Excellent." Lucifer wished he had been present to watch, but one cannot be everywhere at once. "Send her on the hunt. When she discovers the boy, inform me immediately. I will personally oversee the extraction of the book."

⚘

Jak could not believe his eyes. The boat hogged the plateau; it was huge, at least as big as an ocean liner, and the only water around was a small waterfall cascading down the mountain behind it.

"No wonder the sign says 'Fool's Point.' This guy is crazy!" said Jak. "You'd have to flood the whole valley to get that thing to float."

"He must have a good reason for building it," said Gramps. "It's a lot of work building something that big, especially without all the fancy tools we have in our time."

"Clarence," said Mr. Nettor, "what reason could there possibly be for building a boat that big in the mountains? Clearly the man is deluded."

Blackey and Whitey pulled them away from the hill, following the Thread into a small village, if it could be called a village. It was more a collection of houses fringed with a herd of goats and sheep. Four women surrounded by an assortment of two-handled clay jugs huddled around a hole in the ground. One sat on a rock that looked like a beach ball, while another pulled a dripping rope hand over hand from the hole until a bucket emerged, filled to the brim with water. She wobbled it to the side of a jug that was held by a third woman and sloshed the water over the edge.

A big yellow dog raised his head from where he slept in the sun and barked at the approaching wagon, but he didn't bother getting up. Macy did though. She jumped up and put her front paws on the edge of the wagon and emitted a short yip.

One of the women looked up, put down her jug, and hurried over. Her face was almond-shaped and tanned brown, a stark contrast against her teeth, which smiled a bright white. A brown shawl with a black fringe was draped over her shoulders.

"Travelers," she said, "welcome to our little village. Come, rest yourselves," she said, beckoning to the well.

"It must be time to stop," said Jak. "The Thread is floating right above her."

"I don't know about this," said Tess. "The last time our hosts were happy to see us was because they were going to sell us as slaves."

The woman returned to the well and then approached them again, this time with a cup brimming with water. "Drink, drink. The water is good and cold, and you must be hot and thirsty."

Gramps climbed down from the wagon a little more slowly than he had when they first began the trip. "Thank you," he said, nodding kindly at her. "We are thirsty." He drained the cup and gave it back to the woman, who filled it and handed it to Tess.

"My name is Tisrah," she said, "and this is Azras, Vim, and Rispel." She pressed her hands together and bowed. "We are happy you have joined us."

"We can't stay long, ma'am," said Gramps.

"I know," said Tisrah. "You are following the Thread. I saw it come to the well and knew travelers would not be far behind."

"You *saw* it?" said Jak, surprised.

"Yes." Her brown eyes danced as she spoke, and Jak immediately had a sense they could trust her. "I always see the Thread when it comes, for as long as the travelers are with us. It goes when you go."

"Maybe you can help me then," said Jak. He rummaged in the book bag and pulled out the deck of cards. "I'm looking for someone, a man." He held up the laughing-man card. "Have you ever seen him before?"

She pulled it close and smiled. "Yes, I know him quite well."

"You do?" asked Jak, glad he was finally getting somewhere. "Where can I find him?"

She pointed to the boat at the top of the hill. "Up there."

347

CHAPTER 47

Thread Card #2 Finds its Match...
Sort Of

Jak looked at the card again, then up at the tiny figure moving around the boat at the top of the hill. "You mean the man up there building the boat?"

Tisrah nodded. "Yes. He is my husband."

"Your husband?" said Tess, crinkling her nose.

Jak felt the same way. It was no wonder the guy on the card looked like he was laughing – he was crazy! He hoped the Thread would get moving right after he captured his words so they could get away from there as soon as possible.

"When will he come back down?" said Jak.

"The sun has almost finished its trek through the sky, so they will return soon for the evening meal. Would you like to wait for him? Otherwise Rispel could take you up right now."

"Going up right now sounds good to me," said Tess, sounding like she wanted to get it over with. "Let's go."

But Jak wasn't so sure he wanted to go right away. His heel didn't feel very good at the moment. That same pain was beginning to build up again, he could sense it, like water pressing against a dam. On the other hand, the Thread had taken them straight to this village, and there was no way of knowing how long it would stay in this particular moment of time. He had to at least try to capture the laughing man's words while he could. "Alright," he said, "but I may need some help. My foot is killing me at the moment."

"What's wrong?" asked Tess.

"The same thing that happened back at East Eden, like a boiling hot dagger is stuck in my foot, trying to get out."

Nal inspected the skin on Jak's arm. "Your skin isn't yellow, so at least you're not going mad again."

"Well, that's a relief," said Jak. "It's always nice to know you're not going mad."

"That's what I always say," said Mr. Nettor. "If you don't mind, though, I'll stay here and tend to the donkeys while you climb the hill." Nettor mopped his forehead again with his handkerchief and disappeared behind the wagon, humming the song the people on Fool's Point had been singing.

A young woman in a dark red shawl stepped forward, at least she appeared to be young, maybe twenty-five years old. But since looks were deceiving in this world, Jak wasn't sure how truly young she was. In reality, she might be 200 or 300 years old. "I am Rispel. I will take you up to meet Noah."

"Noah?" said Jak.

"Yes, Noah, the son of Lamech."

The Thread followers froze.

"Lamech?" said Tess.

"Yes, the son of Lamech."

They couldn't believe it. The Thread had led them straight back to Lamech's family. For all they knew, he could be inside one of the houses having tea or maybe even up on the hill helping his son. Even if several hundred years had passed since they escaped Enoch, he would certainly remember them.

"Would you excuse us for a moment?" said Tess.

"Certainly." Rispel went back to pouring water while Jak, Nal, Tess, and Gramps huddled back by the wagon.

"What do we do?" said Jak. "If Noah is half as bad as Lamech, we're in serious trouble."

"I say we jump in the wagon and leave," said Tess.

"But where would we go?" said Gramps. "Not only did the Thread lead us here, but he's the next Thread card person. If we run away, the Thread might not come with us, and even if it did, it would only lead us straight back. At the very least, we have to get this fellow Noah to touch the card. How about if I stay down here and keep a lookout, and if I see something fishy, I'll come on up and let you know, and we'll hightail it out of here."

There was no win-win solution to this dilemma; Jak had to get Noah to touch the card.

"Alright," he agreed. "Tess, Nal, and I will go up, and you stay here. Don't let Mr. Nettor get too comfortable. If he sits down and we have to move quick, it'll be like trying to get an iceberg moving."

"Don't worry about him. Just go on up there and see Noah," said Gramps.

Jak, Tess, and Nal stepped back toward the well. "Okay, Rispel. We're ready now."

Rispel swept her long dark hair behind her head with both hands and led the way to a well-beaten path that led up the slope. It was a sort of shallow stairway made out of slabs of rough stone stacked on top of one another like jagged pancakes. Macy ran ahead of them, jumping up the steps, then back down behind them, then ahead of them again, sniffing and barking at anything that moved. She was obviously glad to be out of the wagon.

"Be careful," said Rispel, "Just last week, my husband Shem slipped and gashed his shin on the rocks. Their edges bite and tear like badgers."

"How long has Noah been working on the boat?" asked Jak, picking his way up the hill.

"Oh, let's see...it was ninety-five years when Grandfather Lamech died, and—"

"Lamech's dead?" said Jak.

"Yes, four years ago. It's still a bit of a mystery. One day he was fine, but the next he fell to the fever. For three weeks, we watched his skin shrivel up, and then he died. Some think it was the Black Serpent, but I don't think so. His skin didn't turn yellow, and his eyes were bright to the end, although I suppose it could have been the beast. The stories say there's only been one who survived the Black Serpent's bite, but that was a long time ago."

"How long ago?" said Jak, curious to know who else had survived.

"More than an entire lifetime."

Back home, Jak could have safely assumed she meant about eighty years, certainly less than a century, but here, her answer didn't mean anything. "And how long is that?"

"More than a thousand years. My great grandfather told me about it, although he hadn't been born then either. He heard about it from his grandfather. It was a boy, a Thread follower like you. The serpent bit him in the heel, and by the time he made it to East Eden, his skin had yellowed and his eyes were sunken in. He should've died, but he didn't. He kept following the Thread. No one knows what happened to him, although my father said he met him once."

Jak's heart skipped a beat. "He did?"

"Yes, when he was a boy. He and my aunt had been captured and were to be sold as slaves in Enoch. The Thread follower stole the key from the guard and freed them. Later, they heard that some of the old women believed this boy was the Quelcher, the same Thread follower that was bitten by the black beast in Eden."

Jak's mind whirled back to the room with the slave children. The boy he had heard crying was Rispel's father! Tess caught Jak's eye and shook her head, and Jak knew what she meant. He wanted to tell Rispel that it was him, but he agreed with his cousin's silent advice and kept his mouth shut. Even though Lamech was dead, Noah could still carry out his father's wishes, so they had to stay undercover. "So, where's your father now?"

Rispel shook her head. "Dead. Raiders killed my parents last year. They wiped out the whole village. Shem and I had just come back from visiting them. We'd be dead, too, if we had stayed but one more day."

They climbed the rest of the way in silence, the weight of death pressing down on each of them. Finally, they climbed the last set of rocks and saw the full boat stretched out before them on the plateau. It looked even more imposing up close.

"Wow!" said Jak.

Nal gave a low whistle.

Rispel laughed. "I forget what it must look like to a fresh pair of eyes. I'm so accustomed to seeing it up here that it's just a part of the mountain to me."

The hull loomed above them as tall as a four-story building, as long as one and a half football fields, and as fat as a ten-lane highway. Huge planks extended from the ground up to the ship to keep it from rolling over, and a roof, slanted like the roof of a house, ran for the entire length of the ship.

Halfway down, a gangplank extended from the hull of the ship to the ground like a sideways bridge. Smoke rose from a fire at the edge of the hill, scenting the air with the musky odor of burning pine.

Two men at the edge of the mountain swung axes at logs in a steady *thud-thud*, the same sound that had awakened Jak in the wagon before rounding Fool's Point. The thuds were almost in rhythm with the taunts that sifted down from the drunken crowd on the rock above the plateau.

"All hail the King of Stupidity!"

"Watch yer step, old man. Yer brains spilled out on the floor a long time ago!"

Jak didn't know how the men could work under the constant jeering. "Don't they ever go home?"

"Who?"

"The drunks on Fool's Point." Jak pointed to the rock..

"Occasionally, but only to get more wine. I've gotten so used to their yelling that I hardly even hear them anymore." She paused. "What were we talking about again? Oh yes, how long has Noah been working on the boat. Let's see, when Grandfather died, I remember Noah saying it had been ninety-five years. The next year, we began gathering supplies, and that was three years ago, so that makes it ninety-eight—no, ninety-nine years. Yes. Ninety-nine years he's been working on it."

"He's been building this boat for ninety-nine years?" said Tess.

"Hard to believe, isn't it? I remember as a little girl coming to see crazy Noah. Back then it was just a wooden skeleton."

Jak knew he would get in trouble with Tess if he asked Rispel what he wanted to ask her, because his mother had once cautioned him that it was as bad as asking a woman how much she weighed, but the question wouldn't stay in his mouth. "How old are you, Rispel?"

A great smile spread on her face, and she proudly announced, "I am exactly eighty-four years old as of last Thursday. I just had a birthday. You missed a great party with lemon meringue pie and fried coconuts and wheat cakes with honey. It was wonderful. We might have some of the wheat cakes left, or we could just make some more. It isn't difficult, and it's been a while since Threaders like yourselves have stopped by."

"Rispel!" A man tripped down the gangplank and ran toward them. He was stripped to the waist and wore only a pair of blackened linen pants. Sweat ran down his face and chest, digging furrows in the dirt smeared on his body.

He kissed her, leaving a black smudge on her cheek. "What are you doing up here?"

"We have company, Thread followers looking for your father. Jak, Tess, and Nal, this is my husband Shem."

"I would kiss you as well," said Shem, "except that I don't think a kiss filled with pine tar is the best greeting. But welcome to our home and welcome to the grand project." He swept his arm toward the ship. "Come along! My father is inside. We are just about finished pitching the inside of the ship."

"Pitching the ship?" said Jak. Jak had pitched plenty of baseballs, but he had never heard of pitching a ship.

"Yes, pine pitch. You see the fire over there? My brothers Ham and Japheth are splitting gopher wood into thin strips. We throw it into the fire, melt the pitch into tar, and use it to seal the ship so it won't flood with water."

The first thought that came to Jak's mind was *What water?* The only water around was the waterfall further up the hill, but there was no way it could flood a ship that size.

"Come on," said Shem. "I'll show you inside."

They followed him up the gangplank and entered the boat ten feet off the ground onto an enormous wooden deck, with a stairway on the other side opposite the gangplank. The musky odor of the smoke intensified once they were inside the ship, as if a swatch of pine needles had been suddenly stuffed up their noses. Above them, a deck wrapped around the inside of the ship like a giant donut. The planks that made up the walls were streaked along the seams with the same black that streaked Shem's body.

"See?" said Shem, pointing to the walls. "That's the pitch."

"Shem?" a voice boomed from above. "Who're you talking to?"

"Rispel brought some visitors up."

"Visitors?" Something clunked to the floor on the highest deck, followed by the sound of feet pounding down the stairs. A face fringed with a heavy brown beard and full head of brown hair peeked over the railing of the deck above them. It looked exactly like the face on the card except upside down. "Visitors, you say?" The face whisked away, and the sound of feet pattering across the floor and down another staircase echoed in the boat until the face reappeared on the same deck they were on. He also wore a pair of blackened linen pants, but with a matching blackened linen shirt.

"Visitors! I love having visitors, as long as they are here to enjoy the work we are doing and not make fun of it. Which of the two are you here to do?" He drummed his fingers together and leaned forward a bit. The wrinkles along his eyes crinkled up as he smiled and waited for an answer.

"They're looking for you, Father," said Rispel.

"And we're here to enjoy your work," said Jak. "This ship is amazing. Rispel was telling us about it on the way up the hill."

"It is quite a work," said the man, "but you came to see me?"

Jak held out the card, wanting to get it over with and get back down the hill so they could leave. "Yes. The Thread brought us here. Is this you?"

"The Thread? Hmmm. I haven't seen the Thread in a while." He took the card in his hand and scrutinized it. "Yes, I believe this is me. I don't often see myself except in the occasional pool of water or a bad dream, but I do believe this is me." He held the card up next to his face and smiled. "What do you think, Rispel?"

"Except for the pitch all over your face, yes, it is definitely you," she said.

He placed the card back in Jak's outstretched hand, but it didn't look any different, just the same man laughing at him with no letters, no sparks, nothing.

CHAPTER 48

The End of the World

Jak was flabbergasted. This was not the way it was supposed to work. The words should have been captured as soon as he touched it. *This is going to be harder than I thought.*

"Father," said Rispel, "this is Jak, Nal, and Tess, and this..." She put her hand on the man's arm and turned toward the three newcomers, "this is my father-in-law, Noah."

"Welcome to the grandest project on Earth," said Noah with a sweeping bow. "Plans came straight from Yahweh. This boat is to be 450 feet long, 75 feet wide, and 45 feet tall. There are three decks, making plenty of space for every kind of animal on the Earth. Would you like the tour?"

"We'd love to," said Tess, "but—"

Jak stepped in front of Tess. "That'd be great."

"Good. You've already seen the first deck, so come upstairs. The view is marvelous." He danced over to the stairs and took the stairs two at a time, humming and talking to himself.

357

Jak limped after him with Tess and Nal close behind.

"What are you doing?" Tess whispered. "Remember Lamech?"

"Yes, I remember," said Jak, "but nothing happened to the card when he touched it. Look!" He handed her the card as they trudged up the steps.

She took it and stared at the empty black box. "Nothing happened? But he's got to be the laughing guy. It looks just like him."

"I know, but nothing happened, so we're stuck here for a while. We don't want to make him mad by refusing the tour."

The walls of the second deck were also lined with pitch. A collection of wood cages and rods were lined up next to the railing that overlooked the first deck.

"This is the second deck, specifically for birds and smaller animals. You can see the cages and roosting rods. We'll push them back to the wall when the pitch has finished drying." He bounded up the stairs to the third floor deck. In the front of the boat was a wide space with the windows thrown wide open, catching the sun and the cool mountain breeze. The back half of the boat was closed off, with a narrow hallway splitting it in the middle.

An old man with short gray hair sat on a three-legged stool along one wall with a dripping bristle trembling in his hand, slowly spreading black tar across the seams of the planks.

"Grandfather," said Noah, "we have visitors."

"What's that?" said the man, cupping his free hand to his ear without turning around.

"VISITORS!" shouted Noah.

"No thanks," said the man. "I'm not hungry right now."

Noah laughed, grabbed the man's shoulders, and turned him around. He had a gray beard that stretched to his middle, and his face was creased in wrinkles. Noah pointed to Jak, Nal, and Tess.

The old man peered at them and then lifted his hand and pointed. "Noah, we have visitors."

"That's what I said," said Noah. "This is Jak and Tess and—"

"Jad and Bess?" said the old man.

"No, Jak and Tess."

"Jap and Mess?" the old man tried again.

"No! JAK AND TESS."

The old man peered at Noah's beard and pointed. "You've got some pitch in your beard, son."

Noah smiled and laughed. "This is my grandfather, Methuselah. He's a little hard of hearing, but he normally does a pretty good job of reading lips."

"You have him up here pitching with you?" said Rispel. "I thought he was just watching."

"We tried that," said Shem, "but it's like trying to keep a dog away from a bone. He wants to help, and this is the first thing in years he actually can do."

Noah ambled over to the aft half of the deck and and pointed down the hallway. "This is where we'll stay. Food supplies and sleeping quarters are in the back, and there is plenty of room for us in the front." The quarters were small, and none had windows, but there was plenty of space in each room for a couple of people to set up camp.

"What do you mean, where you'll stay?" asked Jak. "Are you moving into the boat, like a house?"

"You could say that," said Noah. "Haven't you heard? I thought for sure the fools on Fool's Point would have told you. There's going to be a flood."

"A flood?" said Jak. "Like with water?"

"Yes. Yahweh told me almost a hundred years ago that there is going to be a flood. It shouldn't be too long now. We're getting close to being done."

Suddenly it began making sense to Jak. A boat would have to be humongous to put a bunch of people on it. "Is that why it's so big, so you can fit everyone on board?"

The smile left Noah's face, and his brows furrowed. "No, no, not that at all. That's why the flood is coming in the first place." He tugged at his beard, pressed his lips together for a second and then said, "Everyone on the Earth is going to die."

CHAPTER 49

Lamech & Lamech

Jak wasn't sure he had heard correctly. He thought Noah had just said everyone was going to die, but he didn't see how that could be right. "Everyone's going to die?"

Noah nodded his head.

"You mean everybody everywhere?"

Noah nodded his head again. "Yes."

Jak couldn't believe it. "But...but why?" he stammered.

"Evil," said Noah, shaking his head in frustration. "All the evil on the Earth. It's everywhere. Criminals steal and kill, and the judges who are supposed to make sure justice happens look the other way for a bribe and let the guilty go free. Entire villages are wiped out at the whim of a few spear-happy men. Children are kidnapped from their homes in the dead of night to either be sacrificed or sold. And men and women carouse with whomever they please, and then drown it all in a jug of whiskey. That's just the tip of the evil. The poison from the mouth of the serpent runs strong in our blood. Rebellion is our nature and El has had enough."

"Are you saying Yahweh is going to *send* the flood?" asked Tess.

"Yes, I am sad to say it, but he told me I am the only one on the Earth who follows him now. All the old fathers are dead except for my grandfather, and death will come for him soon. The old ways of calling on the name of Yahweh are mixed up with calling on the Lights and doing whatever one pleases. Everything that was pronounced good has been perverted, and Yahweh is angry." Noah tugged on his beard again. "And sad."

It was certainly true that ever since they had left East Eden, it felt like they had been walking in a land soaked and dripping with evil.

"So why's the boat so big then?" said Tess.

"For the animals," said Noah, the twinkle returning to his eyes. "Yahweh said we are to take two of every kind of animal, a male and a female, and seven of the clean animals, the kind we use for sacrifices."

"You mean sacrifices for Remembrance Day?" said Jak.

"You have celebrated Remembrance Day?" Noah's eyebrows lifted.

"Yes, but only once, when we first arrived in East Eden." said Jak. "It was during the Remembrance Day Feast, and Adam sacrificed a lamb."

Noah's grandfather struggled up from the stool and pointed a trembling finger at Jak. "Heh. So you've been to see Adam? That Thread sure takes you through time. Adam was my great-great-great-great-great grandfather."

"He was?" said Jak.

"Yep. It's been... let's see, he died about fifty years before Yahweh took my daddy, so it's been 725 years."

"So death finally got him," said Jak.

"Yep. Death finally gets everybody, 'cept my daddy."

"But didn't you just say that Yahweh took your dad fifty years before Adam died?" said Tess.

"Sure did, but he didn't die. He got sucked up into the sky. It was the strangest thing I ever saw. One moment we were walking down by the fields, and the next he was walking on air, waving goodbye, got taken straight into the sky. So it was kind of like death, 'cept without the actual dyin' part. I never saw him since."

"It's a strange thing," said Noah. "People normally get to live with their ancestors for quite a while before death steals them away, but I never even met my great grandfather Enoch."

"Enoch?" said Nal. His whole face had perked up. "Did you say Enoch?"

This was the second time they had run across someone who knew an Enoch. There was a chance Noah was talking about the Enoch from the city of Enoch, but maybe not.

"Was that the guy the city of Enoch was named after?" said Jak.

"Goodness, no," said Noah, shaking his head in disgust. "That city is a hotbed of rotten onions. None of our folk have ever lived over there. This Enoch was the son of Jared, the son of—"

At this, Nal stumbled backward. "J-Jared?" he stammered. "Is he alive?"

"No. Jared died long ago," said Methuselah.

Jak wasn't sure how much to say, but if Methuselah knew anything about Enoch, Nal needed to know. "When we first got to East Eden, we met Jared and his son Nal."

"Yep, that'd be my grandfather and my uncle," said Methuselah.

Nal and Jak exchanged glances.

"Nal had a twin brother named Enoch," said Jak, "who was taken by the Black Serpent five years before we arrived, but if Enoch is your father, that means he wasn't killed after all."

"Good thing too," said Methuselah. "Otherwise, there wouldn't be anybody to pitch this boat."

"But how did he come back to life?"

Methuselah chewed on his whiskers. "It's been seven hundred years since he left, so a few details may have slipped my mind, but as far as I can recall, he said somebody came to get him, and when he got back, my Uncle Nal was five years older than he was."

"Five years older?" said Nal. "But how can that be? Enoch is my twin...I mean, Nal's twin."

"Don't know. That's the mystery of it."

"But if none of your family ever lived in Enoch," said Tess, "that means your dad isn't the same Lamech who lived in Enoch."

Noah laughed a deep belly laugh. "Absolutely not! My father was a good man. Stand him next to that crooked beanpole in Enoch and you'd see the difference between them right off."

"So you're not going to sell us as slaves to the Lights?" said Jak.

Noah burst into laughter again, this time so hard he could hardly talk. "Sell you...to....the Lights?"

Shem put his brush in the tar bucket. "What ever gave you that idea?"

"Rispel said Noah's father was Lamech, and the only Lamech we knew was the one we stayed with in Enoch. He betrayed us and was going to sell Tess to the Lights as a wife and me as a slave, but I overheard his plans, so we escaped."

"Ah, I see," said Noah, wiping the laughter-tears from his face. "Lamech and Lamech."

"I don't think he's still alive," said Shem, wiping up a splotch of tar that had landed on the deck. "You must have been in Enoch several hundred years ago."

"His son Jabal, the livestock man, died not too long ago as well," said Rispel.

"Those three boys of his weren't too bad," said Methuselah, still chewing his whiskers, "but most of the descendants of Cain were always up to no good."

"Cain?" said Jak. "Which Cain are you talking about?"

"You traveled through time so fast it looks like you missed out on some history lessons," said Noah. "When Yahweh made Cain a fugitive, he left East Eden and headed into the land of Nob, east of the Yarti, and he had himself a family. He built a city and named it after his son Enoch. Enoch grew up and had kids of his own, and they had kids, and so on down to Lamech. Lamech made a name for himself though because of the scar on his face. Did you see it?"

Jak nodded his head.

"A headstrong young man with a brain the size of a pea attacked him with a knife one day over a certain ring Lamech had procured in a shady deal and cut him from the temple to the jaw."

"That's not what he told me," said Jak. "He told me he sold some grain and the man was trying to steal the coins."

"Figgers he'd say that," said Methuselah, "that lying bag of onion-breath."

Noah laughed and kept going. "So Lamech walloped him with a rock and smashed his head in. Then Lamech announced to the world that if his great father Cain was protected by a seven-fold revenge from El, then he was protected by a seventy-fold revenge. It was a fancy blown-up way of sayin' 'Don't even think about trying to kill Lamech'—a bit arrogant if you ask me, but then again, that's how Cain's family kept getting into trouble. Pride and arrogance breed evil just like stagnant swamp water breeds mosquitoes."

"I can't believe it," said Jak. "The Thread led us straight to Cain's home city."

A bell rang from down the hill, and Jak and Nal both tensed, sure it was a warning of another Black Serpent attack.

"Dinner," said Rispel. "Come along. We're having bean biscuits and rice, green peas, and hot potato soup."

Jak and Nal relaxed. They made their way down the stairs and back to the plateau. The two men who had been splitting wood were waiting for them at the bottom of the gangplank.

"Ham, Japheth," boomed Noah, "This is Jak, Tess, and..." Noah stopped as he came to Nal. "I'm sorry, I don't recall your name name, son."

Nal took a deep breath, obviously nervous about saying who he was. "I am Nal."

"Ahhh," said Noah, his eyebrows arching, "just like my great uncle."

Nal smiled. "Yes, sir."

When they got to the bottom of the hill, the Thread hadn't moved; it still hung over the wagon, glowing a soft red light. Jak introduced Noah's family to Gramps and Mr. Nettor and then filled them in on what they had discovered up in the boat.

"That's quite a story," said Gramps.

"I still can't believe Yahweh would do such a thing to the very people he supposedly created in the first place," said Mr. Nettor. "It seems a bit barbaric."

"Barbaric?" said Gramps. "I'd say selling people who've been guests in your own home as slaves is a bit barbaric, wouldn't you? Or maybe sacrificing your own son just to get a year's supply of olive oil. Doesn't that sound barbaric? Or how about wrapping a rock with a string of skulls? Anything strike you as barbaric about that, Rail?"

Mr. Nettor didn't respond with anything more than a "Humph," and then retreated to the silence of combing Blackey and Whitey.

Even though dinner was once again fit for vegetarians, it was a fantastic meal. The bean biscuits were spread with butter and honey, and when it was dipped into the potato soup and the peas, it tasted like chicken pot pie. During dinner, Gramps and Noah talked about them staying with Noah's family until the Thread moved on.

"We sure could use the help," said Noah, wiping a bit of soup from his bowl with a biscuit. "It's a lot of working pitching the boat, a lot of dirty work. And pitching the outside of the boat's going to be a lot harder than the inside. We're going to have to either build scaffolding or hang from ropes."

"Well, if we're going to be pitching," said Japheth, "I vote for the scaffolds. Hanging by a rope that high up gives me the heebie-jeebies."

"I agree," said Ham, his mouth half-full of potato soup. He swallowed. "There's no way I'm going up on a rope."

Both Ham and Japheth were built like bears, so it was easy to see why they did not relish the thought of hanging from the boat by ropes.

"Well," said Noah, "the ropes would be a lot faster, but the only one here nimble enough to do the job would be Shem." His gaze rested on his oldest son.

"That's fine," said Shem, brushing biscuit crumbs off his fingers into the grass. "I don't mind."

"I can do it too," said Methuselah, raising a skinny withered hand in the air.

"You will do no such thing," said Tisrah. She passed a bowl of potato soup to Rispel, who handed it Azras. "A 969-year-old man hanging from the top of the boat by a rope is out of the question."

"Nonsense! I'm as nimble as a monkey," said Methuselah.

"Oh, yes, definitely," laughed Noah, "an old deaf monkey with arthritis in his elbows and knees."

"What'd you say?" said Methuselah, cupping one ear in Noah's direction.

"I said," Noah boomed, "that you can be the pitch handler on the ground. You get to keep the buckets full and hot, then attach them to the ropes so Shem can hoist them up."

"Alright," said Methuselah, "but if the boy falls, I get to take his place."

"We're not even going to talk about Shem falling," said Tisrah. "He'll be fine. It's Yahweh's boat and Yahweh's job. No one's been hurt yet, and we'll keep asking that he keep it that way."

"I can help," said Jak with a touch of hesitation. He didn't know what they would think about a kid pitching the gigantic boat, but he wanted to at least offer. "I don't mind heights, and I'm pretty good with a rope."

"What about your foot, Jak?" asked Tess.

The daggers in his heel had faded, and he felt pretty good. "I'll be okay." Noah looked at Gramps.

"He's right," said Gramps. "He does well with both. I've seen him shimmy up the rope in the back yard plenty of times. He'd be good help."

"Alright then. Tomorrow Papa, Shem, Jak, and I will finish pitching the inside of the boat, and then we'll begin pitching the outside."

Gramps spread a pile of honey on a well-buttered bean biscuit. "Tess, Nal, and I can pitch in wherever you need us. No pun intended."

"Alright," said Noah. "You can help Ham and Japheth. Making the pitch is the bottle neck because it takes several hours just to get it flowing. Boys, can you get up there right off in the morning to heat up the leftovers from today?"

"Sure," said Japheth. He smashed a pile of peas in between two biscuits and bit into the veggie sandwich.

"Shem and I will get the ropes ready while you show Clarence and Nal what to do. Tisrah, you and the girls can continue drying fruit and the other food supplies. I have no idea how long we'll be on that boat, so just keep collecting food. We're going to have to trust that however much we gather will be enough."

Mr. Nettor hadn't said a word the whole time. He just kept shoveling mouthful after mouthful of biscuits and gravy and peas into the gaping hole in his head, listening to how everyone else would be helping. He wiped his mouth with the back of his hand. "I think I'll, um, ah, come up the hill after I finish caring for my animals, of course, and make sure my business supplies are in order, and then I will, ah, I will supervise Jak and Shem. I have much experience as a supervisor, and I am sure you will be pleased with my work." He pasted a cheesy smile on his face and then plugged his mouth with another biscuit.

Noah merely nodded his head and continued with dinner, as if he knew Mr. Nettor's offer was halfhearted at best.

Jak watched Macy and the yellow dog each chewing a bone. He couldn't stop thinking about the card. It sure seemed Noah was the right guy, but if he wasn't, then time was running out. Soon the flood would destroy everyone on the Earth, and Jak would never be able to find the right guy. But the Thread hadn't moved an inch, which meant they had to stay where they were. *So now what?*

CHAPTER 50
The Watcher in the Waterfall

Jak and Nal slept in Ham and Azras's house, Gramps stayed with Japheth and Vim, and Tess went with Shem and Rispel. Mr. Nettor slept in the wagon, saying it didn't feel right sleeping anywhere else.

Jak and Nal almost wished they had slept there as well because they couldn't get to sleep at Ham's house. They were lying in a room that had been built on the flat roof of the main house. Normally it was used for drying fruits and vegetables, but Ham had cleared out enough space for the two boys to lie down.

Ham and Azras must have thought they were asleep because the two were arguing in a whisper below them.

"My friends don't even speak to me anymore in the market," said Azras. "They ignore me as if I have lice."

"And what am I to do about it?" demanded Ham. "I cannot force them to talk with you any more than I can keep the flood from coming."

"You can tell your father to stop going into town and preaching the way he does."

"It would be easier to force water to flow uphill."

"You haven't even tried," said Azras with disgust. "There's a reason no one will work for him anymore. They all think he's a fool, and I don't blame them."

"Shut your mouth, woman. You cannot speak that way about my father."

There was tense silence for a moment.

"I am only saying," said Azras, "that he brings some of the ridicule down upon his own head—and upon ours as well—by telling everyone he meets to change their ways or die in the flood."

"But that's the whole point. They *do* need to change or Yahweh will send the flood. Did you hear about Atuh? Two days ago, he was knifed in the market in the middle of the day for no other reason than they wanted his sandals. His sandals! They left his body propped up against a wall in plain sight of everyone walking by, bleeding and shoeless. Nobody tried to help him, and nobody questioned the killers. The thieves could have gone to any vendor in the market and paid a few shekels for the exact same pair, but they wanted his, and now he's dead. It has to stop."

"Maybe so, but people are sick of hearing your father's talk. Sooner or later, they won't just be making fun of him. They'll do something worse to him...something worse to *us*. We might end up propped up on a wall bleeding ourselves if he keeps it up."

No more was said after that, and Jak and Nal finally fell asleep.

Jak woke before the sun did with the book hot against his belly. He had taken to removing the book from the book bag at night and stuffing it under his shirt just in case someone tried to take it while he was sleeping. It wasn't comfortable, but it felt safer. He got up and stole out into the early-morning air. It was cool and crisp with a heavy dew that drenched his toes. His foot felt pretty good, and he hoped it would stay that way.

Jak loved the freshness of morning with nothing yet awake to spoil the quiet. He wiped a spot on the table as dry as he could and sat down with the book in his hand. Immediately, the wind kicked up and blew the pages open.

> Yahweh protects those who trust him
> like a child trusts his father;
> I was facing death, and then he saved me.
> Now I can rest again, for
> Yahweh has been so good to me.

Jak stopped reading. How many times had Yahweh saved him from death so far? Once back in Eden as he was climbing the vine up Split Falls, once in East Eden when Scorch attacked at the Tigris River, once when he escaped being sacrificed, once when Scorch attacked at the Yarti River, once when he accidentally set Scorch free at the pools, and once when he escaped from Lamech, although technically that was slavery, not death, but he felt okay about including it in the tally. And then once when the mob was chasing them as they escaped the city of Enoch. That was seven times in the past two weeks, eight if he included the miraculous healing at Remembrance Day, but he wasn't sure if Yahweh had anything to do with that or not.

There was no way of knowing for sure if Yahweh had helped him with *any* of the escapes. He knew Yahweh had sent Guardian at just the right time to help him escape the sacrifice, but maybe he would've fallen into the crevice at the pools anyway, and perhaps overhearing Lamech and Cain was pure coincidence. He still didn't know who sent the warning note though. *Did Yahweh have anything to do with that?*

Whoever wrote the poems that the wind kept finding in the book sounded like he had plenty of scrapes with death as well, and Jak wondered if he was still alive.

"You're up early, Jak." Tisrah unloaded a tray of fruit onto the table next to him.

"I like morning."

"Me too. It's unspoiled and full of possibilities."

"Bad possibilities as well as good," said another voice.

"Good morning, Azras," said Tisrah with a heavy sigh.

"It's true, isn't it?" said Azras, fixing her hair with a pin the size of a knitting needle as she walked. "Maybe the water will come today. Hopefully not, because the boat's not done, but what if Yahweh is tired of waiting? Or maybe the Fool's Point crowd will decide to start throwing things like spears and rocks instead of just rotten tomatoes."

"Yes, you are right," said Tisrah patiently. "The fools at the Point could decide to do anything, and the water could come at any time. However, we have not gathered the animals yet, so I do not think Yahweh would do such a thing. And he will keep us safe from the fools as well."

"I hope you're right." Azras spun on her heels and stomped off.

"So much for the unspoiled morning," said Tisrah, shaking her head.

Jak went back to Ham's house and stuffed the book bag under his blanket. He had thought about taking it up to the boat with him, but he didn't want to risk getting tar on it. Gramps and Nal thought it would be okay to stuff it under his blanket, so that's what he did. He hoped it would be safe there.

The day began with a quick breakfast of pomegranate, rye bread, and cheese, and then the boat crew headed up the hill. Halfway up, Japheth and Ham split off and led Gramps, Nal, and Jak across a path that cut straight across the hill.

"You go with Japheth and Ham," Noah had told Jak. "I think you'll like seeing how it's all done. When you're finished, come on up and we'll get you hooked up to the ropes."

The path led to a smaller plateau where two craters sat in the rock, as if someone had dropped a truck-sized basketball onto the ground, leaving two big perfectly round dents. At the bottom of each crater was a hole the size of a softball.

"We can't place the tar kilns too close to the boat," said Japheth. "Too much danger of the boat catching fire, and we don't want to lose a century of work," said Japheth. "It takes plenty of gopher tar to pitch a boat this big, that's why we have two kilns."

"Gopher tar?" said Jak. "Do you have to catch gophers and squeeze the tar out of them?"

"Squeeze the tar out of a gopher?" Ham burst into laughter. "Yep, that's the way we do it. So before you can climb up one of those ropes you have to catch a dozen gophers and bring them back."

"Gopher," said Japheth, rolling his eyes, "is the name of the tree we make pitch from — gopher wood. It's a kind of pine tree. That's one reason Father built the boat here. The hills are filled with gopher wood." Japheth pointed up to the foothills.

The hills were covered in a thick carpet of the pine trees with the bushy fingers stretching to the sky, except for the foothills closest to the boat. The trees here were much younger and shorter. The main feature on these closer hills was the waterfall that shot out of the rock and plummeted twenty feet, only to disappear into a hole in the ground.

"So all he had to do was cut the trees, roll them down the hill, and make lumber out of them. Not that that was an easy job, but at least he didn't have to cart them over the top of the hills. And in the beginning, he was able to hire help, which was great. Yahweh said to make the whole thing out of gopher wood, so that's what Father did." Japheth picked up a shovel and dug a pile of ash out of the first kiln. "Unfortunately, we can't hire anybody anymore."

"Why not?" said Nal. "Did you run out of gold?"

"No. No one will work for us — everybody thinks we're crazy," said Ham, twirling one finger around his ear. "Nutso, brainless, loony." Ham bugged his eyes out as he was talking.

Japheth nodded his head. "Yep, that's why. So we do all the work ourselves now." He put the shovel down. "Anyway, while one kiln burns, we clean the other one out and get it ready for cooking another batch. Yesterday, Ham and I split several gopher logs into slivers no fatter than my finger. Today, we'll show you how to stack them into the kiln, then cover the whole thing with a layer of moss from the forest. After that, we cover the moss with a layer of black dirt a foot deep, and then we build a bonfire on top of the dirt and wait till the wood slivers heat up." He pointed down over the edge of the rock. "That's when the room below us becomes very important."

He led them down a stairway cut into the slope in between the craters and, at the bottom, turned left to a small door underneath the crater. Japheth stooped through the doorway and led Jak into a short, skinny room, barely big enough for two people. Gramps and Nal poked their heads through the doorway.

One pumpkin-sized iron pot sat on the floor, and another sat on a stump in the middle of the room. They were both covered in sticky black pitch, as was the stump. Jak's sandals kept sticking to the floor as he shuffled inside. Since no wood was piled up on top of the crater above them, a column of light poured through the crater's hole into the pot on the stump.

"You can hear the slivers clear across the field a couple of hours after the fire is lit," said Japheth. "The bubbling and popping sound of the pitch as it heats up shoots straight through this hole and echoes in this chamber. Soon after the noise begins, the pine tar begins to flow, hot and black, down the crater above us and down through this hole into the pot. When the pot is half-full, we pull it away and put an empty pot in its place. Never let it get over half-full or it'll be too heavy to handle. There's nothing worse than trying to move a full barrel of hot tar. Although Shem had to do it once when Ham forgot to check it."

"I had to go to the bathroom," Ham called from outside. "What can I say?"

"Shem didn't like that much because some of the tar sloshed out and burned his arm. He never lets Ham forget it."

"And that's it," said Ham, poking his head through the doorway. "Nothing more to tell here except for stacking techniques, but you don't need that, Jak. You'll be swinging from a rope like a monkey." Ham stuck his lips out and made monkey noises.

Japheth rolled his eyes again and shook his head. "He definitely lives up to his name. Jak, you can head on up to the boat now to start pitching. Just follow the trail back to the main path up the hill."

"I can find it," said Jak.

And he did. He hobbled back the way he came, past the stacks of wood, down the trail, and up the main path until the boat loomed before him.

☙❧

A pair of large yellow eyes gleamed in the dark, and a black tongue flickered in excitement. Scorch thought she had smelled him the day before, but she had been deep in her cavern, and the smell had been only a speck in the breeze. But this scent was full and strong, a tongueful of boy—the right boy this time, she was sure of it.

The waterfall on the mountainside had always been a place of rest. No one ever came down into the cave; no one even knew about it—not even when the human began cutting down the trees. Sometimes people came to get water or to cool down in the spray, but no one ever ventured further to see where the water actually went after its brief appearance on the mountain.

She never snatched any of them. She knew if she ate them, her home would be overrun with humans hunting her down, so she just watched. Most often when she was home, she stayed in the depths of the cave, coming out only at night to hunt for sheep or deer or whatever she fancied that day.

But this was where she always brought the boys, although they almost never knew it. She always bit them with the her smallest fang, the one with that filled them with just enough poison to put them to sleep without actually killing them. Then she could eat at her leisure. It was different with her other meals. She always gobbled them down where she caught them, unhinged her great mouth and swallowed them whole, then slithered to a cool spot in a river or pond to digest them, but the boys were different. They were like candles lit in a stale room, filling her entire chamber with the smell she had been pursuing ever since the garden. It was never the exact same smell, but close enough to satisfy her for a while, at least until her hunger took over. But the right boy—this boy on the plateau—was the one she had been hunting. The same salt and hot pepper, the same sweat, the same breath in his mouth: she could smell it all with the tips of her tongue.

She had smelled him a few times before but never managed to catch him. Now that he was within her grasp, she had to move with stealth or he would run again. If he ran, it could be years before she smelled him again. *Slow and sly, sly and slow,* her instincts told her. *And when I gets him...*

Her ears flared, and she belched an angry blue flame into the water that dripped from the cavern wall. When she caught him, she had to bring him to her mate, her ex-mate, the one who had abandoned her so long ago. Her brain wasn't big enough to think the thoughts that went along with the anger, but she felt it deep in her bones, and it drove her mad. She could not disobey; she was compelled to carry the boy back to the sea just as she was compelled to hunt the boy in the first place. She had no choice. But first she had to catch him.

CHAPTER 51

The Preacher and the Impromptu Zoo

Four ropes as fat as the stumpy end of a carrot hung over the side of the boat. At the top of the boat, each rope slipped through a pulley and then cascaded back down. Shem, Noah, and Methuselah stood on the ground fiddling with one of the rope ends. They had woven it through what looked like a giant child swing made out of sheepskin and were now trying to tie a knot to secure the swing.

Seth and Noah were doing the actual tying while Methuselah chewed on his beard and offered advice. "Don't tie that too tight or you'll never have to worry about changing a diaper. It'll squeeze you right off," he said. "Who showed you how to tie knots anyway, Noah? Doesn't look like you could tie down a dead rabbit with that mixed-up piece of rope."

Noah chuckled. "You showed me this knot almost six hundred years ago, Papa, when I was just a boy."

"I did?" Methuselah's bushy gray eyebrows shot up.

"Yep, and I'm tying the exact same knot now that you showed me then."

"Oh." Methuselah chewed a few more whiskers. "Well, you're doing a fine job then. Keep it up." Methuselah turned to Jak and changed the subject. "So, Jak, you looking forward to pitching this here monster of a boat?"

Jak shrugged. "I don't know, I've never pitched a boat before."

"I'm sure you'll like it. And the good news is that it'll only take about six months to finish the job." The old man's head nodded up and down as he talked. "You're not heading anywhere real soon, are you? If you are, I can take your place." He flashed a mostly toothless smile. "Monkey boy. That's what they used to call me when I was young."

"Because of the way you smelled?" said Shem.

Methuselah frowned and poked Shem with his walking stick. "No, smarty pants, because of the way I climbed."

"Well," said Noah, "let's see how our two monkey boys here do with these ropes."

Noah helped Jak into his harness and tightened it so that the sheepskin hugged him like a giant sock. The wool was soft, and it felt like he could sit in the harness for hours, which was good, because that's exactly what he would be doing.

"How's that? Too tight?" asked Noah.

"No. I think it's good."

"Alright. Then here we go." Noah pulled on one of the ropes, and Jak sailed above their heads, twisted around, and slammed his back into the side of the boat.

"We're trying to pitch the boat," shouted Methuselah, "not bang a hole in the side."

Jak's face turned red.

"Give him a minute to get used to it," said Noah. "He's never done this before. Jak, turn yourself around and spread your feet against the side of the boat."

Jak tried to swing his legs around, but his body kept swinging the opposite direction. *If only I could use my right foot like I used to,* he wished. It hung like a dead pendulum from his knee and would not turn in the correct direction until he kicked it with his left foot and pressed it against the boat.

"Okay. Now I'll take you a little higher." Noah pulled again, and Jak shot another five feet up. "You okay up there?"

His body had stayed turned in the right direction, and his feet walked up the boat like he was climbing up a cliff. "Yeah, I'm fine."

"The harness feel okay?"

Jak tugged at the straps; it seemed solid enough. "It's all good."

"Alright then," said Noah, lowering him down to the ground. "We're good to go. All we need now is the pitch. Ham should be up soon with the leftovers from yesterday, then we'll work together upstairs on the third floor. Won't take long with four pair of hands. After that, we'll come out here and Papa and I will pitch the boat from the ground and you'll pitch from the air."

Before he had even finished speaking, Ham trounced up the path with two steaming buckets in his hands. "Snack time," he said. "I caught a dozen gophers, just as you suggested, Jak, and squeezed the tar outta them." He held out the stalk of a hollow weed. "Anybody want a swig?"

Pitching wasn't so bad. It was just like painting, except instead of brushing on a smooth coat of blue or yellow paint, he was slopping on sticky black tar. The brushes weren't really brushes either; they were more like sticks with a flat fat glob at the end that splattered tar wherever he slapped it.

By the end of the morning, Jak felt like he had taken a bath in black honey, and by early afternoon, when they finished pitching the walls of the third deck, a smoky wood flavor took over his nostrils and tongue and he felt like he had been snacking on the pitch.

It was several hours till supper, so they brought the supplies outside and hooked up to the harnesses. Shem and then Jak went flying up with brush and bucket until they were fifteen feet in the air. From this vantage point, Jak had a great view of Gramps and Nal splitting gopher wood into slivers for the tar pits, and a great view of the crowd on Fool's Point.

"Nice diapers!" one of the men on the point called down while the rest of the crowd laughed and launched rotten tomatoes from small catapults they had installed in the rocks. Thankfully the catapults weren't quite strong enough and the tomatoes fell short.

Jak tried to ignore them, but he couldn't help feeling like he was the entertainment at a variety show. It also felt a little strange to be hanging in an oversized baby swing next to a boat bigger than a football field. Jak had thought Methuselah was kidding when he said it would take six months to pitch it, but when he looked down both flanks of the boat, it didn't look like they would ever finish.

"Start there," said Noah, "and when you're done with a section, I'll pull you up to do the one above it."

Jak pulled the brush out of the bucket and slapped it against the boat.

◈

Scorch's tongue flickered to taste the air. The boy was out again, just as he was every day. In the heat of the sun, his scent filled the breeze, but it was too hot for her to go and grab him. The sun boiled her blood to the point of agony. If she was going to capture the boy, it had to be in the shadows. She considered once again following his scent down the hill in the cool of the day, but if she did not find him right away, she risked being discovered, and then the boy would run. She had to wait and keep waiting until the right moment.

◈

The days passed quickly into weeks. The Thread did not move but stayed where it was hovering over the house of Noah and Tisrah.

Jak kept busy pitching the boat; Nal and Gramps kept busy splitting, stacking, and burning gopher wood into pitch; and the crowd on Fool's Point kept busy shooting rotten vegetables from their increasingly stronger catapults. Noah and his boys ignored the pelting and continued working despite the rain of rottenness. Tess helped Tisrah and the other women cut fruit and dry it on the rocks on the south side of the slope. Mr. Nettor kept busy trying to keep busy.

Jak had invited Mr. Nettor many times to come up to help pitch the boat, but Mr. Nettor always told him that strapping him into a harness would be like hanging a boulder from a string and that he would probably smash a hole in the boat. Occasionally he drove Blackey and Whitey up the winding path on the other side of the plateau to watch the progress.

"Mr. Nettor," said Methuselah on one of Mr. Nettor's excursion to the plateau, "sit down and tell me about yourself."

"Me? Oh, there's not much to tell." In reality, no one had ever asked Mr. Nettor that question before, and he wasn't sure what to say. He was accustomed to haggling with customers, not spilling stories about himself.

"Then take this," said Methuselah, handing him a tar-filled brush. "Swinging a paint brush has a way of loosening the lips."

Mr. Nettor stared at the dripping brush, not sure what to do.

"Take it," demanded the old man.

Mr. Nettor stood and slowly removed his dark blue outer robe and laid it on the seat of the wagon. Then he sat back down, took the brush, and began swabbing it over the seams of the boat, oblivious to the black spots spattering on his white linen under robe.

"That's right," said Methuselah. "Back and forth. Squeeze that tar right into those cracks so the water stays out and the boat stays dry."

After that, Mr. Nettor seemed to find his way to the plateau a bit more often to sit side by side with Methuselah, pitching and talking, an odd couple of skinny and stout. But for the most part, he fiddled with his fabric and traveled to nearby towns to sell his wares and purchase new cloth. When the need arose, Noah went with him to purchase various supplies such as knives or fresh rope, but Mr. Nettor always seemed a bit reticent to let the boat builder accompany him, as if he didn't want to be seen with him in the same wagon.

After returning from a trip to one of the larger villages with Noah, Mr. Nettor pulled the others aside to his wagon as soon as dinner was done.

He looked both ways before speaking. "I do not mean in any way to spoil your adventure with the Thread," he whispered, "but do you know what is happening in the villages?"

"They're buying lots of fabric?" said Nal.

"Besides that."

"What's happening, Rail?" said Gramps.

"They are angry, bubbling mad, at Noah."

"At Noah?" said Tess. "Why? What's Noah done?"

"You do not know?" He rolled his eyes, and the jowls under his chin quivered. "Oh, then I am sorry to be the one to tell you."

"Tell us what?" said Jak.

Mr. Nettor peeked out of the back flaps to make sure no one was listening. Satisfied, he whispered, "Noah is out of his mind."

"What are you talking about, Rail?" said Gramps. "Noah is not crazy."

"Oh, but he is, Clarence. You do not see him in the villages, ranting and railing and shouting out a storm of accusations and threats. Here in his own home, he is a nice enough fellow, but out there..." Mr. Nettor shuddered. "He is a different sort altogether."

"What sorts of things is he saying?" said Tess. "I can't imagine Noah hurting anyone. I admit, building a huge boat out in the middle of nowhere is a little strange, but he's a nice guy."

"Well, that is the man who stays here by the boat, but in the villages, a different man appears."

"But what does he *say*?" said Jak.

"First he goes from business to business purchasing the items he needs. And then he goes to the village square and stands on whatever he can find and begins shouting."

"Shouting about *what*?" said Jak. If he had to ask Mr. Nettor one more time what Noah was saying, he was going to smack him with an apple.

"About the end of the world. He tells them how evil they are and that if they don't stop hurting each other, Yahweh is going to send a flood to kill everyone. And he doesn't just say it once. He says it over and over again in a hundred different ways. He tells stories like the man who set fire to a house and killed everyone inside just because one of the children made a face at him or the woman who sliced off another woman's arm because she wanted the woman's bracelet. Story after story after story, he will not stop and the villagers are tired of it. They like the money he brings when he buys their goods, but when their patience grows thin, I am afraid they will slice off his head."

"Are the stories true?" said Nal.

"True? It doesn't matter if they are true or not," sputtered Mr. Nettor, going red in the face. "The point is that Noah is making trouble."

"I thought you said he was out of his mind," said Gramps.

"He *is* out of his mind," insisted Mr. Nettor. "Come now, Clarence. The man is building a boat the size of a village on the side of a mountain and claiming that a flood will kill everyone on the Earth. Does that sound sane to you?"

"Well, what if it's true? What if Yahweh is tired of all the evil on the Earth and is going to wipe them out if they don't stop? Noah does not want anyone to die in the flood, so he shouts so everyone has a chance to change their ways. You can't deny that blood spills quick and easy around here."

"Oh, it's not that bad," said Mr. Nettor.

"Yes it is," said Jak. "I overheard Ham telling Azras about a friend of theirs who was killed just for his sandals. Killed dead, left lying in the street in the middle of the day; no one even stopped to help him."

"Alright, alright. Perhaps it is bad in some areas, but not everywhere."

"If you don't like what's happening, you are welcome to leave at any time, Rail," said Gramps.

Mr. Nettor's face immediately softened. "Oh, no, no, no, no, no. I don't mean to imply I want to leave. I only wanted you to see a side of Noah that is not readily apparent here in his own home."

Just then, a wail cut through the air, and Rispel hurried down the path from the plateau weeping and crying out, "He is dead! He is dead!"

Tisrah and Vim ran to Rispel, who had collapsed in a heap at the bottom of the stairs. "Who? Who has died?"

"He was up in the perch —."

"Did Shem fall?" asked Vim, her voice shaking.

Rispel shook her head.

"Rispel," said Tisrah, kneeling and holding Rispel firmly by both shoulders. "Who died?"

Rispel took a deep breath and let it out. "Papa."

"Papa," repeated Tisrah. She released Rispel's shoulders and slumped to the ground. "What happened?"

"He was coiling up the ropes in the perch when, all of a sudden, he looked at Noah and said, 'I think you're going to have to float this big tub by yourself, son.' And then he slumped over, dead."

Noah and Shem arrived at the bottom of the hill, carrying a person-sized bundle covered with a wool blanket. Ham and Japheth followed, solemn-faced, right behind them.

Tisrah immediately stood and broke out in a wail, followed by the other women.

It sounded eerily like a repeat of Shale's funeral.

They didn't work on the boat at all the next day and instead spent the time building a funeral pyre next to the tar kilns.

"Papa loved this boat," Noah had said. "It's only right he goes to Yahweh near it."

The jeers from Fool's Point did not stop, though, which only intensified the grief.

"Hey, did the old man finally kick off?"

"Guess he wasn't good enough, right?" Rotten potatoes rained down on them even as they built the pyre.

Japheth fumed as they built. "They even have no respect for the dead. I'll be glad to see them swept away in the water."

"Japheth!" said Noah, "Do not say that. They are trapped by the evil that runs in their veins. My greatest hope is that they will be saved from the water and join us on the boat."

That night when the mist came, Methuselah's body was put on the pyre. He was dressed in his finest clothes, which weren't anything special, just an old pair of baggy white linen pants, a patched brown tunic, and a blue vest. His face looked just like Gramma Josie's: waxy and unreal, like an old house that had recently been vacated and had no need of a sign in the front yard that read "Nobody home."

They gathered around the pyre as the light faded from the sky.

"Yahweh," Noah called out, "You are the giver of life, and now you have taken it away. We live in the hope of the serpent and evil and death themselves dying and new life springing up once again." He lifted a coal to the kindling at the edge of the pyre, and they watched the flames lick up the wood and grow into a roaring bonfire.

Jak stared into the heat of the blaze, his hand automatically scratching behind Macy's ears. This was his third funeral, if he included the one for Shale. Death would not stop until he made it to Megiddo.

The next day, the day after that, and all the other days following were different now, filled with urgency. Methuselah was gone, the boat was almost finished, and a steady stream of animals began showing up at the boat as if someone had arranged an exclusive party for zoo creatures. Most of them came in pairs consisting of one male and one female, but some showed up in sevens, like the goats and sheep and doves. Some climbed over the mountains and some crawled up the paths by the houses, but there was no fighting between them; they were focused on one thing: getting into the boat. Somehow they knew exactly where to go. The elephants settled in their stall in the middle of the first floor, the mice scuttled to their nest on the second-floor cages, and the bats hung from a corner of the atrium ceiling above the elephants.

Tess wasn't too wild about the bats because there was no way to avoid seeing them. "Hanging rats," is what she called them.

Jak wondered if Tess knew that the real rats were curled up in a box directly beneath where she would sleep, but he figured it was probably not the best idea to tell her. She could hardly handle being in the same room as his gerbil.

By now, the Thread followers had come to the conclusion that they were going to be entering the boat with Noah and his family. The Thread had not moved, the laughing-man card had not changed, and with the sudden appearance of the parade of animals, even Mr. Nettor admitted that something strange was going on. Noah's grand delusion could no longer be labeled as a delusion. There was no denying it – the flood was coming.

CHAPTER 52
Plunging through the Waterfall

The day had finally arrived when they would finish pitching the boat. It had been two weeks since Methuselah's funeral. A week after that, Yahweh had told Noah that the flood was coming in seven days, and the seventh day was today.

Jak woke up nervous. There was only one section left on the corner closest to the waterfall that would take no more than a few hours, and then they could get on the boat and wait for the water to come.

He stretched his arms. They had become hard and knotted with muscle from pulling himself up and down and across the web of ropes. The hardened muscle felt good – he felt like a man. He had been doing the same work as a man and, even with his bum foot, had almost been able to keep up with Shem.

Everyone else had finished loading the boat with the food they and the animals would need for a long journey. Sacks of wheat, barley, and flax filled the granary on the second floor, and hay and straw were stacked from the floor to the ceiling in the rooms next to it.

Pears, pomegranates, peaches, peas, and a host of other fruits and vegetables that did not start with the letter P filled the grocery room, the biggest room on the boat. Fat red potatoes, carrots, beets, yams, and other root vegetables were stored in barrels along the wall, along with the hard fruits like apples and mangoes. A whole selection of melons filled another section of wooden boxes, and the soft fruit like cherries, oranges, and pears were stored in nets hanging from the ceiling. They had enough food for themselves and the animals for at least a year, Noah figured, maybe more.

"You ready, Jak?" said Shem.

"Yep." Jak fastened his harness, hung the pitch bucket, and pulled himself up. From his crow's eye view, he could see the crowd on Fool's Point was larger than usual, and it looked like they each had an ax or a shovel or some other tool. "Shem, do you see the Point?"

Shem shaded his eyes from the sun and nodded. "Looks like we're in for a bit of trouble." He cupped his hands around his mouth to make a megaphone. "Father!"

Noah's head appeared in the window.

Shem pointed to the crowd. "Trouble's brewing on the Point!"

Noah nodded his head as he peered at the point and stroked his beard. "I am not surprised. I visited Enoch yesterday to trade for spices and couldn't help but talk to a few people."

"A few people?"

"Well," the lines on Noah's face cracked into a smile, "maybe a few more than a few."

"How many?"

"I don't know," Noah shrugged. "I stood on the railing in the square."

"Father!" Shem shook his head.

"I had to get their attention, Shem. The flood is coming today. If they don't turn from evil, they're all going to die."

"But it's been almost one hundred years. They're not going to change. That's just the way it is."

"Perhaps not, but I can't stop trying. Even if on the very last day just one person decided to turn to Yahweh and begin doing what is right, it would be worth it."

Jak slathered on another layer of pitch, one eye on the brush, and the other on Fool's Point. The herd of people there looked like a bunch of restless cows when a storm was approaching. They bustled here and there, brandishing their weapon of choice, shouting, and pointing at the boat. The man who stood on the rock shook a bow and yelled louder than the rest. Jak recognized him as the same man they had heard leading the Fool's Point song before they had met Noah.

"Azril's got 'em brewing today," said Shem, dipping his brush in the bucket.

"Who's Azril?"

"The one on the rock. He's Azras's brother."

"Her brother? You're kidding!"

"Nope."

"Why isn't he here with us?" said Jak, slapping at another crack. "He should be helping, getting ready to get on the boat."

"He thinks we're a bunch of lunatics," said Shem, dipping his brush in the bucket. "Says the flood's already come and washed out our brains."

"What does he say about Azras?"

"He doesn't say much, but he was never happy that she married Ham in the first place."

Jak couldn't help but wonder if Azras was happy she married Ham either. He wiped his brush on the side of the bucket. He was hot, and the sweat was beginning to run down his face. There was only one small square left, and the entire boat would be pitched. He looked down the length of the boat and felt proud. They had done a good job, and it had only taken two months.

Shem placed his brush in his bucket and stared intently behind Jak, his eyebrows knit together in confusion..

"What's wrong?" asked Jak. He stopped slathering pitch and turned to look in the same direction.

Shem pointed to a puffy layer of white clouds on the horizon. "Do you see that? The white in the sky?"

"You mean the clouds?'

"Clouds? They are called clouds?"

"Yeah. You've never seen a cloud?"

"No. The sky is blue in the day and black at night, but never white."

Come to think of it, Jak had never seen a cloud there either. It had never rained. The mist in the evening always provided more than enough water for the plants.

"What do clouds do?" asked Shem, still staring west.

"They drop water on the ground. It's called 'rain.'" Jak faced the boat again and attacked one of the remaining tar-free boards with pitch.

"And what do black clouds do?" Shem sounded a little nervous now.

"Black clouds? They can be dangerous. Wind, lightning, hail and lots of water. Why do you ask?" Jak turned around, expecting to see the same fluffy white, but there weren't any white clouds left. The entire western horizon had suddenly filled with towering black clouds rapidly sailing in their direction. A low rumble vibrated in the distance accompanied by a cold brisk wind.

A shiver ran down Jak's spine. "It's here! The flood is coming *now.*" He threw his brush in the bucket. "Hurry and finish pitching. I have to go warn the others."

He untied the line that secured him in the air and zipped like a dropped rock to the ground. His bad foot twisted at the bottom and he fell over, tipping the tar bucket and spilling pitch on his pants, but Jak didn't care. It didn't matter anymore.

❦

An unnatural gray crawled along the ground. One moment the sun shone hot on the rocks, and the next it was gone. Scorch tilted her head up and sniffed the air with her tongue, and a flood of adrenaline coursed through her veins. *Water.* Water and coolness were coming from somewhere. She had been watching for a day like this for weeks. The boy was still down there, waiting for her, and now she could go and get him.

She slid through the falls and slithered down the slope.

❦

Jak slid to a stop at the heavy wooden gangplank. His twisted ankle ached, but he ignored it. "Ham, Japheth! We have to get everyone on the boat right now."

"We're working on it, Jak," Japheth grunted. He was shepherding a pair of nervous yaks as they bellered and kicked their way up the gangplank.

"But the flood is coming!" cried Jak.

"We know," said Ham, trying hard to not get kicked as he pushed the yaks from the other side. "It's been coming for a hundred years."

"No, I mean it's coming NOW." Jak pointed toward the ugly bank of clouds, and their eyes grew wide.

"What is that?" said Japheth, awestruck.

"They're called clouds, and they're full of water, ready to dump it all here."

A pair of ringtail lemurs scampered up side of the boat and through the door, followed by a pair of mountain lions. The animals had never been so frantic to get on board. Stragglers zoomed, scampered, hopped, and crawled on the boat like something was after them. The only ones who seemed even remotely normal were a hen and rooster pecking the last mouthfuls of bugs from the ground near the end of the gangplank.

"Where is everyone?" said Jak.

"They went back home to finish packing."

"Run down and get them. Tell them to bring only what they can carry or they may be too late. Those clouds are moving fast."

But before Japheth started down the hill, Macy barked, and Tess, Nal, and Gramps crested the top of the hill, each carrying a bundle of blankets.

"Jak, the storm!" said Gramps.

"Yeah," said Jak. "I saw."

"The women are on their way up." He handed Jak his book bag. "I grabbed this for you."

"Thanks." Jak quickly checked inside to make sure everything was still there. "What about Mr. Nettor?"

In answer to Jak's question, a donkey brayed, and the blue wagon pulled around the keel of the boat . Mr. Nettor walked in front of Blackey and Whitey, tugging on their reins.

"I know you don't much want to bring the wagon up to the boat, my dears," he called to Blackey and Whitey, "but you must. You simply must. I will not leave a thousand gold pieces worth of fabric to be buried in water, no sir." He mopped his forehead with his handkerchief, but it did little to stem the flood of sweat springing from his skin.

The giant black serpent scraped along the rock in the crevice where the bottom curve of the boat met the ground. Not only was this the coolest spot, but it was also the darkest and most hidden. The boy's scent was growing stronger with each slither. Her mouth was wet with saliva, and her tongue flickered in and out, flinging specks of spittle, tasting the air and digging a hole of hunger deeper in her belly.

The chickens stopped scratching the dirt and stood still.

Scorch loved chickens—for lunch. Any other time, this would have been the moment to snatch them up, but Scorch stayed as still as the chickens. At this close distance, her tongue painted a clear picture of each bird, down to the number and color of their feathers.

The chickens broke from their spell, squawked, and scurried up the gangplank.

Stupid birds.

The boy's image was quickly filling in as well, a delicious picture of blue eyes and unruly brown hair – this was definitely the boy she'd been seeking for so long. Now she just had to wait for the right moment.

"Come on, Whitey," said Shem. He pulled on one rein while Japheth pulled on Blackey's, but the stubborn donkeys refused to put one foot on the gangplank and even attempted to back away from the boat.

"What is wrong with you?" said Mr. Nettor. "We've been up here countless times before, but you choose right now to become shy?"

"Maybe it's the other animals on board," said Jak. "We've never had other animals on the boat when they've come up."

"Humph," said Mr. Nettor, wiping his forehead again. "There aren't any lions up there, are there? I don't trust lions."

"Yes," said Tess, "right next to the tigers and the bears."

"Humph," he said again. "Has anyone stopped to evaluate how safe it will be for us humans on board this boat?"

"Certainly," said Noah, "and we have come to the conclusion that it will be much safer than not being on the boat. I hear drowning is bad for your health."

"Maybe they need a little encouragement from someone sitting in the wagon," said Jak. He jumped from the gangplank to the ground, intending to climb into the wagon's seat and help, but he never made it that far.

If Jak had two strong legs, perhaps things would have turned out differently, but as it was, he misjudged the distance and only had one leg to absorb the shock of hitting the ground before he thought he would. His body crumpled at the same moment that something heavy scraped across his neck, screeching. His head was forced to the side as the strap of the book bag pulled across his face and flew off his neck.

The donkeys reared, braying, and the women screamed—or maybe it was Mr. Nettor—Jak couldn't tell. But the reason they were screaming was clear.

A giant black serpent writhed hissing at the edge of the hill. Its thick head loomed ten feet off the ground, shooting sparks and trying to fling away the book bag that was stuck in one of its fangs.

"Scorch?" whispered Jak. It had to be her. The white diamond on her head shone clearly against her black scales. She was a lot uglier now. A pair of gnarled black stumpy horns grew out of her head, and her body bore the scars of untold battles.

Macy darted in between Jak and Scorch, baring her teeth and growling, with her hackles raised and her tail spiked toward the sky.

"Everyone stand back," Jak commanded in a low voice. "She wants me and me alone. There's no reason for any of you to die too. You *can't* die. That's why you built the boat."

"You can't die either, Jak," said Gramps. "You've got to carry the book." He edged toward the gangplank.

"At the moment," whispered Jak, "Scorch has the book." Scorch lunged toward Jak, but Macy jumped at the same time and nipped her in the eye. The snake pulled back for a moment but almost immediately lunged again.

Macy darted once more at the serpent's eye.

Scorch screeched and black dribble oozed down her face.

Macy stood her ground, still growling.

She's really trying to kill me, thought Jak. This was not a game. This was not his friend from the garden. She was now a twisted wreck intent on killing him, and he was sick of it, sick of the whole thing. It had to stop—no more missing children and no more attacks in the river. Today he had to be the Quelcher.

Scorch's nostrils flared, shooting a stream of green smoke into the air. She lunged a third time, only this time, she didn't aim for Jak. She snatched Macy in her jaws, turned and raced up the mountainside.

"Macy!" cried Jak. He jumped to his feet and ran after the snake.

"Jak, get back here!" shouted Tess. "Scorch wants you to follow her."

"She's got the book *and* Macy!" Jak shouted back, "Get on the boat. I'll be back, I promise."

"I'm going with you," yelled Nal, hefting his lance.

Several others shouted at him as well, but Jak ignored whatever it was they were trying to tell him and followed the snake past the boat up the naked mountain, watching as her tail disappeared through the waterfall.

Breathless, Jak and Nal arrived at the falls, looked at each other for a moment, and then plunged through after her.

CHAPTER 53

The Smiling Cocoon and a Half-Eaten Candy Bar

It was dark in the cave behind the waterfall. Weird shadows danced on the wall, and water dripped like great drops of sweat. The roof was covered with upside-down spikes that Jak recognized as slack-ites or slag-er-nuts or something like that. A series of faint barks bounced around the cavern, mixing with deep guttural groans from the Earth, making it impossible to tell where Macy was.

"Where did she go?" said Nal. He held his lance poised and ready.

"I don't know." Jak blinked several times, trying to get his eyes to adjust to the darkness.

They followed a rocky outcropping down toward a gorge and peered over the edge, but the bottom was nowhere in sight.

Jak kicked a rock over the edge. It fell almost ten seconds before they heard a distinct faraway splash.

"We're not going that way," said Jak. They backed up and kept climbing down along the wall until they found a small cave entrance just big enough for them to drop through. Air coursed through the hole and blew into their faces as they let themselves down.

It was a tunnel. One end of it was hidden in shadows, but the other was open, and that was where the breeze was coming from. The open side ended at a cliff, from which yawned the same gorge they had seen from above.

Bones littered the ground—some short, some long. Clearly, they had stepped into some large animal's dining room.

"What kind of bones do you think they are?" said Nal.

"Not sure. Whatever they are, the animals had long legs."

Then Jak saw something that made him want to throw up: a skull, just like one from the garland of skulls at Skull Rock. "They're human bones," said Jak, pointing at the skull. A thought occurred to Jak. He picked up one of the leg bones and held it up to his leg. They were about the same size. It was the same with the arm bones. Pieces of the puzzle began to fall into place, and Jak felt even sicker.

"Nal, this is where Scorch lives. This is where she brought the boys she stole." The bones were brittle and dusty, though, and it looked like she hadn't been there in a long time. Besides, she was so large now that she would hardly be able to squeeze through the entrance to the cave.

"Jak," Nal whispered, pointing his lance to the back where the tunnel came to a dead end. A large shadow hung sideways like a giant cocoon attached to the walls of the cavern. It glowed a soft red, the same red as the Thread.

They followed the trail of bones to the back, and Jak hesitantly reached out his hand until his finger pressed into the cocoon. It was like squishy canvas, tough, yet soft. Suddenly the cocoon began to shift and move, and a sideways crack appeared in the middle, like a giant smile.

Jak and Nal backed toward the entrance to the tunnel as the lips began to open, revealing a gaping black hole. Nal stood with his lance poised in case a creature darted out and attacked, but as the mouth opened wider, they realized it wasn't a mouth at all, but a kind of hammock. And on the hammock was a boy.

Nal rushed forward and stared into the boy's face. It was smooth and fine, like the face of a ten-year-old. "It's him, Jak! It's him! He hasn't changed a bit. Enoch? Wake up, Enoch! It's me, Nal!" He shook the boy, but the boy did not move. He was cold and looked dead, the skin white and waxy like Gramma Josie's and Methuselah's.

"ENOCH!" shouted Nal. He wrapped his arms around the boy and lifted him from the hammock, breaking into sobs and rocking the body back and forth. "Please don' be dead, please don' be dead," he repeated over and over again.

But Enoch didn't move.

"It's been a long time, Nal," said Jak quietly, "almost a thousand years. There's no way he could—"

"I know," said Nal, tears streaming down his face. "I s'pose I should be happy I even found his body." He buried his face in his brother's chest and sobbed.

The hammock glow grew a more intense shade of red for a moment, and suddenly, the boy's face flushed pink. He opened one eye and yawned. "Nal?"

Nal's head shot up. "Enoch?" He looked in Enoch's eyes and saw them staring back at him. "Yer alive?"

"Of course I'm alive," said the boy, raising his head and looking around, confused. "When did you get here?"

"Jus' now!" Nal bit his lip, the tears still flowing, but for a different reason now, and smiled. "I jus' got here." He wiped his eyes on his sleeve. "I've been lookin' fer you."

"Where are we?" Suddenly, Enoch's eyes went wide with fear and his head snapped in the direction of the front of the cave. "Is it here?" he whispered.

"No." Nal shook his head. "We're safe for the moment."

Enoch relaxed, but his eyes were still afraid. "It had me in its mouth and took me through a tunnel filled with water, and we ended up here, in this cave. He threw me on the ground, then turned around and watched me. His teeth were so big, and I was so scared, Nal! I thought I was goin' to die, so I asked Yahweh to help me, just like Father said, and then something exploded, and half of the cave disappeared. The Black Serpent fell with it. The only thing left was the cliff, and I was alone for a long time, jus' me and the bones. I looked and looked but couldn't find a way out and I din't know what to do. Then I saw this hammock in the back of the cave, so I lay down, and I must have fallen asleep. That was yesterday...I think."

"Yes, yesterday," said Nal. "Jak, this is my brother, Enoch."

"Yeah, I kinda figured he must be."

A rock clattered down the hill outside the cave.

Jak climbed up to the entrance and peeked his head through to make sure Scorch wasn't slithering down to the hole. She wasn't, but something else was. The shadow of a figure stood at the mouth of the cave, silhouetted in front of the waterfall.

"Nal," whispered Jak, "someone is here."

"Who is it? Did Noah follow us?" Nal grabbed his lance.

The man started picking his way down through the rocks.

"I don't know. I can't tell who it is, but he's coming this way," said Jak. "Quick! Hide in the back." Enoch began to whimper.

"Shhh," said Nal. "Quiet now, Enoch." Nal gave the lance to Jak and hurried his brother behind the cocoon.

A moment later, the man dropped quietly into the cave. He walked to the edge of the floor and craned his neck over the edge of the cliff as if he was looking for something, then came toward the back of the cave. He opened a small jar, dipped his staff in it, then put a coal to the tip. The end of the staff burst into flames.

In the light of the torch, Jak could see a patch of skin on the man's cheek that showed through his beard. And the longer Jak looked at the mark, the more it resembled a half-eaten candy bar.

CHAPTER 54

The Golden Sword

Jak shuddered. *How had Cain tracked him here?* It was bad enough that he had to get Macy and the book back from Scorch, but now he had to face off with Cain too.

Cain stared straight at the hammock. "You might as well come out, boy. I know you're back there. I can hear yer blood pumpin' through yer veins."

Jak didn't move and didn't say anything. He didn't think Cain could really hear his blood, although it was pumping pretty hard.

"The serpent has taken another path down to the bottom of the gorge," said Cain, shifting his gaze to peer into the corners behind the cocoon, "but we cannot stay here. It won't be safe for long."

Still, Jak did not move.

Cain moved a step closer to the hammock.

"Listen to me. The flood is beginnin'. The waters below are heavin' up. Can't you hear them? 'Twon't be long before the cave fills."

Enoch sniffled and burst into tears.

Cain knew for sure they were hiding now, so Jak stood up cautiously with the lance extended. "Stay back or I'll—"

"Put down the lance, boy. I am here to help you "

But Jak didn't budge. The sweat on Cain's face looked like red rivers flowing down, or perhaps the scarlet scales of Beelz.

"Don't listen to him, Jak," said Nal. "He's every bit the snake that Beelz is."

Cain nodded. "Twas true, yes. At one time, I was full o' the same anger as the snake, but—"

Jak cut him off. "You can't have the book. That's the reason you're here, right?" Jak didn't have the book anyway, but he didn't want Cain to know that on the off chance that Cain would get it back from Scorch before Jak could.

"Yes. That's the reason I'm here, but I'm not lookin' to take it from you."

Jak's eyes narrowed. What Cain said didn't make any sense. "Then why have you been following us?"

"To help you." Cain looked as if perhaps this was the first time he had ever uttered those words.

"Liar!" Jak fired back. "I heard you and Lamech in his house. I was outside the window and heard it all. You were going to sell Tess to one of the Lights and me as a slave."

Cain's face contorted as if Jak had stepped on his heart. "You only heard one part of the story. Yes, I was with Lamech, and, yes, he was going to sell you, but that was not *my* plan. Who do you think sent you the note to get you out of Lamech's house? I didn't know if you would come or not, so I had to keep pretendin' in case I had to make other plans."

"*You* left the note for me?"

Another bark echoed off the cavern walls, followed by a screech. The rocks beneath them rumbled and shook, and the sound of running water got closer.

Jak wished he could rush to the edge and look for Macy, but he didn't trust Cain.

"Why didn't you just tell us?" said Nal.

"Would you have listened to me, a murderin' Beelzin?" Cain spat on the ground. "Why do you think the men showed up at the Yarti to trap the Black Serpent? I knew you were headin' there, and I knew the beast was in the river headin' there too. She's been trackin' you e'er since Eden."

Jak's head was spinning. On one hand, it made sense, but on the other, it was crazy. *Why would Cain be helping us?* He tried to think. His arm was beginning to shake from the weight of Nal's lance.

"Listen to me; we don't have much time." Cain's face didn't look so sour anymore. "The beast is riding on the water from the bowels of the Earth. Soon she'll be here, and if she don't kill you, then the water'll drown you. I've spent almost four hundred years with the blood of my brother on my hands. I can't bring 'im back from the dead, but if what you said at Remembrance Day was true, you can. You 'er my only hope of being able to beg forgiveness." His eyes were no longer cold, but pleading.

Jak lowered the lance. It made sense. It was crazy, but the whole story made sense. He knew what it was like to ache for forgiveness. If that little second grader had drowned in the river Jak would have been racked with guilt forever.

"I know you want yer dog back," said Cain, "but she's a sacrifice you'll have to make."

"It's not just Macy," said Jak. "She took the book."

"Yer dog took the book?" said Cain.

"No. Scorch did. I don't think she meant to. It got stuck in her—"

Jak was interrupted when a tremor rocked the cave so hard that he could hardly stay on his feet. An avalanche of stone slid into the entrance of the cave, raining down rocks and dirt, and sealing off the exit. At the same time, the gurgling outside the cave began to grow louder and more intense.

Cain ran to the edge. "She's coming! I can see the flames from her mouth, and the water's pushing her up fast. Now we're stuck, and we'll have to kill the beast or be killed ourselves."

"But we can't kill her," said Jak. "Her scales are too hard."

"True enough," said Cain. "Hard as iron 'cept for a few—those white ones that make the diamond on her forehad. Tis a soft spot, like that on a baby. Hit it hard enough with a rock or a lance, and it'll pierce her skull."

The diamond, thought Jak. *Of course!* That's how the muzzle had calmed her in Enoch, and that's how Jak had made her purr in the garden. It made him sick to think that the very thing that used to bring her so much pleasure would be used to kill her.

Suddenly, Scorch's head flapped onto the floor. She was snapping and flicking her tongue back and forth violently, as if the scent of Jak was driving her into a feeding frenzy.

Enoch screamed as Jak and Cain scrambled to the back of the cavern.

The beast's front flippers scrabbled at the rock floor as she tried to pull herself up into the cavern, but the water wasn't high enough and her flippers were too weak. Scorch's chin slid across the floor and disappeared over the edge with a screech.

Tears streamed down Enoch's face, and his whole body shook. "It's goin' to eat us," he wailed.

Jak felt the same way.

"The Earth is pushin' the water up and then pullin' it back down again, gettin' ready for a big burst," said Cain. "I'm goin' to stand next to the cliff. When the beast comes on the next crest, I'll drive my lance into her brain. If I miss, I'll be dead, and it'll be up to you," he said, looking at Nal. Cain knelt on one knee and put his hand awkwardly on Enoch's shoulder. "Hush now, child, and be brave."

Enoch sniffled and wiped his hand across his nose. "I want to go home."

As soon as Enoch said the word "home," the hammock flashed bright red, and the space where Cain, Nal, and Enoch had stood was now empty.

Jak's stomach sank. *What had happened?* "Cain? Nal?" he said, frantically looking around.

No one answered.

Jak took a deep breath and let it out slowly to try and calm down. He was alone in a cave that was about to be attacked by a killer leviathan and flooded with water at the same time. *What are my options?* He spied Cain's staff lying on the floor. The flames still flickered at the tip, lighting up a small rectangular object on the floor.

Jak picked it up. It was a card, just like the cards in the deck, with a picture of a sword on it. As soon as he touched it a blue thread wound around the edge, just like all the other cards. He was sure it must have appeared when the red light flashed. *But what am I supposed to do with it? Give Scorch a paper cut?*

A watery *whoosh* sounded behind him, and he whirled around just in time to see Scorch's neck flash past the mouth of the cave, followed by a wall of water that surged into the cave like a tidal wave. The water ripped Jak's feet from underneath him, flipped him upside down, and twirled him around. He could see and hear nothing besides the pinch and gurgle of the water pulling him toward the edge of the cliff.

Jak scrabbled at the walls trying to find something to hold onto, but they were smooth and slimy. He twirled the staff sideways, hoping it was long enough to catch both sides of the cave mouth before the water flung him into the gorge.

A moment later, a vicious tug yanked his arms, and he stopped moving – the staff had caught. His head broke free from the water as it receded, and he sucked in a lungful of air. *If I can just hold on long enough for the water to empty from the cave.* Just then, a blast of hot air hit him in the neck.

He turned his head and came eye to yellow eye with Scorch. The bag still hung from her mouth. She hissed, and Jak knew he only had a half-second before the she attacked. There was only one way he could think of to stay away from her teeth.

Jak let go of the staff, lunged for her horns, flipped his body over her head, and held on for his life.

Scorch roared and jerked back.

Jak gripped the horns as hard as he could, but they were so slick with water that he flew into the air. The same jerk that knocked him off also ripped the bag out of Scorch's mouth and sent it flying in the same direction.

Jak saw the bag splash a moment before he hit the water hard in a belly flop. The water knocked the wind out of him and forced its way up his nose at the same time. He flung his arms out to steady himself and scanned the water in desperation for the bag.

Something bobbed in the water, and he swatted at it. A strap tangled in his arm. He grabbed the bag and swam toward an overhang in the wall just as Scorch twisted and struck the water where he had been a second before.

The words *"Yahweh is my protection and my strength"* ran through his mind, and then he had the clear image of the book and the three pockets in the front of it – one for the Adam card, one for the Noah card and one for...

In that instant he knew what the third pocket was for.

Jak frantically opened the bag, pulled out the book, and tried to peel apart the sopping wet cloth, but his fingers were so cold and shaking that it was nearly impossible.

Scorch was swimming in circles, screeching and nosing through every inch of water to find him.

Jak hugged closer to the wall, hoping that her eyes were still terrible and that she could not smell him very well in the water.

The cloth pages finally parted, and Jak stuffed the sword card inside. A red thread stitched the pocket shut, and the book bubbled gold and scarlet and then exploded into a glimmering yellow sword. Jak was so surprised that he bobbled the sword and it tumbled from his hands and sunk into the water. He dove in after it and grabbed the shining hilt before it disappeared in the dark, then gave a tremendous scissor-kick to get his head back above water, gripping the sword with all his strength. *A sword! Gramma's book turned into a sword!*

It seemed a hundred times bigger than Gramps's biggest knife, and glowed bright yellow, as if light had been infused with the metal. He was a bit nervous holding it, but a sword was exactly what he needed right now.

Jak scanned the water for Scorch. He couldn't help thinking that the last time he and Scorch had been in the water together was the night before she changed. That time she had nuzzled his arm. This time she was trying to eat him. *Why did Adam and Eve have to eat from the Knowing Tree?*

Something hit his leg, and the water beneath him surged. He dove down and opened his eyes. In the light of the sword, he saw Scorch turn around and begin corkscrewing toward him, her white diamond glowing like a target.

Jak twisted and pushed off the rock wall with his good foot, bringing the sword down hard toward her head, but it only caught water. Both of them had missed.

He surfaced and got another breath. Scorch was on the other side of the cavern, screeching as she twisted back. *Here we go again, the matador and the bull.*

The water was being sucked back into the gorge faster now, so Jak edged his body into a cleft in the cliff wall as the water sank lower, hoping to stay out of Scorch's reach. He had to send a message to Yahweh. Seven times saved from death was a pretty good average, and he hoped it would become eight. "Yahweh, if you can hear me, I need—"

But that's all he had time to say before Scorch exploded from the water twenty feet below and shot through the air toward the cliff. With her mouth wide open, Jak couldn't even see the diamond, and if he stayed where he was, she would have a clean chance to bite him, so he jumped.

Scorch snapped at him as he passed her in the air, but missed. Half a second later, Jak hit the water, kicking hard to surface as soon as possible. When his head was above water, he looked up.

Scorch was falling backwards, screeching and twisting in the air. She was going to land right on top of him.

Jak churned away from the middle of the cavern just as her tail met the water. Scorch's head followed the rest of her body, plummeting through the air upside down, the white diamond glimmering against the black scales.

Without even thinking, Jak lurched the sword out of the water and thrust it above his head. He felt it tear into soft skin, heard the crunch of bone, and then the sword ripped away from his hand. Scorch's body pushed him down, and he somersaulted across her front flipper. Her claw ripped through his shirt and sliced him open from his belly button to the top of his sternum.

Jak gasped, choked back the water, and sank.

CHAPTER 55

River Rider

Jak's lungs ached for air and Scorch had ripped a foot-long gash in his belly, but he was alive. He tried to press the gash shut, tying his sash as tightly as he could around his middle. It was all he could do for the time being.

He had settled on the floor of the canyon, but he couldn't move. The retreating water pressed him down as it sped back to wherever it had come from. A faint yellow glow wavered through the water above him, outlining a serpentine body sinking toward him. But he still could not move, for the force of the water was too strong.

All he could do was watch the leviathan's coils slowly drape across his legs, a scaly anchor trapping him at the bottom of the flooded cavern.

His lungs screamed for oxygen, and he had a flashback of being trapped in the river back in Grantsburg. He had to breathe; he had to get rid of the polluted air in his lungs.

The golden sword stuck in Scorch's forehead illuminated her face. Two fangs on either side lay exposed, but her mouth was closed, and the fire had left her eyes. She was dead, and soon Jak would be too.

&9

The door of the boat slammed shut, sending a boom like a thunderclap echoing around the valley. Noah spun around, startled. That door was so heavy it would have taken the strength of four men to lift into place.

He hurried up the stairs to the third floor. He was the last one in the boat. All the animals and people were safe on board, except for Jak and Nal and Jak's dog. He sent another message to Yahweh, asking him to bring them back safely.

"Father?" called Japheth. "Are you okay? What was that sound?"

"It was the door," said Noah, making his way to an open window. "Yahweh must have shut it for us. It is now that the flood begins."

The mist of the evening was heavier than normal. It had substance and form and fell from the sky in fat pellets.

Shem reached his hand out the window and caught some in his hand.

"It's water," said Shem, "Falling from the sky, just like Jak said."

"That's impossible," said Ham. "Water doesn't fall from the sky."

Noah stuck his hand out as well and caught the droplets in his hand too. "This water does."

"It's called rain," said Gramps. "In our day, water comes from the sky all the time. As a matter of fact, it was raining the day we left home. That's how the Earth is watered."

"That's the silliest thing I've ever heard," said Mr. Nettor. "How do you keep things from getting wet? This must be the spray from a river. It is—"

Suddenly, Mr. Nettor's body glowed red for a moment, and then he disappeared.

"Rail?" said Gramps.

Tess's eyes darted around the room. "Where did he go?" she said, a touch of panic in her voice.

"The Thread," said Noah. "It took him." His eyes wandered to the waterfall on the hill. "Something is happening in the heart of the mountain."

Down at Fool's Point, heavy wet drops shot from the clouds and stung Azril's face and eyes, and fear seized his bones. Something was not right with this day: there were the black things in the sky, the door on the boat closed all by itself, and now this strange water was falling from the sky. He had to move quickly or it would be too late.

"The water has begun!" cried Azril. "Noah is favored by Yahweh. As long as he is on the boat, we will die. We must destroy it!" He blew a horn and began screaming. "Attack the boat! Destroy Noah's boat!"

The crowd roared and surged off of Fool's Point. They streamed down to the plateau with sickles, rocks, axes, and anything else they could find and began hammering away at the planks of the boat's hull.

Those on the boat watched as the fools from Fool's Point clambered down the embankment to the plateau. The steady *thunk* of metal on wood echoed all the way up to the third floor.

Tess twisted her hair around one finger and wrinkled her forehead with worry. Jak and Nal still hadn't returned, and now the boat was being attacked. She turned to Noah. "They'll destroy the boat. What are we going to do?"

Noah shook his head. "We shall do nothing but wait. Don't worry. The planks are triple thickness in the bottom hull. This boat was built just the way Yahweh said to build it, and he has promised us safety. This boat will be our savior."

"Or our tomb," muttered Azras.

Suddenly, the waterfall on the mountain vomited a tidal wave of water. It thundered down the mountain and across the plateau, cutting into the crowd like a bulldozer. Screams filled the air as the hackers scrambled to grab rocks, stumps, people next to them, or anything that could anchor them to the ground, but it was no use. They were swept downhill along with all the other debris, and only one man straggled back up to safety on Fool's Point.

But it wasn't just water that gushed out of the waterfall. There was one more thing, and when Tess saw it, she laughed and cried at the same time. A boy in a black-stained tunic rode with it.

CHAPTER 56
The Gorilla and the Scarecrow

A moment later, the water finally broke over Jak's head, and he gulped air into his lungs. He would never take another breath for granted again. He would even be thankful for the air around Tess's mom, Aunt Terri, and Jak was pretty sure she took showers in perfume that was also used to fumigate bugs.

Jak strained to pull his legs out from underneath Scorch, but it was as useless as trying to lift a truck. She was too heavy, and every time he pushed, it felt like a knife was ripping through his chest. He knew it would only be a few minutes before the water surged again, and there was no way he could hold his breath long enough to survive.

The light of the sword flickered, and the words that Guardian had given him in the garden bounced into his mind again. *"Yahweh is my protection and my strength."*

If he ever needed protection and strength, it was now. "Yahweh, I don't know if it was you or not, and I don't know if you can even hear me from down here, but seven times I've escaped death, and now I'm stuck again. I don't

411

want to die, and I haven't gotten the book anywhere except down in this hole with me."

A tongue flickered in his ear, and his eyes flew open, terrified that Scorch wasn't dead after all. He swung his fist in the direction of the tongue but stopped mid-swing when he heard a familiar whine.

"Macy?" he said. There was no way Macy could have escaped Scorch or drowning, yet there she was, warm and dripping and happy to see him. He wrapped both arms around her, and for just a second, everything was okay. He had Macy and the book back. Now they just had to get out of the cave...alive.

"Macy," he whispered. Even though Scorch was dead, he didn't want to risk waking her up. It felt right to whisper. "My legs are stuck under Scorch, and I can't get up. We have to push her off me."

The dog must have understood, because when he began pushing against Scorch's body, she put her paws against Scorch and began pushing too, but it was no use.

So this is it, thought Jak, a lump growing in his throat. *I start from the beginning of time and travel 1,500 years only to drown in a hole in the ground.* He wondered if dying there meant he was really dead, or if he would wake up at home and get to live the rest of his life in normal time until death finally tracked him down.

The ground beneath him shook, and water began trickling up his legs.

He sat up. The next swell was coming.

The light from the sword suddenly doused, and the book tumbled from Scorch's head onto Jak's lap.

Great. Does this mean Yahweh has left me on my own? Maybe it's like a punch card for lunch. You get only so many lunches, and when the card is punched out, you have to get a new one. How do you get a new card from Yahweh? Jak knew it was too late now, and he would have to fight it out on his own.

He stuffed the book in the bag and grabbed Macy tight. "Hold on, girl. It's just you and me now."

She licked his face and nestled in his arms.

By this time, the water was up to his waist, and quickly made its way to his chest. It was freezing cold, and Jak's teeth began to chatter. Then, deep beneath them, the ground heaved, and the water shot up as if the Earth was belching.

Jak grabbed a thick lungful of air before his head was engulfed.

At the same moment, the weight of Scorch's body on his legs released for half a second.

Jak scrambled back, yanking his legs out from underneath her. Immediately his body was swept up in the swell of water. It was like someone had popped the cork off a giant bottle of champagne, and he and Macy were the bubbles rushing up.

Excitement rushed through Jak. *Maybe we're not going to die!* But then he remembered the upside-down rock spikes at the top of the cavern. If they didn't slow down pretty quick, they would be skewered.

A light shone above them to the side. Jak assumed it was the waterfall and began swimming toward it, but the water was pushing them toward the spikes too fast.

However, as soon as the column of water hit the top of the cavern, a powerful surge pushed them towards the light. They broke through the waterfall into the welcome open air.

Jak took a deep breath. They were out!

The skies were dark, and heavy droplets of rain pelted his face. He and Macy were riding a river that flowed down the mountain toward the boat. Now all they had to do was get on it. But the boat was surrounded by a mass of people frantically trying to escape the sudden river. *Why don't they just get on the boat? The door is right there. All they have to do is run up the gangplank.* Jak looked again. There was no door and no gangplank.

The water crashed into the crowd and swept them screaming over the edge of the hill. Only two men survived by clinging to the beams that supported the boat while the river rushed by.

Jak was almost to the support beam closest to the doorway, but still the door was nowhere to be seen, only the smooth hull.

His stomach dropped. He wasn't going to be able to get on the boat after all. In a minute, he would be swept over the hill like everyone else, and the water was moving so fast that he would never be able to make it back up.

The water carried him past the beam and on to the next. With his one free hand, he collared it and held on. A sharp pain rippled through his chest as the river knocked him back and forth, trying to pull him downstream, but he held tight.

He gritted his teeth and glanced up the beam, wondering if he could climb it. It jutted up from the ground at a forty-five-degree angle and anchored into a small support on the boat halfway up the hull. It would be a miracle if he had the strength to pull himself out of the river, and even if he made it to the top of the beam, he didn't know where he would go from there.

Jak craned his head back as far as it would go and peered at the top deck of the boat to the windows. One of them was open, and he could see Tess's head poking through it. "Tess!" he screamed. "Tess!"

She waved at him.

"Open the door! Let me in!"

"You'll never get in, boy!" cackled a voice.

Startled, Jak looked up at the third beam where a lanky man clung. Bushy yellow hair poked out from underneath a black hat and he looked very much like a drowned scarecrow. He cackled again, "They won't open the door for the likes of us. The water's begun. Ends up Noah was right, and now we're all going to die in one big pool party." He got a wicked grin on his face and wagged his tongue at Jak.

"Aren't you's that kid?" shouted a second voice. A heavyset gorilla of a man with black hair sprouting in tufts from his shoulders and neck clung to the first beam. "Aren't you's the one who helped pitch this here boat?"

Jak nodded. "I'm supposed to be on board."

"Ahhh, that's too bad," said the scarecrow, his mouth drooping into a frown. "'Tis a shame they left you behind." He gave another high-pitched skinny cackle.

Jak sputtered a mouthful of water. *They don't care! They don't care that I'm almost drowning.* He had seen them before, too, up on Fool's Point with the rest of the hecklers, but what were they doing down here?

Each man had an ax imbedded into the beam above their heads, the handles sticking out like a pair of sore thumbs.

It struck Jak as odd that they would have axes. There weren't any trees to cut around the boat His gaze swept across the hull and stopped at a patch of fresh gouges marking the wood underneath the door.

The blood rushed to Jak's face in rage as he realized what the axes were for — they were trying to smash a hole in the boat!

He wanted to climb the two beams the men rested on and knock them into the water. They could have come down from Fool's Point at any time and helped build the boat. They could have heeded Noah's warning and boarded the boat to escape the flood, but instead they chose to try and destroy the only thing that would keep anyone alive.

"While the three of us wait to die," said scarecrow man, "let's play a little game, shall we? It's called 'Spit on the Boy.'"

Jak tensed and gripped the beam even tighter. He wondered why Tess and the others were taking so long to get him inside. It was hard enough staying above water, but now he had to deal with these two idiots as well.

"Oh, I's going to like this game," said the gorilla man. He snorted and spat a huge green wad at Jak.

The wind blew it wide, and it splatted into the water.

"You missed, idjit. My turn." Scarecrow man hacked and spat but also missed.

With each attempt, they inched up the beams a bit, repositioning their axes so their feet could prop them up.

They weren't just playing a game. They were still trying to destroy the boat.

"He's down there!" said Tess. "See? He's holding onto that beam."

Shem, Gramps, and Ham peered through the rain.

"There's no one left down there except those two men on the beams," said Ham.

"No," said Shem, "she's right! Look on the second support, through the waves. That's him. We have to open the door for Jak."

"We can't," said Noah. "Yahweh is the one who shut it, not me. We could not open it even if we wanted to."

"Sure we could," said Shem.

"Perhaps," said Noah, "but who's to say Yahweh will shut a second time what he has already sealed once?"

"But we can't just leave him out there," said Japheth. "He'll die."

"Better him than all of us," said Azras.

Japheth gave her a disgusted look and Tess's eyes narrowed.

"I can't believe you just said that!" Tess spouted. "You are the most selfish, pigheaded..."

Before she could finish her sentence, Shem cut her off. "There must be something we can do."

"I can only think of one thing," said Noah. He lifted both hands to the sky. "Yahweh, will you help the boy?"

A heavy silence hung among them. Furious, Tess stood by the window, letting the rain pelt her in the face as she watched her cousin struggle. The waves beat over his head again and again. Every time his head disappeared under a surge of water she would hold her breath until he reappeared. If someone didn't come up with an idea soon, he would be just as doomed as the rest who were not on the boat.

Suddenly, Gramps snapped his fingers. "Rope!" he said. "Get the rope. He's spent the past two months hanging from a rope pitching this boat, so he can certainly hang a minute more."

"Yes, get the rope!" Tess shouted. "Hurry!"

Shem burst down the hallway into the supply room and returned a minute later with a coil of rope. Japheth tied one end to a post on the deck, and Shem tossed the other end out as far as he could into the river ahead of Jak.

"Yahweh," he said, "please send the rope to Jak."

Why aren't they opening the door? He was going to drown if he stayed out here. Through the sheet of rain he could just make out Tess's face in the window, but she wasn't doing anything. *She must not be able to see me,* he thought.

Jak had given up shouting. His voice was hoarse, and his strength was giving out. He had to concentrate on staying alive in the torrent. It didn't make it any easier that the bag was strapped around his neck and Macy was tucked into his shirt. She was an extra twenty pounds to manage, and the fact that she was pouched in the front made it difficult for Jak to hold onto the support beam. *If only I could stuff her in the book bag.*

Just then, a dark line shot out the window above, slapped the water upstream, and began floating toward him.

He twisted his arm around and grabbed at it as it floated near, but it sank down and reappeared on the other side of him. He grabbed again, this time snagging it with his fingers. He could hardly hold onto it because his fingers had gone numb in the chill of the water.

It was a rope. They were going to try to haul him out of the water.

Jak slid his hand up the rope and wrapped it around his wrist the same way he had done a thousand times before. The cold made it much trickier, though, and he'd never tried to pull himself out of an angry river. In order to make it, he'd have to let go of the one thing that had kept him alive so far - the support beam.

"Whatcha got there, boy?" said the scarecrow man, peering through the rain. "A rope!" Scarecrow man stretched for the rope as far as his skinny arms would go, but his fingers fell short by a foot

"A rope?" said gorilla man. "Look at that, Noah comes through and throws us a rope. This calls for a double celebration."

Both men coughed up and spat at Jak. One missed, but the other hit him in the ear.

Macy growled and barked, which didn't help the situation because now Jak's ears were ringing as well.

Jak tried to ignore the men. He had to concentrate on letting go of the beam and grabbing the rope in one fluid movement, but the water was cold, so cold that his hands felt like clumpy blocks of ice. If only he could take a thirty second rest to drink a cup of hot chocolate and warm up. But there was no hot chocolate, and there was no rest. He had to work with what he had: the rope and two cold hands versus a raging river.

If he missed, the river would drag him away and dash him against the rocks at the bottom of the hill. If he somehow survived the rocks, the volume of water gushing down the hill was so much that there was no way he would be able to make it back to the boat.

He only had once chance, but it was a risk he had to take.

The river had a tiny ebb and flow – forward, back, forward, back. He needed to wait until the right forward flow to make his move, but he had to do it soon or he would begin to lose circulation in the arm already entwined in the rope.

"You know you're never getting up that rope, right, boy?" said Scarecrow.

"That's right," said Gorilla. "We gonna grab you and throw you back down so fast you won't know what hit you. If we's dying in this flood, so's you. The water eats you up, same as us."

Jak tuned them out until their words blended into the roar of the river.

Concentrate. Forward, back, forward, back, NOW!

He jerked his hand away from the support beam, threw his body up as high as he could, and wrapped his left wrist into the rope. The rough fibers bit into his hand like a saw, but he didn't slide and managed to stay firm. The river clawed at his waist, pulling him down and searing the muscles in his arms, but

Jak held firm. He unwound his right hand and reached as high as he could, then rewound it into the rope.

His chest hurt, and the rope bit into his flesh once more, a thousand pinpricks on the freezing skin. If it had only been his weight, he could have gone much faster, but Macy and the wet book felt like a pile of bricks. He was going to have to tough it out.

He reached up with his left hand, pulled himself up and felt the river let go of his legs, his feet dangling a breath above the water. But the release of the river also meant the rope was free to swing like a pendulum, and that's exactly what it did. As soon as his legs cleared the water, Jak swung straight toward gorilla man.

"There you go," said gorilla man. "Come to Papa."

Jak's body was still too low for gorilla man to reach him, but the man grabbed the rope with one gargantuan arm and began to shake it.

"Once upon a time," said Gorilla, "there was a little spider who got caughts in the rain. He tried to climb up, up and away on a tiny strand of web, but he couldn't hold on." Gorilla shook the rope so hard that Jak thought his arms were going to tear out of the sockets, but he held on.

At that moment, the rope slapped taut against the side of the boat. Something pulled at it from up above and tore it free from Gorilla's grasp. Jak's body swung like a yo-yo higher into the air and in the other direction, straight toward Scarecrow.

Scarecrow smiled in glee and reached his spidery fingers out to pull Jak off the rope, but as soon as Jak got close, he kicked his left foot straight into Scarecrow's nose. The man howled and plastered one hand to his face. His other arm flailed as he desperately tried to keep his balance, but gravity won, and he tumbled into the river.

Jak swung back other direction, back toward Gorilla, but whoever was manning the rope up above had pulled him even higher now, and he sailed past, almost brushing the man's head with his feet.

Gorilla swung his ax and grazed Jak's leg. The ax thudded into the beam.

"Get back here, you blasted monkey." He jerked his ax out of the beam and held it in one hand, a gleam in his eye as he waited for Jak to pass again.

Jak tried to twist his body so he could lift his legs out of reach, but his back hit the boat hard, sending him spinning. There was nothing he could do to keep Gorilla from chopping off his foot or worse.

Yahweh, help me.

At that moment, the beam shook, rocking back and forth as it was seized by the river.

The man dropped down to the beam and hugged it tight, his eyes still trained on Jak who swung over his head, too high now for the ax to reach him.

Gorilla cocked the ax back to fire at Jak, but the beam tipped and he dropped it. He bellowed as the ax plunged into the river.

Whew, that was close, thought Jak. He jerked his body around so both feet squared off against the boat. The rope continued to pull him higher. He walked up the side of the boat like a mountain climber, careful not to crush Macy and moving his bum right leg as fast as he could to keep up with the pace of the rope. For the first time in a while he began to believe he might make it.

THWACK. An arrow imbedded itself into the boat above his head. *THWACK* went another one just below his feet.

"Ha!" shouted Gorilla. "Hangin' like a monkey on a rope for target practice, Azril'll have you drinkin' river water with an arrow in your gullet." He laughed like a hoarse hyena.

Jak turned his head far enough to see Azril on Fool's Point fitting a third arrow to his bow, but the arrow never flew. Another burst of water exploded from the cavern, swept over the point and washed Azril over the cliff. The rest of the water crashed furiously toward the boat.

Gorilla saw the wall of water as well. He hesitated for half a second before scurrying topsy-turvy up the rest of the beam and lunging into the air with his wet hairy arms outstretched toward Jak.

CHAPTER 57
A Tinge of Red

Jak yanked his feet up, and Gorilla's hands grappled at the empty space. He thudded hard into the boat and dropped like a rock into the water. The swell thundered by the boat and Gorilla was dragged under the water.

Jak was sorry that the man would die, but he had brought it upon himself.

Now the only thing keeping Jak from the safety of the boat was the boat itself. His hands were numb, and he didn't know how much longer he could hold on. The cut on his belly burned, and his heel was beginning to act up again as well, that old alien pain scraping into his veins.

He thought he was almost to the short rail that lined the top of the boat. It wouldn't take more than a minute to get there if he were feeling well. He could hear voices shouting at him, but he was dizzy, and could no longer feel the rope in his hands. Suddenly, two pair of hands grabbed him under the arms and pulled him and Macy onto the deck.

Jak had never been so happy to set foot on gopher wood. The windows were closed, and the rain beat against the boat instead of against him. He huddled shivering with a blanket on the floor next to Tess. The pain from the cut was intense. It mingled with the ache in his foot and amplified into a thumping vibration in his blood.

"Where did you go? What happened?" asked Tess.

"The waterfall. Scorch had a lair in the waterfall... and Enoch and Cain and Nal are gone... and Scorch is dead and she scratched me and..." Suddenly he was overwhelmed by shivering and he couldn't talk any more. He closed his eyes.

"You're hurt," said Tisrah. She unwrapped his arms from his chest. His robe was drenched red. She pulled it back and took a sharp breath in. There was less blood than expected, but a yellow pus that smelled like rotten onions had begun to form. A dark shadow crossed through Tisrah's eyes. "Rispel, get me the rosewart."

Rispel came back with a dried gourd. From it, Tisrah poured a red powder over the cut until it looked like dried blood crusted the wound.

Numbness washed through Jak's chest, curbing at least some of the pain.

"I'm sorry, Jak," said Tisrah, "but there is nothing more I can do. The rosewart may overcome the poison, but nothing is certain. A simple cut we could at least sew together, but the beast's poison has taken over your skin and worked its way into the surrounding flesh. If it was your arm or leg, we could cut it off, but on your chest...I'm sorry."

"What do you mean? What are you saying?" said Tess, wide-eyed.

"I mean he may not live," said Tisrah slowly, "It is up to Yahweh."

"Pour some more rosewart on. Try something else. There must be something somebody can do!" Tess demanded.

Tisrah shook her head. "If this were normal snake venom, perhaps, but this is the poison of the serpents." She shook her head again. "It is connected to the heart, and that is something I cannot begin to touch with the medicine I know. Yahweh and only Yahweh will decide whether or not Jak lives."

"We must ask him," said Noah. "We must ask Yahweh to spare Jak's life. Come." Noah grabbed Tisrah's hand and lifted their arms up into the air. "Yahweh, the poison of the beast seeps into this boy's flesh and threatens to steal away his life. Will you heal him?"

Suddenly Jak remembered the seed. It had healed him back at Lamech's house, and it would heal him now. "Gramps," he said through chattering teeth, "get the seed. If I nibble a bit, I bet I'll get better."

Gramps dug in the bag, underneath the book, and deep into the pocket. "It's not here."

"It's not there?"

"Nope – just the book and the deck of cards."

Jak sighed. "The water in the cave must have washed it out." Tears pricked at the corners of his eyes and he covered his face. Not only had he lost the only way for his gash to heal, but it also felt like he had lost a friend. To him, it was not just a seed from the Tree of Life, but it was a seed of hope that better days would come.

"What happened behind the waterfall?" Gramps gently prodded.

The shivering had begun to calm down and Jak finally felt like he could tell them everything that had happened. Scorch was dead. He really was the Quelcher. He had crushed her head with the sword, just like it said in the Promise, and now it would be paradise again. He leaned his back against a post and, as best as he could, told the story. When he was done, everyone looked at him in shocked silence.

"That's why Nettor disappeared," said Gramps. "He glowed red for a moment, then he disappeared. Must've gone back with the others."

"Cain was on our side?" said Tess. "I can't believe it."

"Even the blackest hearts can be washed clean," said Noah. "It is a tragedy that more did not change. If they had, perhaps none of this would have happened."

"But I don't understand how Papa's father has been in the cave this whole time," said Japheth. "If he was in there as a ten-year-old boy, he hadn't gotten married or had any kids yet, so how could we exist?"

"It's the Thread," said Noah. "It deals with time in its own way. Somehow it preserved Enoch as a ten-year-old for over a thousand years and now has brought him backwards in time to his family. He'll grow up normally and father your great grandfather."

"I don't understand a lick of that, but paradise sounds good," said Ham. "From what you've told us of the garden, I'd like to live there. No more backbreaking hours in the hot sun fighting with the weeds for the same patch of ground and all the fruit we can eat hanging from the trees, free for the plucking – yes sir, that's the place for me!"

"So you believe you are the Quelcher?" said Noah. "You have crushed the serpent's head and paradise waits for us under all this water?"

"I guess so," said Jak. "I don't know what else to think. El brought me here for something special."

"But I thought that had to do with the book and the cards," said Tess. "Isn't that what Guardian said?"

She had a point. While Jak had been so wrapped up in saving Macy from Scorch, he hadn't thought about the fact that the book was not yet complete. "Gramps," said Jak, "will you get the book and the Noah card?" He closed his eyes and waited while Gramps fished around in the bag and pulled out the soggy book and dripping deck of cards. "Noah," said Jak, "will you touch the card again?"

Noah took the card from Gramps, but once again, nothing happened. There were no sparks and no wriggling frog—just a soggy card.

"I...I don't know what to think," said Jak. *Could paradise come again if the book wasn't finished yet?* he wondered.

"Jak, you're sure the beast is dead?" said Gramps. "She's not just knocked on the head, unconscious, ready to wake up as soon as she realizes she's dead?"

"The book changed into a sword, Gramps, like I told you, and I stabbed her in the forehead. Check the pouch for the sword card. I saw the sword stuck in her forehead. She's *dead*."

"We'll just have to wait and see," said Tisrah. "One thing is for sure. It isn't paradise out there yet."

The light that filtered through the vents under the eaves had ebbed away. They huddled together in the darkness, a steady downpour thrumming louder now against the roof. Jak was glad he and Shem had pitched the roof as well, even though Shem had argued against it. "Water does not come from the sky. Why do we need to pitch the wood that will never get wet?" But against Shem's complaints, Noah had insisted and it was a good thing he had.

The rain pounded steady and hard for forty days and forty nights. For Jak, each day blended into the next. He was sick for most of it, a heavy fever pressing into his head, dreams of the scarecrow and gorilla men climbing up the veins in his leg, axes poised, ready to hack a hole in his heart. Like Tisrah said, the venom went for the heart.

On the twenty-seventh day, the boat shifted and rolled into the water, bobbing up and down like a huge bar of soap in a bathtub. On that day, Tess anointed a chamber pot with seasickness and they learned the importance of tying items to the deck of the boat.

Barrels of grain tipped and rolled across the floor like bowling balls, knocking over nine-pins of apple baskets and almost striking out a squirrel monkey who was exploring the apples. They spent the next two days going from deck to deck, pen to pen, making sure everything was tied down.

On the forty-first day, Jak woke up and felt fully awake. His fever was down—not gone, but down. The rain had stopped, and sunlight climbed through the vents under the roof. Jak pushed himself out of bed. He was hot and sweaty and felt like he'd been hit by a truck. His fingers probed the line across his stomach. It was still raw and tender, and the familiar alien presence still strained to get at him. He could feel it, but he could also feel something else inside of him pushing it back, like a dam protecting his heart.

He was sick of lying in bed. He had to get out of his room and see what was going on, so he pushed the blanket off and and stumbled dizzily down the hallway to the great room.

"Jak, you're up!" said Tess. She jumped to her feet, sending the squirrel in her lap to look for a new admirer, and hurried toward him. "The rain's finally stopped and the..." She stopped and looked him in the face. "You look terrible."

Jak gave her a weak smile and swayed from side to side. "Thanks. I feel like a million bucks."

"You should be back in bed," said Gramps. He put his hand on Jak's arm to steady him.

The entire group stood on the top deck as Noah opened the window to see what the world looked like. Blue had once again claimed the sky, but blue was the only color they could see – blue sky and blue water. There were no brown mountain peaks, no green trees, nothing except blue and a steady whistling wind...and a tinge of red.

CHAPTER 58

The Whirlwind and the Warm Fuzzies

The Scarlet Thread zoomed through the window and wrapped itself around Jak, Gramps, Macy, and Tess until they were encased in a giant red cocoon.

Tess's eyes darted wildly as the silken strands closed around them. "What's happening?"

"Settle down, Tess," said Gramps. "I'm betting the Thread is doing a little time travel, that's all. Relax. We'll be fine."

At first it felt strange to be wrapped up by the Thread, but they weren't wrapped up tight like a mummy. It was more like a big closet, with plenty of room to breathe and move around. They were only in the cocoon for a moment before the Thread unraveled and they stood on the top deck once again, only now they were alone.

The rocking motion of the boat was gone, replaced by a solid stillness. They had grounded, but the boat was the only thing that was still. Brays, caws, moos, and hisses filled the air, as did the sound of clomping and stomping hooves, scrapes, and shouting. Sunlight flooded up the stairway from the second deck.

"The door is open!" said Jak. "That means paradise is here - the garden is back!" He hopped toward the stairs, but the pain in his chest stopped him short, and he winced. If this was how he was going to feel in paradise, he was in trouble.

"Jak, do you need to sit down?" said Gramps.

"No, I'm ok," he claimed, but he let Gramps help him down the stairs after Tess and Macy.

The mice and ferrets and other small animals ran circles in their cages, pressing their whiskers through the bars, twitching, itching, and anxious to get out.

Through the atrium, they could see Shem and Japheth on the first deck, directing a pair of elephants out the door with long switches.

"Shem!" Gramps called down.

Shem's face angled up, and he smiled. "Clarence, you're back! We were wondering when the bag would open. It's been a year since the Thread wrapped you up and we thought we might have to leave you on the boat. Come on down. We just opened the door. It's time to unload."

The air pouring through the door was crisp and clean, like the air of the garden. Outside there had to be groves of fruit trees, animals frisking about, the clear open blue sky, and most importantly, the Tree of Life. Maybe another Knowing Tree would be there as well, but Jak hoped not. If somebody got the bright idea to eat the fruit, they would wreck paradise all over again. Jak decided that if there was a new Knowing Tree, he would chop it down and burn it. He wondered why he hadn't thought of that in the first place.

Gramps helped Jak out the door, but what he saw was not at all what he expected.

They were at the top of a mountain. The boat lay wedged in a ridge, held fast by a row of rocks. The grass grew thick on a field that sloped gently down one side of the mountain, but nothing frolicked or played there. The animals huddled in pairs around the boat, antsy and unsure of themselves. One of the elephants had wrapped his trunk around his ear, just like Tess did with her hair when she was nervous.

"What's wrong with the animals?" said Jak.

"Don't know," said Japheth, shaking his head. "It's like they're afraid of us or afraid of something."

"They're nervous," said Shem, showing Jak a gash on his forearm. "The tiger swiped at me as she got off."

"Some paradise," said Ham. "The boar took a nick out of my leg."

"Yes, Jak," said Azras. "Where is this paradise you spoke of? The flowers are drab, the sky is dull, and even the sun shines less here."

"Hush, woman," said Noah. "We are alive. Be grateful for the air that fills your lungs."

"I...I don't know," said Jak. "The Promise says—"

"The Promise is nothing more than a pile of fluff that old women stuff into their heads. I'm sick of it, sick of the whole thing," said Azras. She turned and stomped off in the other direction.

At Azras's words a bolt of pain spasmed through Jak's body. It felt like something shifted in every molecule and cell, and then he dropped to the ground.

"Japheth, get your mother," urged Tess, pushing Jak's hair back from his face. "His eyes have sunken and his skin is turning yellow. It's the same thing that happened back in East Eden."

Tisrah laid Jak on a bed of straw in a cave not far from the boat. It was the only place to get out of the wind, but still Jak shivered. The rosewart did nothing to ease the fire in his blood – if only some of the fire would transfer to his skin. *Where is Yahweh?* he thought. *What is he doing? Doesn't he care that I'm sick?* He'd been sick with the poison ever since the moment Scorch had bit him in the beginning, yet he was supposed to carry this book to Megiddo so evil and death could die. But it appeared that instead of him killing death, death was going to kill him. *So much for Yahweh's grand plan.*

"Has anybody seen the tree?" muttered Jak.

"What tree?" said Tess.

"The Tree of Life."

Tess shook her head. "There is no tree like that here. There are only normal trees." She looked away; tears brimming over her eyelids and running down her cheeks. "Why did you have to go after Scorch? This time you might not make it."

"I had to, Tess," he mumbled. "For Macy, for the book, for..."

Noah entered the cave and took a long look at Jak. There was no laughter in his face now, only sorrow. The sounds of the animals outside echoed in the cave, but one sound seemed louder than the others — the bleat of a sheep. It worked its way into Jak's head, matching the bleat of a sheep in his memory.

"What day is it?" said Jak.

"What day?" said Tess. "I don't know. Monday? Does it matter?"

"I mean," Jak whispered. "It's been a long time since Remembrance Day." It was becoming difficult to talk, difficult to draw in the breath. His lungs were closing off.

"It's been over a thousand years," said Gramps.

"Maybe if we kill a lamb...like Adam did..." He stopped talking as a fit of coughing overtook him.

"He's right," said Tess. "At Remembrance Day in East Eden, when Adam sacrificed the lamb, that's when Jak got better!"

"I was going to offer a sacrifice to Yahweh anyway," said Noah, "to thank him for sparing our lives. We will prepare another sacrifice, and it will be a Remembrance Day as well."

"Go quickly," said Tisrah. "The end is near."

When the older man ran out of the cave, a snake slithered to the mouth of the cave where Jak lay. He wasn't a big snake, only three feet long and covered in brown scales, flecked red and black to blend in with the rock. His tongue flickered, and he swung his head in both directions to make sure no one was watching, and then slid inside the cave.

"Shem, Ham, and Japheth, gather together one of each type of clean animal," instructed Noah.

"Why?" said Ham.

"Just do it quickly. We don't have much time." The three brothers returned a few minutes later with an ox, a goat, a turtledove, and a lamb.

"Are we offering all four of them?" asked Ham.

"Yes," said Noah. "It is a thanks offering...and a Day of Remembrance celebration."

"Day of Remembrance? Is it the Day of Remembrance?" said Japheth. "I lost track on the boat."

"It is not exactly the Day of Remembrance, but it is close enough." Noah sharpened a long knife on a whetstone, occasionally testing it on his finger. "Jak is near death; the serpent's poison is taking him. Mother took him to the cave in the hill to rest. We don't expect him to last much longer."

"So quickly?" said Shem. "Then I must go see him."

"No! We must prepare the sacrifice. The last time he was this ill was in East Eden on Remembrance Day. When Adam offered the sacrifice and Yahweh lit the fire, he became well. Stack the rocks into an altar."

"What would the Remembrance Day sacrifice have to do with healing Jak?" said Ham, heaving a large stone into place to create a foundation for an altar.

"I do not know, but we will make the sacrifice and see what happens."

While his three sons worked together to build the altar, Noah took the lamb in his arms. It had been born on the boat with clear eyes, no spots, and no lameness; it was a perfect lamb. He hated to part with it, but this is exactly what Remembrance Day required—a perfect sacrifice. Without perfection, the transaction could not occur. Human guilt could not be transferred to the animal, nor could the animal's innocence be given to humans.

The lamb licked his hand and bleated.

Noah's breath quickened. *Do it now.*

He gently grasped the lamb in his arms and drew the knife across its throat.

Jak had stopped talking, and his breath became raspy and uneven.

Death was in the room. Tess could feel it. A ripple of goosebumps erupted on her skin. Death was there, slowly sucking the life from Jak's lungs.

Jak's eyes darted around the cave, a spastic pair of sunken pinballs shrouded by a yellow face. Even though they had piled wool blankets on top of him, he shivered violently underneath. Death was stealing his heat as well.

Tess knelt next to him with tears streaming down her face. Macy lay with her head on his leg, whining, and Gramps sat next to Jak's head, stroking his hair. They all knew it – the end was near.

⁂

The brown snake slithered back out of the cave and glided up over a rocky path to a secluded pit distant from the boat. A tremendous red serpent coiled in the bottom of the pit, its body as thick as a tree trunk, with a head like a squashed horse. Wisps of black smoke trailed up from its mouth.

The brown snake trembled in fear, yet he did not retreat. He had been commanded, summoned, and so he came.

Beelz raised his head as the snake approached and snorted. *"It isss about time. Tell me what you have ssseen."*

The snake cowered in the dirt. *"Little man...dying. Ragged air, leaving him, dark hole ssstench, death."*

Beelz wheezed and spit out a laugh. *"Ssso death isss at the door. I am not sssurprisssed. Even the ssstrongessst of the humansss iss asss a gnat underfoot an elephant, and thisss isss only a boy. Then the time iss ripe. Did you ssee the bag with him, or were you too ssstupid to noticcce sssuch a thing?"*

The smaller snake pulled its head back. *"Sssaw."*

"Return and retrieve the book from the bag. He no longer needsss it, and I do. Do not let them sssee you."

"How?"

Beelz could not believe the stupid creature was one of his own descendants, and he wondered if there would ever come a day when they would learn to think for their pathetic selves. *"With your mouth, idiot, the only tool you have."*

The brown serpent slithered away before Beelz had finished speaking, which was probably the wisest course of action considering Beelz wasn't in the best of moods. He had spent over a year treading water in the flood, and it had left him waterlogged and cross. One of the flaps on his left ear canal had leaked, and he was still trying to clear the water from his brain.

But this was a fortunate turn of events. He did not need the female leviathan nor the Beelzin to track the boy now, which was good because they were all dead. The boy had come to Beelz on his own, a wandering fly landing tired and unsuspecting on a Venus fly trap. *How very convenient.*

It would only be a matter of time before the book would be stolen away by the enemy, but there was much to be gleaned from perusing its pages to see exactly what Yahweh was up to. The boy was on a mission—a mission different from any other person who had followed the Thread—and Beelz was determined to know how Yahweh intended to carry that mission out. Yahweh would not stop merely because one of his fools expired. He would find another human and try again.

Noah struck the flint as Shem, Ham, Japheth, and their wives stood around watching. The lamb lay on top of the sticks, a whole sacrifice, and everything except the intestines remained on the altar. It was offensive to burn the lamb's excrement, so Ham had dug a hole and buried it.

An orange flicker caught in the small pieces of straw at the base of the sticks, and Noah blew gently, just enough to give life to the flame so it could lick the sticks.

It had been over a year since they had lit an open flame – no fire on the boat except in the stove – that was the rule. It seemed silly to Noah that he had even made the rule. Who of his children would be so foolish as to light a fire on a wooden boat all because they craved a roasted banana? Ham's wife, Azras, came to mind and Noah suddenly was glad he had made the rule.

The thin kindling crackled as the fire grabbed hold, and then it burst into flame. Stick by stick, log by log, the fire grew until the lamb was engulfed in orange and yellow. The acrid odor of burning wool stung the air but then gave way to the roasting meat.

"Yahweh," whispered Noah.

Tisrah stood. The breeze from the abrupt movement made the flame of the lamp flicker and sent ghostly images dancing on the walls. "I am going to Noah. The sacrifice must be made *now* or it will be too late." She turned and hurried out of the cave.

Jak's breathing was no longer ragged; it had slowed so much that his chest barely moved.

"Hold on, Jak," said Tess. "Remembrance Day, remember?" She didn't think he could hear her. He was so far gone now that perhaps he had already died in his head and all that was left was for his body to follow.

Suddenly Jak gasped and sat straight up, like a corpse returned from the dead.

Tess screamed and jumped back.

His lungs sucked in great gulps of air.

"Jak!" Before she knew what she was doing, Tess threw her arms around him and squeezed. "You're breathing!"

Jak stopped breathing again for a second. "I was till you squeezed me."

"Oh, sorry." She let go.

Jak's eyes looked straight ahead, no flitting back and forth, no longer sunken in their sockets. The yellow had disappeared from his skin. He stretched his arms up and out, but he jerked them back down when a twinge ran up his chest. "My chest still hurts, but the other than that, the sick feeling is gone."

"And you're sitting up!" said Gramps, wiping tears from his cheeks with the back of his hand. He thumped Jak gently on the back. "I'd say that's a vast improvement from near death, don't you think?"

The brown snake paused behind a rock at the entrance to the cave. Something was not right, for laughter filled the cave. The snake flicked his tongue out. The smell of death was gone. He poked his head cautiously along the ground into the mouth of the cave but yanked it back just in time to avoid being stepped on by a pair of feet that belonged to....the boy!

The snake hissed to itself. His instinct told him not to deliver this piece of news to the great red serpent. He slithered off to find his mate, hoping they could make an escape from the wrath of Beelz.

◈◈

The fire roared now, and the lamb was almost completely burned up.

"Tisrah! Noah!"

Noah turned around, and his face lit up at the site of Jak hobbling up to the altar. "You are well!" said Noah.

"Yes. One minute I was almost dead, and the next I —"

A bolt of lightning split the sky, accompanied by the heavy rolling of thunder. A whirlwind of light circled toward the Earth, the same sort of light Jak had seen back in the garden.

Jak could hardly stand still. He was sure this was El. At any moment, the wind would turn warm, flowers would burst from the ground, and then the thing that Jak wanted more than anything would happen – the dead would come back to life. Certainly Yahweh would make it happen now that the serpent's head was crushed. He felt a twinge of remorse for Scorch; it would have been better if she had not had to die.

The whirlwind touched the ground, and a brilliant figure dropped down the middle.

A flush of excitement came over Jak. Today he would see Yahweh. Finally, after fifteen hundred years, he would see El.

When the figure reached the bottom, it stepped through the whirlwind of light.

Jak tensed, waiting for the burst of warm fuzzies that used to radiate from the garden whenever El spoke with Adam and Eve. But it never came.

As soon as the figure emerged, the brilliance faded and became a man, a plain old normal man.

CHAPTER 59

Pocket Number Three

Well, not entirely normal. His skin was smooth, brown, and lined like a burlap sack, kind of like the way El had appeared after Adam and Eve ate the black cherries. But his hair was white—not white like old man white, but white as in a blinding reflection of the sun on a sheet of snow. And his eyes were definitely not normal; they burned the intense white hot of a blacksmith's fire.

Jak was sure something wasn't right. If this was El, light should have exploded from the tower as soon as he came out, and the air should be full of the warm fuzzies, but it wasn't. It still blew with the chill of the wind.

"Noah," the figure said. The voice sounded the same as El's though, like the rushing of a river.

Noah and the others dropped to their knees and pressed their faces to the ground. Jak, Gramps, and Tess followed suit.

The figure approached Noah and touched him gently on the shoulder. "Get up, my son. You have done well. You have obeyed and been saved from the flood."

Noah stumbled to his feet. "So it is true then? There are none left but us?"

"None. I took no pleasure in cleansing the Earth, but it was the only way."

Jak stared into the man's flesh. *Who is this?* There was a certain warmth that came from the figure, but it was a distant warmth, not the up-close-and-personal warmth Jak had expected.

Even the animals surrounding them seemed unsettled by the figure. A restless energy flowed through them, and they fidgeted and coughed and pranced back and forth as if they wanted to run away.

"The Earth is once again empty," the figure said, "a vast expanse of jungle and dirt, ready to be explored and shaped into a home for many people. So I give you the same instructions I gave to Adam and Eve. Fill the Earth. Multiply yourselves so that every corner is filled with the laughter of children and the love of a man and a woman."

Jak turned the man's words over in his mind. If this man was the one who gave Adam and Eve the instructions, then it *had* to be El. But if this was El, then where was paradise?

The tigers paced back and forth, and the elephants kept stamping their feet. The ferrets flitted in figure eights while the flamingos flapped their wings and kept edging back. The tension among them hung as thick as a morning fog.

For the first time since the garden, fear of the animals prickled down Jak's spine. If the tension didn't lift, an elephant might go mad and trample them to death, or the tigers might snap and pounce. One of them had already sliced Shem open.

"But you will find life different in this Earth," said El. "The animals will be different."

As soon as he finished speaking, the zoo encircling them exploded into a barking, whistling, and growling chaos. The elephants reared on their hind legs, pointed their trunks to the sky, and trumpeted. Then they thundered back to the ground, almost squashing the flamingos into the rock, and stampeded down the slope. The flamingos squawked and flapped their wings desperately to avoid being run over by the hippos that followed right behind the elephants.

It was now a true stampede, and it appeared certain that some of the animals would die in the attempt to leave the mountain. The rhinoceroses thrashed their heads back and forth, narrowly missing the giraffes that ran next to them. One of the giraffes stumbled as it darted away from the rhino horns, and his back foot nipped a tiger in the face. The tiger roared and leapt over the crowd, landing on top of the rhinoceros that had started the trouble in the first place. The rhinoceros grunted, dropped to the ground, and the two began rolling down the hill and out of sight.

It was fifteen minutes of mayhem during which the humans huddled around El, until the only creatures left were a pair of monkeys, somersaulting in a circle like a confused pair of circus clowns, screaming and pinching each other, until they, too, broke away and followed the dust down the mountain.

"The animals," El continued, "will no longer desire to be with you. Instead, the terror of you will fill them, and, as you have just seen, they will run, fly, and swim away."

"But why?" said Noah. "What have we done?"

"It is not what you have done, but what you *will* do," said El.

"What will we do?"

"You will eat them. Instead of companions, they will become your food."

"What?" said Noah. "Eat the creatures?"

"Yes. As I gave you the fruit and the green plants before the flood, now I give you every creature that moves as food."

Now it was the humans' turn to fidget. A curious hunger swept over them and clawed at their bellies. It was not a hunger that could be satisfied by bean stew, lentil salad, or wheat bread. There was only one thing that could curb such a hunger, and that was meat.

When Jak heard this, his stomach applauded at the thought. Steak, chicken, fish, and ham just got added to the menu, and he had been craving a good burger ever since they arrived. Maybe tonight would be the night, except now they would have to go and find a cow.

"Only do not eat the flesh with the blood still in it. The blood is the creature's life and must be returned to the ground, back to the dirt, where it came from."

El's eyes flickered burnt orange. "And you must be careful to teach your children and their children and their children's children to live in peace with one another. No violence, no spilling of the life-blood. For you have been made in our image, and you each bear the very image of El. Violence against another human is violence against me. Anything, human or animal, that spills the life of a human, I will require his blood as payment."

The flame in his eyes changed back to yellow, and he smiled. "Listen, for I am about to make a promise both to you and your descendants and to all creatures with breath in their nostrils, a promise guaranteed by my own name, that I will never again send a flood to cut off life from the Earth. And this is the seal of my promise." He waved one hand in the air.

The huge cumulus that had hidden the sun for the past half-hour floated away, and light burst through the remaining piddle of clouds, but it wasn't just light and clouds in the sky. Something else arched brilliant against the blue. A tremendous half-circle of color—red, orange, yellow, green, blue, indigo, and violet—stretched from behind the peak of the opposing mountain down to the fleeing stampede of animals on the plain below.

"This is the sign between you and me forever," said El. "Whenever I bring a cloud over the Earth, the bow will appear, and I will remember my promise. Never again shall the waters flow as they have this past year. Do you understand all that I have said?"

Noah nodded. "Yes, my Lord."

"Good. Then all will be well between us." However, the look on El's face did not match his words. The wrinkles around his eyes and mouth were sad.

Jak stepped forward. "Excuse me, sir?"

"Yes, Jak?"

Jak caught his breath when he realized that El knew his name. El had *said* his name. "What about paradise?"

El cocked one eyebrow and peered into Jak's eyes. "Paradise?"

"Yes. The place where the dead come back to life and I can see my grandmother again. When does it begin? The legend says when the Quelcher crushes the head of the serpent, paradise will live once again, and I did that. I crushed the head of the serpent."

"Ahh, yes, young Quelcher, you *have* crushed the head of a serpent. I watched you, and you wielded the sword well. But there is another."

"Another Quelcher or another serpent?"

El smiled. "Now you are asking the right question." He stepped backwards toward the tower of light. As soon as he touched it, the spinning beams tore at the burlap-sack skin, ripping away small chunks so that patches of starlight burst through.

"The legend runs deeper than you know," he said. "Soon there will be room for paradise. Don't give up, Jak. Death does not belong here." He grinned. "You might want to check that card again." He stepped back into the whirlwind. It sucked him up and he immediately turned into a rocketing pocket of light, pulling the whirlwind up along with him until nothing was left in the sky but the rainbow.

Jak pulled the deck out of the bag and slipped the top card out. Nothing had changed. The same laughing face adorned it. It still looked like Noah, and there still was no red thread around the edge. He hesitated and then held the card out to Noah. "Will you try one last time?"

Noah took the card. As soon as his fingers touched it, it wriggled and jerked like the Adam card had, but Noah held tight.

Finally, thought Jak. "What does it say?" he asked, eager to hear the next step of Yahweh's plan.

"It says nothing," said Noah.

There were no words in the black box, but the box was also no longer black; it was a collection of red, orange, yellow, green, blue, indigo, and violet.

"A rainbow?" said Jak. "Why would El put a rainbow on the card?"

"Why did he put one in the sky?" asked Gramps.

Jak thought for a moment. "It's a promise to never send another flood to wipe out life on the Earth."

"So maybe that's why he put it on the card. He could've wiped out everybody, but he didn't. This is a chance to start over."

"But what does that have to do with the promise to Adam and Eve?" said Tess.

"Guardian never said anything about that promise," said Gramps, "He said the journey is to complete the book in order to wipe out death and evil and Beelz. Are there any more Thread cards, Jak?"

"Nope—just Adam's and Noah's and the sword card," said Jak.

Jak took out the book and slid the Noah card in the slot next to the sword card. The red thread appeared and sewed the card inside the pocket. As soon as it was done, the book began to shake in his hands, and the cover turned from black to a brilliant glowing blue, the same blue as the gate at the entrance of the garden. Then the vibrations and the blue faded away, leaving the normal black book in his hands.

"Looks to me like this part of the journey is done," said Gramps.

"But if it's done, then where do we go from here?" asked Jak. The Scarlet Thread had not reappeared since it had wrapped them up in the boat, and Jak had no idea where to go or what to do. Neither Adam's nor Noah's cards seemed like they could do anything to give the book any special power. Jak's head began to swim, and he put his hand out to grab Gramps's arm and steady himself. His chest hurt too. It wasn't as bad as before, but a dull ache quivered along the slice.

"You okay, Jak?"

"I...I don't know. I just got dizzy all of a sudden"

"Tisrah," said Gramps, "we're going to take Jak back to the cave to lie down. I think he got up too quickly."

"I'm hungry," said Jak, rubbing his stomach. "I'm really, really hungry."

"Well of course. I don't think he's eaten a decent meal since he got on the boat," said Rispel. "He needs food. You help him lie down, and I'll bring a banana cake."

⊗

Beelz blew one last ring of smoke, adding to the burnt odor that hung in the hollow. It drifted up, turned a lazy somersault, and then dissipated into the air.

Where isss that blasssted sssnake? He thrashed his tail into the mountain, smashing a pile of rock into slivers of rubble. He never should have sent such a sniveling creature to do such an important job, but he couldn't send a Beelzin because they had all drowned in the deluge, and he couldn't send a Light because they had left the Earth to wait out the flood on another planet.

By now, the boy must be dead, he reasoned, and he was wasting time. He knew it would not be long before El sent one of his weasels to retrieve the book, so he uncoiled himself from his warm spot in the sun and scraped across the rock toward the cave.

CHAPTER 60

Paradise and Poison

Jak lay back down on the straw. He was so sick of being sick. Ever since the book came into his life, it had been one thing after another. But it wasn't really the book's fault; it was the poison, the incessant, unstoppable poison.

"There. You just lie there for awhile," said Gramps.

Jak nodded his head. "Yeah, I think I just need something to eat and to rest for a bit."

"I'll be glad when you're better," said Tess. "And when you are, will you please stop getting hurt?"

Jak laughed. "Trust me, it's not like I'm trying to get hurt."

"I know, but first your heel, then the burns, and then your chest. Gosh, Jak, you're a walking accident."

Something moved in the back of the cave. Macy growled, and the three peered into the dark.

A spiral of light glimmered and then materialized into the head of a lion resting on top of the torso of a man and the legs of a bull. Giant brown wings scrunched against the roof of the cave.

The lion's head roared and then suddenly stopped as if someone had unplugged it.

"Woops, sorry, wrong head." The lion head spun to the left, revealing the head of a man with wild black hair

"Guardian!" said Jak and Tess at the same time.

Jak's spirit soared. If Guardian was here, that meant the Tree of Life must nearby. Maybe it was in a tiny grotto on the mountain, just a little spot for the tree and the few who found it. When El said soon there would be room for paradise, he meant that, over time, the rocks could be cleared, more trees and flowers planted until, eventually, the garden would flourish again.

"Hullo." Guardian smiled. The black hairy legs morphed into human legs, and he pulled his wings in until they disappeared behind his back.

"What are you doing here?" said Tess. "Aren't you supposed to be guarding the tree?"

"In case you haven't noticed," said Guardian, "the Earth's had a bit of trouble lately, and the tree has been relocated to a pile of muck somewhere in the bottom of the ocean. Either the fruit has been squashed to a nasty pulp, or there is a school of fish in the deepest recesses of the ocean having the time of their lives getting zinged." He raised his right hand. In it he carried a branch as long as a yardstick with bunches of leaves soaked in blood.

"Let me help you, lad." With his other hand, he tore away Jak's shirt, revealing the gash on his chest. The yellow pus had dried up and sat in crusty flakes upon the ridges of the wound, but the skin had not sewn itself back together.

"The sacrifice wiped away the toxin that built up over the ages in your veins, but you'll need a bit of direct contact with the lamb's blood for this wound to heal." He held the branch over Jak and snapped it down, jerking it back shy of Jak's chest, splattering blood over the cut. Guardian pinched the skin with his other hand for a moment and then let go. When he did, the skin remained glued shut.

"There. Now the food will actually do you some good."

Jak sat up. The dizziness had gone away, and now only his stomach hurt. His appetite was definitely back. But before he could eat, he needed an answer to a nagging question.

"This isn't it, is it," said Jak.

"Tisn't what, lad?"

"Paradise."

Guardian shook his head. "Not yet. Someday."

"But why can't El start over now? The evil people are gone. They were killed in the flood."

"You do not understand what it would mean for El to start over."

"What are you saying?"

"Starting over requires more than just wiping out those you consider evil and re-creating the garden. It requires cleansing the poison from human blood."

Jak swallowed hard. "But didn't that just happen in the flood?"

Guardian pulled a knife from his pocket and in one swift movement, sliced clean across Jak's wrist. Blood spurted to the ground.

"What are you doing?" cried Tess.

"All blood," said Guardian.

Suddenly Jak understood.

"If El restored paradise now," he said slowly, "I could not be a part of it. He would have to destroy me first, along with Tess and Gramps and Noah and the rest."

Guardian nodded. He clamped his hand around Jak's arm, and the bleeding stopped. "That is why you have to keep going. The Earth has been washed clean of thousands of dead rebellious souls, but evil still flows in your veins. You know that, Jak. You feel the weight of evil in the world more than anyone. Humans must be cleansed in order to make room for paradise, and you carry the weapon for cleansing."

Jak fingered the book. "So I just have to keep going?"

"Yes."

"But what about the Thread? I don't see it anywhere."

"It will come when El is ready." Guardian stood and dug something out of his pocket. "Here," he said, flipping it in the air to Jak. "I believe this is yours."

Jak caught it with surprise. It was the seed, complete with one chipped corner. "Where did you get it?"

"Found it floating on the sea on the way here. Thought you might like to have it back." He winked and unfurled his wings.

"Wait! Where are you going?"

"Got to get back to guarding."

"But you said the tree is gone."

"Yes, 'tis, but I've been given a new assignment."

Jak looked at him in confusion. "Another assignment? What are you guarding now?"

His face cracked into a smile. "You." He leapt straight up and disappeared into the rock ceiling.

Immediately, a heavy stench of smoke filled the cave, choking their nostrils so they could hardly breathe.

CHAPTER 61

The People at the Bottom of the Stairs

A violent wind ripped through the cave, turning the smoke on its head in upside-down swirls, and then rocketed down an open door.

An open door? The cave doesn't have a door....or windows or a blue linoleum floor. Where are we?

Macy yipped and scratched at the floor, sending her ball skittering under the kitchen table. The smoke alarm above the sink blared as the pancakes on the griddle smoldered to death.

"We're back!" said Gramps. "Just in time to flip the pancakes."

Tess coughed and grabbed a spatula off the counter. "That's right – straight into the garbage."

Jak's mind raced back to the day they left. The freight train of wind still tore through the kitchen, which meant...

He rushed down the basement steps and saw another Gramps, Macy, Tess and himself huddled around a book next to the orange sofa. And then, they were gone.

Acknowledgments

This story began a long time ago with the seed of an idea for a picture book that stretched and grew over the years until finally becoming what it is today. A whole bunch of thank you's must be said to many different people who have been a part of this process.

First of all, thank you, thank you, thank you to my wonderful wife, Julie, for walking with me through the many ups and downs of this journey. I am a better man because of you.

Thank you to Dr. Jeannine Brown for Hermeneutics 101, where the idea for "Jak" was born.

Thank you to Margaret Terry for encouraging me to "write a few paragraphs" so kids knew a little bit about Jak. The paragraphs never stopped coming, which is how a picture book ended up as a novel.

Thank you to the Bill and Jeanne Westerlund, George and Stephanie Sreckov, Shawn and Carmen Balding, Steve and Char VanSlyke, Sam and Jeri Ann Helfenstine, and Tim and Kara Pitchford for helping to make this project possible.

Thank you to Janelle Solberg for her always insightful and patient critique, and to Autumn Conley for editing (any remaining mistakes are mine).

Thank you to the many, many friends who read manuscript drafts and gave me feedback and encouragement.

Thank you to Switchfoot, Relient K, Steven Curtis Chapman, The Robbie Seay Band, Bebo Norman, Sarah Groves, Third Day, Ginny Owens, Brandon Heath and Chris Rice for providing the musical inspiration to write.

But most of all, thank you, El, for giving us the Scarlet Thread.

If you'd like to leave me a comment or keep up with what's going on in the **Jak & the Scarlet Thread** series, you can visit my website, www.bighungryplanet. com. You can also follow me on Twitter @NathanAndersonJ or find me on Facebook. Thanks for reading!

Nathan J. Anderson

Nathan J. Anderson is a writer, speaker, musician and cancer survivor who spends a lot of time thinking about both this life and the next. He produces a radio show called Nite Lite for kids (you can listen online at his website), and is an adjunct professor for Lakeland College. If you'd like to invite Nathan to your event either live or via Skype, contact him at www.bighungryplanet.com.